Praise for
Victoria Christopher Murray

"Murray has always impressed me with her ability to live the life of her characters and make them come alive with each turning page."
—*Indianapolis Recorder*

"Victoria is an exceptional writer who knows how to deliver a story."
—Kimberla Lawson Roby, author of
Changing Faces

Praise for *The Ex Files*

"A moving-on song in four part harmony."
—Donna Grant and Virginia DeBerry,
authors of *Tryin' to Sleep in the Bed You
Made* and *Gotta Keep on Tryin'*

"My girl, Victoria Christopher Murray, has done it again! I love her work and this book will bless you, so read it."
—Michele Andrea Bowen, author of
*Church Folk, Second S....., and
Holy Ghost C......*

"The lessons of growth, love ....oria does best. . . . [An] excellent ....est-selling ....n Needs a Wife*

"The engrossing transitio...........n go through make compelling reading. . . . Murray's ....d portrait of how faith can move mountains and heal relationships should inspire."
—*Publishers Weekly*

"This is a book everyone can enjoy . . . and more important, this is a book that can reach out to the brokenhearted no matter who they are and where they are."

—Book Bit (WTBF-AM)

"Reminds you of things that women will do if their hearts are broken . . . Once you pick this book up, you will not put it down."

—UrbanReviews.com

"Murray does it again and definitely delivers a great story. This one will grip your heart."

—APOOO Book Club

"Victoria Christopher Murray continues to confront real-life issues in her latest novel. . . . A heartfelt read."

—AOL Black Voices

Praise for *A Sin and a Shame*

"As with Murray's previous novels, *A Sin and a Shame* is intriguing and well written. If you loved and hated Jasmine in *Temptation,* you'll love and hate her again."

—*Indianapolis Recorder*

"Victoria Christopher Murray at her best . . . A page-turner that I couldn't put down as I was too eager to see what scandalous thing Jasmine would do next. And to watch Jasmine's spiritual growth was a testament to Victoria's talents. An engrossing tale of how God's grace covers us all. I absolutely loved this book!"

—ReShonda Tate Billingsley, *Essence* best-selling author of *I Know I've Been Changed*

Praise for *Grown Folks Business*

Also by Victoria Christopher Murray

Too Little,

Too Late

Victoria Christopher Murray

A TOUCHSTONE BOOK

Published by Simon & Schuster

New York   London   Toronto   Sydney

Touchstone
A Division of Simon & Schuster, Inc.
1230 Avenue of the Americas
New York, NY 10020

Copyright © 2008 by Victoria Christopher Murray

First Touchstone trade paperback edition June 2008

TOUCHSTONE and colophon are registered trademarks of Simon & Schuster, Inc.

For information about special discounts for bulk purchases, please contact Simon & Schuster Special Sales at 1-800-456-6798 or business@simonandschuster.com.

Designed by Mary Austin Speaker

Manufactured in the United States of America

10   9   8   7   6   5   4   3

ISBN-13: 978-1-4165-5252-9
ISBN-10:   1-4165-5252-9

To my sisters, Michele, LuCia, and Cecile.

Thank you for always reminding me that this author thing is just
what I do and not who I am.

Jasmine and Hosea

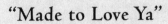

JUNE 2006

"Made to Love Ya"

—GERALD LEVERT

✳ ✳ ONE

EVEN WITH THE COLD METAL of the gun's barrel pressed hard against her temple, Jasmine's feet would not move.

"I want you out of my house."

Jasmine wanted to plead for her life. Beg for forgiveness and give him at least one hundred of the good reasons she had for telling her husband all of those lies. But her lips, like her feet, were frozen with fear.

"I said get out of my house."

The venom in his voice turned her fear into fight. And she fought with her words. "Please, Hosea, please forgive me for not telling you the truth before. But I'll tell you now; I'm forty-three, not thirty-eight."

The gun cocked.

She dropped to her knees and cried. "And I didn't tell you that I was married before because—"

Hosea pushed the metal into her skin.

"Please," she begged more. "Please."

He pulled the trigger.

Jasmine screamed. Shot up straight in bed, her skin dripping with the same sweat that drenched their satin sheets for the many nights that this nightmare invaded her sleep.

"Darlin'?"

She heard the calm of her husband's voice, then felt the warmth of his arms. "Darlin', it's just a dream." The kisses he planted on her forehead were meant to soothe, but that didn't work.

"It's all right, darlin'," Hosea kept saying. "Just another one of those bad dreams."

He's wrong, she thought as she settled back in bed. *This was not just a dream.*

Even as the rhythm of Hosea's sleep breathing returned, Jasmine's eyes stayed wide open. She knew if she surrendered to unconsciousness, Hosea's words would come back. And those words—far more than the gun—made fear rise like bile within her.

In her nightmare, Hosea was as cold as the gun he held. As cold as he'd been on the day, about eighteen months ago, when he'd *actually* told her he'd wanted nothing more to do with her—right after she revealed that he wasn't the father of their daughter.

For the millionth time Jasmine wished that her lies had ended there. But they didn't. And she knew if her secrets were uncovered her nightmare would turn into reality.

This dream was a sign, a warning—she was sure. She'd had it two or three times over the past year. But in the last two weeks, the ghost of her deceptive past haunted her with an almost daily vengeance.

She knew the reason why—it was because in ten days she and Hosea were renewing their vows.

"I want us to stand before God again," Hosea had told her when he first came up with the idea. "I want us to recommit."

Her eyes had widened with surprise. "Baby, don't people wait until their tenth or twentieth anniversary to do that?"

"There're no rules." He'd embraced her. "What's most important is the reason why. And with the way we started . . ." He'd stopped right there. Jasmine had closed her eyes and remembered the wonder of their first six months of marriage, and then the beautiful birth of their daughter. But when Jacqueline was barely twenty-four hours old, Hosea had walked away—from both her and the baby. Yet God's grace had found its way to her through Hosea's heart.

"I forgive you" was all Hosea said when he came back to her. He'd held her and Jacqueline and explained that it was God who had put them together, so they were divinely obligated to work through whatever challenges they had.

From that day, he'd loved her, claimed Jacqueline as his own, and together they'd lived in matrimonial bliss. But in the middle of her heaven, she wallowed in hell, terrified that one day the rest of her lies would be revealed.

Now, the fact that Hosea wanted to renew their vows so that they could start afresh made her tremble in terror. How could she stand before God—again—and pretend that all was well?

I've got to find a way to tell Hosea.

But even as her spirit longed to stop the lies, she didn't have the faith—or the guts—to tell the truth. It was too risky; she could lose Hosea, this time for good. No, she couldn't take that chance. Her secrets would have to stay tucked away in the dark, and she'd just pray that they never came to light.

TWO

THE MISSION: TO KEEP ALL of her secrets hidden.

And there was only one person Jasmine knew who could make sure that task was accomplished.

"Good to see you, Mrs. Bush." With his thick Lithuanian accent, the doorman greeted Jasmine as if he hadn't just seen her last week.

She waved to Henrikas and scooted into the elevator. Although she, Hosea, and Jacqueline had moved away a year ago, this Park Avenue building still felt like home. A minute later, the apartment door opened before she even had the chance to knock.

"I thought you were coming yesterday." Mae Frances spoke in her signature grumpy tone. But her eyes sparkled.

"Hello to you, too, Nama," Jasmine said, calling Mae Frances by the name that eighteen-month-old Jacqueline had given to the woman who, just three years ago, had been nothing more than the cantankerous old lady who lived across the hall. But now, Mae Frances was part of their family and the only grandmother Jacqueline would ever know.

Jasmine kissed her cheek, then swept into the apartment. She stopped, a déjà vu moment—back to the first time she'd entered this space. She'd been shocked when she'd walked into this drab apartment that didn't match the woman who was always drenched in diamonds and furs and who was chauffeured through the city in a limousine. She remembered her pain when she discovered that it was all a façade, that Mae Frances was a woman living in poverty with a prideful heart too hard to ask for help. Mae Frances had been an unsaved soul whose eternal doom had already begun right here on earth.

But that was then. Now there was no darkness inside Mae Frances's residence. Today, the sun's rays pressed through the massive windows framed with designer drapes that Jasmine had bought and Hosea had hung. The aged, raggedy furniture was gone, replaced with the chic pieces that had once graced Jasmine's apartment.

"What are you grinning at?" Mae Frances grumbled, standing as erect and elegant as a dancer.

"Your apartment looks good."

"Umph." Mae Frances smoothed the new silk skirt that Jasmine had bought her last week before she settled onto the sofa. "I'm just holding this furniture until you and your husband move. You need to get out of that penthouse and find a home with a yard for my granddaughter." Her eyes scanned the room. "Then I'll give you back all of this fancy stuff—I don't need it. What's this ugly color, anyway, aqua?"

Jasmine didn't bother to answer. She'd come to learn that this was just Mae Frances's way. Her tone, her words had nothing to do with her heart.

"I'm just doing this as a favor for you." Mae Frances continued her rant. Still, she was stiff, but her smile matched the light in her eyes.

"And we thank you."

They both knew she'd given Mae Frances the furniture. But while the woman Jasmine had come to love like a mother had changed much over the years of their friendship, her pride still remained. So, Jasmine let her keep her dignity and went along with whatever role Mae Frances wanted to play on any given day.

In an instant, Jasmine's smile was gone. "Do you have the information?"

Solemnly, Mae Frances nodded and handed Jasmine a slip of paper.

She took a moment before she glanced at the note: Kenny Larson. And next to her ex-husband's name was a number with a 678 area code.

"How did you get this?"

Mae Frances waved her hands in the air. "One of my connections."

Jasmine shook her head. She'd grown closer to Mae Frances than anyone besides Hosea. But still, her friend was a mystery. She had no idea how Mae Frances always had the hook-up. It was one of her connections who had helped Jasmine almost get away with keeping her daughter's paternity a secret. Dr. Jeremy Edmonds, an Upper East Side ob/gyn, had twisted the truth, making sure that Hosea believed Jasmine's lies—all for a fee, of course.

Mae Frances stopped Jasmine's memories. "You need to make this call."

"What should I say?"

"Find out his intentions. Make sure he has no plans to mess up your life." Mae Frances tilted her head. "I still can't believe you were married before."

She nodded. "Kenny was my high school sweetheart. I was a cheerleader and he was the star of the football team, on his way to the NFL."

"Hmph. Guess that didn't happen."

Jasmine shook her head. "He got hurt in college. Messed up all our hopes of becoming rich and famous. We never even got close—he ended up being nothing more than a numbers cruncher."

"So explain to me why you never told Preacher Man?" she asked, referring to the name she'd given Hosea the moment she'd met him.

"I don't know why," Jasmine whined. That was the truth. She had no idea why she'd told that lie. It made no sense now. But back then, when she was determined to become Hosea's wife, she was convinced that the lie was necessary; sure that Hosea—a minister—would never consider making a divorced woman his wife. She knew now that she'd been wrong. But what she wasn't so certain of was what Hosea would do if he found out. Even if he could forgive her for the lie, would he forgive how—and for how long—she'd hidden the truth?

That's why she had to make this call.

Jasmine's heart pressed hard against her chest as she dialed. She wasn't afraid of her ex—just of the secret that he unknowingly held.

"Hello."

Jasmine didn't know why a woman's voice surprised her. "May I speak to Kenny?"

"Who's calling?"

None of your business was what Jasmine wanted to say, the Jezebel rising in her. She wondered what other words she could say to make this woman—whoever she was—even more insecure. But then, Jasmine remembered; she was no longer the woman who went after another woman's man.

"Tell Kenny it's an old friend."

The pause told her that explanation wasn't good enough. Still a moment later, she heard "This is Kenny," and the rich, familiar tone made her smile.

"This is Jasmine." Then there was nothing, and Jasmine wondered if she was going to have to remind her ex-husband that she was his ex-wife.

"Wow. Jasmine. It's been a long time. How are you?"

"Fine." Jasmine stopped, not knowing what to say next.

There was a time when Jasmine had loved herself some Kenny Larson. But being married to a middle-manager in an insurance company was a hard life for Jasmine to live. An even harder life to accept. Especially when her best friend of thirty-five years—Kyla Jefferson—had married a successful doctor, and had a life full of the accoutrements that Jasmine had always known would be hers.

Jasmine sighed. There was no need to travel down that lane of memories. Life was perfect now—with Hosea. She just had to make sure it stayed that way.

She searched for words to say to her ex. "I've been fine and . . . I was just . . . I was thinking. . . ." She stopped again, calmed down. "It's good to hear your voice," she said and meant it.

"Good to hear you, too," he said with a warmth that came from his heart. "So, you still in Los Angeles?"

She said, "No, I left a while ago," and settled into the conversation like she was talking to an old friend. "I'm in New York." Behind her, she heard a deep cough. She glanced up and her eyes widened.

Mae Frances stood at the entry with the extension phone pressed to her ear. She covered the mouthpiece and hissed, "Don't tell him where you live. Don't tell him anything!" Then she motioned for Jasmine to continue.

It took a moment for Jasmine to turn her attention back to Kenny. "So . . . you're in Atlanta."

"Yeah, I've been here since I got married. Or remarried, I should say."

"You like it down there?"

"Yeah, I have a son."

That made Jasmine smile. Kenny had wanted children. She didn't. Not when he was earning only fifty thousand dollars a year. "Is he playing football yet?"

Kenny laughed. "He's only two, but give me a couple of years, I'll have him out there. What about you? Did you ever change your mind? Decide to have kids?"

"Yeah, I have—" The loud cough stopped her. Made her only say, "Yeah, I changed my mind."

He said, "So, what are you up to?"

"Not much. I work with my godbrother—"

The cough came again.

"I'm just living life." She paused and old memories played again in her mind. Of how Kenny had taken care of her when her mother passed away. How he'd tried to rescue her from her agony. How he'd been the only one who could. How even all of that had not been enough to rescue her from the mundane life she'd lived, the glamorous life she craved. "I know you're surprised to hear from me," she said, her voice softer now, filled with the love that she once had for him. "I'd been thinking about you and wondered if you were okay. And happy."

"I'm good. Very happy."

"I'm really glad to hear that."

"I hope you're happy, too," he said.

It didn't even take her a moment. "I am." Another long silence sat between them. "Well, I really didn't want anything more than to say hello."

"Listen, let me get your number."

"No!" she exclaimed. She could imagine that now. Kenny calling. Hosea answering. The ex-husband introducing himself to the present one. She said, "I think we should just leave things right here."

"O . . . kay," he spoke slowly.

"It's just that even now, hearing your voice, I know that I did a lot of things wrong. There's not a lot I want to remember."

"So you're saying I remind you of all the bad times," he said with no hostility in his tone.

"It wasn't all bad, Kenny. And it wasn't all you."

He chuckled. "There was a time when I would have paid big bucks to hear you say that."

"I'm sorry for all we went through. I know you tried, but I guess I wasn't happy with myself, so I couldn't be happy with you."

"Hey, it wasn't all bad and it wasn't all you."

She smiled as he repeated her words. "I wish you all of God's blessings."

By his pause, Jasmine knew she'd surprised him with those divine good wishes. "You too, Jasmine. Take care."

She held on to the phone a moment longer, remembering. But Mae Frances's cough reminded her that she needed to forget.

Mae Frances growled. "Well, *that* didn't work."

"Why were you listening?"

"Good thing I was. You were about to give up all the info that you're trying to hide."

"At least now I know."

"Know what?"

"I know where he's living, that he's married, that he has a son. And that he's happy. I don't have to worry about him showing up here in New York. I'm good."

Mae Frances twisted her lips in doubt. "Here's hoping."

Jasmine smiled. For the first time in weeks, she looked forward to snuggling in bed next to Hosea. Her secrets were safe.

She leaned back against the sofa's edge, but Mae Frances slapped her arm, making her sit up straight. "Take your head off my couch," Mae Frances scolded. "With all of that gel in your hair, you're gonna mess up my furniture."

Jasmine rubbed the space where her skin still stung. But she couldn't get mad. There was nothing in life that could change Mae Frances.

"No problem. I don't wanna mess up your furniture." She jumped up. "Gotta go, anyway. Are you okay for dinner? Do you want me to pick up something?"

"No, thank you. I don't need nobody looking after me like that. I'm not an old woman, you know."

"I know, but I will always take care of you." Jasmine kissed her cheek. "We'll pick you up for church in the morning."

"Okay," Mae Frances grumbled. "But I'm only going because of that ridiculous bet. Don't make no sense that someone should blackmail someone else into going to church."

Jasmine chuckled. Mae Frances had been saying those same words every week.

Both of them knew that the bet they'd made—that Mae Frances would go to church if she and Hosea reunited—was long ago over. Mae Frances had kept her end. She'd marched into church that first Sunday—in between Jasmine and Hosea—with her head high and her lips poked out. And now more than a year later, Mae Frances was still sitting in the pews at City of Lights at Riverside Church every Sunday, that is, when she wasn't in the choir stand draped in her burgundy gown, belting out tunes of old Negro hymns with the Senior Choir.

"See you tomorrow, Nama. Love you," Jasmine yelled over her shoulder. She couldn't wait to get home and start planning their second wedding. She was ready now to renew her vows, commit to Hosea again. Start all over. And this time, there would be no lies.

✳ ✳ THREE

Hosea adjusted his tie. His second wedding—that made him smile. He wondered if he and Jasmine would ever do this again. Maybe fifty years from now.

That made him suddenly remember. He closed his eyes. Went back. To another time. Another wedding—that almost was, but never happened. Hosea sighed and wondered why that memory came to him now. He never thought about his past. Didn't want to start thinking about it now.

The door creaked open.

"Well, you don't look nervous."

Hosea grinned at his father. They hugged before he said, "No, Pops, I'm good. I don't have to wonder whether Jasmine will show up. She can't change her mind." Hosea held up his hand, wiggled his fingers. The diamond chips in his wedding band glittered.

Reverend Bush beamed, but his smile widened when the door swung open again, this time banging hard against the wall. Jacqueline scurried into the room.

"Dada, Dada," she squealed before she jumped into her father's arms.

"There's my pumpkin." He lifted her, pressed his lips against her neck, and exhaled.

She giggled, then wiggled from his arms and ran to Reverend Bush. "Pop-Pop!"

She raised her arms and her grandfather lifted her up. "Look at you, all dressed up, pretty in pink."

"Speaking of pretty . . ." The voice came from outside the room, but a moment later, Mae Frances paraded in wearing her own pink chiffon dress that fluttered around her ankles as she moved.

"You're beautiful, Nama." Hosea kissed her cheek.

She tossed her hand in the air and smoothed over her French roll. "Really? I grabbed this ol' thing from the back of my closet."

Hosea grinned. He knew Mae Frances remembered that he was with her and Jasmine when they'd bought this dress a week ago. He said, "You're going to be the most beautiful woman in the church. After my wife, of course."

Reverend Bush said, "Is Jasmine ready?"

"She is. We're just waiting for Preacher Man."

"Peeker Man!" Jacqueline imitated.

Reverend Bush and Mae Frances laughed, but Hosea didn't. "Nama, don't call me that. I don't want Jacquie growing up calling me Preacher Man."

"Peeker Man!" Jacqueline echoed.

Hosea shook his head as he took Jacqueline from his father's arms.

"I'm going to check on Jasmine," Mae Frances said. She pushed back her shoulders, raised her head high like the queen she knew she was. "Reverend, do you want to join me?"

Reverend Bush gave her a half-smile. "If it's okay to see the bride before the ceremony."

"It is. You're not her husband. In fact, last time I checked, you were single; isn't that right?." She looped her arm through Reverend Bush's before the two left the room together.

"Dada!"

Hosea rested Jacqueline on his lap and hugged his daughter. He was grateful for this day. Grateful that he and Jasmine would start again. Without the secrets and the lies that had tainted their union the first time.

Remembering their first wedding made him pull back and

glance at his daughter. She ignored him; her focus was on the ribbon in front of her dress.

Just looking at her made him smile—except for moments where that small corner of his heart ached. And now, as he'd done so many times, he searched Jacqueline's face for just a hint of himself. It was ridiculous, he knew that. How would he ever see something that couldn't be there?

"You are my daughter," he whispered. Legally, she was. His adoption of Jacqueline had been complete for months.

"Dada," she said.

"Yes, I am."

Jacqueline really was a beauty, from her honey-colored eyes to the sharp angle of her jaw, down to her full lips. She bore no resemblance to him and if he hadn't witnessed her birth, he would have even questioned her maternity. But Brian Lewis—that man Jacqueline did not deny. She wore her biological father's DNA on the outside.

That was his sentence—a lifetime of looking at the daughter he loved so much and seeing what he hated most. His wife's sin. Though he had long ago forgiven, it was a battle to forget. All he could do was remember. The sin.

"My dada," Jacqueline said.

Hosea looked at his daughter. Her smile was gone, and now her thick eyebrows were bunched together like she was deep in thought.

Hosea smiled. There it was—that was his part of her. His serious, studious nature. She was a beauty, but her brains—she'd get that from him. At least, that's what he'd pretend.

He lifted her up. "Did I ever tell you that I loved you before you were even born?"

Jacqueline nodded and laughed.

He knew she didn't understand. But one day she would know his unconditional love for her.

He let her legs drop to the floor. "Okay, my pumpkin. Let's go get married."

"Git marry!"

Just one look at Jasmine made him forget her sins.

"*I was made to love ya . . .* "

Gerald Levert crooned through the speakers and Jasmine sauntered down the aisle as Hosea's favorite singer told how every part of him was made to love his woman. There were times when Hosea just knew this song had been written about him.

He was made to love this woman who was moving slowly toward the altar, her eyes filled with light just for him. Two years, a multitude of sins, yet he loved her like nobody's business. And she had never looked more beautiful than she did today, in the pink gown she wore.

His wife had complained about the twenty extra pounds she carried since she'd given birth. But Hosea couldn't see it. Whatever size she was now—a ten, twelve, fourteen, twenty—it didn't matter to him. He loved every inch—from her shoulder-length auburn-streaked hair to her toned legs that would have been the envy of any sprinter, she was the perfect woman, the one created by God just for him.

His eyes left Jasmine and he glanced down at Jacqueline, standing at his side, waiting. When he looked up again, the look of total devotion that Jasmine wore let him know that he could do this, he could take these vows and then put it all—her past, the sin, his hurt—behind him. After today, he wouldn't think about or remember any of it anymore.

"Mama, come!" Jacqueline's demand broke through the majesty and they all laughed.

"Sorry I took so long," Jasmine said before she moved into

place at the altar. She stood on the other side of Jacqueline and took her hand, the bridge between husband and wife.

"Well, here we are again." Pride was inside Reverend Bush's smile as he stood before his family. "I have done a few of these ceremonies, but I've never done one so early into a marriage. But therein lies the beauty—there is no definition as to when one can stand before God and reaffirm love that has deepened with not only the passing of time, but also the living of life." He paused. "Hosea and Jasmine, when you first stood at this altar two years ago, little did you know that trials would come that would test your faith, and your love—for each other and for God." Reverend Bush paused and Jasmine and Hosea both glanced at Jacqueline.

Clearing his throat, Reverend Bush continued. "But you kept your promises, to each other and to God, understanding that this commitment is not for a limited time, but for a lifetime.

"So, I am proud to be here, in front of two people—" he grinned at Jacqueline, who still stood holding her parent's hands "—excuse me, three people, who not only love God, but know God. Who understand that their union is ordained by God. Who understand that anything that God puts together, no man can take apart."

Hosea took a breath. As long as he remembered these words he'd be fine. This wasn't about him. Never was. This was about the love that God had placed in his heart—for Jasmine. This was about the life that God created—in Jacqueline. This was about living the life of blessings that God had—for all of them.

Minutes later, when Reverend Bush announced, "Hosea, you may kiss your bride . . . again," Hosea had never been happier to hold his wife. *Thank God,* he thought as their lips met. *Thank God for new beginnings.*

. . .

"May I have your attention, I'd like to say something."

The murmur of chatter ceased as the thirty-some-odd guests turned toward Hosea.

Jasmine grinned as she moved to his side. "What are you going to say?"

He answered with just a smile as his eyes scanned the space. This was so different from their first reception. Back then, they'd celebrated with two hundred guests in a private room at Tavern on the Green. But today, only the people dearest to them were here, and they celebrated in the church's reception hall.

Hosea had been surprised when Jasmine insisted on a simple ceremony. "Just our family," she'd said.

His wife had grown so much. Faith and family—that was most important to both of them. He had to talk her into including more guests than just his father, Mae Frances, and her godbrother, Malik. Now, as he glanced at the gathering—from Mrs. Whittingham, his father's assistant, to Brother Hill, one of the head deacons at City of Lights, he was glad they'd included their friends.

"First," Hosea began, taking Jasmine's hand, "thank you for sharing this day with us. For me, today is even more important than the first time. Because two years ago, I loved Jasmine, but I didn't know Jasmine. And it was the same for her with me. But now, through time, trials, and triumphs, we know everything— the good, the bad, the ugly. We even know each other's nightmares."

Soft chuckles filled the space, but Jasmine's smile went away.

"I want everyone to know how much I love my wife and my daughter. So in front of family and friends," Hosea raised his glass in the air, "let me say to Jasmine Larson Bush, thank you for making me the happiest man on earth again. I look forward to our years—not without some tears—but with mostly love and laughter. This is our beginning. Clean, fresh, new." He lifted his flute higher.

Glasses clicked and "Cheers!" followed.

"I have one more piece of news," he said loud enough to get everyone's attention again. "My wife and I are going to take an extended honeymoon."

"Get out!" Jasmine exclaimed. "A vacation?"

"Well, not exactly a vacation, but you're going to love it. We're going to Los Angeles!"

"Oh, that's nice," Mrs. Whittingham said, and the rest of the crowd agreed.

Hosea chuckled when he glanced at his wife, her face long with confusion. "I know this won't compare to our honeymoon in Bermuda," he said to her, "but you're still going to enjoy it because we're going for three months."

"Wow," rang through the group. There were more smiles, more cheers. Happiness from everyone. Except for Jasmine.

"Some of you know Triage Blue, my friend and the other executive producer on my television show. Well, Triage is making major moves. He's gone from rapper to talk show host and now actor. He's starring in a new Spike Lee movie, taping in L.A. So instead of finding a temporary cohost, we're taking the show on the road."

"Los Angeles," Jasmine said, still not able to find any joy.

Hosea turned to Malik. "Bro, do you think you can manage for three months at the club without my wife?"

"You know she runs the place." Her godbrother smiled. "But we'll work it out. I'm sure Rio will still be standing when you guys get back." Malik raised his glass, toasting Hosea and Jasmine. "Don't worry. The two of you," he paused and looked at Jacqueline, who was sleeping in her grandfather's arms, "the *three* of you go to the Left Coast and have a great time."

Hosea squeezed Jasmine's hand. "A great time. That's exactly what we plan to do for the rest of our lives."

FOUR

Jasmine tucked Jacqueline underneath the blanket, kissed her cheek, then tiptoed from her bedroom.

"Is my pumpkin asleep?" Hosea asked, meeting Jasmine in the hallway.

She nodded. "Your pumpkin had a long day."

He grinned as he put his arm around Jasmine and walked beside her. "You haven't said much about my surprise."

Jasmine turned toward the massive living room windows that overlooked Central Park. Even in the night hours this tenth-floor view of the park's southern border was a natural wonder. But the beauty didn't bring her the peace that it normally did.

"So, what do you think about L.A.?" Hosea settled onto the couch. "Pretty exciting, huh?"

More like scary. "It could be."

"That's not the right answer. What's wrong?"

She didn't have to turn around to know that his face was now creased with concern.

She pasted on a smile, took a deep breath, and faced him. "I was thinking . . . is it necessary for me to go to L.A. with you?"

His frown deepened.

"I mean," she continued, "if you're only going to be there for three months, do we need to pack up everything?"

"We're not moving. All we have to do is take a few bags. The show's going to pay for our place; they're looking at apartments at the Fairmont for the staff."

Years ago, she would have walked from New York to Los Angeles to spend one night in that five-star hotel in the San Fernando Valley. But that kind of stuff didn't matter anymore. All she cared about was her husband and her daughter. And keeping her husband happy. She couldn't do that if she were in Los Angeles.

"But it's more than packing a few bags, Hosea. We'll have to disrupt Jacquie—"

"From what?"

"From her life."

Hosea chuckled. "Jacquie doesn't care where she sleeps as long as Mama and Dada are in the next room." He paused. "I thought you'd be excited."

"I am." Jasmine lowered her eyes. "But I can't imagine leaving my job for three months."

"Malik said the club would be fine."

"Only because you put him on the spot. He didn't have time to consider it. I run that place. What's going to happen to Rio if I'm gone for that long?"

"So you don't want to go to Los Angeles?"

After a moment, she looked at him. "We can do the commuter marriage thing. Jacquie and I can come on weekends. And sometimes, maybe, you could come home."

His eyes narrowed, his mind in thought. "I don't like this. I would miss you and Jacquie. And what about the baby?" He wrapped his arms around her. "I was thinking L.A. would be better for us. Less stress, a prolonged vacation. We'll make a baby in no time out there."

Inside, Jasmine sighed. It wasn't stress that had stopped her from getting pregnant. She suspected that it had more to do with her being forty-three and not thirty-eight. Five years—not a big difference in the overall spectrum of time. A big difference—if you were trying to conceive.

"Sweetheart, first of all, three months is not going to stop us from getting pregnant. And, if you're right about it feeling like a vacation, we'll be fine on the weekends." *And it will give me time to come up with some medical reason for this not happening.*

"You really don't want to go with me?"

"I *want* to go. I just think it would be better if Jacquie and I stayed here."

He took her hand and pulled her onto the couch. It took a few minutes for him to say, "I don't like this, but if it works for you, then I'll make it work for me."

She exhaled. Her wish, granted.

But only seconds, and then, "Are you sure there's not another reason why you don't want to go to Los Angeles?"

She closed her eyes, didn't move. Stayed inside her husband's arms and marveled at his discernment. He was right—she never wanted to go back to Los Angeles, the city where her sins began.

He asked, "Does this have anything to do with Brian?"

There—he'd said it. For the first time since he'd come back to their marriage, he had spoken her sin aloud and said Jacqueline's father's name.

She told him the truth. "Brian never crosses my mind. I only love you."

He lifted her chin, looked into her eyes. "I know that. I don't have any doubts." He paused, but the way he held his lips together, Jasmine knew he had more to say. "About Brian," he began again. "One day we're going to have to talk about him. And we're probably going to have to see him."

She frowned. "Why?"

"Because of Jacquie. We're never going to lie to her. When the time's right, we're going to tell her about her father."

Jasmine jumped from the couch, crossed her arms, and looked down at Hosea. "You're her father."

"I know that," he spoke calmly. "But we have to face the fact that when she learns about Brian, she may want to know him."

Know what about him? Know that she was conceived in lust, not love?

Jasmine whipped her head from side to side. *We will never tell her* was what she wanted to say. But she knew her husband. He would never lie—not by commission or omission.

Hosea stood and rested his hands on her shoulders. "Whether we like it or not, Brian Lewis will always be a part of our lives because of Jacquie."

Still, Jasmine did not agree. She loved her daughter and wouldn't change a thing about her—except for her paternity. To her, Jacqueline was Hosea's. That's how it would always be. She didn't know how she would do it, but she would make sure that Brian Lewis never got close to her family.

"Are you sure you don't want to go to L.A.?"

She shook her head. "We'll be fine. I promise."

"Will you miss me?"

She nodded.

"Show me how much." He pressed his lips against hers, then lifted her into his arms.

She squealed.

"Ssshhh, you'll wake my pumpkin."

Their lips met again and as they edged toward their bedroom, Jasmine began the silent prayer that she'd said every time for the last year: *Please, God. Let tonight be the night. Let us make a baby.*

 FIVE

THE KISSES WERE LIKE butterflies sweeping against her cheek.

"Mama." Jacqueline giggled.

Jasmine moaned before her eyes fluttered open.

Hosea stood over her, holding Jacqueline in his arms. "We just wanted to say good morning. I'm going to take my pumpkin back to Mrs. Sloss," Hosea said, referring to their live-in nanny.

Jacqueline laughed as Hosea lifted her high above his head, then settled her onto his shoulders.

"By the way," he began, "are you sure you don't want to go to the luncheon today? It's the last time the entire staff will be together before we go to L.A."

She shook her head. Now awake, her "Monday To-Do List" was already scrolling through her mind. "No can do. I have a full day," she said, scurrying to the bathroom.

Inside, she hopped into the shower, sighing as the warm spray soothed her. Leaning against the pebbled tile, she closed her eyes and relaxed under the water's massage.

Go.

Jasmine's eyes sprung open. She glanced through the foggy glass. She heard nothing more than the shower's rain. She leaned back, closed her eyes again.

Go.

Gentle. Guiding.

Jasmine tilted her head. Called out, "Hosea!"

He opened the bathroom door. "Yeah?"

"Did you say something?"

"I didn't say a word, darlin'. Watch out now, don't be hearing things that aren't there." He chuckled and closed the door.

She turned off the water. Stepped cautiously from the stall onto the heated floor. She listened for a moment, then pressed the button to turn on the in-wall speakers. If she was going to hear voices, she wanted them to be real.

But even through Brent Jones singing Hosea's favorite song, "My Heart's Desire," she heard it again.

Go.

Is that it? Jasmine wondered. It was the first time that she'd heard that voice. That voice that so many others spoke about. Especially Hosea—he said that God talked to him all the time. But she'd never heard a word from above. So how was she supposed to know if this was Him?

Go.

"Go where?" Jasmine asked the air. She stayed in place for a minute, then opened the bathroom door.

"Babe, what time is the luncheon?"

Hosea stepped from inside his closet. "You changed your mind?"

She thought about the voice. "Isn't that a woman's prerogative?"

He laughed. "It's in the Rainbow Room at noon. Want me to pick you up?"

She shook her head. "No need for you to come all the way downtown. I'll call for a car." She closed the door and wrapped herself inside her towel. She wasn't sure if it was God she heard, but she wasn't taking a chance. If God was talking to her, she was certainly going to listen.

✳ ✳ SIX

"Hey, darlin'." Hosea opened the Town Car's door.

Jasmine stepped out and into her husband's arms. "I didn't expect you to be waiting for me."

He kissed her. "Whenever I get the chance, I walk side by side with my wife." Slipping his hand into hers, the two weaved through the lunchtime throng outside of Rockefeller Center.

Chatter and laughter greeted them when the elevator doors opened on the sixty-fifth floor. Jasmine and Hosea mingled with the *Bring It On* team, until the restaurant's staff directed the guests to sit for lunch.

"I'm glad they put us at a table together," Jasmine whispered to Deborah Blue. "I thought they were going to have a dais or something."

"This is so much better," Deborah agreed as she sat at the table set up for four. Then she called to her husband. "Honey, you and Hosea see each other every day, but you're worse than me and Jasmine."

Hosea and Triage—the other executive producer of the show— turned toward their wives and laughed.

"We're busted." Triage kissed his wife, and as he sat, he turned to Jasmine. "Hosea just told me you're not going to L.A."

Jasmine stiffened. "I can't get away right now." She took Hosea's hand. "But I'll be visiting when I can."

"I'm sorry to hear that," Deborah said. "I'll be in L.A. the entire summer recording a new CD and I was looking forward to showing you the city."

Before Jasmine could tell Deborah that she was born in Los

Angeles, Stephen Hager, one of the top executives with the network, stood at the microphone. "I'd like to thank everyone for
coming today. This is an exciting time for the show. Our ratings
have steadily increased, which means more advertising dollars."
He paused. "And those Emmys we got earlier this year certainly
helped."

Applause filled the room.

"This is a good time for a celebration. That's what this lunch is
about. No long speeches, just an enjoyable time with colleagues.
Now, before they serve lunch, I do have one announcement." He
turned toward Hosea and Triage. "I have to congratulate you two
for the wonderful job you've done."

More applause.

"You've both expressed your thoughts about the show in L.A.
and we agree with you—*Bring It On* should thrive in Hollywood."

The crowd nodded.

"To help with that, we've hired another producer. An award-
winning news journalist . . ."

Jasmine leaned forward, whispered, "Did you know they were
hiring someone else?"

Hosea shook his head. "But Triage and I did request another
producer after Mary Magdalene left. We wanted someone with
news experience."

Jasmine sat back. That made sense. Hosea was always saying
that he wished the show had a bit more of a news/current-events
focus.

"Ladies and gentlemen, let me introduce the newest member
of the *Bring It On* team, Natasia Redding."

"You're kidding!"

Jasmine frowned as her husband shouted, then jumped from his
seat. A tall woman draped in a red Tadashi V-neck sheath sauntered into the room, paused at their table as if she were at the end
of a runway, and then wrapped her arms around Hosea's neck.

Jasmine's glower deepened; she was not feeling this scene.

"What are you doing here?" Hosea asked, when he stepped back.

"Didn't you hear?" Natasia responded in a voice that came from her throat. "I'm joining the show."

"Hosea," Stephen began, "we were in the final stages of the interview when Natasia realized that you were one of the hosts and a producer. We understand you know each other."

"Yes," Hosea said, "we do."

When the woman slipped her hand through Hosea's, Jasmine jumped up and stood in front of her husband.

"Oh, Jasmine," he said, as if he'd forgotten his wife. "This is an old friend, Natasia."

Natasia laughed, her chuckle sounding even sexier than her voice. "Old friends? Is that what you call it?" Her fiery fuchsia-colored lips spread into a wide smile as she turned to Jasmine. "Please, I'm the first woman he ever loved and I still have the engagement ring to prove it." She held out her hand to Jasmine. "Do you work with Hosea?"

Jasmine stared at Natasia's hand, left it dangling in the air, then crossed her arms and glared at her husband.

Hosea cleared his throat and embraced Jasmine. "Natasia, this is my wife, Jasmine."

"Really? I didn't know you were married." She paused, her eyes wandered over Jasmine, up, then down, before she turned back to Hosea. "I can't believe you came to New York and turned into a star," she said as if Hosea's wife didn't exist. She hooked her arm through his. "We must catch up."

Natasia slipped into the chair where Jasmine had been sitting and pulled Hosea down next to her. Jasmine's eyebrows raised, her mouth opened, but before she could say a word, Deborah was at her side.

"Here, take my seat," Deborah whispered.

"Oh." Natasia stopped her chatting. Looked up. "Were you sitting here?"

"Yes. I was sitting next to my husband."

"That's okay, darlin'," Hosea said. "Sit here." He patted the seat Deborah had been in. "I'll get another chair."

"Triage just went for one." Deborah took Jasmine's hand and guided her into her seat.

Natasia giggled. "Isn't that cute? You call her darlin' too." Before Jasmine could say a word, Natasia continued, "So tell me about the show," she said, ignoring everyone else. "I couldn't believe it when I found out this was you. What a coincidence." Natasia paused, leaned in closer, the deep V of her dress right in front of Hosea's face. "Oh, that's right, you don't believe in coincidences." She paused again. Lifted his glass of water and took a sip as if the glass and Hosea belonged to her. "So, it must be fate. We were meant to be."

Jasmine began a slow rise from her seat, but Deborah's hand on her shoulder held her down. "Girl, don't even worry about it," she whispered.

"Oh, I'm not worried. I just don't play that."

"You know I understand, with the hoochies throwing themselves at Triage all the time," Deborah said. "But this is business." She looked around the room to remind Jasmine where they were. "And Hosea is going home with you."

"So, what have you been up to?" Natasia asked as the waiters placed salad plates in front of them.

Through lunch, dessert, and speeches that followed, Natasia chatted with Hosea as if it was just the two of them. And Jasmine sat, seething in her seat.

"Darlin', are you ready?" Hosea finally asked.

Jasmine's eyes darted between Hosea and Natasia. "Oh, I've been ready."

Natasia smiled. "It was so nice to meet you . . ." She paused, squinted. "What did you say your name was?"

"Jasmine," Hosea responded for her. He took his wife's hand. "Natasia, it was really good seeing you."

"Oh, sweetie, this pleasure was definitely all mine." She opened her purse and pulled out a card. "Let me give you this. I'm staying at the Ritz and they give you these." She tucked the business card into Hosea's hand. "That's the number to the hotel. Call me before you stop by."

Jasmine's mouth opened wide. She could not believe that she was going to have to beat down this woman right here, right now.

"I won't need this."

"Sure you do." Natasia grinned. "How else will we catch up?"

"We'll do that in the office."

"But my hotel room is much more . . ." she paused, looked at Jasmine, "private."

"No." Hosea's voice was stern this time and he handed her back the card.

With a smirk, Natasia shrugged. "Whatever." She smiled at Hosea, but when Natasia turned to Jasmine, all signs of her cheer were gone. "I guess we'll be seeing quite a bit of each other."

"You can count on it," Jasmine said before she took Hosea's hand and marched out the door.

 SEVEN

HEAT ROSE FROM EVERY PORE of her body.

Hosea asked, "Do you want me to drop you at your office?"

"Aren't you going home?" Jasmine managed to ask, although it was difficult to talk and breathe and fume at the same time.

"Yeah, I told you, I'm going to hang out with Jacquie today."

"I'm going home with you." She stared straight ahead.

She couldn't look at her husband, because if she did, she'd remember the way he looked at that woman. But even as she stomped toward their car, she knew there would be no way to forget Natasia Redding. Everything about that woman was unforgettable; she may have been working behind the scenes, but Natasia could have easily made her fortune in front of the camera. Svelte and striking, she had the undivided attention of every man and the undeniable envy of every woman in that room.

"Darlin', are you all right?" Hosea asked as they strapped on their seat belts.

She wanted to tell him never to call her that again. "I'm. Fine."

Hosea glanced at her with raised eyebrows, shrugged, then inched the car from the parking garage.

All Jasmine could think about was Natasia. Her looks. Her charm. The way she commanded Hosea's attention as if she knew him. She *did* know him—well.

I'm the first woman he ever loved.

Jasmine bounced back against the seat. "Why didn't you ever tell me about Natasia?" she demanded, still not looking at him.

Hosea shrugged. "There was nothing to tell. Neither one of us talked about our past relationships."

Jasmine was ready to pounce, but thoughts about her ex made her slow her roll.

"But you were *engaged*," she said, her tone softer now.

"But never married." He took her hand into his. "I married the woman I wanted."

Inside, she sighed, softening more. She wanted to forget all about this, but the vision of that woman in her mind wouldn't stop.

"You should have mentioned her."

"Why? She would still have shown up today. And that's the problem you have, right?"

Jasmine twisted in the seat to face him. "Yes. Hosea, she was all over you."

"Come on, you're exaggerating."

"No! I'm not. There were a couple of times when Deborah and Triage had to hold me back. I was ready to take her out."

He laughed. "First of all, you don't belong to that group of women."

She softened even more. "I know. But back in the day, she would have found herself laid out on the floor."

"Well, I'm glad I didn't know you then because that's not the kind of woman I want."

Jasmine sighed.

"Darlin' . . ."

She cringed when he said that.

"It doesn't matter what Natasia's sellin' 'cause I ain't buyin'." He squeezed her hand. "How am I gonna have time for someone else when I got you?"

He was extending an olive branch and she wanted to take it. Just lean back and forget. But she had to add, "I don't trust her."

"No need to trust her. Trust me."

"It's not always about that."

He pulled his hand away, and glanced at her sideways. "It's always about trust. And you'll always be able to trust me."

She was quiet until they pulled in front of their apartment building. The doorman greeted them and Hosea tossed him the car keys.

Inside the elevator, Jasmine asked, "Are you sure there's not another reason why you didn't tell me about Natasia?"

Hosea sighed. "I don't want to talk about this anymore."

"But I need to."

"There's no reason. I've told you all there is."

"Are you sure?"

He stepped to the side, tilted his head. "I've told you the truth, Jasmine," his voice stronger now. The elevator doors opened. "Secrets are your M.O., not mine," he said before he stomped from the elevator and into their apartment.

Jasmine stood at the window, staring at the full foliage of Central Park. Hosea had taken Jacqueline to the pond, but thoughts of the lunch were still with her.

Hosea was right. She should trust him. And she did. But she didn't trust Natasia. She'd been in the game long enough to recognize a player. Natasia was definitely a player and the game had already begun.

"It must be fate. We were meant to be."

Those were Natasia's words, but Jasmine knew that Natasia being in New York was no coincidence. How could it be? She was the kind of woman who did her research, of that Jasmine was sure. She was convinced Natasia knew everything about Hosea Bush—including that he had a wife.

"That woman is definitely after my husband."

"You say something, darlin'?"

Jasmine spun around; Hosea stood at the door with Jacqueline in his arms.

"I didn't expect you back so soon."

"My pumpkin is knocked out. Let me lay her down."

Jasmine nodded, then waited for her husband on the couch. Even though the June sun beamed heat into their apartment, she shivered—every time she thought of Natasia.

"Our daughter ran me ragged." Hosea plopped down next to her. "I'm gonna take a nap myself." He picked up the newspaper. "So what did you do while we were out?"

"Not much. Was just thinking."

"About what?" He sighed. "Or should I even ask?"

She paused. "I've decided to go to Los Angeles with you."

He nodded slowly. "Well, that's a good thing."

"And I'm taking Mrs. Sloss." Jasmine expected Hosea to ask her why she would need their nanny since she wouldn't be working. But watching Natasia was going to be a full-time job.

"That's fine." He grinned. "Is there any particular reason for this change?" he asked, though through his smirk, Jasmine was sure he knew her reasons why.

"Only that I couldn't stand the thought of missing you." She kissed his cheek, then pushed herself up. "You said you needed a nap; I think I want one, too."

He tossed the newspaper to the floor. "I'm right behind you."

She took a few steps, then stopped. "We're staying at the Fairmont, right?"

He nodded.

"Make sure that Natasia is not in that hotel." Before he could say a word, she added, "That's not open for discussion." Only then did she smile. And take his hand leading him into their bedroom.

EIGHT

HOSEA STOOD AT THE OPEN door for a moment. Natasia's head was bent low, her eyes focused on whatever she was reading. Every inch of her desk was covered with pads, folders, binders.

The ends of his lips turned upward. This was the Natasia he remembered, the woman he'd loved. They'd worked together, played together. Lived together, loved together. It was the last thought that kept him standing there. It was the memories of their bedroom romps as the midday sun burned through the windows of their fifteenth-floor Lake Shore Drive apartment that kept him staring.

"Hey, you."

Her voice tugged him away from Chicago. Brought him crashing back to New York. He hadn't noticed that she had looked up and was now staring at him.

He cleared his throat and his thoughts; strolled into her office. He sat, and she rose from her chair. Leaned across her desk toward him. His eyes strayed from her face, her lips. Moved to take in the curves of her body that weren't hidden beneath her lavender dress. He inhaled and memories of her rushed back.

Her chuckle was deep and low as if she knew his thoughts. She tossed her hair over her shoulders and sauntered around to where he sat. Perching herself on the edge of the desk, she crossed her legs and both of them watched her hemline rise.

"Was there anything you wanted?" she asked.

"No." He forced his eyes back to her face. "I mean, yes. We're going to lunch, right?"

"Oh, sweetie," she started, making Hosea raise his eyebrows.

She chuckled. Held up her hands. "Sorry. Old habit." She started again, "Hosea . . . I was going to call you. I'm still inundated with these files."

"No problem." He stood, turned toward the door. "We can do lunch . . . whenever."

"Oh, no you don't." She grabbed his hand. "You're not getting away that easily. Let's do dinner."

He shook his head, and then noticed she was still holding his hand. He pulled away.

She said, "Dinner would be much better because I'm in the middle of all of this and I don't want to stop."

"Keep going. We'll do lunch tomorrow."

"That won't work." She grabbed her desk calendar. "I'm meeting with Steve tomorrow." She pouted. "Getting together with you is not all pleasure. I have so many questions."

"They're lots of people here who can help."

"But I trust you." When he added nothing more, she sighed. "All right. I'll just pick up after lunch. It'll be harder. I was on a roll—"

He held up his hand. "Okay, we'll do an early dinner."

"Thanks, sweetie." This time there was no apology for that term of endearment.

He said, "I'll make reservations. How's six?"

"Eight would be good. Nine would be better."

"I'll make reservations for seven." Even though Jasmine was used to these last-minute dinner meetings, he added, "I need to get home."

"Okay."

Hosea stepped into the hallway and with his hands stuffed deep into his pockets, he rushed into his office. Wondered about this dinner. Thought about all he'd been remembering. Decided that this was all about nothing—just a recollection of history.

He reached for the telephone, but then pulled back. He needed a moment. A little time before he called his wife to tell her that he wouldn't be home for dinner.

The flood gates opened and Hosea was submerged beneath the memories . . .

"Minister Bush."

Hosea turned around and his heart bumped harder against his chest.

"Hello." The woman held out her hand. "I'm Natasia Redding. I just wanted to add my welcome to all that you've received." She smiled, her hand still dangling in the air. When Hosea finally grasped her hand, she said, "Welcome to Crystal Lake Cathedral."

It took Hosea a moment to say "Thanks."

She glanced down at their hands, still together.

He pulled away, even though he didn't want to. He could hold her hand forever. He searched his mind for more words, but he couldn't think of anything.

She came to his rescue. "I work with the audiovisual team, so if there's anything I can do to help you get settled, let me know."

Again, he wanted to say more than "Thanks."

Again, she was the one to free him from the silence. "You know what," she began, "do you have any time now? There's something I'd like to ask you. And if you're free . . . we could do brunch."

Hosea wanted to turn around to see who was watching. Surely, this was some kind of ministerial hazing. Why would this woman who should be gracing the cover of fashion magazines ask him to go out on his first Sunday at the church? But within the hour, he was sitting across from her at Oceanique.

"Are you from Chicago?" he asked.

"Lived here all my life," she said between bites of her pasta. "Only left once—to study in London."

"College?"

"Kind of. I went to undergrad here at the University of Chicago. Then I went to Oxford."

"Ah." Hosea sat back. "A Rhodes Scholar."

She shrugged, as if she were embarrassed.

"I'm impressed."

"Don't be."

But he already was. Beauty and brains. And, she was a Christian, wasn't she? His hope was rising. He asked, "How long have you been going to Crystal Lake Cathedral?"

"A couple of years. When my fiancé moved to Chicago . . ."

It was hard to listen to more after the word "fiancé" sucked the air from his hope.

"Your fiancé?"

She nodded. "I'm engaged."

Only then did he notice. The ring. It was an itty-bitty thing. Too small to sparkle or shine. A man trying to claim this woman as his own should have covered her with diamonds. At least that's what he would have done.

She said, "I wanted to talk about your newspaper."

That's what this is about.

"I'm a producer on the NBC morning show and I've been looking for projects for our cable stations."

For the next hour, she told him her thoughts of using the newspaper *The Christian Times,* where he was editor, as the format for a talk show. But he'd had difficulty concentrating as he watched her lips move.

Why are you engaged? was what he wanted to ask her.

Finally, he agreed to give her proposal some thought.

Outside the restaurant, she handed him her card. "I'll be looking to hear from you."

He hailed a cab, held the door while she slid inside, then he watched the car roll away before he walked in the opposite direction. It was good that only God knew his thoughts.

But something had come out of that brunch. It had been five years since his mother had passed and for most of that time, he'd lived as a monk.

Then today, Natasia had stirred thoughts and feelings that he'd almost forgotten. Maybe God was telling him to get back into this game called life, and Natasia was God's messenger . . .

"I'm ready if you are."

Hosea turned from the window and his memories. Automatically smiled when he looked at her. It may have been the end of the workday, but Natasia looked as fresh as the morning. Her lips gleamed with gloss and she glowed as if she'd just come from the beach.

He glanced at his watch. "It's only five-thirty."

"I finished early and thought we could have drinks before dinner. So," she continued as she moved toward him, "I made reservations and ordered a car."

"We could've caught a cab."

Natasia sighed. "You haven't changed a bit."

"Oh, I'm very different." He made sure he was looking into her eyes. "I'm a husband and a father now."

She paused, nodded slightly. "But in every other way, you're the same." His face spread with surprise when she adjusted his shirt collar. "You're a star now, sweetie. You should act like one."

Gently, he pushed her hands away. "Natasia, you cannot call me sweetie."

"I know," she whispered. "It's not professional."

He shook his head, then moved toward the door. "I made reservations at the Bistro."

"Would you mind if we changed that? I made reservations at Tavern on the Green," she said, brushing past him. "I've never been there."

He followed her into the hall. Tavern on the Green—it was just a restaurant.

. . .

"Good evening, Mr. Bush."

"How're you doing?" Hosea asked as the young man poured water into their glasses. He grabbed his menu and studied his choices even though he almost knew this menu by heart. Taking a quick glance at Natasia, he wondered if she knew this was the place where he and Jasmine had their wedding reception.

"So, the fact that the staff is calling you by name means that you've been here before, huh?" Natasia grinned.

"Yes, quite a bit." He put down his menu. "In fact, this is where Jasmine and I celebrated after our wedding."

She stared at him. Said nothing at first. Then, "So, what's good here?" as if anything that had to do with his marriage was not worth mentioning.

He let a moment go by. "Just about everything. Guess it depends on your mood."

Without looking up, she said, "I'm in the mood for a lot of things. But I'll settle for the seafood cocktail and a salad."

Hosea gave their orders to the waiter and when they were alone, she asked, "I guess we're having the early dinner that you wanted."

"Yeah." He spread the napkin across his lap. "Like I said, I want to get home to my family."

"A few drinks wouldn't have stopped you from going home." She gave him a half-smile. "Or would they?"

It was hard to turn away from her gaze. "I don't drink."

"I haven't forgotten that." She leaned on the table, closer to him. "I haven't forgotten anything."

Hosea cleared his throat. "So how have your first few days been?" he asked, taking them straight back to business.

"Great. I love New York, but I'm looking forward to L.A. I think that's going to breathe new life into the show."

He nodded. "I still can't believe we'll be working together."

"Believe it. The network wanted a top producer and I'm one of the best."

"The best and so modest." *Just like I remember.*

She shrugged. "Tell the truth, shame the devil."

He chuckled. "I just never imagined that our paths would cross like this."

"Really?" She took a long sip of water and then leaned back in her chair. "Come on, Hosea. You didn't think I'd give up that easily, did you?"

He raised his eyebrows. Was this an admission that this reunion had been planned? "Give up? You sound as if there's something you can get back."

Her lips curled into that smile that he remembered. That smile that used to melt him. The waiter broke through their silence, laying their plates in front of them.

Natasia reached for her fork, but Hosea took her hand, bowed his head.

"Sorry," she whispered.

He began. "Heavenly Father, Jesus Christ, our Lord and Savior. Lord, we thank you for this food we're about to receive. May it be used for the nourishment of our bodies in order for us to do Your will. We give You thanks for this meal and for so much more. In the name that is above all other names, Jesus Christ, we pray. Amen."

Even when they opened their eyes, she held onto his hand until he pulled away. And he turned right back to business. "So, where were you working when they found you?"

"At NBC. On the nightly news, and I was producing some specials."

"And winning Emmys."

"Seven over the years, but who's counting." She slipped a shrimp to the edge of her mouth, sucked on the cocktail sauce. "I'm most proud of the Emmy I got for my series on adoption in Africa."

He raised his eyebrows. "I didn't know that was you."

"It was me. All me. From the idea straight through to production. I even got to take a couple of trips to Africa and now I'm on the list to adopt."

"Really?" He grinned. "That's terrific."

She nodded. "It's been a while, though. Lots of bureaucracy. And since I'm not an actor rolling in the bucks . . ."

"I'm sure it'll happen."

"Let's hope." She raised her glass and took a sip of wine.

"So, winning Emmys, planning on becoming a mother . . . you have quite a full life."

"You sound surprised. As if you thought I'd fall apart without you."

He didn't miss a beat. "Not at all. I knew you'd be fine."

"Is that why you walked away leaving me only a note?" Her smile was gone—from her face and her tone.

He hesitated. Wondered if he should take them back to business. Finally, "That's not what happened."

"That's what I remember. I came home from that business trip and you were gone. The only thing left was that note on the kitchen table."

"You knew I was moving out."

"That wasn't supposed to be for another two weeks."

"I got a chance to get that apartment."

"And it couldn't wait?"

"No."

She pushed her plate away. Looked him straight in the eye. "That was a coward's way. You never even said good-bye."

He took a moment to think. "I did what I thought was best."

"No you didn't. You left then because you couldn't face me. You knew that if I was there, you'd never be able to walk away."

He shook his head. "I wanted the break to be easy."

She laughed, but there was no joy in the sound. "How could

breaking up ever be easy? Especially with the way I loved you."
She reached across the table, but he left her hand alone. "I thought
you loved me, too."

This was supposed to be a meeting between colleagues. But a
while ago, they were so much more, and because of that, Hosea
knew this conversation had to happen.

"I did love you, Natasia. If I hadn't, I wouldn't have asked you
to marry me."

"But then, you took it back," she said, as if she was still
shocked by their break-up. "And I just want to know why."

"Why are we going over this again?"

"Because even after five years, I still don't understand."

He shook his head, spoke softly. "We weren't meant to be."

"No matter how many times you say that, it doesn't make
sense. Not with the way we were."

He nodded slowly. There was a time when he couldn't understand it himself. Even now he couldn't explain it in clear English.
For four years they walked the path that both were sure would
lead to marriage.

And then it was over.

She was right; it didn't make sense.

Except—it was God. God spoke to his heart. Told him she was
not the one. He had wrestled with God, at first. Refused to listen.
But finally, he'd done what he had to do.

"So," she said. "Can you explain it to me?" When he stayed
silent, she added, "That's what I thought."

"I may not be able to explain it any better than I have, but I
know we did the right thing."

"How can you say that, Hosea? We were magic."

He fought to keep those magical moments from his mind.
"Natasia, we were not what the other needed."

Her voice rose a bit. "You were exactly what I needed." Then she softened. "What I wanted." She grabbed his hand. "And you're exactly what I want . . . now."

He looked down at their hands together and remembered Jasmine's words.

"I don't trust her."

Natasia said, "I loved you then and I love you now."

He drew his hand away, as if he'd been bitten by a snake. "Natasia, this is crazy. You and me . . . it's long over."

"Are you sure?"

"How can you ask me that? I'm married."

"You didn't answer my question."

"I don't love you. I'm in love with *my wife.*"

She shrugged away his words. "I was engaged when we met."

His eyes thinned. "That was different. Your fiancé died."

"And sometimes I feel like I went through two deaths!"

That hit him hard. He had to wait for her words to fade away before he spoke, "I'm sorry. I thought by now . . ." He paused, and his eyes scanned her face. "Natasia, maybe this isn't going to work."

She frowned. "What are you talking about?"

"You. And me. Working together. It's going to be a problem."

"Not for me."

"But what you're saying . . ." He stopped for a moment. "I never meant to hurt you."

In her eyes, he saw all of her anger-hate-sorrow. She stared right through him, giving him no relief. Then, "I asked you a question, you answered. From now on, it'll just be business." She pulled a folder from her portfolio.

Hosea watched as she scanned through the papers. "Natasia."

She looked up.

"Are you going to be able to handle this?"

"Handle what?" Her anger simmered. "Handle you throwing

away the best thing that ever happened to you?" She shrugged. "Of course."

"If what we used to be is going to get in the way . . . because I don't want any drama."

She tossed the folder onto the table. "You've known me longer than you've known your wife. There's never been any drama with me, Hosea." She paused. "Look at me. Do you think I'm going to have a problem moving on? I told you how I felt and you told me how you feel. It's done. From now on, it's all about business." She leaned across the table. "It's all about . . . *Bring. It. On.*"

He saw something in her eyes—not defeat, not retreat.

She settled back in her chair. "I have questions about the L.A. show format," as if the rest of their conversation had not happened.

Hosea pushed his plate aside. As she talked, inside, he prayed. He really wanted her to stay on the show, but their personal relationship had to end right here.

He prayed that Natasia could handle that. If not, then Jasmine was right. Natasia would have to go.

NINE

JASMINE GLANCED AT HER WATCH; she had at least an hour before Hosea returned. Stepping from the elevator, she pulled open the glass doors to the *Bring It On* offices.

"Hi, Brittney."

"Hey, Jasmine." Hosea's assistant swiveled in her chair. "Hosea's out. He had a doctor's appointment."

"Oh, yeah. I forgot," she lied. "I wanted to surprise him for lunch, but I'll wait in his office. I have some calls to make."

Brittney nodded, turned back to her computer.

"By the way," Jasmine paused. "I wanted to say hello to Natasia. Is she in?"

"Yeah, her office is two down from Hosea's."

"Thanks." Jasmine kept her smile until she turned around. Two doors down wasn't far enough. She'd make sure that Natasia was farther away once they got to Los Angeles—preferably in another building altogether.

She marched into Hosea's office, adjusted the photos of her and Jacqueline atop his desk, then strolled back into the hall. But when she peeked inside Natasia's office, it was empty.

Jasmine was tempted to walk in, sit down, and wait. But then this meeting wouldn't appear coincidental.

Moving toward the coffee room, Jasmine heard the voice before she slowly stepped inside.

Natasia stood across the room, her cell phone gripped between her ear and her shoulder, her back to Jasmine.

"What do you mean there are no apartments at the Fairmont?"

Silence as Natasia listened and Jasmine grinned.

"No," Natasia continued, her tone heavy with frustration. "I'll be there too long to have a regular room." Then, "How far away is this other hotel?"

The way Natasia sighed, Jasmine wondered if the hotel was in another state.

"All right, but keep me on the list at the Fairmont." She clicked the phone off, then whipped around.

"Hello, Natasia."

Natasia twisted her lips into a smile. Folded her arms and leaned against the counter. "Jasmine."

"Ah." Jasmine reached for a coffee cup. "You remember my name today."

"Are you here to check on your husband?"

Jasmine poured her coffee. "Not that it's any of your business, but I'm having lunch with Hosea."

"Really? I'm surprised he's hungry . . . for anything. After the," Natasia paused, "what should I call it . . . dinner we had last night."

It took both of Jasmine's hands to keep her cup steady. "Well, it's a new day, and he wants to have lunch with his wife."

Natasia grinned. "Good for you."

"So, is everything working out for you here?" Jasmine asked in a "I hope not" tone.

"Definitely. It's more than I could have hoped for."

"I'm surprised you left such a high-powered position in Chicago to take a temporary gig with *Bring It On.*"

"Who says this is temporary?"

"I'd consider a three-month contract temporary."

Jasmine knew she'd scored a point when Natasia's smirk disappeared. She'd have to thank Deborah for that information.

"It's a three-month contract for Los Angeles," Natasia came

back. "But there's an option to continue as a consultant when the show comes back to New York."

Now it was Jasmine who lost her smile. "You'll be consulting from Chicago?"

"I could, but I haven't decided yet. I'm keeping all the doors open, because New York is looking pretty wonderful right now. Especially after dinner at Tavern on the Green with Hosea, there's more than just my career at stake." She sauntered past Jasmine. "Think about that and then try to have a nice day."

Her first thought was to throw the hot coffee she held right into Natasia's face. But that would be a hard accident to explain.

Jasmine still heard Natasia's chuckles even as she dumped the rest of her coffee into the sink. *It didn't mean anything.*

Hosea had called last night and told her he had a meeting. He just didn't say it was dinner with Natasia.

Jasmine marched toward Hosea's office. He had some explaining to do. But as she paced, she calmed. Confronting Hosea was not the way to handle her husband. He wasn't the problem anyway. She needed to cut out this cancer at its core.

She was just going to get rid of Natasia.

TEN

JASMINE RUSHED THROUGH THE doors of the church where her father-in-law was the pastor and half-waved to Mrs. Whittingham. Reverend Bush's longtime assistant barely gave Jasmine a nod.

Time couldn't change everything. Even though she had been married to Hosea for more than two years, Jasmine knew Mrs. Whittingham still didn't like her. Still thought that Jasmine only wanted Hosea for his money and status and power.

But Jasmine didn't care what the silver-haired, wide-hipped biddy thought.

"Is Mae Frances in?" Jasmine asked.

"Yeah," was all Mrs. Whittingham said, not even taking her eyes from the computer.

Jasmine headed toward the room that had been converted from a storage closet.

"It's about time you showed up," Mae Frances huffed.

"I'm ten minutes early."

"Whatever. I don't know why you couldn't take the time to have lunch with me."

"Because," Jasmine began before she sat, "I've got to get some work done before we leave for L.A. Do you have the information?"

Mae Frances slid a folder across her desk.

Jasmine's eyes scanned the pages. "Where did you get this?"

"Where do you think? From one of my connections."

Scrolling through the report, Jasmine wasn't sure whether she should be delighted or deflated. One thing was sure, she'd been right.

The dossier, with photos, was thorough—including Natasia's family history, employment record and reviews, even awards she'd received and the fact that she had an outstanding application with AFAA, an international adoption agency that specialized in placing African children in homes around the world.

But the part that made Jasmine shudder were the pages that highlighted Natasia's road to *Bring It On*. The story that Natasia concocted about being pursued by the network wasn't close to the truth. That part wasn't a shock. But the extent to which Natasia had courted the execs made Jasmine know for sure that this woman was trouble. She'd called for meeting after meeting, week after week, writing proposals and giving presentations on how she could take the show to the top. It wasn't until her agent insinuated to the network that she might not renew her contract that the relentless pursuit paid off.

"That Natasia Redding sure is a beauty," Mae Frances said.

Jasmine's stomach churned. "Thanks for sharing," she said, not raising her eyes.

Mae Frances folded her hands. "Are you going to tell me now what's going on?"

Jasmine started to speak, but then paused when she looked up. What a difference two years—and salvation—made. Here Mae Frances sat with her own office inside a church. A place where Mae Frances used to say only hypocrites resided.

She was never quite sure what Mae Frances did here at City of Lights. Special projects, was what Reverend Bush called it. Apparently, Mae Frances did research for his publishing ventures. Her current assignment: to examine how God used women in the Bible.

No matter what Reverend Bush said, Jasmine knew this was a trumped-up job, designed to keep Mae Frances in church and reading the Bible. Because of the reverend's example, Mae Frances had a new heart. She glowed, she smiled. She laughed, she loved. Mae Frances had been changed.

"Answer me!" Mae Frances growled. "Tell me about this woman!"

Jasmine shook her head. There were a few things not even salvation could fix.

She told Mae Frances the story of Natasia. "She's after Hosea," she said finally. "And this," she held up the papers, "proves it."

Mae Frances waved her hand in the air. "Please, Preacher Man ain't going nowhere."

"I told you, they were engaged."

"So? He married the woman he loved. And Lord knows there ain't many men capable of love." She leaned closer to Jasmine, her face and voice softer. "Preacher Man's the real deal. And his daddy is too."

Jasmine tilted her head. "Mae Frances, you got a thing for Reverend Bush?"

"Oh, please. That man ain't nothing but a kid. I'm old enough to be his . . ." she patted her hair, "older sister. Any way, I'm not interested in that man. I'm only sayin' that Preacher Man comes from good stock. He couldn't care less about that model-looking toothpick."

Her description of Natasia didn't make Jasmine feel better. Made her think even more about the twenty or so extra pounds she carried since she'd given birth.

"If Natasia means nothing to Hosea, why didn't he ever mention her?"

"For the same reason you never mentioned your ex to him. Forget about that woman."

"I can't because I know her."

Mae Frances frowned. "From where?"

"From my past. I *was* Natasia. When I went after a man, I got him. And a wife was no deterrent for me. In fact, I think sometimes a man being married made it more satisfying when I got him. Believe me, I recognize the game," she said, her concern apparent. "And you have to be a little bit crazy to play it. That makes her even more dangerous."

Mae Frances nodded slowly. She stood, walked across the carpeted office, and locked her door. Then she looked back into the eyes of the woman she loved like a daughter. "Do you want me to take care of her?" she whispered.

Knowing exactly what she meant, Jasmine's eyes widened. Here they were, sitting in the church, surrounded by shelves overflowing with Bibles. Here Mae Frances stood, with her new heart, suggesting old remedies. Here Jasmine sat, considering it.

Jasmine's ringing cell phone stopped the conversation. She flipped it open. "Mrs. Sloss, is everything okay?"

"Oh, yes, Ms. Jasmine. Jacqueline's fine, but I have some bad news. I won't be able to go with you and Mr. Bush to Los Angeles. My daughter just called." Mrs. Sloss sniffed. "She found a lump. It's cancer. And I can't leave my family right now."

"I'm so sorry."

"Thank you, Ms. Jasmine. We're hopeful. We're a praying family, you know."

"I know. I'll come home right now."

"Oh, no. Just come after work. I want to give my daughter and her husband some time tonight. But I want to spend the night with them tomorrow."

"Definitely." Jasmine clicked off her phone and told Mae Frances the news. "Mrs. Sloss's daughter makes my problems seem so trivial." Jasmine rose from her seat and sighed. "I don't know how I'm going to watch Natasia without Mrs. Sloss being there to help me with Jacquie."

"Jasmine Larson, this woman has you so frazzled you're forgetting your resources. I'll go to Los Angeles with you. We'll take care of Natasia Redding together."

Jasmine scurried around the desk and wrapped her arms around her friend. "Thank you!" She kissed her cheek.

Mae Frances grumbled. "I'm only doing this so that I don't have to be part of this bet we have going. In L.A., I won't have to worry about going to church." She paused and with laughter in her eyes, she asked, "Or do you plan to force me to go to church out there, too?"

"I'm sure Hosea will find a church for us, Nama."

Mae Frances sucked her teeth. "Well, if I have to go, I will. But tell Preacher Man to find a good church. With someone who knows the Word. And who's preaching it. Like his daddy."

Jasmine laughed. With Mae Frances by her side, Natasia Redding didn't stand a chance.

"You're working late," Malik said.

Jasmine pushed away from her computer and glanced at her godbrother standing at the door. "I'm trying to get as much done as I can before I leave." She motioned for Malik to take a seat. "Thanks for not having a problem with this."

"No biggie. Your team will hold it down. And there's always the telephone."

"And airplanes. If you need me I'll be on the first thing smokin'."

"I may take you up on that." Malik loosened his tie. "And you can always work from de Janeiro," he said, referring to their sister club in Los Angeles.

She shook her head. She wasn't going anywhere near that place—where she met Brian Lewis. Where their affair started. "No, I'm staying far away from there."

"Because of Brian?"

"Because my life is about my husband and daughter. I don't want any part of anything that might bring drama."

Malik nodded. "I'm really proud of you, Jas. You're handling this marriage thing."

"That's why I'm going to Los Angeles. To keep my marriage straight."

He frowned, and for the second time that day, she told the story of Natasia. She ended by saying, "So, I'm going to keep an eye on Natasia and if God is on my side, I'll get rid of her, too."

His lips were pressed together as he studied her words. "I hear what you're sayin', just keep your hands on top of the table. In plain sight. For everyone to see. Especially Hosea."

"I'm not sure that's possible with someone like Natasia."

"Stay clean." He spoke slowly, his warning in his tone. "Remember, no secrets from Hosea."

Jasmine sighed. "Wish that were true."

He held up his hands. "I don't even want to know."

"You already do," Jasmine said. Indeed, Malik knew all of her secrets. She'd told her godbrother about her lies, even about Hosea not being Jacqueline's father, before that secret had been exposed. "I haven't told any *new* lies."

"Why don't you just tell Hosea that you were married before? And that age thing . . . that's no biggie. Lots of women . . . and men lie about that."

Jasmine pushed herself from her chair and strolled to the window. Like the summer day that was just now taking its bow, Jasmine wished her past would fade away as seamlessly. In her mind, she could almost see that happening. Over and over, she played the scenario where she would go to Hosea and confess the truth. But that's where the tape ended. She could never get to the part where he held her. And loved her. And forgave her—again.

"I wish to God that I'd never told those lies, Malik. And now I wish I could tell the truth. But I can't, especially not now. Not with Natasia in the picture. I can't do anything that could give her an in with Hosea."

"Natasia doesn't have anything to do with your marriage. Hosea's not like that." Malik joined her at the window. "Promise me you'll really pray about this, because I don't want to think about what would happen if . . ."

He stopped, but Jasmine knew what his next words would be. This was a warning, just like the one he'd given her on the day her world came tumbling down . . .

It was supposed to be the best day of her life—eighteen months ago, the day Jacqueline was born.

But hell had opened up when Malik came to visit at the hospital bearing flowers and condemnation.

"The only reason I keep harping on you telling Hosea the truth about the baby is because I know that the longer the secret goes on, the worse it will be," Malik had said as the two sat alone in her hospital room.

At that moment, Jasmine had been sorry that she'd ever confided in Malik about her baby's paternity. "Why do you keep insisting that Hosea will find out? He won't."

"Jasmine, secrets never stay silent."

Then she'd blurted out, "Hosea will never find out that he's not Jacqueline's father!" right before Reverend Bush walked in.

She had wanted to die right there. The reverend had heard everything. And he had forced Jasmine to tell Hosea the truth.

"I know you blame me for that secret coming out." Malik interrupted her memory. "And I'm sorry."

She turned away from him, but he didn't stop.

"It's just that before your dad passed away, I promised him that I would take care of you and Serena." He paused when she faced him. "Your sister's easy. But you . . ."

Now Jasmine smiled. "I don't blame you, Malik." When he raised his eyebrows, she said, "Okay, I did blame you, but I don't anymore. It all worked out then and I'm going to be fine now. Don't worry. I have everything under control this time."

Malik nodded, although she knew that he still didn't agree. But all he did was embrace her, and with his arms, told her that he hoped she was right.

ELEVEN

Jasmine was brilliant.

At least, that's what she kept telling herself. Her grin was spread all across her face as she rode up in the elevator.

It was an inspiring idea that had come to her in the middle of the night. So inspiring that for hours she'd lain awake, counting the minutes until morning.

Then at the day's first light, she'd jumped from bed, even as Hosea reached for her. "Sorry, babe." She scurried toward the bathroom. "I've got an early meeting."

It was a lie, but just a little one. She did have a meeting—of sorts—with the woman who always rescued her.

"Jasmine Larson," Mae Frances began the moment she swung open the door. "What's got you all fired up?"

"I've figured out how to stop Natasia before she gets started." Her voice was shaking with excitement.

"How?"

"I know how to end her games right here in New York. Make sure that she doesn't even get on that plane to Los Angeles."

"Would you stop babbling!"

"We're sending Natasia to Africa!" Jasmine beamed.

Mae Frances frowned. As Jasmine paced, she explained.

"You're gonna call Natasia, pretend you're some president or prime minister or tribal chief or something, tell her that you've personally taken an interest in her case—because of all of her accomplishments—and then get her on a plane to Africa." She spread her arms open wide. "I am brilliant."

With her hands planted on her hips, Mae Frances looked at

Jasmine as if she wondered when her brain had stopped working. "And she's gonna get on a plane to Africa because . . ."

"Remember she wants to adopt a child? So here's her chance."

"Ah!" Slowly, Mae Frances began to nod.

Jasmine said, "She'll buy a ticket, take a long, long flight, and while she's in Africa, we'll be in L.A." She fell back onto the couch and laughed. "Won't that be great?"

Mae Frances didn't yet share her joy. "What's going to happen when Natasia Redding gets off that plane in Zimbabwe or Kenya or wherever, and she realizes there's no baby?"

"Not our problem. By the time she figures it out, the show would've hired another producer and Natasia will be stone-cold out of a job." She kicked her feet in the air. "I am brilliant."

Finally, Mae Frances smiled. "Yes, you are, Jasmine Larson." She patted her hand. "I've taught you well." She moved toward her desk. "Let me get working." Pulling a black book from the drawer, she said, "While I would love to call Natasia Redding myself, this call has to come from Africa or else she won't believe it." She flipped through the pages.

"You have a connection in Africa?" Jasmine's eyes were wide with admiration.

"No, but I know someone who can make the call *look* like it's coming from Africa." She waved her hand toward the door. "Get out of here. I don't need no eyes watching while I'm taking care of business."

Jasmine was almost skipping by the time she got to the lobby. She strolled down the street and then stopped in front of the shop where she used to pick up her morning coffee when she lived in this Upper East Side neighborhood. She glanced at the Lotto poster in the window: $325 million.

Why not? she thought as she pushed open the door. Maybe she was more than brilliant. Maybe she was lucky, too.

TWELVE

HOSEA STOOD AT THE WINDOW in his father's office and watched the water pour from the sky. He loved the rain, had for many years. It had started that night with Natasia . . .

On that day, he had peeked into Pastor Case's office. "See you tomorrow," he said to his boss, the head pastor of Crystal Lake Cathedral.

"Wait!" Pastor Case called before Hosea could take a step. "I'm doing a counseling session; can you sit in?"

Hosea glanced at his watch. Although he hadn't taken time in the year that he'd been at this church to socialize, tonight he had a big date. In front of his television. Monday Night Football. The Bears versus the Giants. It didn't get any better than that for a New Yorker living in Chicago.

Pastor Case asked, "Can you stay?"

"Sure." He'd be home by the second quarter.

"Great." The pastor motioned toward the sofa. "You know, my goal is to turn over these counseling responsibilities to you."

"I'm ready," Hosea said. "Who are you seeing tonight?"

The soft knock on the door stopped the pastor's response. "Pastor Case?" Natasia peeked into the office. "Oh, I'm sorry. You're in a meeting."

"No, come on in, Natasia. We're ready."

She moved with tentative steps, her umbrella dripping with rainwater. As she shook off her coat, she eyed Hosea and passed him a smile. "Hi, Minister Bush."

Hosea nodded, his lips frozen with the rest of his face into a stiff smile.

In the weeks following their brunch over a year ago, the two had only exchanged a few pleasantries. And then shortly after, Hosea had heard the news—Natasia's fiancé had died in a bungee-jumping accident. Time after time, he'd pulled out her card, wanting to offer his condolences, but it didn't seem like their one encounter was enough to reach out that way.

Pastor Case said, "I hope you don't mind, I asked Minister Bush to join us."

"I guess it's okay." She looked from one man to the other.

"Just as an observer," he added. "Minister Bush is going to be in charge of our counseling ministry."

The look on her face made Hosea say, "Natasia, if you'd feel more comfortable with just Pastor Case . . ."

She held up her hand. "No, I'm fine." She lowered herself onto the couch.

"So, how are you?" Pastor Case asked.

Hosea sat back. Kept his eyes trained on the pastor. But his glance kept shifting to the woman next to him. It was just jeans and a simple sweater that she wore. And her hair was tucked under a leather cap. But she was as elegant today as she'd been when she'd first taken his breath away.

"I feel really good," Natasia said.

She spoke, but Hosea's glance stayed on the pastor.

"I know grief is a spirit," she continued, "and I'm determined to walk away from this place."

Hosea tried to remember all that he'd learned in his Ministry and Ethics class.

"I think the thing that's slowed me down a bit," Natasia said, "is the way Doug died."

Hosea wanted to close his eyes. But not even that would keep her image away. *I'm not supposed to be thinking like this.* But it was difficult to remember that he was a minister when she sat so close. She was clearly a woman. Who reminded him that he was a man.

The minutes crept by. Pastor Case questioned. Natasia responded. And Hosea sweated, his eyes on the clock.

Finally, "Well, we can call it an evening," Pastor Case said. He'd barely spoken those words before the telephone rang.

As the pastor rushed to answer, Natasia stood. She glanced at Hosea, bit the corner of her lip. Smiled, then turned away. He smiled back, and turned his attention to his hands.

She whispered, "I'm going to run to the ladies' room."

He watched her dash from the room. Only then did he exhale. Maybe counseling wasn't for him. Or maybe it was just counseling Natasia that was the problem.

"Oh, boy," Pastor Case said as he rushed toward his closet. "This rain has caused havoc on my roof. It's leaking."

"That doesn't sound good."

"Nope." He grabbed his coat. "Where's Natasia?"

"In the ladies' room."

"Would you mind seeing that she gets to her car and then locking up here?"

"Sure, Pastor."

"Okay, son. I'll see you in the morning."

Hosea waited, paced, and reminded himself that he was the minister.

"Where's Pastor Case?"

She'd been gone for just minutes, but Hosea marveled at how much more beautiful she seemed. She'd done nothing—just looked better with the passing of time.

"Pastor had an emergency at home."

"Oh." It was a long stare that she gave him. Then, like before, she turned away. She slipped into her coat, and said, "Looks like it's still coming down out there."

"Yeah; are you okay driving?"

She nodded. "I'm from Chicago. I've driven in much worse than this. Plus, I actually love the rain. To me, it's God's way of just washing us up a little."

He grinned. "I'll never look at the rain the same way again."

She grabbed her umbrella. He clicked off the lights and followed her out. At the door, they stood together, watching the rain pummel the earth.

"Okay," he said. "I'll hold the umbrella and we'll make this dash. Got your keys ready?"

She patted her coat pockets. Frowned, then dug inside her purse. "I can't find my keys." After more moments, "Maybe I left them in the car."

"Okay, let's check." Hosea held the umbrella as they darted through puddles to her Volvo. He tested the doors—locked. She checked the windows—closed. They peered inside—no sign of keys. Without a word, they raced back into the church.

"I can't believe this!" Natasia exclaimed, shaking the water off.

"They've got to be here somewhere. I'll check Pastor's office. You check the ladies' room."

Within minutes she was back, searching through her coat pockets and purse again. "This is ridiculous." She released a long breath of frustration. Then her eyes widened. "Maybe Pastor Case picked up my keys." She nodded. "Yes, I dropped them on his desk when I was taking off my coat. He probably picked them up by accident."

Hosea looked at her. *Maybe.* "Okay, so I'll give you a lift."

She hesitated. "I don't want to leave my car here. I have a meeting in the morning downtown."

Hosea moved toward the phone. "Then I'll call Pastor Case."

She stopped him. "You said he had an emergency; I don't want to bother him." She grabbed her PDA. "I've done this before, so I know my auto club has a master key. Would you mind if we waited for them?"

As Natasia made the call, Hosea hung up their coats and then wandered to the small kitchen. He set the coffeemaker, and then wondered how keys that were here just minutes ago, were now gone. It almost seemed like a trick—like the many he'd had to endure over the year from half the single women in the congregation.

He shook his head. *Not Natasia.* She was way too classy to resort to something like that. Plus, she had just lost her fiancé.

By the time Natasia joined him, he agreed with her theory that Pastor Case had mistakenly lifted the keys.

"I don't have great news," she said, as she grabbed the mug Hosea had prepared for her. "It may be a couple of hours because of the weather."

Hosea took a sip of his coffee.

She said, "I hope you didn't have plans tonight."

"Actually, I did."

"Sorry," she said, although she didn't sound regretful at all.

He looked at her for a moment. "I'll bring my plans right here."

She frowned and followed him down the hallway. Inside the pastor's office, he turned on the television and laughed when Natasia clapped her hands.

"This is exactly what I planned to do," she said. "I am such a Bears fan."

"Really?"

"Since I was a little girl."

"Well, we're going to have a big problem. Because the Giants are my boys from way back."

"It's on now." In one motion, she sank onto the floor, crossed her legs yoga-style, and smiled up at him. "Wanna wager?"

He laughed. "We're sitting in the middle of God's house and you're talking about betting?"

"Not for money. Just a friendly wager between friends."

"Between friends, huh?" he said. And then, he noticed it. The pounding in his chest, the sweaty palms, were gone. Now all he felt was normal. They were just two people waiting out a storm.

She said, "Tonight you're not my pastor. We're just friends—"

The slam of the door didn't take Hosea away from that long-ago memory, but his father's voice did.

"Hosea!" When he faced his father, Reverend Bush said, "Seems like you were in another place."

Another time, he thought. He hugged his father. "Just got a lot on my mind."

"Guess so. It has to be exciting, although can't say your leaving makes me happy. I'm gonna miss you guys."

Hosea nodded solemnly, then broke into a grin. "It's not me . . . or Jasmine you're going to miss."

Reverend Bush laughed. "I can't believe you're taking Jacquie away." He leaned closer to his son. "Come on. Just leave her here with me."

"Yeah, right. Talk to my wife about that."

He shook his head. "You can't blame a grandfather for trying." Reverend Bush motioned for Hosea to sit down. "So, you didn't say what you wanted to talk about."

"Nothing, really. Just wanted to spend some time with you before we head for La La Land."

Reverend Bush pressed his fingers together and peered at his son. "Talk to me."

Hosea shifted. "About what?"

The reverend leaned across his desk, his face stretched with concern. "Everything okay with you and Jasmine?"

"Oh, yeah. We had our big problems right up front so we know that our marriage can survive anything. We're good."

Reverend Bush nodded. "Glad to hear that. It took me a while to get here, but I'm convinced God has big plans for you two as husband and wife." Reverend Bush stopped, stared again. "But there's something you're not . . ." He rotated his hand in the air as if that motion would complete his question.

Hosea glanced out the window. The rain continued to plummet in sheets, making him want to remember again. "There's nothing more to tell, Pops." Then, after a moment of silence, he said, "Natasia's in town." Reverend Bush frowned and Hosea repeated her name, this time slowly to bring her back to his father's memory.

"What's she doing in New York?"

"Getting ready to go to L.A. She'll be working as a producer for *Bring It On.*"

Reverend Bush's eyebrows rose. "You hired her?"

"Not me. The network. I told you we wanted to build the show's news element, and there's no one better than Natasia."

Reverend Bush sat, thoughtful. "Does Jasmine know?"

"Of course."

"Not that Natasia's going to be on the show . . . does Jasmine *know?* About your past relationship?"

"Like I said, of course. I don't have any secrets from my wife." Hosea leaned forward, rested his elbows on his knees. "Jasmine knows everything, Pops. And she knows the most important thing—that I love her."

Reverend Bush clasped his hands as if he were about to pray. "I don't think working with Natasia is a good idea."

Hosea frowned.

Reverend Bush continued. "Marriage is difficult enough. Don't bring unnecessary complications to the table."

"Natasia's not a complication. She's one of the best producers in the business."

"She's not the only one."

"True, but if the network wants her, why should I make it an issue? She knows that whatever we had was over long ago. She knows that all that's left between us is strictly business." He paused. "And she knows that I'm married and I love my wife."

"Seems like she knows a lot."

"I told her all of this."

"Seems even more interesting that you had to have that kind of conversation."

The images came, floated through his mind. Natasia at Tavern on the Green. Her hands on his. Her lips professing that she would always love him.

Hosea said, "Yeah, we talked. I wanted to make sure she understood."

"I know how much you loved Natasia."

"Key word—loved. But I was able to walk away when God told me to." Hosea relaxed in his seat. "Pops, you're making something out of nothing."

"It has to mean something. If not, you wouldn't have mentioned it."

"I only mentioned it because . . ." He wondered why he'd brought up Natasia's name. Wondered why he thought of her so much these days. "I only mentioned her because I tell you everything. I got this, Pops."

Reverend Bush nodded. "Then, if you say you've got it, that's all I need. You know how I am. We talk once, then I'm done. After that all I do is pray."

Hosea smiled. "That's all I need."

"Just remember, son, there's a reason why your mother named you Hosea. She knew when you were still in her womb that you would hear the voice of God."

He smiled. It had been over ten years since his mother had passed, and finally, he'd found a way to have joy whenever she was mentioned.

"I hear Him, Pops. All the time."

"Just make sure that you listen. Especially in situations like this. Especially with your marriage."

"Always do."

"And know that you can always come to me."

"That I know."

The two men hugged as if all was okay. And inside, Hosea prayed that all he'd told his father was true.

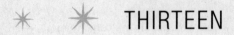

THIRTEEN

"YA WANNA WALK OUT TOGETHER?"

Hosea glanced up and tried not to smile. But he couldn't help it. Every time he looked at Natasia, memories stretched his lips into a grin.

"Yeah." He stood. "I'm ready to get going. I'm sure Jasmine has a ton of things for me to do before we get on the plane in the morning."

Natasia nodded. "I've gotta pack myself. Can't say that I'll be sorry leaving the Ritz. Not that I don't love that place, but even the best hotels get old after a week. It'll be great to have an apartment in Los Angeles." She paused, looked at him. "I just wish I was going to be staying at the Fairmont with you. Are you sure there's nothing you can do?"

Before he could respond, her cell rang. He pressed the elevator button as she flipped her phone open.

"Yes, this is Ms. Redding."

The elevator pinged and the doors slid apart. Natasia held up one finger, asking Hosea to wait.

He nodded. And listened.

"You're kidding," she said.

She frowned, and he did the same.

"No, I mean yes. I'm still interested. Definitely. I've been waiting a long time." She paused, looked at Hosea, bit the corner of her lip. "Tomorrow? Well, that's not possible." More silence. A deeper frown. "I understand. Can you give me a couple of hours?" When she closed her phone, her face was etched with worry.

"What's wrong?"

She waited as if she wasn't sure what to say. "That was the adoption agency. Actually one of the connections from Africa." She started at him and said, "They have a baby for me, Hosea," in a tone that sounded like she didn't believe her own words.

He was as stunned as she was. "Wow."

"And they want me to come to Malawi. Tomorrow."

"Wow."

"I know," she said as they stepped into the elevator.

He waited until they got into the lobby before he asked, "What are you going to do?"

She shook her head. "I don't know." She walked out of the building with slow, halting steps. She was in a trance. "I've been waiting, but I don't know . . . is this the right time? What about my job? What about this show?"

He shrugged. "I don't know what to tell you."

"I need to talk to Steve. Maybe I can work this out, at least with my job in Chicago. I should be back in a few days . . . or weeks. I don't know." Her eyebrows bunched together.

Gently, he held her arm. "Do whatever's best for you, Natasia."

She looked down to where he held her. When she glanced back, he wasn't sure what he saw in her eyes—regret, fear. "I'll call you."

He stood still as she walked, still unsteadily. And after just a few steps, he wondered if he should follow her.

No, he decided. This was her life. He didn't need to be part of it.

When she was out of sight, he began walking north and he thought about how quickly life changed. Natasia had come back to him, and just as fast, now she was gone.

Maybe this was a sign. Maybe his father had been right. He didn't need any complications in his life.

All he would do now is call Natasia in a few days and wish her well.

✳ ✳ FOURTEEN

JASMINE STROLLED TO THE front of the plane with a wide smile. With Natasia gone to another continent, she had no concerns. She'd even tossed away her fears about running into Brian. Los Angeles was too big a city for that to happen.

She plopped into the seat next to Hosea and strapped herself in. She'd been waiting for Hosea to tell her that Natasia had left the show, but he'd said nothing. She wasn't worried, though. After days of planning, the call had been made yesterday. And this morning, Natasia was on her way to Malawi.

Glancing at her watch, she figured that her nemesis was probably forty thousand feet in the air on her way to adopting a child from the same country as Madonna had. Maybe one day, Natasia would call the mega-star to arrange a play date—if she could find her own baby. Jasmine chuckled.

"What's so funny?" Hosea lowered the newspaper he was reading.

"I was just thinking about something Mae Frances said."

"Is she settled in back there?"

"Not really. She's fussing about having to put Jacquie down. And she's threatening to curse out anyone who tries to make her strap her grandbaby into that big ol' seat." Jasmine half-sighed, half-laughed. "You're going to have to handle her."

"I'll take care of Nama." He leaned closer to his wife. "But first, I want to take care of you."

The moment their lips touched, a voice spoke from above. "Hey, guys."

"Natasia!" they exclaimed together.

"What are you—" Jasmine stopped. She wasn't supposed to know anything about Natasia not being there. But Hosea asked the question for her.

"What are you doing here?"

Natasia lowered her voice, speaking only to him. "I decided this wasn't the time. Being with you, I mean, being on the show is where I'm supposed to be."

"What about the baby?"

"Believe me, there are plenty of people waiting. And I'll have another chance." She paused. "Don't worry. I'm fine. I'm doing the right thing."

Jasmine bounced back in her chair. Folded her arms. Did nothing to hide her disdain.

"Well, at least you made the flight." He glanced at his watch. "Just in time. We're gonna take off soon." Hosea pointed toward the rear of the plane. "There're a couple of seats back there."

Natasia's glance followed Hosea's finger. She frowned. "I need to be sitting with you."

Jasmine eyes widened.

"I'm sitting with my wife."

"But I have work to do."

"Then you *will* be more comfortable in the back. You can use the tables."

Jasmine inched to the edge of her seat. She was ready to bounce up and smack her if Natasia said anything else.

Hosea said, "I'll check with you once we get in the air."

With a deep sigh, Natasia took another look at Jasmine. "Okay . . . darlin'. I'll be waiting for you."

Jasmine pressed her legs into the seat, willed herself to stay in place and not show out on this corporate jet.

Once alone, Hosea leaned over and kissed Jasmine's forehead. "Sorry 'bout that."

"I thought . . ." Jasmine pressed her lips together. She couldn't even ask what she wanted to know.

Hosea said, "We'll be taking off in a few. I'm going to check on Mae Frances and my pumpkin."

Jasmine tried to breathe herself back to calm. She didn't really need to ask anyone what had happened. Natasia had decided not to adopt the child. Had decided that being with Hosea was more important.

It was clear—she was not giving up. And she proved it with the way she'd just thrown herself at Hosea right in front of Jasmine's face.

Jasmine shook her head. Even in her wildest days she'd never been that blatant.

"Well, it took some work," Hosea said, sliding back into his seat. "But Jacquie is strapped in and so is Mae Frances."

As the three flight attendants demonstrated the safety procedures, Hosea held Jasmine's hand. She wanted to pull away, punish him for ever knowing Natasia. But she had no reason to be mad at him. He wasn't the one who was acting like crazy was part of his DNA.

When the jet angled into the air, she reached inside her purse and pulled out the lottery ticket she'd purchased the day she formulated the plan to send Natasia back to Africa.

She looked at the numbers and then tore the paper into tiny pieces. It was obvious, any kind of luck she'd had had run out. Now she was going to need some special kind of blessings to take care of this woman.

Hosea took a sip of the soda the flight attendant handed him. "You okay?" Jasmine nodded and once again, he reached for her hand. "Listen, I know Natasia is a little difficult to take."

"Is that what you call it?" She paused, lowered her voice. "It's a lot more than that, Hosea. She's crazy."

"Don't you think that's a bit of an exaggeration?"

"No. And when someone who's crazy is after you, let me tell you, she'll do anything to get you."

He grinned. "You sound like you're speaking from experience."

She pouted. "Baby, don't make fun. I'm being serious."

"I know you are. But it doesn't matter what Natasia does. There's nothing she can do to get me. She could stand up here butt-naked twirling a hula-hoop around her belly and one around her neck, and I wouldn't care."

Jasmine couldn't help it, she laughed.

"There's nothing Natasia could say or do that would take my eyes away from you."

"But, Hosea, she's so disrespectful."

"Okay, I'll talk to her. Because if it bothers you, it bothers me." He squeezed her hand. "I'll tell her I ain't having it."

"Thanks, babe."

"Now, I've got something for you." He grinned. "Wanna become a member of the Mile High Club?"

Another voice spoke before Jasmine could respond.

"Excuse me."

She didn't have to look up to know the devil hovered over them.

"Hosea, I wanted to go over the schedule so that I can tell the staff it's a go in the meeting tomorrow," Natasia said.

"Tomorrow? No one's going into the studio until Thursday."

"That's your schedule. But I've called a meeting with the producers."

"Natasia, give everyone a chance to enjoy the Fourth of July before we work them to death."

"You may have time to relax, but I don't. So anyway, can I have just a bit of your time now?"

Hosea shook his head, but Jasmine said, "Babe, it's okay. I'll check on Jacquie and Mae Frances." She whispered, "Maybe you can talk to this heifer about showin' some respect. And after that, you can talk to me about that Mile High Club thing." She kissed him.

She didn't bother to look at Natasia. Just strutted by her as if she knew her game and didn't even care.

"Mama!" her daughter exclaimed when Jasmine settled into the seat next to Mae Frances.

"Hey, baby." She lifted Jacqueline onto her lap. "You having a good time with Nama?"

Jacqueline nodded and leaned against her mother's chest.

Mae Frances tilted her head close to Jasmine's. "I guess she decided against Malawi," she whispered as she peeked toward the front of the plane.

"I guess she wants Hosea more than she wants a child."

"She's sure determined. Had her eyes on you and Preacher Man the entire time while the plane was taking off. Almost fell out of her seat trying to see what you were doing." She paused. "I don't know, Jasmine Larson. This one might be real trouble."

Jasmine turned her glance back to where her husband sat. The high seat-backs restricted her view; she could only see the top of their heads. Hosea and Natasia sat a little too close, but she was determined to stay right where she was. She needed to give Hosea time to give Natasia the message that he wasn't interested in her little games. And she needed to give Natasia time to know that she wasn't concerned about her two-bit tricks either.

After a few minutes, Jasmine stood and rested her daughter in Mae Frances's lap. "You're still okay with Jacquie being back here with you?"

Mae Frances nodded. "I'll take care of this little darling. You go take care of that skank."

"Mae Frances!"

"What? That skank oughta be glad I prayed the Sinner's Prayer or else I'd be up in her face telling her what's really on my mind." She paused. "Hmph, good thing I'm saved."

Jasmine laughed and turned toward the front cabin. She was going to do exactly what Mae Frances said. She was going to take care of that skank.

FIFTEEN

MAE FRANCES YELLED FROM THE hallway, "Are you guys ready?" and with her fists, she banged on the door.

"Nama!" Jasmine grabbed Mae Frances and pulled her inside the suite. "Are you trying to get us evicted? The Fairmont is not that kind of place."

"Hmph." Mae Frances paraded into the suite across from hers. "This ain't no better than where I live."

Jasmine couldn't deny that. The Fairmont was an elegant hotel that housed short-term-lease apartments on the top levels. But the elite Park Avenue building where Mae Frances lived was equal in splendor to this place.

Mae Frances stood in the middle of the living room and folded her arms. "You guys aren't ready? You got me out of my bed so that we could do this. I'm only going because you bugged me."

"Really? I thought you were going because you wanted to see Los Angeles."

"I live in New York!" Mae Frances growled. "Why would I want to see Los Angeles?" Then Mae Frances glanced out the window that overlooked Griffith Park. And she smiled at the view.

Jasmine called out to Hosea and he came, carrying Jacqueline on his shoulders.

"Nama!" Jacqueline giggled.

"How's my heart?" And then, "How're you, Preacher Man?"

"Peeker Man!" Jacqueline cheered.

Hosea rolled his eyes. "Are you ready?"

"I've been ready," she huffed. "Just waitin' for you slow folks."

"Slo' pokes!" Jacqueline said and they all laughed.

Jasmine grabbed her bag just as the telephone rang. Still chuckling, she answered, "Good morning!"

"Let me speak to Hosea."

That voice took all of her cheer away. "Who is this?" Although Jasmine already knew.

A sigh. "Natasia."

"I'm sorry, but we're on our way out," she said as if she were talking to a telemarketer. "May I take a message?"

"Let me speak to Hosea, Jasmine. I don't have time for your little games."

My little games? Oh, this hussy is about to be cursed out.

"This is about work," Natasia continued, "and it's important."

Jasmine rolled her eyes. What she wanted to do was hang up, pretend this call never happened. Instead, she waved her hand toward her husband.

"What's going down?" Hosea said into the phone. A second later, his eyebrows rose. "Natasia, I'm not coming in. It's the Fourth of July and I have plans."

Jasmine held her breath and prayed that her husband would fight for his freedom and his time with his family.

"Who called this meeting?" More silence. Then, "Is Triage there? Let me speak to him."

"Mama," Jacqueline called, trying to take her attention away. "Look!" She held up her teddy bear.

Jasmine smiled at her daughter, but quickly turned back to her husband.

"Triage, what's happening?"

By the time Hosea said good-bye, Jasmine knew her day was ruined.

"I have to go into the office. Looks like the studio wasn't expecting our team for another two weeks."

"How did that happen?"

"I don't know. Natasia caught the mistake."

"She's the one who probably caused it."

"Anyway," Hosea continued, as if he hadn't heard his wife, "she's called in everyone to redo the schedules." He sighed. "Sorry about this, darlin'. But you and Mae Frances go on to Disneyland."

"No." Jasmine pouted.

"Please don't make me feel bad. I'll get to the office, take care of business, and then I'll catch up with you guys down there."

"No." Jasmine shook her head, unwavering in her discontent. "We'll just stay here."

"No we won't," Mae Frances piped in. "You go to work, Preacher Man. I'll take care of your girls."

"Thanks, Nama." Hosea turned to Jasmine, kissed her forehead. "I promise I'll make this up to you."

Jasmine was still standing in place, arms folded, when Hosea rushed from their suite. "I can't believe this. She calls, he runs."

"That's not what happened. His work called. And he's been running to that job since you met him. That's nothing new."

"But what's new is Natasia." Jasmine paused, chewed on the corner of her lip. "She has more power than I thought. Just working on the show gives her too much access to Hosea."

Mae Frances waved her hand as if Jasmine's words meant nothing. "You're the only one with access to Preacher Man. Look, we've been in L.A. for one day and haven't even begun to fight. She'll be gone soon enough."

Jasmine nodded, although she felt far from confident.

"Mama!" Jacqueline ran to Jasmine and wrapped her arms around her mother's neck. "Dada?"

Jasmine lifted her daughter and hugged her. "He's at work," was all she said, even though her thoughts continued. *He's at work. And he's with Natasia.*

SIXTEEN

TRIAGE GLANCED AT HIS WATCH. "Okay, this is all straightened out now, right?"

Natasia nodded. "We're done." She slammed the binder shut. "It's only taken four days."

"Yup," Triage said, shrugging on his jean jacket. "The days that I had planned to relax before I began pulling double duty on this show and the movie."

"Sorry," Natasia apologized.

"Wasn't your fault," he said, then turned to Hosea. "You're gonna get out of here?"

"In a minute. I just want to look over this one more time because there's no way I'm coming in tomorrow. I want one day with my family before we begin on Monday."

Triage waved. "I'm out. Call me if you need me, but I don't want to hear a word from you until Monday." He chuckled as he rushed from the conference room. "Peace."

With a sigh, Hosea rested his elbows on the table and massaged his eyes. "These have been the longest days."

"I know." Natasia stood and Hosea noticed that even in skinny jeans, a T-shirt, and sneakers, Natasia still sashayed as if she were on a runway. When she stood behind him, she said, "Just think, on Monday we'll hit the ground running." She rested her hands on his shoulders and massaged with the tips of her fingers.

Seconds ticked by before, "Don't do that."

"Relax," she whispered, not stopping.

He raised his hand to meet hers. Held her still.

She sighed, but her hands stayed in place. "Don't let this be about your wife, Hosea. I'm not doing anything. I know how you feel about her."

"I don't *feel* Jasmine. I love her," he said without turning around.

"Didn't mean to use the wrong word."

"It's more than the wrong word." Finally, he faced her. "You need to understand that I love Jasmine."

She sat in the chair beside him. "Why do you feel the need to keep telling me?"

"Because you don't seem to be hearing me."

She shook her head as if she didn't understand. "What have I done to make you say that? You told me how you felt three weeks ago and I said fine. Now, we've been in L.A. for four days, working all kinds of hours—and the key word is *working.* So what have I done to make you think that I'm not hearing you? My God, Hosea," she said with more than a bit of annoyance in her tone. "I was just giving you a little massage because you looked tired. Don't make a big deal out of it."

"It's not just me." He didn't back down. "My wife's not happy with this either."

She raised her hands in the air. "Not happy with what?"

"With you."

"Oh, please. I can't believe you find insecurity attractive."

"She's not insecure. Look, Natasia," he said with a sigh, "I want this to work. If I wasn't sure before, the way you've handled the last few days proves that we're blessed to have you. But I won't do a thing to risk my marriage."

She half-smiled. "Thought you said *nothing* could risk your marriage."

"That's what I said. That's what I meant. And anything and anyone that gets close to being a risk will have to go."

She pressed her lips together, but after a moment, she softened. "Okay." She held out her hand. "You said it, I heard it. Let's shake on it."

He glanced at her hand as if it were a trap. But then he took hers inside his. "I want this to work. I want us to be friends."

"Me too." After a moment, she added, "Now, as a friend, would you mind if I massaged that little spot right there." She pressed through his sweatshirt to the top of his shoulder blade. "You're really tight."

She smiled that smile.

He melted.

"As a friend," she repeated.

After a long moment, Hosea nodded.

Slowly, she rose. Sauntered around him and returned her hands to his shoulders. "I'm going to make you feel all better."

Hosea closed his eyes, tried not to moan with pleasure, and never saw the grin that filled Natasia's face.

SEVENTEEN

JASMINE STEPPED FROM THE shower, yawned, and wondered why she felt so sluggish. Wasn't like she'd exerted much energy since they'd arrived in Los Angeles. Hosea had worked from dawn to way after dusk every day since Natasia had called on the Fourth.

"We're going to spend the whole day together tomorrow," he'd announced when he'd climbed into their bed last night just before midnight. But when he'd leaned over to kiss her, she had rolled away.

Now, as she stood in the steam-filled bathroom, she still felt the same way—she was mad. Although she didn't really know why. It wasn't as if Hosea hadn't worked long hours before. And there were many times when he'd had to sit in for her with Jacqueline when she stayed late at Rio for a special event.

But this wasn't about work anymore. This was about work with Natasia.

"Morning, darlin'." Hosea stepped into the bathroom.

Jasmine didn't turn around. Just wrapped the towel around her, reached for her toothbrush, and turned the water on blast.

"Morning," Hosea repeated.

Jasmine's mumble didn't sound a bit like English.

"Come on."

Another grumble.

From behind, Hosea grabbed her, edged his lips to her neck, and blew soft breaths onto her skin.

Jasmine fought hard not to feel anything. "Stop it, Hosea," she said, keeping the sharpness in her tone. "I'm mad at you!"

He backed away with a grin. "Thanks for telling me, 'cause I wouldn't have known. So fill me in. Why?"

"Because we've been here for four days and we haven't seen you for four hours."

"But you know why."

"I know, but I'm mad anyway."

"Aww, I'm going to make it up to you today."

"How?" She still pouted.

"Well," he stepped closer to her, "first, we'll go to church. And then, we'll have lunch somewhere fabulous in Beverly Hills."

Jasmine yawned as if she were bored.

"And while we're in Beverly Hills, we'll stop in a few stores . . ."

Jasmine's mouth snapped shut and her eyes opened wide.

He continued, "I wanna buy something special for my wife."

She bit her lip, tried to keep her smile away.

"And then," he embraced her again, "we'll come back here, find something for Mae Frances and Jacquie to do. And when it's just you and me . . ." He pressed his lips against her neck, and with his tongue made her moan. "So, how does that sound?"

"It sounds . . . okay."

Hosea's eyebrows rose. "Just okay? Well, maybe I needed to shake things up a bit." With a quick motion he whipped her towel away.

"Hosea!"

"What? You don't like being butt-naked by yourself?" He shrugged his robe from his shoulders and pulled her close again.

"What are you doing?"

Hosea laughed. "If you have to ask, then I've definitely been away too much."

She protested when he kissed her, "I've got to go check on Jacquie."

"I just checked. She's still sleeping." His tongue tickled her neck once again. And then, he moved downward.

"But suppose . . ." Jasmine tried to remember what she was

going to say. "Suppose . . ." She leaned against the sink and closed her eyes. "Suppose Jacquie wakes up?"

"Then . . ." he said before he pushed her onto the floor.

Jasmine shrieked.

"We'll have to make this quick." With no more words, he returned to his business.

Jasmine tried to remember the thousands of reasons she had for being angry, but all that came to her mind were the millions of reasons she had for loving her husband so much.

Jasmine tugged at the tapered jacket that was riding above her waist. She sighed as she took in her reflection; she wanted to lose the extra pounds she'd carried since Jacqueline was born.

Behind her, Hosea said, "Darlin', we have to get going."

She grinned at him. "Don't blame me for being late. I was minding my business when you . . ." She adjusted his tie. "Where's Jacquie?"

"In her bedroom with Mae Frances."

Jasmine grabbed her purse. "What church are we going to?"

"Hope Chapel, in Inglewood."

Hope Chapel. Jasmine's eyebrows knitted together. "Who's the pastor?"

"Beverly Ford. She's a friend of Pop's and she's dynamite."

Jasmine had to force herself to keep breathing, keep thinking. "But Inglewood. That's so far."

"Only about thirty minutes away, which is why we have to leave now." He moved toward the bathroom, then paused. "Didn't you grow up in Inglewood?"

She shook her head. "No, in Ladera." *Think, Jasmine, think.* "I'll go get Jacquie and Mae Frances."

Rushing to Jacqueline's bedroom, she inhaled deep breaths. She needed the oxygen to think because there was no way she could go to that church.

"Mae Frances!" she exclaimed the moment she walked in. The way Jacqueline jumped in Mae Frances's lap made Jasmine lower her voice. "I'm sorry, baby," she said to her daughter, then crouched in front of the rocking chair where Mae Frances held Jacqueline.

"Goodness, Jasmine Larson," she said through the veil on her hat that covered her eyes. "What's wrong with you?"

"I need your help." Jasmine pasted a smile on her face when Jacqueline looked at her. She whispered, "Hosea wants to go to this church and we can't."

Mae Frances stood, put Jacqueline on the bed, and then came back to Jasmine. "What're you talking about?" she asked, as she adjusted her hat.

"Hosea wants to go to Hope Chapel, but we can't because that's the church Kyla and Jefferson go to."

Mae Frances frowned. "Who're Kyla and Jefferson?"

"Kyla was my best friend." She spoke quickly, knowing that Hosea would be bellowing for them soon. "But we're not friends anymore, because I slept with her husband."

Mae Frances's penciled eyebrows rose. "When did you do that? We just got here!"

"Mae Frances, that was years ago. When I lived here. That's not who I am now."

"Oh, I forgot."

"Anyway," Jasmine stood and paced the room, "the problem is, Alexis goes to that church, too."

Mae Frances shook her head, more confused than before. "Who's Alexis?"

"Kyla's best friend, and," she turned and looked at Mae Frances pointedly, "Brian Lewis's wife." Jasmine watched her words sink in, saw Mae Frances's eyes widen with understanding.

Mae Frances glanced toward Jacqueline. "Her father."

"Don't say that!"

"Why not? She doesn't understand."

"She understands more than you think and even if she doesn't, I don't want those words in her subconscious. Hosea is her father."

"Jasmine!" Hosea's voice echoed from the other side of the suite.

She peeked into the hall. "We're coming, babe." Closing the door again, she turned to Mae Frances, desperation filling her eyes.

"Well, is this really a problem? Preacher Man already knows everything."

"But Brian doesn't. If he sees Jacqueline . . ." She stopped and both of their eyes turned to the toddler. To the little girl who looked nothing like the people she called Mama and Dada.

"Jasmine!" Hosea called again.

She took a breath before she opened the door. "We're coming, babe. Jacquie spilled juice on her dress and Mae Frances is changing her."

"Hurry up," he shouted.

She whispered to her friend, "What am I going to do?"

Mae Frances thought for just a moment. "Pick up Jacquie," she directed. "Let's go."

Jasmine's eyes widened.

"Jasmine Larson, have I ever let you down? Do what I say."

Her heart was pumping hard when she held Jacqueline in her arms. She glanced back at Mae Frances, standing regally in a fuchsia suit that was fit for a First Lady. Mae Frances lowered the veil of her hat, then nodded for Jasmine to move on.

"Finally," Hosea said when they entered the living room.

"We're ready now," Mae Frances said, "to go hear some good preaching—" She stopped suddenly, leaned against the sofa, and released a moan.

"Mae Frances!" Hosea rushed to her side.

She moaned again.

Hosea lowered her onto the couch. "What's wrong?"

"I don't know. I think it's my stomach . . . or my head." With sad, sick eyes she glanced up at him, her hat now tipped to the side. With a deep breath, she said, "Okay, let's try this again."

Hosea held her arm. "Take it slow."

Barely two inches off the sofa, she groaned so loud, Jasmine wondered if something was really wrong with her.

"Okay, that's it. You're not going anywhere," Hosea said.

"I'm fine." Mae Frances held one hand to her head and the other rested near her stomach. "I don't want to miss church."

"You're missing it today, Nama."

"All right," she said, disappointment dripping from every part of her. "I'll rest a little and will probably feel fine—right about lunchtime. We're going to Beverly Hills, right, Preacher Man?"

"Don't think about that right now." Hosea took her arm, helped her to stand.

She moved slowly, cautiously, as if pain could come with her next step. "I'm so sorry," she said as she passed Jasmine. "Why don't you guys just go on to church without me?"

Jasmine's mouth opened wide, but before she could scream obscenities at her friend, Hosea said, "We're going to stay here. Just in case you need us."

Mae Frances glanced over her shoulder and winked.

"I'll be right back, darlin'."

The moment the door closed, Jasmine collapsed onto the couch and hugged Jacqueline to her chest. That would have been some major drama—running into Brian and him seeing Jacqueline.

She shuddered, held her daughter tighter.

Her focus on Natasia had left her soft, but that wouldn't happen again. She would keep her family right here in the Valley. Brian and Alexis and Kyla and Jefferson could have the rest of the city.

As she kissed the top of Jacqueline's head, she made mental notes. One: Find a church in the San Fernando Valley. Two: Get rid of all the drama in her life, especially Natasia. Three: Don't add new drama, stay away from Brian. And four: Find a way to pay Mae Frances a million dollars for saving her life once again.

Jasmine held the silk sheath dress up and posed in the mirror. "Babe, don't you love this?"

Hosea peered at his wife over his reading glasses. "How long are you going to primp like that?"

"All day, every day until I have someplace to wear this bad boy." She jumped onto the bed and kissed Hosea. "Did I ever tell you that you're the best husband?"

He grinned. "You've mentioned it." He took off his glasses, rubbed his eyes. "It was great hooking up with Sebastian," he said, referring to the designer who had made her wedding dress. "I'd forgotten that his studio was up here."

"Aren't you glad I called him?"

"I think you mean, aren't *you* glad?" He chuckled. "I'm sorry, though, that we didn't get the chance to hang out in Beverly Hills."

Jasmine wasn't sorry at all. She'd carefully waylaid their plans to go into the city, insisting that they stay in the Valley and visit Sebastian.

"There's nothing special about Beverly Hills anyway. I've been there thousands of times. And lunch at Jerry's was better than any of those stuffy restaurants."

He nodded. "That pastrami sandwich was tight."

"The corned beef was good, too. Just wish I hadn't eaten so much." She rolled off the bed and stood in front of the mirror again, her eyes gazing at her hips. She'd been shocked when she discovered last week that she couldn't fit into a pair of size twelve jeans. When the salesclerk had asked if she wanted a larger size,

Jasmine had rolled her eyes and stomped right out of the Bloomingdale's fitting room. "I need to lose some weight." She sighed.

"No you don't."

"Easy for you to say, Mr. I've-lost-twenty-pounds-and-passed-them-all-to-my-wife."

Hosea patted his belly. "I do look good, don't I?" His laughter made Jasmine pout. "Ah, darlin', you know I love every extra inch, every extra pound of you."

"Hosea!"

"I do, I love me some you. There's just a little bit more of you to love."

"Are you trying to make me mad?"

"No, I'm just telling you the truth. Anyway, you only need to look good for me, and I say you look doggone good."

"I want to get back in shape."

"As long as you're doing it for the right reasons."

"I'm doing it because I don't like competition."

He let her words stay between them for a moment. "You don't have any," he said slowly.

"Natasia looks like a model."

"And you look like the woman I adore."

"Spoken like a husband."

"Spoken like a husband in love." He reached for her and she moved to the edge of the bed. "Don't let Natasia get to you. She'll be gone in three months."

"A lot of damage can be done in that time."

"Not to us." He pulled Jasmine onto his lap. "Trust me, because I really don't want to talk about her anymore."

Jasmine nodded, but not because she agreed. Hosea was right—there was no need to talk about Natasia anymore. Her back-to-Africa plan had failed, but she already had another one in mind. And this time, she was sure it would work.

EIGHTEEN

"Is there anything else?" Hosea asked as he glanced around the conference table. Their Los Angeles production team was much smaller than the New York staff—only two producers with him, Triage and Natasia serving as executives.

Wendy and Myra, the junior producers, shook their heads.

"I have something." Natasia paused, a dramatic moment. "I just got off the phone with Dr. Joseph Marshall and it's official, I've booked him for the show."

"You're kidding!" Hosea exclaimed. "We've been trying to get him for a year."

"You mentioned that," Natasia said.

"Yeah," Triage added, "I thought after *Oprah*, he wasn't interested in doing other shows."

"Well, I got him." She looked straight at Hosea. "For you." Then, "The only stipulation is that he wants to meet with one of you before the taping. He wants to do it on Friday."

"Well, I'm out," Triage said. "I'm on set for the rest of the week. Can you handle it, bro?"

"I'd love to." Hosea faced Natasia. "Tell Dr. Marshall I'll meet him anywhere he wants. He'll be in L.A. all day Friday?"

"He's not coming to L.A. He wants you to come to Oakland."

Hosea's eyes narrowed.

"He'd like to have," Natasia glanced at her notes, "a late-afternoon planning meeting to talk about the show and to have you tour his studio and facilities. He thinks that'll give you a good feel for his program, *Street Soldiers*." She jotted something onto her pad. Without looking up, she continued, "Brittney, make the flight arrangements. Oh, and of course, you'll need a producer with you, Hosea." She looked up, smiled at him. "So, I guess it's a plan."

"Sounds like it," Triage said. He leaned over and gave her a high-five. "Thanks for hooking that up."

"That's why you're paying me the big bucks." She glanced at Hosea, who sat without a smile, as the rest pushed their chairs back. "Are you okay?"

He took a moment, then nodded. "Yeah."

Triage said, "If that's it, I'm out." He bumped knuckles with Hosea.

As the producers and Brittney followed Triage out, Natasia stood. "I'll prepare a complete dossier—"

"Wait," Hosea interrupted her once they were alone. He motioned for her to close the door.

As she moved toward him, he didn't miss the way the hem of her sundress fluttered around her knees, the perfect frame for her bare legs. She leaned against the edge of the conference table and held up her hands. "No applause, please. A simple thank you will do." When he didn't comply, she frowned. "I thought you'd be ecstatic. I really worked on Dr. Marshall because I knew he was the one guest *you* wanted. So, what's wrong?"

He sighed. "We've been over this a million times."

Her frown deepened. "Over what?"

"I know what this is about. Dr. Marshall, the trip to Oakland; I know what it's all about."

"What?" She shook her head as if she was confused.

"I'm not going to Oakland with you. We're not going to be alone anywhere together. *This* has got to stop."

She folded her arms. "And by *this* you mean?"

"All these discussions. And now this trip, this trick. It has to stop. I'm married. Happy. I wish you would get that so that we can move on."

With raised eyebrows, she asked, "Are you finished?"

"Yeah," he said, still annoyed.

She paced the length of the conference room. "If I hadn't known you for so many years, I would slap the crap out of you." It was his turn to be shocked. "How dare you, Hosea! I worked my behind off to get Dr. Marshall and all you can think is that I arranged it to get to you?" Her hands folded into fists. "I am so pissed right now I don't know what to do. I'm not desperate, Hosea. I don't have to trick a man to be with me.

"Before this meeting, I'd already told Wendy that *she'd* be going to Oakland," she said, still stomping. "I have a breakfast meeting downtown on Friday. Then, I'm taking the cameras to the Sony lot to tape some footage of Triage, and then I'm meeting with Stephen to discuss the extension of my contract—which I can tell you will not happen now. You couldn't pay me enough to stay here.

"So, you see, Mr. Bush, I can't go to Oakland, don't want to go to Oakland. Don't want to be anywhere, at anytime alone with you! And frankly, after this, I don't even want to be on this show!" She grabbed her portfolio and marched away.

"Wait!"

Natasia pulled the door so hard, it slammed against the wall.

"Natasia, wait. Please."

She paused, her back still to him.

Slowly, Hosea stood, moved toward her. He closed the door and slid in the small space between her and the wall. "I'm sorry," he whispered. "I thought—"

"That's the problem." She stared straight at him. "You thought . . . too much."

The anger in her eyes made him clear his throat and inch away. "It's just that . . . I don't know. Maybe some of this is me. I was imagining . . . and I just went with that. I'm really sorry."

She considered his words. "You need to lay off the soap operas."

"Is that your way of saying you accept my apology?"

Slowly, she nodded. "But Hosea, I don't want to have this conversation again. I'm not after you. And I'm tired of the accusations."

"It won't happen again."

She locked her eyes with his. "I hope not, because in this business things happen and I don't want to explain myself every couple of days."

He held up his hands. "I'll never question you again."

Finally, she smiled a little. "You'd better not."

He grinned.

"Okay, so I'll work with Brittney on the reservations for you and *Wendy*."

They walked shoulder-to-shoulder toward the door, but she stopped before they stepped into the hallway. "By the way, I wasn't thinking about you or Oakland, because after that long day on Friday, I'm meeting Mario Walters for drinks."

His eyes widened. "The actor?"

She nodded. "So, you see, I did everything I could not to go to Oakland . . . with you." She wiggled her fingers in a wave.

Hosea watched as she sashayed, like poetry in motion, down the long hallway. And he released a long sigh.

They held each other in the dark and Hosea kissed the top of Jasmine's head.

"I'm going to Oakland on Friday," he stated the fact. "For the show. Meeting with Joe Marshall."

"An overnight trip?"

"No, but it will be all day."

"Hmmm."

He squeezed her tighter, then said, "Go ahead, ask."

Jasmine hesitated. "You said you didn't want to talk about her anymore."

"But I want you to ask me."

"Just tell me what you want me to know."

He kissed her before he said, "Natasia's not going with me. She didn't even want to. Did everything she could to get out of this trip."

Her head was still resting on his chest when she said, "I don't believe that."

"It's true. She doesn't want to go because she has a date with Mario Walters."

After a moment, Jasmine said, "She's slumming now."

"Slumming? I said Mario Walters."

"So? I mean, yes, he might be finer than Denzel, funnier than Will, sings like Luther, and dances like Usher. But he's no Hosea Bush."

He chuckled. "Spoken like a wife."

"Spoken like a wife in love."

"So does this prove that I was right about Natasia?"

She slid her bare leg up against his. "This proves that I was right about you." She paused. "I love you, Hosea."

"Ditto." He pulled her closer, their two bodies almost one. "I was made to love you."

He kissed her again, and then in the dark, they stayed in place, just thinking, just holding, just loving each other.

NINETEEN

JASMINE HAD ALREADY PRAYED this morning, so now it was time to give God a little help.

She tucked Jacqueline in for her noon-day nap before she settled into the living room. She picked up the phone, but before she made the call she wanted to, she dialed the number she had to.

"Talk to me!"

"Hey, babe," she said. "How's it going?"

"Hectic."

"You started taping yet?"

"No, but we're about to. What's going down?"

"Nothing. Just want you to know that I love you."

"Ditto! I hope you have something fantastic to do today."

"Babe, you have no idea."

After a quick good-bye, she hung up. Good! She wouldn't have to worry about Hosea returning to the hotel and overhearing her conversation. That's how Hosea had discovered that she was pregnant. He had walked right in when she was scheduling an abortion.

The memory made Jasmine shudder. Made her try to imagine life without Jacqueline. Made her feel so blessed that Hosea *had* walked in and saved her baby.

That time, the intrusion had worked out—eventually. But being overheard would never happen to her again.

Searching her PDA, she found the number, then clicked the track wheel. If a baby hadn't appealed to Natasia, big bucks certainly would.

"Jasmine, great to hear from you," Annika exclaimed, her Swedish accent thick. "How's the married life?"

"Absolutely wonderful." She sank into the sofa's thick cushions. "Hosea and Jacqueline are my joy."

"And Malik? Is he still single?"

Jasmine laughed. "Yeah, he is. You should give him a call."

"Don't tempt me. Your godbrother is the walking definition of phine!"

Jasmine laughed. Annika Eklund had been in the U.S. for only ten years, but she spoke as if she'd been born in New York—deep in the heart of Harlem.

Annika continued, "So, are you and Malik looking for new candidates?"

"No, we're not hiring, but I do need you. As a headhunter and as my friend."

"How can I help, hon?"

"I need you to find a job for someone."

"A friend?"

"An enemy."

"Ooohhh, chile, this sounds wonderfully juicy. Details, details."

For minutes, Jasmine explained to the executive recruiter who'd become a good friend Hosea and Natasia's past, and how she'd ingratiated herself into their present.

"This crazy trick is after my husband, Annika. And I want her gone. Can you help?"

"It'll be my pleasure. So, where would you like Natasia to go?" She paused when she realized what she'd said and the two shared a long laugh.

"As far away as you can find," Jasmine said. "Somewhere like London, Paris, the deep caves in Russia. And don't worry, I'll pay your normal fee."

"Are you kidding? I'll do this for free. It's a brilliant idea. I wish I'd thought of this when that skussy, Helena, came after my ex."

"Skussy?" Jasmine laughed. "A Scandinavian term?"

"No, purely American. I always called these kinds of low-life women hussies. But then when I came to the States, I heard the wonderfully descriptive word 'skank.' So I combined the two, and bam! You got skussy."

Jasmine laughed. "I love it!"

"So, hon, this one's on me. Just hang onto that fine husband of yours. I'll take care of Natasia. Give me her contact information."

Jasmine gave the number to the studio.

"Okay, give me a week, two tops."

Jasmine hung up and for the first time since she'd heard Natasia Redding's name, she felt complete relief. Sure that now that skussy was on her way out.

✳ ✳ TWENTY

Hosea saw the placard with his name scribbled across the front before he saw the little man who held it.

"I'm Hosea Bush." He slung the strap of his computer bag over his shoulder and resisted the urge to ask the man who wasn't even five-feet tall how old he was. He wasn't too worried; he suspected the gray that edged his hairline made him old enough to drive.

"Do you have any luggage?" the driver asked in a voice that was as small as he was.

"Nope, this is it."

He nodded. "We have to walk. They don't let us park close anymore."

"Lead the way." Hosea slowed his stride to match the man's steps. They moved only a few feet when his cell phone rang.

"Talk to me."

"Hey, Hosea," Brittany said. "Did you get my message?"

"Nope. Just landed. What's going down?"

"There's been a mix-up with Dr. Marshall's office. They thought the meeting was tomorrow."

"Tomorrow? Saturday?"

"Yup. Apparently, Dr. Marshall's in meetings all day today."

Hosea sighed deeply. "How did this happen?"

"I don't know. Natasia handled everything."

Natasia. "Okay, I'll just have to make this work."

"I'm already on it. I made reservations for you at the Palace in downtown San Fran."

"Great. Is Wendy staying there, too? She's on the flight behind me, right?"

"Well, that's another change. Wendy was on her way to the airport when I caught her. She can't come up there now. Remember, she's flying back to New York tomorrow? Her sister's getting married on Sunday."

"Oh, that's right. So, Myra's coming?"

"Triage said Myra's too junior. Natasia's coming."

He frowned.

Brittney continued, now with a lower voice, "I gotta warn you, though, Natasia threw a fit when Triage told her that she had to change her plans."

"She doesn't have to change her plans. She can come in the morning."

"I guess she had plans for the whole weekend."

Hosea wondered if those weekend plans included Mario Walters and then he wondered why he cared. He thought about insisting on Myra, but knew it would be better to have Natasia. "Okay, arrange Natasia's flight for the morning and make sure a car picks her up."

"Should I have her meet you at your hotel?"

"No! Have her go to Dr. Marshall's. Order a separate car for me and I'll meet her there."

"Okay, Boss."

Hosea clicked off his phone. He had to lean forward to see the top of the driver's head. "Plans have changed," he said, hoping the man could see over the steering wheel. "I'm going to the Palace."

The driver nodded.

"The station hired you for the day, right?"

"Yeah."

"Okay, I'm gonna need to dash to a mall to pick up a few things. But I want to check in first."

"No problem."

Hosea leaned back as the Town Car eased onto the freeway.

For some reason they thought the meeting was tomorrow.

How could Dr. Marshall's office believe the meeting was tomorrow when Natasia clearly set it up for today? He shook away the first answer that came to him. This was not Natasia's fault. She'd made it clear that she was over him, and according to Brittney, Natasia wasn't happy about this either.

But still . . .

He flipped open his cell, pressed the speed dial.

"Hey, babe," Jasmine answered. "Did you just land?"

"Yeah, but there's a problem. I'm gonna have to stay overnight. Someone got the meeting with Dr. Marshall mixed up. It's tomorrow."

"That's a pretty big mix-up. If Natasia was with you, I'd think she'd arranged this." Jasmine chuckled and Hosea pretended to laugh with her.

"Well, that means I won't be home tonight and I don't know how I'm gonna sleep without you. You're my pillow."

"Ah. Spoken like a husband."

"Spoken like a husband in love."

"So, you're going to have to pick up a few things, huh?"

"Yeah, I'll buy another shirt, some underwear, a toothbrush." He sighed. Schlepping through a store was not his idea of fun.

"Oh, come on. Give me an excuse to go to the mall." She laughed. "Is Wendy there yet?"

Hosea hesitated. "No. Listen, darlin', I'll call you from the hotel to give you the number, okay? Love you."

"Ditto."

When he clicked off the phone, he loosened the noose that was masquerading as a tie around his neck.

Why did I just lie to Jasmine?

It wasn't a total lie—Wendy *wasn't* there. And even if it was a lie of omission, he'd done it with purpose. No need to upset Jasmine, and mentioning Natasia's name would do that. Anyway, it wasn't like Natasia was going to be spending the night in Oakland. She'd fly up in the morning, they'd have their meeting, and he'd be back in Los Angeles—with his wife and daughter—by dinner. Jasmine didn't need to know any of this. Didn't need to give her any reasons to be suspicious. He had enough wary thoughts for both of them.

Hosea moved the computer from his lap, leaned against the bed's headboard, and closed his eyes, wondering what it was going to take to get his focus back.

It had been this way for the last two hours. He couldn't concentrate because his head was filled with memories of long ago yesterdays . . .

"Are you sure about this?" Hosea asked as he handed Natasia the bowl of popcorn.

She crossed her legs Indian-style and popped open a can of Hawaiian Punch. "This is the best Valentine's Day I've ever had."

He sat next to her. "If you say so."

"Baby, we do what everyone's doing tonight all the time. I think staying in is really special." She pressed play on the remote and the tape began.

Natasia leaned back inside his arms and they chomped on popcorn, sipped punch, and watched her favorite movie, *Love Story*. Suddenly, Natasia pushed herself away from him.

"What's wrong, darlin'?" he asked with a smile.

She lifted her hand to her mouth, then stared at her palm. "What the . . ." She couldn't take her eyes off the ring she'd pulled from the popcorn box.

Hosea shifted until he was in front of her, lifted her chin with his fingers, and said, "Nat, let's do the darn thing. Let's get married!"

She stared into his eyes, her mouth open wide. And then she punched him.

"Ouch," he said, feigning injury. "That's not the way you're supposed to say yes."

"You got butter all over my engagement ring!"

He laughed. She cried. Together they slipped the ring on her finger. And then as Ali McGraw explained love and sorrys to Ryan O'Neal, she had kissed him, then ripped his pants off and told him yes with every part of her body . . .

Hosea bounced from the bed. It made no sense, the way he kept thinking about his past. He was over her, of that he was sure. He loved Jasmine, he was even surer of that. So why all these memories?

He needed relief and grabbed his cell phone.

"Hey, babe."

Just the sound of his wife brought his heart back to where it was supposed to be. "Calling to check on you, darlin'. How's my pumpkin?"

"Jacquie is worn out. She's asleep."

"It's just six. You'd better wake her up or she'll have you up all night."

"I hope she does. Playing with her tonight will keep me from missing you. So, what're you doing?"

"Nothing much."

"You're supposed to say that you're thinking about me."

He remembered the thoughts he'd had just moments before. "I'm always thinking about you."

"That's better." She laughed. "Did Wendy get there yet?"

"Ah, no. All of that will arrive in the morning."

"All of that?" He heard the frown in her voice.

"You know what I mean, all the notes, etcetera. Have you eaten yet?" He needed to change the subject to stop his lies.

"Yup, just a salad. I'm really serious about losing this weight. What about you, have you eaten?"

The knock made him say, "Hold on a sec." He scooted across the room and pulled the door open.

"Surprise!" Natasia stood with her hands in the air as if she'd just jumped out of a cake.

"Babe, who's that?"

That quickly, he'd forgotten the cell phone he held. "Just room service."

Natasia's eyebrows rose as she brushed past him into the room.

"I'll call you back, okay?" He clicked the phone off without giving Jasmine any more.

Natasia swiveled around to face him. "So, I'm room service now, huh?" She grinned. "That could be a good thing."

"What are you doing here?" He didn't share her cheer.

She frowned. "Brittney said she told you about the mix-up."

"I know about all of that." His hands moved in the air with his words. "But what are you doing here . . . now? I thought you were coming in the morning."

"That was the plan, but when I thought about it, this is an important meeting. We need to be prepared."

"We could have done this in the morning."

"Last-minute preparations are not what won me all those Emmys. We're going to do this right. In fact, I was thinking about a new angle. Let's make this a full-hour news show, *Dateline* style. Make this entire episode about Dr. Marshall and *Street Soldiers*. We'll film his facilities, do B roll on his radio show. We're in Hollywood. Let's make this show look like it."

He stared at her for a moment. "So that's why you're here?" His tone thickened the air with tension.

"Yes." She looked right back into his eyes, daring him to doubt her. When he asked nothing more, she said, "I gave up a lot to be here. But my *job* comes before everything. Okay?"

It took him a moment to let it go. "Okay."

"So what do you think of my idea?"

He breathed, relieved. She'd gone right back to business. Surely, this wasn't any kind of trick. "Sounds good. What're you talking about specifically?"

"I have lots of ideas." She glanced around the room and then stared at the bed where he'd been moments before, thinking about her.

"Ah . . . have you eaten?" he asked.

She shook her head. "I guess you haven't either. You're waiting for room service, right?"

"Let's go downstairs," he said, ignoring her words. "We can talk in the restaurant."

"Or we can talk here and *really* order room service, and," she paused, sat on the edge of the bed, crossed her legs, "we can . . . eat . . . right here."

"Let's go downstairs, Natasia," he said stiffly.

She bounced from the bed, laughed. "I'm teasing, Hosea." She pouted. "You used to be more fun."

"Never when it came to business. Where're the files?"

"In my room." She grinned. "Wanna come with me?"

"I'll meet you in the lobby."

"Okay, give me five."

He tried not to watch her jean-covered hips as she moved in front of him. When the door closed, he breathed. She'd asked for five minutes, but he needed more like ten.

Finally it was all about business.

For hours they read and debated. Formulated their plan. And in between, they snacked on hot wings, quesadillas, and potato skins.

Hosea leaned back in his chair and glanced at his watch. "I cannot believe it's almost eleven." He signaled the waiter to bring him another soda.

Natasia picked up a wing and took a small bite. "Yep, but we're ready."

"Definitely." He grinned, but stopped smiling when his cell rang. Flipping his phone open, he turned his body slightly away from the table. "Talk to me."

"Hey, babe. You were supposed to call me back."

"I'm sorry. I'm down in the restaurant, still working."

"With Wendy? I thought she was coming in the morning?"

He paused, glanced sideways at Natasia as she sipped her wine. "Wendy's not here. I'm just eating and working and . . . " He closed his eyes, not believing how easy it was to keep the truth from his wife. "So, did you have a good night?"

"As good as it can be without you."

Hosea glanced at Natasia once again. Her eyes were down, scanning their notes. As she read, she sucked the end of a chicken wing, then the tip of her tongue grazed her lips, wiping away the sauce. When she tossed the bone back onto the plate, she licked each of her fingers. One at a time. Slowly. Thoroughly. Then, she looked up. Directly at him.

"Hello?" Jasmine called through the phone.

He broke his stare. "I'm here. I'm gonna head up to my room. Catch some sleep."

Me too. Will you think about me?"

"I'll do better than that," he said. "I'll dream about you."

"I love you, Hosea."

As if she heard Jasmine's declaration, Natasia cleared her throat, demanded his attention.

"Hosea?"

"I love you too," he said to his wife, although his eyes were on Natasia. "I'll call you in the morning, darlin'."

He clicked off the phone and signaled for their check. Silence stayed until the waiter returned. Hosea signed, then pushed back his chair. "Ready?"

Natasia lifted her glass, emptied the corner of wine that remained. Then said, "Can I ask you something?"

The cheer that had been in her voice all evening was gone. In its place, sadness, a dread that Hosea had heard only once before—on the night he told her it was over.

She said, "What is it about Jasmine? What is it that you see?"

"I see God," he said without hesitation.

She reared back a bit at his words. "In Jasmine?" she asked, as if she couldn't believe his answer.

But he was not moved by her shock. "The moment I met Jasmine, I saw the woman I knew God wanted me to marry."

She nodded slightly, then lowered her head. "How did you know she was the one?"

He shrugged a little. "It wasn't like I saw a burning bush or anything." He paused. "But I heard His voice. Inside of me. Guiding me."

"So with me, God told you no?"

He waited a moment, not wanting to hurt her with the truth. Then, he nodded. "It took me a while to walk away, Natasia. Even after God clearly said no, I wanted it to be you. I was going to force it."

"Why didn't you?"

He sighed. "Because I was tired of running from Him. Tired of not living for His purpose. Tired of doing things that I wasn't supposed to be doing."

"Like having sex."

He nodded. That had been a contention between the two. Hosea was always consumed with guilt afterward—Natasia was not. "I was a minister and living with one of my congregants. No matter how you spin it, it wasn't right."

"I never understood why you took that so seriously. We were in love, in a monogamous relationship, planning to get married."

"And it *still* wasn't right. We were living hidden lives. Lying all the time—I couldn't keep up with the truth. God couldn't bless that. So, He took it away. Turned what had started out as good, bad."

"That's not the way I remember it."

"Natasia, we started fighting all the time—"

"That was just life."

"That was just life without Him." He paused. "I did the right thing. For me. And for you."

She studied her hands. "The break-up never made sense to me, but what's been worse is what happened afterward. I've dated . . . a lot, but I compare every man to you."

He chuckled. "I don't know why."

"Trust me, Hosea." She smiled, although sadness was all over her. "You're special." She stopped and blinked. Slowly moved her hand toward his.

She touched him. He held her.

She sighed. "I've never been able to talk to anyone the way we talked. I've never been able to laugh with anyone the way we laughed." She stopped, spoke slower. "I've never made love with anyone the way we made love. You can't tell me that you don't remember that."

Since she'd come back, he couldn't stop remembering. She'd been his melody. He'd been her harmony. He squeezed her hand, then let her go. "You're going to find that again, Natasia, but you've got to live for now. Not in the past."

"That's what I'd been doing until fate brought us together again." She paused. "Do you ever think about me? Or what we used to be?"

He pushed back the lump in his throat and his memories at the same time. Lied without words—just shook his head, no.

She asked, "How do you know that your life wouldn't be better with me? Better if we were married?"

"Nat," he said softly.

They both stopped and rested in the name that he used to call her. "Let's not do this anymore. I'm—"

She held up her hand. "Stop. Don't say it. I'm sorry." She took a deep breath. "It's the wine. Not me."

He nodded, helped her from her chair. They shared no words as they walked through the lobby. Inside the elevator, they stood shoulder to shoulder, staring straight at the steel doors.

The bell binged on the sixteenth floor and they both hesitated before Natasia stepped forward.

Hosea followed. When Natasia looked at him with raised eyebrows, he held up his hands. "Just want to make sure you're safe."

"You don't have to."

"Yes, I do."

A small smile. "Always the gentleman."

Silence returned, until they stopped in front of her room. Natasia pushed her key into the electronic lock, then suddenly whipped around and pressed her lips against his.

It was shocking.

Soft.

Nice.

Hosea closed his eyes, remembered, and wrapped his arms around her. She leaned into him more.

His heart pounded as his tongue found hers and they kissed the way they used to. His breaths came quicker when her hands slipped from his neck. Then, her fingers moved lower. Lower. Lower.

Her touch made reason return.

He pushed their bodies apart. Her breathing matched his and she turned away, fumbled with the lock. "Come inside," she breathed, finally pushing open the door.

He stayed still.

She reached for his hand, but he took two steps back. Then stopped.

"Please," she said, moving into the hallway.

She stretched toward him again, but he moved from her grasp. Their eyes held as he backed away more. Then he turned and rushed down the hall. He came to the elevators, but kept moving. He didn't want to wait, couldn't afford to stop.

At the end of the hall, he paused at the staircase. Turned. Looked back from where he came. Looked back to Natasia's room. To where she'd stood just moments before.

But now she was gone.

TWENTY-ONE

JASMINE ROLLED OVER. HER eyes fluttered, then widened. "Jacquie!" And she remembered. Her daughter had stayed with Mae Frances last night. This was her morning to sleep in since Hosea was in Oakland.

She lay back down and molded her body into the soft sheets. She felt like she could lie there forever—especially if Hosea was with her. The thought of her husband made her frown. It was after ten and he hadn't called. She reached for her cell, but then the hotel's phone rang. She smiled. All she had to do was think of him and he would call.

She lifted the phone, settled back into the sheets. "Hey, babe."

"Sorry. Jasmine. It's just me," Annika said.

Jasmine laughed. "Hosea's away and I thought you were him."

"I'm not your babe, but I'm calling with great news. I've found a few hot opportunities for your girl."

That made her sit up straight. "Already?"

"Yup. Even one in London."

"You're kidding. Have you called her yet?"

"That's why I'm calling you. I tried reaching Natasia yesterday and was told she's in Oakland on business."

Her blood stopped flowing. Her heart stopped beating. But her brain—that worked. And Annika's words crashed inside her head, over and over.

"In Oakland on business."

That was all Jasmine heard, but Annika continued. "I could wait, but I was wondering, if you had her cell, we can get this party started."

Her brain directed her lips to move, "No . . . I don't . . . have her cell," she stuttered.

"Well, it's not like the positions are going anywhere. I was just excited. I'll call her on Monday."

"Thanks," Jasmine said, and then stared at the phone for long after she put it back in place.

Natasia's in Oakland.

That was impossible.

She went over everything that Hosea had told her—how Natasia wasn't going on this trip, how she didn't want to go, how she was dating Mario Walters.

All lies!

No, Hosea would never lie. Would never cheat. Honesty, loyalty were the most important things to him.

I lied, I cheated.

But Hosea would never stoop to the low things she'd done. Would he?

"Oh, God," she cried and sank onto the edge of the bed. She couldn't have lost the fight already. Natasia couldn't have taken Hosea so easily.

She jumped when the telephone rang, stared at it. There was no doubt who was on the other end this time. Surely, it was the man she loved. But did he still love her?

With a deep breath, she grabbed the phone. "Hello."

"May I speak to Jasmine, please?"

She frowned. "Who's this?"

"Jasmine, this is Brian. Brian Lewis."

She flung the handset across the room as if it was a rattlesnake. What was this man doing calling her? And why now? Why, when her life was falling apart?

She despised Brian Lewis, the man who had almost destroyed her marriage and given her such a gift at the same time. Surely, he had only one reason for calling. And that was to lead her straight back into temptation.

Alexis and Brian

"It's a Man's Man's
Man's World"

—JAMES BROWN

TWENTY-THREE

ALEXIS SLAMMED ON HER brakes, grabbed her coffee mug before it tipped over, then leaned against the horn. The man in the car ahead glanced at her through his rearview mirror, and in her mind, she gave him the finger. But she stopped there. It was hard to curse out anyone with the gold cross that dangled from her mirror.

Still, she slapped the steering wheel. L.A. drivers pissed her off. That guy could have taken the light—it had barely turned yellow. Now, she'd have to hope that Brian got caught at a light up ahead. Chances of that were good since this was the midst of the morning rush.

She took a sip of her coffee and waited. It wasn't like she had to have her husband in her sight. She already knew where Brian was going. This was the third Monday in as many weeks that she had stalked him through these same streets.

The light turned green and she zipped into the next lane and then swerved in front of the guy who'd cut her off. Now she felt better.

But her relief was fleeting and within seconds, her mind was back to asking, "Why? Why? Why?" And her heart was telling her to turn around. She could have easily paid some professional trained to spy on spouses.

The thought of writing that check made her feel like a cliché—a suspecting wife and a cheating husband. She and Brian weren't like that.

So what am I doing? she wondered as she sped down Wilshire. At Morrison Street, she made a left, then a quick right onto Honey Lane.

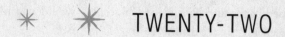

TWENTY-TWO

IT WAS THE CURVE OF HER calves that made Brian sweat. Just the sight of her legs transported him to another place—a room. Any room. With a bed. He could see, even feel her legs wrapped around him. He leaned to the right to stretch the tightness in his neck. Still, his eyes never left her legs.

"Dr. Lewis?"

Slowly, his glance traveled upward. The pharmaceutical sales-woman smiled when his eyes finally met hers. Her grin was welcoming—as if she knew what he was thinking. As if she were not offended at all. As if she thought his thoughts were good thoughts.

Brian cleared his throat and tried to shake off the heat that she carried. "Well, I'll pass all of this information onto Dr. Miller. She's the one—"

The woman held up her hand. "I know Dr. Miller makes the buys. I'm just glad you were free to see me today. I don't know how I got my appointment mixed up like that." She leaned forward and this time, Brian couldn't keep his eyes from her cleavage that peeked through the silk blouse she wore. "I'll just leave these with you." Her voice drew Brian's eyes upward. Again there was that smile. Wider this time.

She stood. Held out her hand. "Dr. Lewis, it was a pleasure."

He took her hand and hoped she didn't feel the moisture that had settled inside his palm. He stepped back, but still, she held his hand a moment longer and with the smallest of movements, her thumb caressed the soft skin between his thumb and forefinger. And with her eyes, she told him this meeting didn't have to end here, didn't have to end now.

She edged her car to the curb just as Brian jumped from his SUV several cars in front of her. She turned off the ignition and slid lower in her seat.

This made her crazy! The way she knew exactly which house Brian would go to. The way she knew how he'd trot up the steps, ring the doorbell, and then step inside once the woman answered the door.

Like the times before, she just stayed and watched, even though every one of her bones wanted to race up to that door and begin her beat down. In her mind, she alternated between beating her husband and his mistress. In her mind, the fight always ended the same way—with both of them spread out on the floor. And her not knowing—or caring—if they were dead or alive.

But she never made that move. And today—unlike the previous times—she wouldn't wait for Brian to come out. She turned on the ignition, swung the car into a U-turn, and pressed toward home. She glanced at her hands gripping the steering wheel, but she felt calm. Really, there was no other way to be. She wasn't going to cry; she had never shed a tear over a man, and now that she had sneaked past forty, she wasn't about to begin. Brian would never come home and find her thrashing on the floor.

She was more like the gun-wielding wife with her weapon aimed at just the right body part. But she wouldn't do that either. God and time's wisdom kept her from making those kinds of time-behind-bars decisions.

"Didn't expect you back so soon," said the doorman of the apartment building where she and Brian lived.

She flipped him her keys. "Yup, Charles, I've got some business at home today."

"Well, have a great day, Mrs. Ward-Lewis."

"I will," she said and meant it. The rest of her great day was already planned. As she stepped into the elevator, she imagined how she would confront Brian. The moment he walked through the door, she'd tell him everything she knew and then hand him his bags that she would have already packed.

But then, she shook her head. She wasn't lifting a finger. She'd confront him and then give him thirty minutes to pack his own bags.

Just before she entered their penthouse, she changed her mind. She'd only give him *fifteen* minutes to get out of their apartment and her life for good.

TWENTY-FOUR

BRIAN DROPPED HIS KEYS ON the desk and flopped into his chair. He bowed his head, exhausted, though it was barely noon. The quick knock on the door made him sit up straight.

"What's up?" his best friend, Jefferson, said as he sank into the chair across from him. "Looks like you had a hard night."

"More like a tough morning." He shook his head.

Jefferson let a moment pass. "You saw her again."

Brian nodded. "I don't know what to do. This guilt's got me twisted."

Jefferson leaned back in the chair; his white doctor's jacket fell open exposing his crisp shirt beneath. "You still haven't told Alexis?"

Brian shook his head.

"That's where the guilt is coming from," Jefferson said. He leaned forward. "You've got to tell your wife."

Brian chuckled, although neither one of them found Jefferson's words comical. "I don't know how many times I have to tell you this, Jay. My wife is not your wife. If Alexis finds out, she'll leave me. I won't get the pass that you got when Kyla found out about your affair."

"Bro, trust. It wasn't a pass. But we did survive. And I believe you and Alex will too." He paused and when Brian offered nothing, Jefferson continued. "You've got to trust God and your wife, because living the way you're living ain't living."

Brian shook his head. Jefferson wasn't hearing him. Maybe he wasn't living well right now, but he had no doubt that he would hardly be living at all if Alexis found out.

"Believe me," Jefferson stood, "tell your wife. It's the only way."

Brian watched his friend walk out the door before he leaned back in his chair. There was no way he was taking Jefferson's advice. He'd already lived through one divorce, leaving two sons behind. He was not going to give up on this marriage. He planned on keeping his promise that he and Alexis would be together until the day of death. No, he wasn't telling her a thing. He'd just have to find a way to trudge through this madness alone.

✳ ✳ TWENTY-FIVE

THE LIVING ROOM WAS DRENCHED with the early evening summer sun, but still, Alexis shivered. She clasped her hands together and her ring pinched her finger. Holding her left hand high, her diamond created a rainbow that danced against the walls.

The memories were still fresh, of the night a bit over six years ago when Brian marched into her apartment, after midnight, wearing a tuxedo. While she wore her bathrobe, he got down on bended knee and told her that he would love her completely, openly, honestly. From that moment, she never questioned his love.

Then, about a year and a half ago, the doubts began. Started right when Brian returned home from that trip to New York. The trip that hadn't made any sense to her when he first announced that he was leaving.

"You're going to New York tonight?" she'd said with surprise. "But tomorrow is New Year's Eve."

"I have to, baby. I'm doing a consultation on a newborn. We're meeting on New Year's Day. It may be a holiday, but that doesn't matter to this family."

Although she thought it strange, she'd accepted his explanation. He was an ophthalmologist, considered one of the nation's foremost infant eye surgeons. So, she'd pushed aside the instincts that told her something was up, and focused on the fact that Brian was a specialist. Told herself that all was well, even when she sat in church at midnight and celebrated the incoming 2005 without her husband.

Then he'd returned suddenly on January 1, walking into their penthouse, both of his arms filled with bundles of roses so thick, their number was impossible to count.

"The surgery was canceled," was his explanation. "And I missed you."

The next day he appeared at her office and against her protests, whisked her away, first for lunch at her favorite restaurant, Heroes, and then an overnight trip to Santa Barbara.

"I needed to spend some time with you" was his explanation this time.

Then the next night at home, he held her in his arms, and told her that he wanted to renew their wedding vows. She told him just how corny she thought that was, told him that you only needed to make that commitment once.

But he'd insisted. "I just want you to know how much I will always love you."

It was only because of her resistance that they never had that ceremony, but the memory of those events had kept her wondering. She knew her doubts were ridiculous—her best friend, Kyla Blake, told her so.

"Girl, I cannot believe you're complaining about this." Kyla laughed when they'd met at Starbucks and Alexis told her that something wasn't quite right. "So let me get this straight—Brian brought you flowers, took you on a trip, and wants to renew your wedding vows. Alex, most women would call that hitting the husband jackpot."

But it was her early home training that played in her head.

"A woman always knows." She'd overheard her mother's gossip fests with her friends many times.

Alexis knew.

Now she knew for sure.

The sound of the key turning in the front door lock startled her, and she sat up straight, keeping her eyes on the window.

"Hey, sweetheart," he said.

She took a courage-building breath before she faced him. But when she did, she had to fight to keep the bile from rising inside. Her eyes shifted from his face to the flowers he carried.

Leaning over, he kissed her cheek. "These are for you. Happy Monday."

She inhaled the fragrance of his guilt before she took the bouquet from him. Then suddenly, she dropped the bunch into her lap.

"What's wrong?"

"A thorn." She picked at the torn skin on her palm, right beneath her ring finger.

"I'm sorry." He lifted her hand and kissed the spot that had been pricked.

She held her breath, willing herself to ignore the ache that crept into her heart. Willing herself not to care anymore.

He said, "Let me put these in a vase."

He took two steps away before she asked, "Did you buy the same flowers for your mistress?"

He stopped. Kept his back to her for a moment, then pivoted and faced her.

She was impressed. Didn't seem as if he'd been shocked by her ambush.

"What are you talking about?" he asked in a what-are-we-having-for-dinner tone.

She stood, squarely faced him. "I'm not going back and forth. I don't want to hear the details or the denials. I just want you to pack and leave."

He loosened his tie as if he needed air to speak. "Pack and leave? For what?"

She folded her arms to stop her heart from crashing through her chest. "I told you," she said as calmly as she could, "I'm not going through all of that. Just pack your . . . just pack and get out."

He tossed the flowers onto the dining room table and rose petals scattered at his feet. He looked down, stayed that way, pulling his thoughts together. Finally, "I'm not having an affair, Alexis."

She sighed; she didn't have time for this.

He said, "You've got to believe me."

"Why should I believe a liar like you?" She stepped closer. "I've been following you."

"What!"

"I didn't stutter. I've followed you for the last three weeks."

"I cannot believe you," he said, his voice rising. "How could you do that? How could you invade my privacy, not trust me—"

She held up her hand. "Oh, no. You will not turn this around, Brian." She stepped closer, pointed her finger in his face. "*You're* the one having the affair. *You're* the low-down-dirty-dog. *You're* the one who's leaving this house tonight."

"I'm not going anywhere; I'm not having an affair!"

She shook her head. "Then I'll leave." She moved toward their bedroom.

"Alex, wait." She stopped, watched his Adam's apple crawl up his throat. "I'm telling you the truth," he said quickly. "Really, sweetheart, it's not what you think."

"Then what is it?"

He paused, searching for words. "I can't tell you."

She laughed. He didn't.

He said, "I can't tell you. Not right now. I can't tell you alone."

Without a word, she pushed past him. He grabbed her. Slowly her eyes moved down to where he grasped her elbow and just as slowly, he dropped her arm.

"Sweetheart, I'm telling the truth," he said softly. "I'll explain it to you tomorrow."

"Explain it to me now."

"I can't. I need . . . help with this."

"That doesn't make sense."

"I know, but that's why I'm asking you to trust me. Just wait for tomorrow and go there with me."

Her eyebrows rose. "I know you're not talking about . . ."

He nodded. "But you'll see. You'll understand."

She crossed her arms and her glower deepened.

"Trust me for one more night. Because I'm telling you, Alex, I'm not having an affair. I love you."

She hated herself already. Hated herself because it sounded like the truth, because she wanted it to be true.

Her eyes were thin slits as she nodded her agreement to do what he asked.

He released a long breath and wrapped his arms around her. But she wiggled from his embrace, pushed him away. "You'd better explain everything to me tomorrow," she demanded.

He nodded.

She turned into their bedroom and slammed the door in his face.

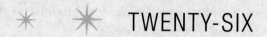 # TWENTY-SIX

BRIAN EDGED HIS CAR AGAINST the curb. He glanced in the rearview mirror; Alexis wasn't behind him. She was there, at the last light. But now she was gone.

He shook his head, wondering if his wife had changed her mind. He knew that was a serious possibility. From the moment she told him this morning that she was taking her own car, he knew that her chances of showing up with him were tenuous at best.

"Why do you want to drive?" he'd asked when she made that announcement as he'd come into the kitchen. He sat at the table and said, "Let's ride together."

She glared at him, then dumped two pieces of burnt toast onto his plate. She stood, towering over him, daring him to speak another word. Finally, he called the truce. Picked up a slice and bit into the hardened bread. Only then did she walk away.

When they'd left home and she'd followed him down Wilshire, he wondered why he'd never noticed her trailing him before.

A car's horn blared behind him. He glanced in the mirror, said a quick prayer of thanks before he jumped from his SUV.

"This better not take long." Alexis swung her purse over her shoulder, almost hitting him with the bag.

"It won't." He led her up the steps to the front door of the house that he'd been visiting for more than a year.

The door opened, and with a sideways glance, he saw Alexis's eyes widen. *Maybe this wasn't such a good idea,* he second-guessed himself.

"Hello," the woman greeted them. With her white-blond hair

set in a stiff bouffant style, all that was missing was the long blue dress. She could have easily slipped into the story book pages as Cinderella.

Brian stepped inside first, the referee between his wife and this woman she did not know.

"Nice to meet you, Alexis." She held out her hand. But Alexis had left her manners at home and the woman's hand stayed alone, hanging in the air. "I'm Taylor Perkins," the woman continued anyway, her voice still breezy as if she was unfazed by Alexis's attitude.

Alexis folded her arms, stared. Still, Taylor smiled, "Follow me," she said.

Together the three moved down the narrow corridor into a room.

With a quick glance, Alexis scoped the space. Took in the desk, and chairs, and shelves stocked with books. Taylor motioned toward the sofa as she sat in an oversized chair facing them.

With her attitude and impatience rising, Alexis asked, "Who are you?" The question was for Taylor, but she directed her words toward Brian.

Taylor said, "I'm your husband's doctor."

It began slowly, the way Alexis's lips spread and then her mouth opened wide. Her glance moved from Brian to Taylor back to her husband. And she sank onto the couch. "Doctor?" she whispered. "Brian, you're sick?"

He looked at Dr. Perkins first before he nodded and sat next to his wife.

Her hand covered her mouth. "Oh my God. Why didn't you tell me?"

Dr. Perkins said, "I've been encouraging Brian to talk to you, Alexis. He's wanted to, but this has been difficult for him."

Alexis paused and swallowed, bracing herself for the worst news. "Baby," she began. She scooted closer, took his hand. "Whatever it is, I'm here. I'm going to stand with you."

"I've wanted to tell you," he said, his head bowed. "But I didn't want to lose you."

"That could never happen. I'm here for you." She paused. Took both of his hands into hers. "Tell me, what's wrong? What is it?"

Slowly, Brian raised his head.

Alexis said, "Whatever it is, we can handle it."

He glanced at the doctor.

The doctor said, "Alexis, actually, I'm a therapist."

Brian said, "Yes, Dr. Perkins is my therapist." He paused. "And she's been helping me because . . . I'm a sex addict."

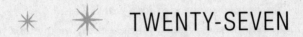

TWENTY-SEVEN

ALEXIS WAS SLEEPWALKING.

Only she wasn't asleep. And she wasn't walking. Instead, she was sitting on some couch, in some office, in some house, in some part of Los Angeles.

But sleepwalking was the only explanation she had for the words she'd just heard.

"I'm a sex addict."

Then, Cinderella said, "It's important for you to know, Alexis, that sexual addiction is not about sex. What your husband has is becoming a medically recognized disease." And now, Cinderella was rambling on about how Brian was recovering well.

What are they talking about?

"Alexis, would you like a glass of water?"

She heard the voice, but it sounded like a distant memory, very far away. "I don't need water, Doctor. I need to know what you're talking about."

Brian exchanged a quick glance with the doctor before he took Alexis's shaking hands into his. "Sweetheart," he said, his volume barely above a whisper, "I've been . . . sick for a while. But I've been getting help."

It was hard to keep his face in focus. "Help? For being a sex addict?"

He swallowed, nodded, waited for her to say more.

She wondered, *What kind of help do you get as a sex addict? More sex?* That thought made her say, "I've got to get out of here." But she didn't move.

"Alexis," the doctor said, "I know this is hard to hear, but your husband has been working on this for over a year."

"You've been a sex addict for a year?"

Dr. Perkins said, "Actually, he's been recovering for a year."

"Baby," Brian said, "I've been faithful to you for this entire year."

She frowned, his words ricocheting in her mind. "Faithful for a year? But we've been married for five."

Silence.

Alexis asked, "So . . . what are you saying?"

More silence.

She answered for her husband, "That means that before last year . . . I've got to get out of here." This time, she jumped from the couch, grabbed her purse.

"Sweetheart, please stay."

"Alexis," the doctor called, "It's really important for you to stay. I've been encouraging Brian to tell you for some time now. Not only because it's best to be honest, but because so much of his recovery depends on you."

Alexis said nothing.

Dr. Perkins said, "I want to assure you that men and women have been healed and marriages have been saved. You'll help yourself and your husband by being part of this."

Alexis shook her head. *She* didn't need any help.

"All right. Maybe this is too much for today," Dr. Perkins said. "Let's set up something for tomorrow. After you've had a chance to absorb this."

"I don't think so." Alexis stepped over Brian, made her way to the door.

"Wait, I'll go with you," Brian said.

Alexis whipped around. "No! You. Stay here." She glared at him. "With your therapist." This time, she ran. Down the hall. Out the door. Onto the street and into the car where she was safe.

She sat frozen, hoping that here, in the quiet, she could comprehend it all.

But when she saw Brian rushing toward her, she floored the accelerator, heard the screech of the tires, and watched Brian leap onto the sidewalk out of her aim.

Even as she drove, her daze stayed. The scene played over in her mind. And there was no sense to any of it.

Sex addict.

Time passed. The fog cleared.

Sex addict.

She remembered when she'd heard those words before. With Halle Berry. And her husband. And she had the same thoughts now that she had then: sexual addiction? Ha! A man's explanation. A man's disease. A man's excuse for being unfaithful.

Halle's man then. Her man now.

What was she supposed to do?

From the corner of her eye, she saw the store and she swerved into the Neiman Marcus driveway just as her cell rang. Glancing at the phone as if it were a rat, she checked the number, then flipped it open.

"Hey," Kyla, her best friend sang. "I called your office, and LaKeisha didn't know what time you were coming in. What's up?"

"I had an appointment." Alexis pushed through the store's glass doors.

"Okay, call me when you finish. Let's do lunch."

"I'm already finished." Inside, Alexis wandered to the first counter she saw—the designer sunglasses.

"Are you heading back to the office now?"

"No, I'm in Beverly Hills. At Neiman's." She motioned toward a pair of glasses and the lady behind the counter pulled the eyewear out for her. "I'm doing a little shopping," she said as she tried on the glasses. Then, to the salesclerk, she said, "I'll take these."

"You, shopping?" Kyla chuckled. "Okay. Something's wrong. Who danced on your last nerve today?"

"I'm shopping so that I won't think about the fact that my husband is a sex addict."

Kyla laughed, and waited for the rest of the joke. When Alexis didn't offer more, Kyla said, "Why are you calling him that?"

"Because that's what he and his therapist just told me. So now I'm in Neiman's having my own therapy."

"Alex." The glee was gone from Kyla's tone. "Back up. What are you talking about?"

"My husband is a sex addict," she said in an anchorwoman's voice. "At least that's the excuse he's giving for cheating on me."

Alexis could tell that the salesclerk was fighting to keep her attention on the four-hundred-dollar sale she'd just made, rather than on what had to be one of the juiciest conversations she'd ever had the opportunity to overhear.

After a period of silence, Kyla said, "Alex, please tell me you're kidding."

"I'm not. That's why I'm shopping. I want to look good for my divorce," Alexis said, signing the sales receipt.

"Alex, come to my house. We can talk here—"

"I can talk and shop at the same time," she said, now browsing through the shoe department. She held up a pair of Jimmy Choo satin sandals. "By the way, did *you* know that Brian was a sex addict?"

"No! Why would you ask me that?"

Alexis shrugged, put down the shoe, and strolled to the Manolo Blahniks. "I just figured that Brian had told his best friend. And if he told Jefferson, I figured that Jefferson had told you. That would make me, his wife, the last to know."

"Alexis, if I had known . . . wow! I'm just trying to wrap my head around this."

"Me too. But shopping is making it easier." She held up two

shoes and motioned toward the clerk. "Size eight," she whispered. Then, back to Kyla, "So, if you think you're having a hard time with this, imagine me."

"I'm coming to Neiman's right now."

"You don't have to. I'm having a grand old time by myself." She slipped into one of the designer shoes that the clerk returned with. "Kyla, you should see these Gucci pumps. They're fabulous."

"You don't like that kinda stuff, Alex," Kyla reminded her.

"I do now. These shoes will go great with the Chanel glasses I just bought. Even if they are," she paused, looked at the end of the shoe box and flinched, "seven hundred dollars."

"Keep your phone turned on," Kyla exclaimed. "I'll be there in twenty."

"Why?" Alexis whined. "You'll just make me take all of this stuff back. And I've just begun my therapy."

But Kyla had already hung up. Alexis snapped her cell shut, tossed her credit card to the salesclerk, then rushed to the store's directory. She had to move quickly. Because when Kyla came, she'd bring good sense with her.

Until then, Alexis needed to get far away from the memory of this morning. And Neiman's and her credit card were going to help her to do that.

Inside Zodiac, Alexis and Kyla needed the table for four where they sat. The two chairs beside them overflowed with Alexis's purchases.

"So, that's all you know?" Kyla whispered, even though they sat alone in their section of the restaurant. "Just that Brian said he's a sex addict?"

"That's enough, don't you think?"

"No! I don't even know what that means."

"It means my husband had sex. Without me. And he wasn't

alone." Alexis grimaced. Inside, she'd been thinking about what Brian's confession meant. But aloud, the words were sharp. Cut. Made her heart bleed.

Kyla exhaled a long breath. "You need to know more. You need to really talk to Brian."

Alexis raised an eyebrow. "About the details?"

"If Brian is an addict, it's not like he's just having an affair. It means he's sick."

"It means that he's slept with other women." The coffee cup shook in her hands. "It's a man's world, Ky. And some man came up with this name for cheating. But I don't care what you call it. Adultery by any other name still means that you can't be married to me."

"Alex, you can't stop here. There is too much love and too many years between you and Brian. Talk to him. At least understand before you do anything."

Alexis sighed, lowered her eyes. "Brian and his . . . therapist want me to meet with them tomorrow. But I don't know if I can sit in the room with him and Cinderella."

When Kyla frowned, Alexis explained.

"Well, no matter what she looks like, she's still a therapist, right?"

"Yeah."

"Then that means that Brian has done everything right."

Alexis raised her eyebrows.

Kyla said, "You caught him getting help. And he took you to meet his doctor. That means he's doing everything he can to save your marriage."

"That's not possible. I can't imagine staying with him now."

"I can't believe you're saying that. You were full of advice about forgiving when Jefferson cheated on me."

"This is not the same thing. Your husband slept with only one woman."

"Only?"

Alexis ignored her friend and continued, "Brian says he's an addict. That means he's slept with . . . " She stopped. Shook her head as she thought about what that could really mean. Halle's husband—weren't there rumors that he'd slept with dozens of women? She said, "Brian is not like Jefferson. Brian's been with more than one woman."

"Did he say that?"

"He didn't have to. Just the definition of sex addiction—that's what it means."

"When did you get your medical degree?" Alexis raised her eyebrows and Kyla continued, "This addiction could be playing out in a number of ways. It doesn't mean he's been sleeping around."

Alexis said, "So, when did you get *your* medical degree?"

Kyla smiled a little, reached across the table, and took her friend's hand. "I just want you to look at the facts. You caught Brian trying to work it out because he loves you. If he didn't care, he would have just continued . . . doing whatever it was that he's been doing. That has to count for something."

Alexis sat unmoved by her friend's words.

Kyla sighed and leaned back. "Okay, this could have played out way worse. You could have been like me and walked into your own house and found your best friend in your bed."

A small smile crossed Alexis's face. "That wouldn't have been good because you're my best friend."

Kyla chuckled. "You know what I mean."

Alexis nodded. Indeed, she did know what her friend meant. It was a time that she would never forget, a time that had been filled with pain for all of them—especially Kyla.

After sixteen years of a solid marriage, Kyla had come home to find her other best friend, Jasmine, naked in her bed. And Jefferson, coming out of the shower. The shock, the pain of the betrayal had devastated Kyla to the point where Alexis had been sure nothing could save that marriage.

But she'd been wrong—God had restored what the devil had tried to destroy. He had put Kyla and Jefferson back together, even better than they were before.

Alexis asked Kyla, "How do you live with it? Does it still bother you?"

Kyla shrugged. "It's been so long now, what, six years? I think about it sometimes." She paused, pinched her lips together as if she were having one of those bad memories. "But it's easier because Jasmine is gone and I don't have to see her face."

"Well, that makes it easier for me, too, because you know, if she were living here, she would have been one of the women that Brian . . . " She shuddered. "I might be facing homicide charges right about now, because if Brian had ever been with Jasmine, both of them would have to die."

"Why are you thinking like that? First of all, Jasmine hasn't been anywhere near Brian. Secondly, you don't even know what he's done and you've convicted him. The man at least deserves a trial." She waited a moment before she encouraged, "Go with Brian to the therapist. Listen to him. Listen to her. Ask questions. Then you can make a decision."

It took a moment for Alexis to nod. "You're a good friend, Ky."

"You taught me how to be one."

"And I need a good friend right now."

She took Alexis's hand. "Don't worry, Jefferson and I will be with you and Brian all the way."

"I know, but I'm talking about *right now.*" She pointed to the chair spilling over with packages. "I need help getting all of this to my car."

"You're going to keep this?" Kyla eyed the shopping bags. "You shopped under duress. You should take some of this stuff back."

"I can't."

"Why not?"

"Because I'm going to do what you said. I'm going to go with Brian and talk to Cinderella. But something tells me that I'm going to need this stuff over the next few days just to make it through."

Alexis stuffed the last bag into the trunk, then hugged Kyla.

"You're going home?" Kyla asked.

"Yeah, my business will have to run itself today." Alexis slipped into her car and waved to her friend. She twisted the car onto the street and then checked her phone. As she scrolled through the incoming calls, she frowned. Not one from Brian. With what he'd taken her through this morning, he should have had the decency to be blowing up her phone. Then she would have had the pleasure of ignoring him.

She glanced at the clock. Barely two; he would be in his office—unless he was out doing his sex addict thing.

She pressed the speed-dial number, then held her breath. He answered on the first ring.

"Sweetheart, are you all right?"

"I'm fine."

"I've been so worried. I wanted to call, but wanted to give you space."

"That was a good idea."

"We have to talk."

"That's why I'm calling." Another deep breath. "Go ahead and make an appointment with your doctor . . . your therapist. I'll be there tomorrow."

She heard his relief. "Thank you, sweetheart. I—"

"Don't thank me for anything, Brian. All I'm doing is going with you to the doctor. I'm not committing to anything else."

"Okay." He stopped, let time pass as if he knew his next words might be the most important ones he'd ever say. "Alexis, I love you."

He waited as if he expected a response. When she didn't say anything, he said, "Are you at work?"

"No."

Again he waited. Nothing. Then, he said, "I want to see you. Let's meet at Heroes."

Alexis sucked her teeth. Like going to her favorite restaurant was going to fix anything.

He said, "I can meet you there now."

"Ain't gonna happen. I'll see you tomorrow morning. At the doctor's office. I'll be there at nine."

"Where—"

She clicked off the phone, not needing to hear anymore, and pressed the power button. This time, she was sure that Brian would call back, wanting to know where she was, where she was going. She had no idea. Only knew that she wasn't going home. She needed to go someplace where she could breathe.

She eased onto the 405 Freeway and then pushed a button on the dashboard. The whirring began and then sunlight peeked above her until the car's top was tucked inside its compartment.

June's heat filled the car, but the coastal gusts kept her cool. She never rode with the top down during the week, hated the havoc the wind caused on her hair. But today was no ordinary Tuesday.

For weeks, she'd thought Brian had been having an affair; now she wished that had been the truth. This idea that her husband loved sex the way she loved coffee was too difficult to grasp. And then, she wondered if he had sex as often as she drank coffee.

She shook that thought away, turned on the radio. Missy Elliott and a few of the other ladies of hip-hop blasted through the car, talkin' 'bout get your freak on.

Sex addict.

She pressed the button for another station.

Beyoncé sang, "To the left, to the left. Everything you own in a box to the left."

Sex addict.

She turned the volume up and sang along, "You must not know 'bout me, you must not know 'bout me."

She pressed the accelerator and took the speedometer way past the speed limit.

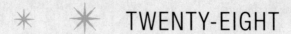# TWENTY-EIGHT

Her plan had been to drive as far as a tank of gas would take her. But after only a few miles, emotional exhaustion set in and Alexis swerved off the freeway, stopping in front of the Fairmont Hotel.

Less than ten minutes later, the bellman led her to her room. "This is one of our best," he said as they entered. He stacked her Neiman's bags on the couch. "This is the Utopia suite."

Alexis would have laughed if she could.

"Will there be anything else?"

"Coffee."

"Right over there." He pointed to the machine on the kitchen counter. "And there's a Starbucks in the lobby."

"Thank you." She handed the bellman a tip, closed the door, then stood on the edge of the room as if she didn't know what to do.

She carried the shopping bags into the bedroom, then wandered through the rest of the suite. But not even the warmth of the buttery-yellow walls and the midday sun that beamed through the floor-to-ceiling windows could thaw the chill that had been inside her bones since this morning.

On the balcony, she stood at the rail and marveled at the magnificence of Griffith Park seventeen floors below. She sank into the cushioned wicker chair and with her legs stretched out on the ottoman, she rested beneath the breeze. There she stayed, getting up only to quench her thirst with coffee, as the summer sky shifted to the evening. Even when the fading day brought the desert night's chill, she didn't move. She didn't want to face the empty room that was waiting for her.

It was driving her crazy—the way she could think thoughts, but feel nothing. She wished she could rant with rage. Or even fall to the floor and wither in wife-done-wrong pain.

But she was numb. Just like when she was sixteen and her father came into her bedroom with the news that her mother had died. The doctors had said then that she was in emotional shock.

Maybe that's what was happening now.

But while her emotions seemed dead, her thoughts weren't. And the images continued. Of Brian, standing at the head of an assembly line—woman after woman marching by. *I'll take that one,* he said. *And that one.* She wondered how many there had been.

And then she wondered if he'd had only one a day. Or if he'd had two. Or if he bedded one woman at a time. Or did he prefer ménage-a-trois?

That thought drove her from the balcony. She grabbed her PDA and with the calculator, added it up. Five years, 365 days. That would be almost two thousand women—if it was just one each day!

Her head throbbed as she stripped naked and climbed into the luxurious bed. But not even the thousand-thread-count sheets brought rest. She twisted through the slow passing of time and when sleep refused her request, she clicked on the television. But the late-night talk shows brought no relief from the thoughts that kept her awake. When she finally pushed herself from the bed, it was only 2:10.

Wearing the hotel's bathrobe, she returned to the balcony. Still, she couldn't feel, couldn't cry, couldn't rage.

Another hour passed, and she stepped back into the room. This time, she didn't give the bed a chance to deny her. She settled on the sofa in the living room. And with the television tuned to BET late-night music videos, she closed her eyes and was granted sleep.

But then she dreamed. She was in a bedroom with Brian. She sat at a round table filled with an endless number of coffee mugs. He lay on the bed, naked and grinning. But not at her. He beamed for the women standing behind her—a line that extended for miles beyond that bedroom.

She picked up a cup. He picked up a lover.

She drank her coffee. He devoured his woman.

She did it again. So did he.

One by one.

Every time she grabbed a new cup, he snatched a new female.

She drank faster. He kept up with her.

She drank more. He did the same.

She was filled to the top with coffee. And then she exploded. Bolted up from the couch with a scream.

She drew her knees to her chest, wrapped her arms around her legs. Remembered her dream. And cried. And ached. And wished that Brian was dead.

Two thousand women? She cried through the thoughts of how she'd shared her husband with so many and what kinds of diseases she might now carry.

Her cries continued until the morning sun rose. And with daylight came clarity.

After a shower, she spread the clothes she'd purchased yesterday across the bed, then chose the dress she'd wear to the place where she and Brian would spend their final hours together as husband and wife. She held up the sleeveless shift in front of her. It was appropriate. It was black.

As she dressed, she imagined what she would say. Brian would understand that she wanted a divorce, since he would never stay with her if she'd slept with two thousand men.

She shuddered. *How did he even have time to work?* But she shook that question away. It didn't matter. That was his life now and had nothing to do with her. She had only one mission.

She'd make her announcement, Brian would agree. They would divorce. This would be short and simple. Quick and easy.

As she waited for the hotel elevator, she wished she'd made herself at least one cup of coffee to go, then decided to grab a cup in the lobby. But after standing in the line and placing her order, all she could think about was her dream.

She twirled the cup she held. Inhaled its fragrance. And then tossed the untouched drink into the trash.

TWENTY-NINE

"SHE DIDN'T COME HOME last night, Dr. Perkins." Brian loosened his tie, paced the length of the office. "This is what I was afraid of."

"Calm down. Alexis said she was coming."

"I don't think so." He shook his head. "Wherever she stayed, she had all night to think and decide that she couldn't stay married to me."

"Brian."

The calm in his doctor's voice didn't ease his anguish.

She said, "The fact that Alexis is willing to be here tells me that she wants to work through this. Believe me, I've worked with patients whose spouses didn't want to hear any more after they heard the words 'sex addict.'"

He stopped moving. "So you think our marriage can be saved?"

"Yes." The doctor leaned forward on her desk. "Everything is working in your favor. Alexis is coming to this meeting. That's her part. You've been doing your part by committing to working through this. Together, you and Alexis have the best of chances."

He sank into the chair, lowered his head. It was difficult to believe her words.

"Let me ask you this," Dr. Perkins said. "If you had cancer, would Alexis leave you?"

His head and his spirits rose. That was a good question. Maybe Alexis could see it that way. That would be his prayer. He'd add it to the prayers he'd been saying all night. Prayers that started from the moment he entered their condominium and wandered through the empty space, until he rested alone in their bed.

He had prayed to God to first keep his wife safe. And then to touch her heart so that she would understand. And forgive him. And stay.

"There is something you should know, though, Brian," the doctor broke through his thoughts, "just like if you had cancer, your wife deserves full disclosure. You're going to have to be completely honest and answer any questions she may have."

Brian frowned. "Suppose she wants to know how many women I've been with?"

The doctor looked straight into his eyes. "Tell her. I'm going to get Alexis to focus on what's important, but anything she wants to know, even names or occasions, tell her the truth."

He nodded, as if he agreed, but he didn't. Truth wasn't something he practiced, and he didn't think this was the best of times to begin. Too many questions from Alexis could lead to Jasmine. And he had a feeling that his wife would rather hear that he'd slept with five hundred women than hear Jasmine's name.

He shook his head. His marriage *might* survive five hundred women, but it would *never* survive one Jasmine.

Every time he thought of Jasmine, he stopped breathing. Just like he had on that New Year's Day, a year and a half ago. The last time he saw Jasmine with her husband in her club, Rio. He had flown to New York just to get with her. But she hadn't been happy to see him. She had faced him with eyes filled with fear. And then he'd noticed her swollen belly and their glances locked again. This time, there was fear in his own eyes. In his gut, he knew the child she carried was his.

It must have been her shock that made her faint. Right there—she'd fallen into his arms. Her husband had grabbed her from his grasp and yelled for someone to call 9-1-1. In the bedlam that followed, Brian had stayed until the ambulance arrived. Then he made his own getaway. He'd headed straight to the airport, not even taking time to stop at the hotel. Just called the front desk of the Plaza and arranged to have his clothes packed and shipped.

His heart was still pounding when he had settled into his first-class seat. He didn't notice the woman who sat next to him. But she'd started the conversation.

"Are you leaving or returning home?"

"Going home." He'd barely looked at her. All he could see, think, was Jasmine and her bulging belly.

After two hours and two drinks, Brian was more amenable. He introduced himself to the lady with the big white hair.

"Nice to meet you. I'm Dr. Perkins."

"Ah, a doctor. So am I."

He told her he was an ophthalmologist. She told him she was a sex therapist.

He laughed.

She shrugged and said, "That's the normal reaction, but I can assure you, I help people just like you do. You help your clients to see better; I help my clients to live better. I counsel them through their sexual addictions."

His laughter stopped. "I've heard people claim they're addicted to sex, but come on, Doctor, is that real?"

"It's as real as the abnormalities you treat. It's just that while most of your clients know they have a problem, most of mine don't, not until their lives get so out of control."

Her words made him shift in his seat. He motioned to the flight attendant for one more drink and didn't share another word with the doctor. Not until they landed.

Reaching toward him, Dr. Perkins said, "I believe in networking. Take my card."

He frowned.

She continued, "Not for you. But you may know someone who knows someone who knows someone who can use my services."

He'd tucked the card inside his wallet, planning to toss it into the trash later.

But that night after Alexis had fallen asleep in his arms, he'd rolled from the bed and pulled out the business card. Stared at it. Thought of Jasmine. Remembered the others.

Curiosity made him tiptoe into their home office and in the dark, search the Internet. The answers came quick—*The symptoms of a sex addict: risk taker, living a double life, willing to endanger professional and personal life . . .* the list went on. But it was the signs that one doctor spoke of—the secret life, the shamefulness, the depression and despair—that had his name written all over it.

Thirty minutes later, he slipped back between the sheets. And resting next to his wife, he made his decision to see Dr. Perkins in the morning.

The ringing door bell pulled him from the past.

"That must be Alexis," Dr. Perkins said, rising.

Brian nodded as the doctor moved toward the front. In just seconds, Alexis would be sitting next to him. Hearing the stories of his secret life. He closed his eyes, told himself to breathe. And said his prayers all over again.

THIRTY

ALEXIS STOOD OUTSIDE, FOLDED her arms, and then with the tip of her mule, tapped the passing seconds. She glanced at her watch, even though she knew the time. She'd been watching each hour pass since she'd awakened.

"Good morning, Alexis." The doctor spoke with a perkiness that belied the early hour.

Silently, she followed the doctor down the hall. There was no need for niceties. She had only one purpose. To get this over with. Short and simple. Quick and easy.

Inside the office, Brian jumped from his seat, took a step toward her, but the pain in her eyes stopped him. He swallowed hard. "I was worried about you."

"No need." Alexis didn't look at him as she sat. She kept her eyes away because she knew if she looked at him, her mission might be thwarted. *Short and simple. Quick and easy.*

But she could still feel his gaze. *Get a good look now*, she wanted to taunt him. Wanted to shout that this was the end.

"First, Alexis," the doctor began, "thank you for coming. This is hard, but it's going to be much easier for you and Brian with the both of you here."

Alexis nodded because she was sure that's what the doctor expected. But all she wanted to do was tell the doctor to save her breath. Tell Brian to pack his bags.

"Before we begin, I want to add one other thing." The doctor placed her arms on her desk and leaned forward. "It's important for you to remember, Alexis, that this is a real illness. It's not an excuse that Brian's made up to explain his unfaithfulness."

Even with her shock, Alexis didn't move a muscle. Those were words she'd uttered to herself yesterday. The thoughts of divorce paused in her head. But after a moment, she snatched the thoughts back. No matter what, Brian had betrayed her.

Dr. Perkins continued, "Do you have any questions?"

Alexis hesitated, thought about the two things she wanted to know: *Were you really with two thousand women?* And *how fast can we sign those divorce papers?*

"I don't have any questions," Alexis began. "But, Doctor, I'm not even sure why I'm here." She didn't miss the exchange between Cinderella and Brian. "I thought about it last night and—"

The doctor held up her hand. "Alexis, I know how hard it was for you to come here. But I'm going to ask a favor. Since you're here, would you mind hearing me out?"

Alexis pinched her lips together. It was as if Cinderella knew her thoughts and was trying to stop her from what she had to say. Breathing deeply, she nodded. There was no harm in listening. She'd make her declaration about divorce soon enough.

The doctor smiled her approval. "What I thought we'd do today is talk about the facts of this illness before we get into Brian's case specifically." She took a breath. "If at any point you feel that I'm getting too technical, or you have any questions, stop me." She glanced at Brian. "And if there is anything you want to add, definitely do."

For the first time, Alexis glanced at her husband. He was pressed back in the chair, as if he were trying to get away.

"Okay, Alexis," the doctor began, sounding as if they were about to have a friendly conversation. "It's important that I repeat this: sexual addiction is not about sex. Addictions are usually severe habits that people form to medicate their feelings based on their need to escape."

Escape? From me? she wondered, and then tossed the question aside. It didn't matter—whatever Brian wanted to get away from, he would soon have his wish. He would be free from her, and she would be free from this humiliation.

The doctor continued, "It really is no different than alcoholism, although it is more similar to an eating disorder."

Oh, God. Alexis wondered if she was going to be able to keep breathing.

"What I mean by that is, with an eating disorder, we don't want you to stop eating. Well, we don't want Brian to stop having sex, do we?" She paused, smiled. "My job is to get Brian to a place where his sex drive is normal, where it's just about making love. The techniques I use are the same as if I were working with someone who was . . . addicted to caffeine."

Alexis frowned. She didn't turn, but in her mind she stared Brian down. He had told on her! He had tried to compare his addiction to hers.

Dr. Perkins continued, "I'm sure you're wondering why Brian is this way. What does a sex addict get out of it?" The doctor answered the questions, "What Brian gets is what drives most of us—endorphins. You've heard that term, correct?"

Alexis nodded.

The doctor explained anyway. "Endorphins are hormones that reduce one's sensitivity to pain. It's a brain drug that affects our emotions." It was the way Alexis inhaled a deep breath that made the doctor ask, "Is this too much?"

I'm not confused, Alexis wanted to tell her. *I'm just ready to go.* "No, it's just that none of this matters."

"Alexis, it's important for you *not* to look at sexual addiction the way the world does. You're in the middle of this crisis and you have to see it the way it actually is. Brian's behavior was just a way for him to medicate himself."

"Medicating from what?" Her tone screamed that she didn't believe any of this.

"Most of the time it's stress, although it can be as serious as trying to escape the memories of past abuse. We've determined with Brian," she paused, looked at him as if she wanted to include him in the conversation, "that his addiction stemmed from stress, but it became what's called a DCM—daily coping mechanism. Brian struggles with the pressures placed on him as a man, especially an African American male."

Great, Alexis thought. This theory better not get out. Or else there would be millions of black men cheating—now, in the name of racial stress.

The doctor continued, "In school, Brian felt he had to perform at the top of his class. With both of his parents being educators, that perfection was expected. Then, he became a doctor, an ophthalmologist, and right before you two were married, he changed his focus to newborns—a high-risk, high-stress specialty. That inside pressure had to have a place to go."

"Come on, Doctor. Lots of people have stress." Alexis stood, paced, and every time she passed Brian, she wanted to slap him upside his head. "I have stress. I own an advertising business with over thirty million dollars in billings. More than twenty people work for me. I have stress every day."

The doctor nodded. "I'm sure you do. That's one of the challenges of our society; the effects of stress are not taken seriously. But Alexis, I'm sure if you weren't so upset, you'd realize that people handle stress differently. Some medicate with alcohol, with shopping, with overeating, overworking, oversleeping . . . and then there are some who do it with sex. Truthfully, one way is not better than others."

If you're married, your addiction can't be sex.

The doctor added, "I don't know how you handle stress, but I can assure you that you do something. You may overexercise, drink excessive amounts of caffeine, or medicate with drugs— marijuana, cocaine, heroin—it's something."

Alexis folded her arms and stood as stiff as a tree. She would never be moved. "I don't do drugs."

Dr. Perkins said, "That's a good thing. I just want you to understand that Brian's need for release is normal. It's how he's handled it that's not normal. But neither is it normal to overeat or overdrink or overspend.

"The blessing in Brian's behavior is that there are many who can't handle stress at all. And those people are the ones who often take their own lives." She stopped, letting the truth of her last words hang in the silence.

Alexis sank into her chair. *It's that serious?* Now she glanced at Brian. And her heart softened—just a bit.

"Alexis," the doctor said, as if she could see her anguish diminish, "you have to understand this to realize that the women Brian's been with," she paused as Alexis cringed, "they weren't sexual beings to him. They were objects to help him release his pressure."

Two thousand objects. Her heart was hard again.

"So," the doctor continued, "understanding the theory will help your marriage survive."

This was her cue. The point where she would tell Brian and Cinderella that no amount of CPR could breathe life back into something that was dead.

The doctor said, "Alexis, I'm sure you have something in common with many spouses. Most want to know who their spouses were with. They want to know names, and times, and places."

And how many!

The doctor continued, "None of that matters . . ."

All of that matters.

The images of her dream rushed back. All of those women. With their hands. And mouths. All over Brian.

"I can't do this." Alexis jumped up.

"I'm sorry," Brian said, jumping from his chair as well.

"I'm sorry," the doctor said, too, though she stayed behind her desk. "Maybe this was too much for today. We can stop."

Alexis shook her head. Tightened her purse strap on her shoulder. "I'm leaving."

Brian said, "We're not finished."

"Yes, we are." She stared straight into his honey-colored eyes. "I can't do this, Brian. I'll have my attorney call you." She spun around, marched toward the door.

"Alexis!" Brian shouted. "If I had cancer, would you leave me?"

His words made her stop.

"Would you?" he asked again.

She didn't face him. But still, she didn't move.

"Would you?" His voice was closer.

Now, she'd even stopped thinking.

"If you had cancer, I wouldn't leave you." This time it was a whisper and she could feel his breath on her ear. "Because I love you, Alexis. Always have. Always will."

She inhaled, forced herself forward, and away from him. She dashed down the hall and out the door. But no matter how fast she ran, she couldn't outrun the question he had asked. The question that shot bullets into the hard shell that covered her heart.

THIRTY-ONE

BRIAN'S BLACKBERRY VIBRATED on his hip. He grabbed the PDA, read the text, then sank onto the barstool. He rested his elbows on the small table and massaged his eyes.

Jefferson slapped him on the back and slid onto the stool next to him. "Maybe you should just go home."

Brian glanced around the sports bar crammed with men in suits, their ties loosened, their hands grasping mugs filled with beer—their release from a long week of work. Around the room, flat-screen televisions featured Friday night baseball games, but no one seemed to be watching.

"I'll be all right," Brian finally said. "Thanks for hanging with me. I needed a break and I don't come to these places alone anymore."

"I was thinking," Jefferson said, scanning the menu, "maybe you should take some time off."

"No, what would I do at home? Alexis hasn't been there since Monday and she just text messaged me. She's not coming home tonight."

"What did she say?"

"For me to stop leaving messages; that she's fine." He sighed. "I don't know what I'm going to do. I've been worrying nonstop not knowing where she is." He paused. "Do you think Kyla knows?"

Jefferson shrugged. "I don't know. But if she did—"

Brian held up his hand. "I know, she wouldn't tell you, 'cause you might tell me." He lowered his head into his hands once again, massaged his temples as if that would make his worries go away.

"What are you gentlemen having?" The waitress flung her waist-length weave over her shoulder, balanced an empty tray on one hand, and planted the other on her hip. She glanced at Jefferson, then smiled at Brian as if she knew he was the one she could get next to. "What can I get you?" She spoke just above a whisper, although the din of men enjoying their time away from work and wives rose above them.

He took in the white blouse tied at her waist, and the black skirt that did little to hide her thighs. But it was her fishnet stockings that made his nature rise. He grabbed a menu. "Ah, Jefferson, what are you having?"

"Just a Coke and a platter of wings." He handed his menu to the waitress. "Make mine hot."

"And what about you?" She turned back to Brian.

"The same." He kept his eyes away from her. "But make mine mild."

"Really? I would think you'd want 'em hot." She laughed. "Okay, I'll put this in for you." She stepped closer to Brian, taking away his space to breathe. "You sure I can't get you anything else?"

"We're sure," Jefferson said, rescuing his friend.

With a smile, she slithered away and Brian breathed. "That's major temptation, man," Brian said.

"Just hold on. The Bible says you'll never be tempted beyond what you can bear."

Brian nodded. "I've been bearing it. Dr. Perkins helped me identify the triggers. There seems to be a point that I get to when I'm under stress where I have to do something." He pulled a candy bar from his pocket. "So now, instead of that candy—" With his chin, he motioned toward the waitress. "I do this." He popped a piece of chocolate into his mouth. "Get my endorphins this way. Seems simple, but it works." He smiled just a little.

"Whatever it takes to save your marriage."

The bit of cheer he had went away. "Not sure that's possible."

"I thought when Alexis talked to Dr. Perkins that would be a turning point."

"It was. Just wasn't the turn I wanted. She hasn't been home since."

"She's just trying to work through this. She'll be home."

He shook his head. "Even if she does come back that won't be the end."

"True." Jefferson nodded. "But with Dr. Perkins you guys will make it."

Brian stuffed a large piece of candy into his mouth as if he was trying to stop more words from coming out. The secret that he held inside had been percolating for over a year. And now it was bubbling over. He needed to speak it aloud. Hear how it sounded. Hear how it might sound to his wife.

He swallowed the last of the candy, then said, "If Alexis comes home, and finds out the complete truth, she won't be able to handle it."

"What can be bigger than what you two are already handling?"

Brian paused, glanced over his shoulder as if he was making sure no one but his friend was listening. He whispered, "One of the women I was with," he paused, lowered his voice even more, "was Jasmine."

It took a moment for his words to make sense to Jefferson. Then with wide eyes, he leaned away from Brian as if he was trying to get away from this news. "Jasmine Larson?"

He nodded.

"Whew!" Jefferson blew a long breath of air. "Man, Alexis hates Jasmine. And Kyla's not too fond of her either."

"That's an understatement."

After a moment, "Why and where—" Jefferson stopped himself. Held up his hand. "It doesn't matter, B. It'll still be fine."

"How can you say that? You just said it yourself . . . my wife hates Jasmine."

"But if Jasmine was just part of the illness and nothing more, Alexis will understand."

Nothing more. There was plenty more.

"But here's the key, B," Jefferson began, leaning closer to give his counsel, "you've got to tell Alexis now because if she finds out on her own . . . " He left his thought unfinished, knowing that Brian knew exactly what he meant. "But if you tell her now, it's all part of the discovery of your illness. It'll be hard, but you two will come through." He paused. "Kyla and I did."

"I keep telling you, your wife is different from mine."

"You must've forgotten how long Kyla stayed away from me after she found me with Jasmine. Remember she left L.A.? I had to go to Santa Barbara to get her. All Kyla could think about was getting a divorce. But I stayed strong. And we made it, with a lot of work and total honesty. You and Alexis can do it. Trust that."

Brian shook his head. He couldn't see it—couldn't see the scene where Alexis would wrap her arms around him and say, "I forgive you," once she heard Jasmine's name. "I'll think about it."

"And think about how when you come clean, there will be nothing left standing between you and Alexis."

Brian lifted his glass, swallowed some water and the rest of his secret.

The waitress sauntered back with their plates and sodas. "Here you are," she spoke to Brian. "Will there be anything else?"

But this time, Brian wasn't even tempted. Just waved her away, then bowed his head. He prayed over his food, but his prayer was for more than what was on his plate.

It was a quick prayer, but he heard his answer. He lifted his head, opened his eyes. He knew what he had to do. It was the only chance he had to get his wife back.

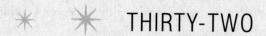

THIRTY-TWO

IT WAS TIME TO GO HOME.

Alexis grabbed her purse, glanced around the suite that had become her asylum, and then rolled her suitcase from the room.

Outside in the hotel's courtyard, she breathed in air that wasn't from the seventeenth floor for the first time in three days.

The attendant opened the car door for her and she smiled her gratitude before she handed him a ten-dollar bill. Then she zipped her Lexus around the circular driveway and onto the street.

She had never planned to stay at the Fairmont for more than one night. But the exchange at Dr. Perkins's office had driven her back to the hotel. And inside that sanctuary, Brian's words had battled his deeds.

His words: *If I had cancer, would you leave me? Because, I love you, Alexis.*

His deeds: Brian and his two thousand women.

The deeds were more powerful. Made her tie up her heart with string. Wrap it securely so that it could never be touched. She would never be hurt again.

If I had cancer, would you leave me?

Still his question stayed, whispering even now in the wind as she sped down the freeway toward home. But she shook away those words and tightened her heart strings.

All she had to remember was that she had vowed to stay with Brian through worse, through sickness, but nowhere had she promised to stay with him through two thousand women.

She felt her cell phone vibrate before she heard the ring. She sighed; she had to call Kyla. Between her best friend and her soon-to-be-ex, her voice mail was full. Picking up the phone, she glanced at the screen, frowned, then answered.

"Alexis?"

"Yes, Pastor Ford." She raised her voice above the wind. "How are you?"

"I'm fine. I'm calling because I need to see you. Can you drop by my office?"

Alexis shook her head before she spoke a word. Her mission would not be denied. "I'm heading home right now—is it something we can discuss over the phone? Or at church tomorrow?" She knew this call was about the program design for the upcoming women's retreat. She had promised to have the first drafts on her pastor's desk by this past Tuesday, but her week's plans had been blasted into the breeze after Brian's addiction confession.

"No, I don't do meetings by phone, and I really need to see you today." The pastor's tone said that she was the one who would not be denied. "How long will it take you to get here?"

The battle of wills was won—Alexis would go to her pastor. She glanced at the clock on the dashboard. "I'm on the four-oh-five. I'll be there in about fifteen minutes." Alexis tossed the cell phone onto the passenger seat. Why did Pastor Ford want to meet on a Saturday? Didn't she know that people had lives? Had business to take care of? Had divorces they had to get started?

Well, it didn't make sense to make a fuss—not with Pastor Ford. She would just go, speak to her pastor, and then be on her way. By tonight, her marriage would be over.

The fragrance of his cologne met her at the door and wrapped around her like a lover's arms.

Alexis turned around, but it was too late to cut and run. Pastor Ford stood at her door as if she were a defensive lineman ready to take Alexis down if she made the wrong move.

"What are you doing here?" Alexis asked, her tone filled with venom.

Brian rose from his chair. "I've been worried about you."

A moment passed before she eyed the door again.

"Alexis!" The pastor said her name as if it were a command. "Brian came to me because you two need help. I want to talk to both of you."

She didn't need help with anything, but she didn't have the strength to battle her pastor. "All right," she said, as if staying was her choice. With her chin jutted forward, she sat in the chair.

Pastor Ford settled behind her desk. Her eyes were soft as she looked at Alexis. "Brian's told me everything." She paused, her sorrow clear on her face. "This has to be tough."

Duh? was what she wanted to say. But good sense came out. "You know me, Pastor, I don't wallow in anything. It is what it is and I'm ready to move on."

"Alex," Brian said before the pastor could respond. "I haven't had the chance to say this to you. I've never had the chance to say I'm sorry for all of this because I love you too much to hurt you."

She kept her eyes away from him and shrugged, as if his words didn't matter. But it took all the will within her to keep those strings tight around her heart.

He continued, "I asked Pastor to get us together because I want you to know everything. How it started. Why I got treatment. It's amazing, Alexis, I didn't even know I had a problem . . ."

Now she faced him. "Really? How many women did you sleep with before you realized you were cheating on me?"

He bowed his head. "I know this is hard to believe, but it was like it wasn't even me. And then afterward, all of those times—"

Alexis flinched.

"All I could do was think of you," he continued. "But not even thoughts of you and how much I wanted our marriage were enough."

"Not enough?" She paused. "Then let's fix this. Let's stop all of this and go straight to the solution." She looked into his eyes and prayed that her words would hurt him as much as he'd hurt her. "I want a divorce."

"Okay, let's pause," Pastor Ford intervened. "I understand how you feel, Alexis, but I'm surprised that your first reaction is divorce."

Alexis was proud of herself. For the second time in minutes, she stopped the "duh" before it escaped from her lips. Instead she asked, "Why? Even God says that you can divorce for adultery."

"No." The pastor's response shocked them both. "For some reason, people think that divorce is automatic with adultery. But that's not God's intent. God always planned for marriage to be a lifetime commitment—no matter what. Now, yes, there are circumstances—because of our sinfulness—where divorce can be the answer."

Alexis smirked, her face lit up with victory.

Pastor Ford ignored her look of triumph. "Here's the thing, Alexis. Never did God want for people to use divorce as a solution."

"I'm not trying to solve a problem," Alexis said. "I'm trying to correct a situation. When we married we said we'd be faithful to one another, and it's obvious that I'm the only one who's kept that commitment."

"That's true," Pastor Ford said. "Brian was unfaithful and you were not. That said, do you feel better?"

Alexis wanted to scream that nothing short of a divorce would make her feel better.

When Alexis stayed quiet, Pastor Ford said, "Brian, you need to tell Alexis everything you told me."

He waited for Alexis to turn toward him, but when moments passed, he spoke to her profile. "There was only one reason why I sought help. And that was because I love you. Even though I never thought you would find out, I wanted help because I wanted to stop. I wanted to be faithful to you."

She faced him now. "And you needed help to be faithful?"

Her words were soaked in sarcasm, but he nodded. "Yes. That's what being an addict is all about."

She turned away. Stared at the bookcases behind the pastor's desk that were stuffed with Bibles and other instructional guides on how to lead a Christian life. She wondered if her pastor had any good books on how to get a Christian divorce.

"Alexis, I love you."

She stayed stiff, kept her focus on her anger.

"But I'm sick. I have a disease."

She took a quick breath. Tried to hold onto the strings she felt loosening around her heart.

He persisted. "That's not an excuse, it's a fact. But it's an illness that I'm going to fight with everything within me. This is not going to destroy me. And I'm going to fight to the end to make sure it doesn't destroy us."

He was pulling on her heart strings again, but she pulled back harder. Made those knots tighter.

He said, "I want to get well because of you."

He never played fair. Even when they played Scrabble, she'd always caught him stealing a letter when she wasn't looking. Now he was trying to steal her heart.

But she fought to hate him like she had all those days in the hotel room. Fought to hate him the way she did when she walked into this office with only divorce on her mind.

The pastor said, "Alexis, I know you're hurt. But try, for a moment, to look past that and see Brian. And his hurt. And listen to his apology and hear his plea for forgiveness."

But what about me?

The pastor said, "Think about what God would want you to do."

Now it was the pastor who wasn't playing fair. Always using the truth of God to try to get people to do right.

Alexis had to pull back the strings. She tried to grab them, tried to wrap up her heart once again. But Brian's words, his apology, his pleas pulled the strings from her. And inside, God tore them away, leaving her heart open.

Pastor Ford walked around her desk and crouched in front of Alexis. Only when the pastor used her fingers to wipe her cheek did Alexis feel the tears in her eyes.

"This is going to be one of the hardest things you've ever had to do. It's going to take courage and strength to stand by Brian."

I don't want to stand by him, her head said, even though her heart told a different story.

"But you already have everything that you need, because you have God."

Alexis was pissed. Pissed that she was crying. Pissed that her heart strings hadn't held up. Pissed that she still loved Brian.

"Don't let pride and stubbornness stop you from doing what God is telling your heart," Pastor Ford whispered before she stood. She leaned against the edge of her desk and spoke to both of them, "I counsel a lot of people, and if there's a couple who can make it, it's the two of you. Alexis, understand that as a Christian, once someone has truly confessed and repented, it is our job to forgive." She turned to Brian. "I applaud you for stepping up. For being in therapy and not waiting until you were caught to handle this. That's proof to me that you're sorry and you're serious. But this is the beginning for Alexis; you have a lot of work to do to help her."

He nodded. "I'm willing to do anything for her to forgive me."

Pastor Ford held up her hand. "It's not just about forgiveness. Sometimes that can be the easy part, because forgiveness is about the past. The difficult step is the future, and that's where reconciliation and trust comes in. It will be a long time before she trusts you again. And without trust, you will never have reconciliation.

"Your job is to help her trust you. If she wants to know where you are every minute, you have to tell her. Whatever she needs, you have to give her. Any question she asks, you have to answer."

"I'm willing to do that."

Pastor Ford nodded. "Just make sure that you're totally honest."

Brian was slow to agree this time.

The pastor smiled. "Alexis, is there anything you want to say?"

Alexis sniffed, shook her head, and wished she'd never answered Pastor Ford's call this morning.

"I'm going to give you both scriptures to study, because the nature of sexual addiction is spiritual. It's the kind of darkness that Jesus has authority over. And you have to stand with that authority."

Alexis thought about her plans—how she was supposed to already be home, packing, leaving.

"Alexis," the pastor said, "do you think you can do this?"

It took her a moment to put the words together. "I don't know."

Inside her heart, she heard a gentle, guiding whisper, *If he had cancer, would you leave him?*

She said, "I . . . I . . . I can try," before her sobs began.

Brian rushed to his wife and held her as their pastor pushed herself from the desk, and without a word, left Brian and Alexis alone.

THIRTY-THREE

He had hope.

Brian couldn't remember the last time he'd left home with a smile on his face and hope in his heart. But that's what he had this morning.

He jumped inside his car, but then sat back and remembered the weekend.

He'd had few expectations when he and Alexis had finally walked out of Pastor Ford's office. He'd followed her home, but even after they'd given their cars to the valet and ridden up in the elevator, she hadn't spoken a word. Hadn't even looked at him.

When they'd stepped inside their apartment, he'd asked, "Alex, is there anything you want to talk about?"

That was the first time she looked at him. But only for a moment before she marched into their bedroom and slammed the door behind her.

At least she's home, he told himself.

For the rest of the day, he'd waited for her to come out. He'd been tempted to knock on the door—to see if she was all right, to see if she wanted something to eat, some coffee to drink. To see if she still loved him. But he'd left her alone, and when the day gave way to night, he wandered into the guest bedroom, stripped, and dropped onto the bed.

He'd been lying awake for hours when he heard the door to their bedroom squeak. He held his breath, waited, wondered if he should get up.

He had his answer when she appeared at the door. In the deep dark of the night, he could only see her silhouette, outlined by the white thigh-long nightshirt that she wore. All he wanted to do was take her into his arms, and make her love him again. But he stayed in bed. Stayed waiting.

"Are you awake?" she whispered.

"Yeah."

He flung the blanket away from his body, but she held her hand up. "Don't."

He didn't move, only because he didn't want to drive her away. After a moment, she inched toward him. Then she sat on the floor, crossed her legs, and rested her elbows on her knees.

Silent, staring moments, then, "I'm willing to try," she spoke softly.

His heart pounded, but he remained quiet, knowing there was more to come.

"I don't like this. I don't understand it. But I think you love me."

"I do." He wasn't sure if she heard his whisper.

"It's taken awhile, but I believe this is an illness. And if you're sick, I can't leave you. I have to help."

"Thank you."

More silent time. "I need therapy, too." She stopped as if her words surprised her. "I want to go to Dr. Perkins with you."

He hesitated, but he wanted to give her anything that she needed. So he said, "Definitely."

She said nothing more. Just sat staring at him before she rose. He moved to get up with her, but she held her hand up again. Shook her head. He had lain back down. Heard his bedroom door close. And he smiled.

In the morning, he'd knocked on the door to see if she wanted to go to church. She didn't answer, and like Saturday night, she'd spent Sunday locked away from him.

It had been difficult to watch the day's hours pass without the sight of her, but he remembered the night before. He held onto that hope.

Then in the middle of last night, she came to him again. She moved toward the bed, pushed the covers aside, and then laid beside him. He wrapped his arms around her as if she were fine china. Even when he heard the steady rhythm of her breathing, he didn't close his eyes. Just held her. And prayed, giving thanks, through the rest of the night.

With a smile now, he backed from his parking space and within thirty minutes, he was sitting in front of Dr. Perkins with a new attitude.

"Things must be going well," the doctor said.

"Yeah," he nodded. He recounted for Dr. Perkins the session with their pastor. "So, Alexis is home. It's awkward. But she's home. And she wants to do some of these sessions with me."

"That's important. We'll still keep it to twice a week, but one of those days will be for both of you."

He nodded.

The doctor said, "You know, when Alexis comes in, she's going to want to know a couple of things—like how did this begin, and what guarantees are there that you won't start this behavior again."

"It won't happen again, Doctor," Brian said.

"That's what you say, and that's what you want. But Brian, we both know that the triggers that caused this addiction are still there. You have a highly stressful life."

"But I'm aware now. I'm not going to relapse."

"I agree that you know how to control the urges. But that won't stop Alexis's questions."

He wondered if his wife being in these sessions was a good idea. "Do you think Alexis will be able to handle this?"

The doctor nodded. "Brian, if this illness was rated, you'd be at the low end. I'm going to make sure she understands that." The doctor paused. "The only thing I won't be able to help with is if you don't tell her everything she wants to know."

Brian clasped his hands together. He already knew what the doctor would say next.

"I've asked you before," she began, "and I let it go because you've been making progress, but I've been doing this long enough to know there's more to your story. Now that Alexis will be joining us, I need to know the whole truth so that I can help."

Brian stood, turned away as if he couldn't face the doctor. He let time pass before his confessions began, "I've been with a lot of women."

"I'll make sure that Alexis understands it was never about other women, never about the destination. Just the journey."

He wondered if his wife would understand the difference. Wondered if his wife would understand that about Jasmine.

"One of the women," he began, "my wife knows."

"A friend of hers?"

"No, an enemy."

When the doctor didn't say anything, Brian turned around. Her face was stiff, as always, not a hint of judgment.

"I had sex with a woman my wife despises. A woman who tried to ruin our best friends' marriage."

The doctor looked at him, knowing there was more.

"I had sex with the same woman that my best friend slept with."

Still, the doctor spoke as if she had no opinion, "That fits the pattern."

Brian chuckled without humor. "Glad to know that I'm normal—at far as sex addicts go."

"So, you remained friends with this woman, but your wife didn't?"

He shook his head. "No. Jasmine . . . she lives in New York." He sat down. "Doctor, talk about the journey . . . it was such a high to get on the plane for the sole purpose of chasing this woman. The thing I'll never understand is I don't even like her.

But the fact that we were on opposite ends of the country, the fact that I knew she didn't want me, made it better," he said, sounding like he was reliving the high.

"Brian, I thought you understood this addiction by now. That is classic behavior. You chose women you couldn't, wouldn't connect with. Women who would never threaten your marriage. The chase was a game—a release from the pressures." Dr. Perkins leaned back in her chair. "It won't be difficult to explain Jasmine to your wife."

"You don't know the history. My marriage won't survive this."

"I think it will. You're past the toughest part with Alexis. She understands that you're sick. Jasmine is part of that sickness."

Maybe.

"Tell Alexis about Jasmine while we're talking about the disease. She needs to see Jasmine as part of the addiction."

Maybe.

"If you wait to tell her or if she finds out sometime later, separate from this therapy, then Jasmine becomes an affair. And that will threaten your marriage."

Maybe it could have been that simple—if that was the end. He said, "You wanted the whole truth."

"Yes, I need to know everything."

"It's not small."

"If it's part of the illness, it is."

He took a breath. "Jasmine had a baby. I think . . . it's mine."

It had taken a year and a half for her emotions to show. For Dr. Perkins to widen her eyes and open her mouth. For her to lean back in the chair and ask, "A baby?" But then, she paused, relaxed, became the composed doctor again. "It's all part of the addiction," she said simply.

"That's all you have to say?" He shook his head. "So what am I supposed to say to my wife—that I'm addicted and I have a baby?"

"That's the only thing you can say. You would have never been with Jasmine, she would have never become pregnant, if you weren't an addict." She leaned forward and in her clinical voice continued, "This is big, I admit it. But you're not the first man this has happened to. Don't even think about keeping this a secret," she warned. "Tie Jasmine to the disease. If you don't tell her, Alexis will know that you're hiding something. I guarantee that after all that's happened, her emotional radar will be sharp."

The doctor made sense. Maybe he could pass Jasmine and her baby off as just one of the effects of his illness: self-loathing, depression, Jasmine, a baby.

Maybe.

"I'll think about it, Doctor."

She nodded. "Okay, let's begin. Are your episodes still decreasing?"

As one side of his mind talked to the doctor, the other side considered her advice. Could he really tell Alexis about Jasmine and keep their marriage intact?

Maybe it was time to honor Alexis with the truth.

But first, he had to find out what *was* the truth. It was only intuition, not a fact, that Jasmine's baby was his. If God was on his side, he was wrong.

Either way, he had to find out.

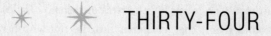 # THIRTY-FOUR

ALEXIS HAD HER OWN ADDICTION—she was a sex-addict fanatic!

It had been three weeks since she'd found out about Brian. And almost every day, she sat in front of her computer Googling for answers. She did the same thing now, scrolling through articles until she found one that was new:

The reasons for sexual addiction fall into one of three categories: biological, psychological, and spiritual. Alexis paused. How could sexual addiction be spiritual?

She closed that window and opened another.

Almost ten percent of the population has some form of sexual addiction—especially with the accessibility of the Internet. Men and women are doing all kinds of things with their computer . . .

Quickly, she closed that window. Went to another.

Sexual addiction is a cycle of excitement, then guilt. Compared to another addiction—bulimia—sexual addiction can also have a binge and purge sequence.

Inside her head, she saw Brian binging and purging on women. Over and over.

She jumped up. Without signing out, she turned off the computer. It was time to get off the World Wide Web.

Kyla hugged Alexis as if she would never let go.

"I've missed you." Kyla pulled back; her eyes wandered up, then down. "I guess I didn't have anything to be worried about. You look gorgeous."

"Don't be fooled. I can work the outside. It's the inside that needs help."

The friends held hands as they strolled into the Woman's Place. At the spa's front desk, they registered and then were led to one of the private rooms. With lavender-scented candles smoldering around them, they changed into the full-length robes and slippers, secured their clothes and purses in the lockers, then settled onto the overstuffed recliners.

A soft knock on the door interrupted their chat. One of the spa assistants peeked inside. "You're having lunch first, right?"

Alexis nodded.

"Okay, what can I get you to drink?"

Kyla said, "Tea for me," and then frowned when Alexis ordered water. Once alone, she asked, "What's up with the water? Boycotting coffee?"

"In a way." Alexis picked up a *Vanity Fair* and flipped through the pages without stopping to read a word. She said, "I discovered there was more than one addict in the family. Only my addiction to coffee wasn't as hurtful as Brian's addiction to sex."

Kyla tried to cheer her friend with her smile. "I guess the family that fights addictions together stays together, huh?"

She sighed. "Why did Brian choose sex as his addiction?"

"I don't think it's a choice, Alex. I mean, people who are addicted to food, do they choose that? Or gamblers, do they choose that?"

Alexis shrugged.

"And remember, this a disease. People certainly don't sign up to get sick."

"I guess . . . I don't know." She paused. "I don't know much these days. I don't know if I've even forgiven Brian. Sometimes I feel like I'm only there because that's what God would want."

"That's a good reason."

"But does it count if I don't have real forgiveness in my heart? If I still have all of this stuff in my head, will God count what I'm doing as true forgiveness?"

"I think He'll count it as you trying."

Alexis shook her head. "I've never been through anything in my life so overwhelming. I don't know what to do, what to think. That's why Brian and I haven't . . ."

Even without the rest of her words, Kyla understood. "Really? Not since . . ."

Alexis nodded. "Not since I found out. I can't even think about letting him touch me that way."

"I thought you were waiting until you had all of those tests."

"That was my excuse, at first, but the results came back last week. We both tested negative for HIV and any STDs."

Kyla's shoulders relaxed with relief. "I didn't want to ask. That's a blessing, you know."

"I know. But still, every time Brian gets near me . . ." She shuddered, closed her eyes, and remembered the nights. The nights when she stayed in her office in Culver City. Or the nights when she stayed in her home office. Always waiting until she was sure that Brian was asleep. Then she would choose the bed in the guest bedroom or sometimes even the couch. Anywhere but the bed they were meant to share as husband and wife.

"The thing that scares me is that Brian and I were really good together and he still cheated on me."

"You're still calling it cheating. Why don't you just accept that it's an addiction?"

"Because the words sound different, but they feel the same." She stopped. "And the bad part of all of this is that I keep thinking that if I don't get back into bed with him, he'll cheat on me again."

"Just stop thinking of Brian cheating before or cheating again. Stop thinking about cheating, period."

If it was as easy as "just" stopping . . . But she couldn't stop thinking—about the women who still taunted her in that dark place. The women who came to her every night, mocked her, and told her that they could have her husband any time they wanted him.

"When Brian and I get back into bed together, it won't be just the two of us there." Alexis closed her eyes, waited for her friend to tell her that she was crazy.

"Girl," Kyla began and leaned closer, "I know exactly how you feel."

Alexis's eyes popped open.

Kyla said, "When Jefferson and I finally got back together after Jasmine, I felt like she was right in the bed with us."

Alexis twisted on the recliner to face her friend. "You never told me that. What did you do?"

"I just kept loving my husband until I kicked the image of Jasmine's trifling behind out of my bed."

Alexis laughed. "That must have been fun."

"It was. Pastor said that in a situation like this, it's important to build back that part of your relationship. But it was so hard. There were times when we were making love and I wasn't even there." Kyla's eyes glazed over for a moment, as if she were remembering. "It was like I was having an out-of-body experience. But slowly, that went away." She paused, brought her thoughts back to the present. "And girlfriend, let me tell you, Jefferson and I may be over forty, but—" She snapped her fingers three times.

Alexis chuckled. "So, I have something to look forward to."

"Definitely. We're in our prime, girl. Don't let nothing steal this joy." Her smile dimmed a bit. "Especially since Brian is trying."

"He is . . ." Alexis paused.

"Sounds like there was a 'but' coming."

"No," Alexis said, deciding to keep quiet about her feelings—because that's all she had. Feelings, nothing more. But she could feel that there was something still separating her and Brian. Something more than his addiction. Something more that he was hiding. The secret—whatever it was—was polluting the air that they shared. "I really do want to get back what we had" was all that she said.

Kyla leaned closer. "I have a great idea."

It was the look on her friend's face that made Alexis smile too. "Tell me, my dear."

"You don't know how to get back into bed, right?"

Alexis nodded.

"Well, get freaky. Forget about the bed!"

Alexis burst into laughter as she listened to her friend's plan.

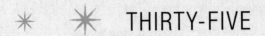# THIRTY-FIVE

BRIAN WAS WEARY.

It was barely noon, but he'd been in the office since an hour after dawn. It had been a restless night once again, without Alexis by his side. This morning, he'd found her in the recliner in the living room. He did what he always did—kissed her cheek. And like a fairy tale, she'd awakened.

He sighed at that memory. She would not sleep with him, but every other part of their life was moving forward. In therapy, he talked, she listened. At home, they ate, watched television, even played Scrabble together. It was just the final act of each day that they did alone.

In those hours when he was left by himself, he thought most about his secret. There were times in the middle of the night when he wanted to tiptoe into the living room, lift Alexis into his arms, carry her to their bed, and make love to her until she forgave him all the way. But the thought in his head—of Jasmine and her baby—stopped him. Because he didn't want to be the one to bring his wife closer . . . just in case hurt was waiting not far away.

He frowned when a knock on the door forced him from his thoughts. He had no appointments, since today was July 3. His schedule was holiday light.

Another knock before he said, "Come in."

His frown deepened when a lady in a black uniform, complete with a hat, entered his office. "May I help you?"

"Dr. Lewis, this is for you." She held up a tuxedo on a hanger, and a small bag.

"I'm sorry . . ."

"And this." She handed him an envelope.

He recognized Alexis's handwriting, pulled out the card: *I'm waiting for you* was all it said.

Slowly, he smiled. The uniformed woman passed him the tuxedo. "Your shoes are in the bag. I'll be waiting outside."

He couldn't change fast enough; his mind was filled with wonder—what was his wife up to?

Within ten minutes, he was sitting in the back of a limousine. "Can you tell me where we're going?"

"No, sir," the driver said, keeping her eyes straight ahead. "But there's another card for you. In the champagne bucket." Then she closed the privacy window.

He beamed as he read: *I'm still waiting. Relax, have a little drink, get ready.* He leaned back into the leather seat. He didn't even want to look out the window. It didn't matter where he was going. As long as his wife was there when he arrived.

Even before the car curved around the winding driveway, Brian was sure of where he was. This was the bed-and-breakfast inn in Oceanside that he'd mentioned to Alexis.

As soon as the car stopped, he opened the door, even before the driver could step out.

"Dr. Lewis!"

But he ignored the driver's call. His eyes (really, every part of him) was focused on his wife. Alexis stood at the top of the three steps that led to the inn's entryway.

From the moment he'd first seen her, all those years ago, he'd wondered why Alexis had never pursued a career in modeling. The eggshell sleeveless dress with its simple princess-neckline fit her five-ten frame as if it had been sewn onto her. And when she turned sideways, he gasped at the deep cut in the back.

With a quickness, he stepped toward her. But just a few feet away, he stopped. Didn't move again until she reached for him. He trotted up the stairs and pulled her into his arms.

"I've been waiting for you," she whispered.

"I . . ." Pressing her finger against his lips, she stopped him, then guided him inside into the wide-open foyer.

It wasn't the artwork from local painters hanging on the wall or the bright-white art deco furniture that had his attention. It was the windowed wall that framed the view of the ocean that made him hold his breath.

Walking in rhythm, their heels echoed against the polished parquet floor until they stepped onto the balcony where the fragrance of the sea greeted them.

"This is beautiful." Brian inhaled. "I've been here five minutes and already I don't want to go home."

"We're just getting started." She motioned toward the sofa on the deck. "Take off your shoes and socks."

He frowned.

She repeated her request, before she slipped off her sandals. He did the same and when he was barefoot, she led him down the steps. Silently, he followed, as they shifted through the sand until they stood at that place where the water met the earth.

"I can't believe we're here," Brian said as a wave left its residue around their ankles.

She turned to him, her face covered with the ocean's mist. "Give me your wedding band."

It was only because she smiled that he twisted the golden circle off his finger. She did the same—removed her wedding band from under her engagement ring and then tucked both into the pocket of his jacket.

She said, "Now is the time for us to renew our vows."

He didn't speak.

"I know you wanted a real ceremony with lots of people, but I think for where we are now . . ." She paused. "I want to do it this way. Just the two of us. Speaking what's in our hearts."

"Alexis," was all he could say, not able to think of a time when he loved her more.

"So, do you want to do this?" she asked. "I know we don't have any vows prepared, but I think we can just say what we want, right?"

"I . . . this is wonderful." He took her hand and a breath. "Alexis, from the first day I saw you, I loved you. And there hasn't been a day since when I didn't love you. There hasn't been a moment when I wasn't thinking of you."

Her eyes wandered away with those words. She gazed into the sea as if she needed that sight to help her believe him. With his fingertips, he brought her back to him.

"I mean it," he said. "I know I hurt you. And I don't have enough sorrys within me to tell you how sorry I am. But I will spend the rest of my life making this up to you. From this day forward, I will love you so that you'll always know you're loved. You will never have a doubt." This time, he caught her before she turned away. "Here and now, this is my vow to you."

For minutes, the water crashed around them, a cool refuge from the heat of July. When Alexis was ready, she said, "The reason I'm here is because I love you. Not because this is right, not because I'm such a forgiving person. Just because I love you. It's love I can't explain. But I know it's real because the love is still there. Even with the pain, even in the moments when I just wanted to die." She paused, wanting him to understand all that she'd been through. "My love is still there. And now, I want to build my love back stronger than it was before." She took a breath. "I want to love you always. Here and now, this is my vow to you."

She'd barely spoken her last word before Brian pulled her into his chest and his lips met hers. Her tongue greeted his. There they stayed. Connecting once again.

When they pulled away, Alexis said, "We forgot something."

"What?"

"The rings. We forgot to put them back on."

He chuckled, pulled the bands from his pocket. Studied the two golden circles. Then, he said, "Do you trust me?"

She took a deep breath.

"Alexis, you can trust me. I can't help what's behind us, but I can tell you that you can trust what's in front of us." He paused. "I know it's going to take time to trust me completely, but can you trust me in this moment?"

She tried to keep her frown away as she nodded.

He looked at their wedding bands once again. "The width, the length, the depth of this ocean is nothing compared to the love I have for you." He tossed their rings far into the water.

Alexis shrieked.

"We're going to buy new ones tomorrow," he said quickly. "To celebrate this."

She was motionless, her hand still covering her mouth.

"I'm sorry," he said. "I just thought this was a great way for us to express this new beginning."

"No, it's fine," she panted. "I was just thinking," she held up her left hand and the diamond's sparkles danced under the sun, "I'm glad I didn't give you my engagement ring!"

She laughed. He did the same. They held hands. Clumsily treaded through the sand back to the inn. Together.

The heat of the Jacuzzi, the hum of the bubbles was lulling him to sleep. But Brian fought the fight; he had to stay awake and wait for Alexis. Tonight, under the rhinestone-studded heaven, there were no thoughts of their pain. All that was on their minds was today.

Brian leaned back and savored the memories of the hours that had passed, their dinner of steak and lobster and champagne they shared on the deck. Then the way Alexis had relaxed in his arms while they watched the sun bow in the horizon. There was only one thing that could make this day better—and that would be this night.

It was more than the way Alexis had planned this day that gave him hope. It was the fact that their room was a single, not a suite. There was no sofa for Alexis to escape to; there was only one place for her to rest. In the bed. Next to him.

But even though just thinking about being with her made the very essence of him almost explode, he wasn't going to touch her in that way. Not until she was ready. And if not tonight, he would be fine. This day was enough—for now.

The door from their room to the patio slid open. *Finally,* he thought. *How long does it take to put on a bathing suit?*

Alexis stepped out, wrapped in a towel.

He greeted her with a smile. She took the two steps to the top of the Jacuzzi, then paused.

Reaching for her, he said, "The water's great."

A moment, then she tossed aside her towel. Wiped his smile away.

She moved, slowly, letting his eyes devour all of her nakedness. Then, little by little, she submerged into the bubbly water and glided toward him.

Although he could no longer see her body, the image stayed with him. And he wanted more.

His heart pumped hard; surely, it was about to blast through his chest when she reached him. Touched him. Wrapped her arms around him.

"I love you," she whispered.

It wasn't human power that kept him from tearing away his swimming trunks and taking his wife right then.

Instead, he relished the time. Kissed her, made her moan. Caressed her, made her whimper. Enjoyed each moment, moved as if it was their first time. When she called his name, he kicked off his trunks, and under the water, he loved her.

Her cries of pleasure became louder and he groaned, joining her melody. For long minutes, they sang. Sang until they couldn't sing anymore. And she collapsed, still in his arms.

His heart's desire was to stay there. Forever. Never leave the Jacuzzi. Never leave this inn. Never go home.

But he knew tomorrow would come. Though now he also knew that they would be fine. He had his wife back.

THIRTY-SIX

ALEXIS PUSHED HER BIBLE aside when she heard the knock on her door.

"Hey." Julie, her vice president, peeped into her office. "The meeting's in thirty minutes."

She closed the door, leaving Alexis alone once more. Of course there was no way she would have forgotten the meeting. How could she? This was the biggest account pitch her ten-year-old advertising agency, Ward and Associates, would be making this year. Twelve million dollars for the Healthy Heart Cereals account. And she was ready. Or rather, her team was ready. Julie and two account executives had worked for weeks to prepare. Normally, she would have been right in their midst, checking every storyboard, working until they had the best. That was her life—until she had learned that her husband was addicted to keeping his pants down.

She glanced at the platinum band that graced her finger. Looking at the new ring made her smile with the memories. And that's what last week's trip to Oceanside was supposed to do. But although she and Brian had connected once again, a mountain still stood between them.

She blamed their disconnect on whatever secret Brian was holding. As hard as he tried, he still wasn't there, especially in their most intimate of times. He'd push her away, not physically, but in the ways that counted. In ways that were difficult to describe, but in ways she could definitely feel.

What are you hiding, Brian?

She'd spent hours trying to figure it out, but had come up with nothing. And now she was sick of it. Sick of thinking about it. Sick of not knowing.

She piled the folders together for her meeting and then bowed her head. She needed to pray—not for the task at hand, but for what she would face later when she talked to Brian. She prayed that he would give her all the answers she needed. And then she prayed that knowing everything was really what she wanted.

Alexis inhaled, took in the aroma of Brian's favorite dish that would greet him, disarm him, and put him at her mercy. At least, that's what she'd been taught.

She was barely four years old when she would climb onto one of the kitchen chairs and watch her mother prepare dinner with the same care that she gave to everything she loved.

"The way to a man's heart, sugah," her mother drawled in her Savannah accent, "is through his stomach. You can get a man to do anything if you first fill his belly with his favorites."

Tonight she was testing this long-ago learned theory.

The key jiggled inside the lock and she positioned herself by the dining room table.

Brian stepped inside, glanced around the wide-open space filled with candles that shimmered, and closed the door slowly.

"Okay," he paused for an instant, "it's not our anniversary."

Alexis pushed all the questions she had from her mind. Stuffed her hands inside her jeans and put on a happy face. "Nope, not our anniversary."

"And it's not your birthday. Or Valentine's Day. Or even my birthday."

She chuckled. "None of the above."

"So, what did I forget?"

"Nothing. This is just something I wanted to do." She stepped closer to him. "We came back from Oceanside and jumped right back into life. I wanted to bring back a little of that magic." She kissed him, then said, "Go in and get changed."

He shook his head. "Nuh-huh, because I can smell it. You made it, didn't you? I don't want to wait."

She laughed. "Go change. By the time you come out, I'll have your plate waiting."

With a grin, he rushed into the bedroom.

She scooped spoonfuls of the shrimp and grits casserole onto their china. Filled two flutes with wine. Sat down and planned her words.

Brian was dressed in a sweat suit when he returned. He sat beside her, held her hand, and blessed the food. Then he took his first bite and moaned.

"I cannot believe you did this," he said. Took another forkful and released more sounds of pleasure.

Alexis stabbed a shrimp with her fork, swirled it inside the grits.

"You're not hungry?" he asked, his mouth full.

She dropped her fork. "Not really." Inside, she prepared her questions, braced for the answers. "You know how I get when I cook."

"Too bad," he groaned. "This is so good." He leaned across the table and kissed her, leaving a trace of grits on the corner of her lip. He smiled as she licked it off. "Oh," he said, "How did the pitch go today?"

"I think we got the account."

He stopped chewing. "Alex, that's terrific."

She half-smiled. "But you never know."

"If you think you got it, then I know you did." He paused. "You don't seem excited."

"It's just that I have so much on my mind. I've been thinking about . . . us."

With his napkin, he wiped the corners of his mouth, then rested his arms on the table. "We're going to be all right."

"That's my prayer."

He took her hand, kissed her fingers. "I will always be grateful for you standing by me through this."

"It's a disease, right?" She took a sip of wine. "There is something I want to know, though."

He turned his attention back to his plate.

"Sometimes I think about you and what you've been through. And in my mind, I'm taken to places I don't want to go."

He nodded, but kept eating.

She frowned. Waited for him to tell her that whatever she imagined was worse than the truth. But he said nothing.

"I imagine you with the women. And that's hard for me."

More nothing.

Her frown deepened. "I need to talk about this."

Still nothing.

"Brian," she called. It took him a moment to look up. "Talk to me. There are things I have to know. About . . . the women."

He stuffed his mouth with a shrimp. Chewed and bought time. Finally, "Our therapy has been going well."

Huh? "It has," she said, slowly, keeping herself calm.

"And in Oceanside, wasn't that a new beginning?"

"It was."

"Then why look back? Let's just go forward."

She digested his words. Felt the disconnect once again. "I can't go forward until I look back."

"You don't need to look back."

"How can you tell me what I need?"

He took a breath. "Because in this situation, it's about what we both need. It's about what's good for our marriage."

Her eyes narrowed as she peered at him, trying to see the parts that he wouldn't show her. She waited a little while, then lifted her glass of wine and strolled toward the bedroom.

"Alex."

She stopped, turned.

"Come back."

"Why?"

"Because in order for this to work, we can't walk away. We have to handle our problems together."

"That's what I was trying to do. But you don't want to talk to me."

He pushed away from the table and walked to her. "That's not true. I just think that some things . . . should be said . . . with Dr. Perkins. So that she can help us work through any challenges."

She thought for a moment. "So you'll answer my questions in her office tomorrow?"

He hesitated. "Yeah, yeah."

Two affirmatives, but neither sounded like a real yes to her.

"Okay." She turned back toward the bedroom.

"Are you fine with that?"

She faced him again. Nodded. Smiled.

"Okay," he breathed, relieved. "I'll clean up and then be right in."

Inside their bedroom, Alexis settled on the bed, sipped wine, and waited for her husband. She wasn't about to kick him out of this room. She was desperate to at least keep their physical connection.

Her lips lingered on the edge of the glass as she pushed all of her thoughts aside. *Let tonight be tonight,* she decided. Tomorrow she would have all of her answers.

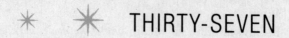# THIRTY-SEVEN

USUALLY ALEXIS ARRIVED AT the doctor's office one minute before she was supposed to be there. Today, she was fifteen minutes early. She scanned through magazines as she waited. And then right at noon, Brian strolled in.

"Hey, sweetheart." He kissed her cheek, then sat next to her.

Dr. Perkins said, "You two are looking well."

Alexis scooted to the sofa's edge, eager to get this session started.

"We're doing good." Brian leaned back against the couch. Spread his arms over the top, and then crossed his legs as if they were just going to chat.

"That's great," Dr. Perkins said. "You're connecting."

"Speaking of connections." Alexis raised her hand as if she needed permission to speak. "I have some questions."

The way Brian shifted let her know that he didn't expect her to ask the questions she'd asked last night. As if the love they shared was enough to make her forget.

Yes, they'd made love with more passion than they'd had since their trip to Oceanside. But the images of the two thousand women were still there, in bed with them. Right next to his secret that always hovered above.

"I'll answer any questions you have," Dr. Perkins said.

"Not you, Dr. Perkins." She turned toward Brian.

Brian glanced at the doctor then clasped his hands as if he was praying. Alexis wondered if he was asking God to keep her silent. But she didn't care what he or God said.

Dr. Perkins looked at Brian, but she spoke to Alexis. "Ask whatever you want to know."

She braced herself, but didn't hesitate for a moment. "How many women were you with?" Then, in her mind, *Please don't tell me two thousand.*

"Alex, that's not important."

"How can you say that?" She glared at him. "It's important because I want to know."

A moment later, "I'm . . . I'm not exactly sure."

"Take a guess."

He shook his head.

"A guess, Brian," she forced it.

"I don't know what a guess will do."

"Let me help you. Are you talking thousands? Two thousand?"

He bolted from the couch. "No!" He paced. "No where near two thousand. Or even a thousand."

She was feeling better until he stopped. "So, nine hundred and ninety-nine?"

He shook his head. "Not even close. But I never kept count. It wasn't like I was collecting them." He paused, but the stiffness of her face told him that she wanted more. "Okay, one hundred, two hundred, I don't know."

There was a big difference between one hundred and two hundred. And based on his response, it could be three hundred or five hundred. She couldn't think of one hundred people she'd invite into her home. Yet, there were at least that many women who had shared her husband.

As bad as that was, she wanted more, wanted it all. "Were you ever with anyone I know?"

He looked at her for a moment longer than she would have liked, then turned away and returned to the path he set on the carpet. "I don't know how any of this helps."

"It helps me." She tried not to tremble as she thought about what his stalling meant. Had he slept with women in church? Or some of her employees? *Oh, God,* she thought. *Please not one of my clients.*

He said, "Why isn't it enough that I'm getting help? Why do you have to know specifics?"

"Because we're not connected, Brian. There's still so much between us, and moving forward is not going to eliminate what's in the past." She waited for him to say something. "Brian, I know you're hiding things from me. And I can't stand it."

He sat next to her. Took her hands into his. "I want to forget about the past and focus on the future with you. Let's just focus on my healing."

"But the past is part of *my* healing."

When he shook his head, she pulled her hands away.

She asked, "What are you hiding?"

"Nothing." But he wouldn't look at her.

"If you're going to keep secrets . . ."

"I don't have any secrets!"

"Then answer my questions!"

"Your questions don't have anything to do with secrets. You're only asking me these things because you don't trust me."

"And that surprises you?" Alexis stood. "If you don't want to let me in, then let me out. I don't need to be in a marriage—"

"Alexis," the doctor interrupted, "it's not a good practice to run when things aren't going your way."

"Doctor, I've sat here for weeks listening to the fact that my husband was so stressed that he had to have sex without me. But even though it was hard, I kept coming because I made a commitment." She turned from the doctor and now faced Brian. "And you made a commitment, too. To help me get through this. To help me understand. To be honest with me." She grabbed her purse. "Obviously, like the way our entire marriage has been, I'm the only one who cares about commitment."

"Alexis," the doctor began, "don't walk out while you're upset."

But she didn't listen. And she didn't look at Brian as she stomped from the room. She heard him calling her, but she didn't turn back. There was nothing more to say if he couldn't trust her with his truth.

✳ ✳ THIRTY-EIGHT

"Do me a favor," Brian said to the receptionist as he rushed toward his office, "hold my calls."

Inside his office, he locked the door. It only took moments to find the number in his BlackBerry.

He thought again about the plan that he'd come up with as he drove from Dr. Perkins's office.

It had been his prayer to just tuck this part of his past away. But the secret he held kept rearing its head, this time with a vengeance. Alexis knew he was hiding something and the way she had walked out on him just an hour before . . . he shook his head as he remembered her face filled with disgust.

Were you ever with anyone I know?

He'd tried to answer, but he just couldn't say the name. Because if he said "Jasmine," at some point he'd have to add "baby." And he didn't even know if that baby was his. Before he did anything, he had to know.

He clicked the track wheel on the phone, then waited as it rang.

"What's up?" J.T. answered.

"Hey, this is Brian Lewis."

"Dr. Brian. What's up, man?"

"Nothing much, what about you?"

"Still hanging. Where've you been? We haven't seen you much around here and I know you miss the honeys. We've got the best in the Valley, but you know that already, don't you?" J.T. laughed.

It was true; Brian did know. J.T.'s nightclub, de Janeiro, was a mecca for women. Many nights—after surgery—he'd gone there, scoped the crowd, ended up with a woman of his choice who had the pleasure of spending a couple of sex-crazed hours with him.

He shivered. He didn't even want the memories. "Listen, I'm calling for business, actually."

"Ah, that's no fun."

"I need to get in touch with your friend Malik. The guy who owns the club in New York."

"You making a run to the city?"

"Thinkin' 'bout it."

Brian jotted down the number, then gave the excuse of a waiting patient to end the call. Still, J.T. wouldn't let him go until he promised to come by the club soon.

He hung up and for minutes stared at the paper. Malik—Jasmine's godbrother. Just one more call and he'd get to Jasmine.

Is this the right thing to do?

It was obvious that Jasmine had claimed her husband as the baby's daddy. And that's the way it needed to be.

Until now.

He sighed. He didn't care for Jasmine; still, he hated bringing this drama into her life. But if she cooperated, they would be able to do this in secret. Get a paternity test and if God was on their side, rule him out as the father.

He tucked the number into his pocket. At least he had that now. But before he did anything else, he wanted to see his wife. Talk to her and convince her that all was well in their world. If she still didn't believe him, then he'd make this dreaded call.

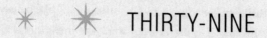 THIRTY-NINE

ALEXIS STOOD ON THEIR BALCONY high above Wilshire Boulevard.

Seldom was she home in time to watch the cars and trucks that crawled beneath her window during the rush-hour exodus. But she didn't notice the street below. Instead, she was focused on memories from this morning. Each time she remembered Brian's refusal to answer her questions, her heart stopped.

What was he so afraid to tell her? What could be worse than him being a sex addict? Whatever it was, it had to be big. She was almost afraid to know. But she was even more afraid not to know.

"Hey."

Startled, she turned around. She hadn't heard him come in. Her eyes fixed on his face. And then his hands. And her heart stopped beating again.

Brian kissed her and offered her the bundle of flowers he carried.

She didn't touch the roses. Just brushed past him. "I didn't expect you home so early." She glanced, once again, at the peace offering he held. This time, there were at least four dozen roses in the bundle. The size of his apology let her know for sure that they were in trouble. "Those are not going to help." She pointed to the flowers.

"I'm just trying to say I'm sorry."

"Instead of telling me you're sorry, tell me the truth." When he didn't respond, she said, "Never mind." Took a short breath. "We need some time apart."

He shook his head. "No. Dr. Perkins said it's important for us to be together now and I agree."

"But if you're not going to be truthful . . ." She paused, giving him a chance to tell all. "What's the point?" she finally asked.

He stood stoic and silent, but his eyes were glazed with sorrow. Made her heart stop beating once more.

What is it? she screamed inside. But she refused to ask him again.

He said, "Sweetheart, I really do want you to know everything."

"Then. Just. Tell. Me."

He waited a moment, as if planning his words. "I need . . . some time."

"You've had nothing but time."

"I need a little more. A few days." When she shook her head, he continued, "I know this is hard, Alexis, but, it's hard on me too." She glared at him, not believing he was trying to convince her that he shared her pain. "It's hard," he continued, "because I've hurt the best thing that's ever happened to me, and I don't want to hurt you anymore."

"Every time I hear something new, I hurt." She paused. "But it's part of the process, because I have to know."

Alexis could see the thoughts behind his eyes. See the way that he was making choices and decisions that would affect the rest of their lives.

Finally, he said, "I know this is a lot to ask, but trust me."

She chuckled, although it sounded more like a groan. Folded her arms. Told him without uttering a word that he hadn't done anything to be trusted.

"Trust me," he said again softly, ignoring all that she'd told him silently. "I need a few days to figure this out. And I promise . . . I'll tell you everything."

His words—the way he spoke them, and his eyes—the way they moistened, told her that she had much to fear.

He pleaded, "Trust me this one last time."

It has to be love, she thought. Love that made her act so stupid. Love that made her want to believe. Love that gave her hope, even when deep inside she knew that it was love that was going to hurt her again.

Love made her say, "Just a few days, Brian. But that's it." She walked away, leaving him standing in the middle of the living room, still holding the flowers.

FORTY

His wife was on the edge.

But it still took Brian four days to build the courage. He'd come to his office on a Saturday so that no one would overhear. Still, he locked himself inside and then dialed the number quickly before he changed his mind.

"This is Malik," the voice on the other end said.

The sound of his voice made Brian want to hang up. But he inhaled, stuck out his chest like a man. "Malik, I don't know if you remember me," he said, thinking that if he'd been forgotten, that would be a good sign. "This is Brian Lew—"

Before he could get his full name out, Malik said, "I know who you are. Wasn't that long ago when we last spoke."

Malik paused long enough for Brian to remember how he'd called and told him to stay away from Jasmine and her baby. Brian had been more than happy to abide by Malik's wishes. His plan had been to stay away from Jasmine forever. But life changed things.

Malik asked, "So what's up?"

Brian took a breath. "I know what we agreed, but I need to talk to Jasmine. I'm not trying to pull anything or to get with her . . . or anything," he rambled. "But this is important. Urgent really, and I don't have her number."

Several beats and then, "Straight business?"

"Yeah."

Another beat. "All right."

Brian frowned. He'd expected more resistance—or maybe more resistance was what he wanted.

Malik continued, "Jasmine and Hosea are in Los Angeles."

"Really?" That was not good news. He didn't want to share this half of the country with Jasmine and her husband—and his wife. "They moved to L.A.?"

"Nah, just there on an extended business trip. They're staying at the Fairmont. Give me your number and I'll call Jasmine. If she wants to talk to you, she'll call."

He gave Malik his cell number.

Another pause, and then Malik asked, "Man to man, this is straight up?"

"Definitely. I'm happily married, faithful to my wife . . . now. Just need to talk to Jasmine for a minute."

"Good, because she and Hosea are happy. No need for drama."

"There won't be any," he said, and prayed that would be true.

"Then I'll call her for you," Malik said before he said good-bye.

For long minutes after he'd hung up, Brian sat, tormented by his questions. Why had Malik been so amiable? Had Jasmine told Malik that she wanted to speak to him? Had she been looking for him? And if she had, why?

Now he needed the same answers that his wife wanted.

Malik had said Jasmine and her husband were at the Fairmont. He called information, got connected to the hotel, and then asked for the Bushes. He said a quick prayer, and made a plan to hang up if Hosea answered.

"Hello."

It wasn't a warm greeting; she sounded frantic. "Jasmine?"

"Speaking."

"Jasmine. This is Brian. Brian Lewis."

He heard the phone fall to the floor and he knew that was a sign. He knew he was in trouble.

Jasmine and Hosea, Alexis and Brian

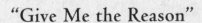

AUGUST 2006

"Give Me the Reason"

—LUTHER VANDROSS

FORTY-ONE

"JASMINE?"

She could hear him calling her through the phone, but all she could do was stare at the receiver that she'd hurled across the room.

"Jasmine?"

Deliver me from evil . . .

She picked up the telephone and squeezed the handset, hoping somehow that would choke the caller at the same time. She found her voice. "Brian, what do you want?"

"Are you all right?"

"What do you want?" she demanded to know.

"We need to talk."

She could not believe this man was calling. Surely he remembered their last encounter in New York. When she was face-up on a stretcher being wheeled into an ambulance.

That should have been the end of him—of them.

"I know you're surprised to hear from me."

"That doesn't even begin to explain it."

"Believe me, I don't want to be calling, but I have a reason."

"You always do." Her next move was to slam the phone down with enough force to cause major damage to his eardrum. Then he'd get the message that she—and her marriage—was not to be played with.

But before she could make that valiant move, he said, "I'm calling about the baby."

Jasmine pressed the phone to her ear. Sank onto the bed. "What baby?" she asked as if she didn't know.

"I need to see you."

Jasmine tried to keep the trembling that threatened to make her drop the phone again out of her voice. "That's not possible."

"I know you're here in Los Angeles."

"How . . . " She stopped. It didn't matter how he found her. All that mattered was getting this man off the phone; out of her life. So that she could get back to what was really important—slaying the other snake, Natasia, who was slithering through her backyard. "There's no reason for us to get together."

"I'm not trying to cause trouble, but I need to see you. Alone."

She frowned. Thought about all the pain their trysts had brought her and the man she loved. Thought about how she'd almost lost Hosea because of Brian. "I cannot believe—"

He interrupted her tirade. "It's not about that, Jasmine. I love my wife."

"And I love my husband."

"Then we're in the same place. But I still need to see to you. And since I want to talk to you about the baby, I know you don't want your husband there."

Ah, she thought, *this must be some kind of shake down.* She couldn't wait to blow up his plan.

He said, "This meeting can stay a secret, but we need to talk."

"I don't keep secrets from my husband."

"You've kept this one—"

"What secret? The one where you're Jacqueline's father?"

She heard his deep gasp.

"He already knows." She imagined his despair as his plan fell apart. But she felt no joy in this victory. She just wanted him off the phone.

"Why . . . did you tell your husband that?"

"Because it's the truth."

"You had a paternity test?" It was his voice that trembled now. "Without me?"

"Didn't need to. Hosea and I were never together while you and . . . " She closed her eyes, tried not to remember.

"So, I am——" he said.

"Jacqueline's father," she finished for him.

"Jacqueline."

She was sorry she told him that. He didn't need to know the name Hosea had chosen for their daughter.

"So," she began, "your blackmail plan is dead before it got started."

"Blackmail? That's not why I called."

"I don't care why you did, but now that you know about *my* baby, you can just go about your business."

"But, my wife. If Alexis finds out——"

"That's *your* drama." She slammed down the phone and prayed that would be the end.

Except it couldn't be the complete end. With the way she was trying to live, she had to tell Hosea about this call. That was the deal——no more secrets, no more lies.

Except now, Hosea had a secret that felt a lot like a lie.

No! This wasn't about Hosea. This was every bit Natasia——she could smell that slut all over this so-called business trip to Oakland. It was a standard skank ploy——tricking somebody else's husband to be somewhere, without his wife, to be alone with you. It was a trap that she'd set herself, when she lived that scandalous life. She couldn't count the number of times it worked.

Just like it worked for Natasia.

Jasmine grabbed the phone, dialed her husband's cell. It went straight to voice mail. What was she supposed to say——get Natasia out of your bed? She left no message.

She hung up, dialed the hotel directly.

"May I speak with Hosea Bush?"

"Mr. Bush has checked out already."

Glancing at the clock, she realized he was probably with Dr.

Marshall—he'd said they were meeting first thing this morning—if that was even true.

She called Hosea's phone again. Voice mail. And then again. Same thing.

There was only one thing left to do.

She dropped to her knees, leaned against the bed. "Lord, I don't know what's going on up there, but You know. Please, Lord, please, keep that hussy away from my husband."

And then she did something that Mae Frances had advised her to do weeks ago.

"This prayer thing really works," Mae Frances had said, as if she'd discovered something new. "All you have to do is pray three times—once for the Father, then the Son, and close it out with the Holy Ghost."

So that's what Jasmine did—prayed that prayer three times before she pushed herself from her knees. Now while God did His thing, Jasmine knew she had to do something too.

It didn't matter that Natasia had a contract. Her happy behind needed to be on the curb by Monday. And no matter what excuse the two would come up with about what happened in Oakland, she was going to make it clear to Hosea that Natasia needed to crawl back to whatever sewer she had climbed out of. This time, Natasia was going, and Jasmine wasn't going to accept any kind of no for an answer.

FORTY-TWO

HOSEA TIPTOED INTO THE SUITE, dropped the overnight bag next to the door, and then moved through the darkness. Careful not to make a sound, he sank onto the couch. And rested.

He had to—he was emotionally exhausted. He was on a roller coaster, a ride that had begun . . . with that kiss.

Last night, when he'd returned to his hotel room, he'd climbed into bed, drunk with thoughts of Natasia. And her lips. And her hands.

Then he thought about his wife. Thought about calling her. But didn't want to call too late. Didn't want to wake her. Didn't want her to hear anything in his voice that would give her a clue that he was filled with guilt.

Although it wasn't like he'd been unfaithful, not really. Natasia had kissed him. And he'd stopped her.

But he couldn't stop the thoughts. Couldn't stop wondering what could have happened. Almost wishing that it might, maybe, perhaps, somehow would happen again.

Then this morning Natasia had knocked on his door, and stepped into his space with confidence.

"We have to meet Dr. Marshall as a team," she began, "and before we go to his offices, I wanted to apologize. About last night."

He'd been nervous, shifted back and forth as if he was trying to be a moving target.

She continued, "I'm so sorry. I shouldn't have kissed you. But it wasn't me."

He frowned, not understanding.

"It was the wine," she said.

He'd said nothing, just watched her lips move.

"I wasn't tryin' to get with you or anything." She continued, "I am very clear that it's over between us."

For the first time he wondered if that was what he really wanted.

"So, am I forgiven?"

He spoke his first words. "All is forgiven."

"Thanks."

"And forgotten."

She laughed. Looked him up and down as if she didn't believe that part.

From that point on, she'd acted professionally. On the car ride to Dr. Marshall's office, she chatted as if she didn't feel the heat between them. Inside the meeting, she talked as if there was nothing more on her mind than Dr. Marshall and his *Street Soldiers.* And as they left the building, she'd waved to someone waiting in a tinted-windowed Mercedes and told him, "Go on to the airport. I'm having dinner with a friend. May not get back to L.A. until tomorrow." Then, she strolled away as if he'd never meant a thing to her.

Seemed like what she'd said was true—it was just the wine.

Seemed like what he'd said wasn't true—all was not forgotten.

Why can't I get her out of my mind?

"You're back."

He turned around and saw his wife's silhouette in the doorway. Even in the dark, he could see the outline of her thighs, barely covered by her short nightgown. "I'm sorry, darlin'," he said softly. "Did I wake you?"

"No. I couldn't sleep. I've been calling you all day."

"Sorry. My phone was dead. I didn't take my charger with me." He reached for the light.

"Leave it off." She stood over him, and they stared at each other before he pulled her onto his chest.

He sighed, relishing her familiar weight. "I missed you," he whispered, and meant it. He kissed her and his hands glided over the satin that she wore. "I couldn't wait to get back to you and Jacquie."

"Is that because you couldn't wait to get away from Natasia?" she asked, as if that was a normal question.

He froze as she stared into his eyes. Wondered if she was searching him for the truth. Wished that she would ask him nothing else.

His wish was not granted.

"Why did you lie about Natasia?"

He was as stiff as a statue. "I didn't lie."

"Was she in Oakland?"

He said, "Yes," and was amazed that he could speak without breathing.

"Then it was a lie. No matter how it happened. Commission or omission, it was a lie." Her voice stayed calm.

"I didn't know she was going to be there," he said, trying to be as cool as his wife.

"But once she got there—"

"I didn't want to tell you because I knew you'd be worried."

"It was worse when I found out from someone else. Then I was really worried. Imagined all kinds of things."

Hosea had to fight to hold his gaze with hers. But he wanted her to look into his eyes, so she would see the truth. "I would never do anything with her. I would never do that to you."

A beat. "I believe you."

He exhaled. "But I am sorry. We promised no secrets. I should've told you the moment she got there."

"Yes. You should have."

"I will from now on."

"No. You won't. Because I want her gone, Hosea. I don't care about the contract. I want her off your show."

He was careful not to push her away as he sat up and turned on the light. Looked into her eyes, clearly now. "Jasmine, not only can I not do that, but there's no reason—"

"There is." Her voice rose a bit. "She tricked you, Hosea. Was there even a meeting?"

He nodded slowly, hating that he had to explain. Knowing that he needed to be patient. "We met with Joe Marshall all day."

"Still, it was some kind of ploy. She's crazy. She's after you and will do anything she has to."

He shook his head, trying not to remember the kiss. "It wasn't Natasia. Dr. Marshall apologized for the mix-up. Someone on his staff messed up."

"With the help of Natasia." Jasmine stood and folded her arms. Hosea's glance followed the hemline of her nightie as it rose. He swallowed, remembering just how much he loved his wife.

She said, "I don't care what you say, I know I'm right. We can't trust her."

He stood and faced her. "You don't have to trust her. Trust me." He kissed her forehead and then turned toward the bedroom.

"Where're you going?"

"To take a shower." He hoped she wouldn't ask him why he'd do such a thing when showering at night had never been his habit.

She said, "We're not finished."

The command in her tone made him face her again. "We don't need to talk about this anymore. Just trust me."

He turned away and then prayed inside that what he'd just told his wife was the truth.

FORTY-THREE

"BRIAN?"

This was supposed to be his sanctuary. He had told Alexis that he had something to do at the clinic this morning. And it had cut his heart when she didn't even question him. Didn't even ask what kind of work he had to do on a Sunday morning.

All she did was shrug and say, "Guess you're not going to church." Then she'd walked out of their apartment without looking back. Left him alone as if she didn't care what he did. As if she knew their days together were numbered.

His marriage was slipping away. Almost a week had passed and he still hadn't told her all that she wanted to know. What was worse was that she'd stopped asking. Like she'd given up.

"Brian." Jefferson called him again. "What are you doing here sitting in the dark?" He clicked on the light, making Brian shield his eyes from the brightness. "Man," Jefferson slipped into a chair across from him, "you look bad, B."

Brian glanced down at the wrinkled shirt he wore. He guessed he did look bad compared to his friend, who was donned in his Sunday best.

"What are you doing here?" Brian asked, tossing the half-eaten candy bar he held onto his desk.

"I came to pick up some files, but it looks like I'll be picking up a friend instead."

"I needed someplace to go, to think." He paused. "My marriage is over."

Jefferson fell back against the chair. "What? I thought everything was working out."

"It was. We've been trying, but . . ." He closed his eyes as he remembered the conversation he had tried so hard to forget. Jasmine telling him the truth. "I just found out something that will end my marriage for sure."

"Wait a minute, your marriage *isn't* over?"

"Not yet."

"Man," Jefferson's shoulders relaxed, "you and Alexis will make it. I'm sure of that."

Brian shook his head. "You don't know what I know."

"So tell me."

This was supposed to be a secret that wasn't to be shared with another soul. But if anyone could help him, it was Jefferson. His friend had been (almost) in the same place he was now.

"I talked to Jasmine."

Jefferson's eyes widened. "B, don't tell me—"

He held up his hands. "Not like that. I've been delivered from being unfaithful." He took a breath. "But I only told you part of the story."

"Okay," Jefferson said slowly.

"Jasmine had a baby."

Nothing more needed to be said between two men who were three-decade-long friends. "Yours," he said, for confirmation only.

Brian simply nodded.

"Man! How did that happen? I mean—"

"Please, no lectures." Brian held up his hand. "I can't handle it over the beating I've given myself."

Jefferson sat, as if thoughts were turning over in his mind. "Are you sure it's yours?"

"That's what Jasmine said."

Jefferson waved his hand in the air. "I know you're not taking her word. If you think it could be yours, you need to have a test."

Brian didn't bother to explain that this wasn't about trusting Jasmine. It was about what she'd said. Deception was more her style, but she'd already told her husband that he was the father. She would have never admitted that—unless it was the truth.

"At least I understand why you're sitting here in the dark," Jefferson said. "Wow, B, this is big. So, how are you planning on telling Alexis?"

"I'm not."

"Whoa! Brian, man, don't try to hide this. It'll never stay a secret."

"It will if you don't say anything." he paused and wondered if Jefferson would be able to keep this from his wife. "I'm telling you, man. You can't tell Kyla," his voice rose.

Jefferson held up his hands. "I don't like it, but I'm not gonna give you up. Think about it, though, 'cause what's done in the dark—"

"If you're careless will come to light."

"That's not the way it goes."

"That's the way it has to go for me."

Jefferson shook his head. "Is there anything I can do?"

"Can you make this go away?"

"I can make the secret go away and help you tell the truth. That's all I know." When Brian said nothing, Jefferson added, "But if you're not gonna come clean, there's not much I can do. Except pray." After a moment, he walked from the office.

Brian knew that Jefferson didn't believe he could keep this news from Alexis, but he already had a plan. First, he would never tell anyone else. Next, he would come up with something to tell Alexis. A lie that she would believe was the secret he'd been hiding.

He stood, turned off the light. Some things were just better done in the dark.

FORTY-FOUR

ALEXIS WAS BONE TIRED OF being stuck.

It wasn't all the weeks of this drama that exhausted her. It was Brian—his deceit and his lies and . . . whatever. She had no idea what to call it, because she had no idea what was going on.

She was through.

She lifted the last box and carried it into her closet, stacking it on top of the others. Then, taking her PDA she scrolled to Tasks and opened the document she'd created: "Things to do for the Divorce." She scanned the items, and noticed the number. Seven tasks. Seven. God's number of completion.

When she heard Brian's key in the front lock, she turned off her PDA, then closed her closet door. It was amazing to her that Brian hadn't noticed the small changes in their condominium. She couldn't really blame him—it wasn't like she was packing furniture or appliances. It was just personal things: family photos, her elephant collection, and of course, her clothes.

"Hey, you."

She looked over her shoulder. Then chuckled, although there wasn't a thing funny. There he stood. Hands filled again. With a bundle of roses. She definitely needed to move out, because Brian's secret was going to drive him straight into bankruptcy with the way he was buying flowers. He needed to save his money. For divorce court.

"These are for you," he said, his voice flat. He didn't even hand her the bunch. As if he was as bored as she was with these floral gifts, he just laid them on the bed. "How was your day?"

She wondered if he sensed something, knew that his wife was

ready to leave him here, alone with all of his lies. Wondered if that was why he was talking to her like they were normal, when they both knew they were not.

"I didn't do much. After church, just came home." She sat on the bed. "Just trying to get things together."

He nodded as if he understood. "That's what I've been doing." They sat shoulder-to-shoulder, silent for a few seconds. "I told you that I had to take care of something at the clinic, but I didn't."

"I'm not surprised."

"I did go to the office."

"That surprises me."

"Why?"

"I stopped believing anything you said a while ago."

He flinched; the sting of her words hurt. "That makes me sad."

"Me too. But I feel like you're lying every time you open your mouth."

"What has to happen for you to believe in me again?"

She wanted to tell him that never, ever would she believe in or trust in or listen to him again. And in a few days, she'd be able to add never living with him to that list. But instead, she said what she'd been begging for weeks, "Tell me what you're hiding."

Slowly, he nodded. As if he was now prepared to tell nothing but the truth. He took her hand. "I'm going to tell you everything."

He'd barely spoken his last word before she began to shake. It could have been seconds or minutes that passed. To both of them, it felt like painful hours. "When it comes to what was going on with me, with my addiction, I haven't lied to you, Alex. But, you're right, I haven't told you everything."

"Omission is lying, Brian."

He nodded. "It's taken me time to admit it, but I know I have to be honest in every way. But first, I want you to know why I've been keeping this from you." He stroked her hands. "Every time I look at you, I see what I've done."

"It's the disease, right?" she asked, as if she was still trying to believe in that theory.

"It really is a sickness, but I hope you can see that I'm handling it. I'm trying to get well, be healed, get delivered . . . whatever you want to call it. I'm over it."

"It seems . . . you are."

"But you're right; there are other things. I wanted to protect you, but I see my holding back isn't good either."

Together, they took a deep breath.

"You asked if I'd ever been with anyone you knew . . ."

Already she was crying inside.

"It's not someone you know well, not someone who's a friend."

She snatched her hands away from him. "Who is it?" Her imagination spun into overdrive. Was it someone she worked with? Or one of her sorority sisters? Or someone she hugged in church every Sunday?

"It was Tonya."

She frowned. Searched her mind for someone she knew by that name.

"Tonya Brady."

There was nothing in her memory bank.

He said, "The receptionist in Gordon's office."

"Our accountant?"

He nodded.

Alexis had to think hard to remember the mousy woman with mud brown hair. She frowned. Was that possible? Was she one of the women her husband had bedded in his addiction?

This really is a disease.

Tonya didn't look anything like the exotic women who traipsed through her dreams. "I can't believe . . . Tonya?" Alexis asked, wanting to be sure Brian was truly confessing to being with this woman.

He nodded. "You asked if there was anyone you knew, and you knew Tonya."

Alexis shifted on the bed, confused by her own emotions—upset a bit, at her own relief. "So, she's the secret? She's what you were afraid to tell me?"

He swallowed hard. Nodded slowly.

She sat silently, her shoulder touching his. She was trying to feel it. The mountain that had stood between them. But it seemed to be gone.

She pondered the revelation. Tonya. A white woman. A mousy white woman. A woman with small eyes and huge teeth. A woman that not many—men or women—would notice.

"From this point on, Alexis," he said, breaking through her thoughts, "no more secrets." He waited a moment, and then moved slowly. As if he wasn't sure if he could touch her. But when she didn't move away, he held her.

Inside his arms, Alexis closed her eyes. Finally, the truth. At least, it felt like the truth—kind of. The mountain was definitely gone and she felt some relief. This had to be the truth, because what else could there possibly be?

But still, there was something, something . . .

She nudged that thought aside. She was tired of being stuck. Either she was going to leave or stay. Believe Brian or not.

She chose to believe him. And it was all because of Tonya.

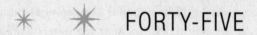

FORTY-FIVE

BRIAN ROLLED OVER, PAUSED as Alexis snuggled into the sheets, then slipped from the bed. He glanced at his wife, her face glowing with her smile.

It was a night of wondrous love after he confessed, and in their bed, she told him that almost all was forgiven. He should have been smiling himself.

But he couldn't find any joy.

He tiptoed from the bedroom, and inside the living room he lay back on the couch. Remembered what he had told his wife and wondered what would happen if he took it all back. But he couldn't. And he wouldn't.

He'd never been a man big on the truth, but tonight his heartache was deep as he thought about the number of ways he'd lied to Alexis.

How do I love thee? Let me count the lies!

He'd told lie after lie. Lies to cover lies. Lied because he loved her. But if God was on his side, these would be the last lies he'd ever have to tell.

Today's lie was almost ridiculous. He'd slept with a legion of ladies, yet he had lied about this one. Lied because he had to come up with something big that Alexis would believe. And though he'd conquered many, Tonya wasn't one of them. Just a lie to satisfy his wife.

Luckily Tonya had moved to Juneau, Alaska, and Brian's hope was that Tonya would never leave the last frontier. That she would stay in Alaska forever and never run into Alexis.

This lie had served him well, had satisfied his wife in ways that

he couldn't have imagined. Not only did Alexis seem to understand why he never confessed to bedding Tonya, but in a warped
way, Brian could tell that Tonya made Alexis feel better about
this disease. If he could have sex with Tonya, surely he was a sick
man.

The lie had worked.

Big time.

Too bad he still couldn't smile.

But he couldn't wallow. He'd done what he had to do. Now,
he'd start telling the truth—but first, he had to create it. And for
that, he needed a different plan. For that, he needed Jasmine.

FORTY-SIX

"SO HAVE YOU COME UP WITH a plan yet?"

Jasmine shook her head. Days had passed, yet the ghost of the Oakland weekend remained.

"I don't know what I'm going to do, Mae Frances. I'm just praying that Natasia will take one of those jobs Annika found."

Mae Frances grinned and sat back on the couch. "I have to admit, Jasmine Larson, that was a good one." Then she was serious again. "But you can't depend on that alone. Not the way this witch operates. You need a Plan C to back up that Plan B."

Mae Frances was right. But she had run out of ideas. And her thoughts weren't on Natasia as much as they were on Hosea and the way he was since he returned from Oakland.

"Well, if you don't have a Plan C, I'll come up with one for you." Mae Frances's eyes were squinted when she stood, as if she was already deep in thought. "I'll call a few of my connections. See if we can find out a little somethin' somethin' on her."

"Thanks, Nama," Jasmine said, although she didn't have much hope. Women like Natasia had little to hide. They laid every card right out front for the world to see. Natasia didn't care who knew about her plans to get Hosea. She wanted him, she would have him. Period.

At the door, Mae Frances stopped. "If my granddaughter wakes up, call me."

"I will, but she's so worn out from the park this morning. Thanks for taking her."

"You know that girl is my heart." Then Mae Frances rolled her eyes. "You need to get dressed. No use walking around here like somebody died, Jasmine Larson," she said before she slammed the door.

Jasmine looked down at the robe she wore, even though it was after three, and she sank onto the couch. She hadn't had the energy to get dressed. Not when she was so consumed with what was happening to her marriage.

It wasn't like Hosea had made any great transformation—just little things that let a wife know that something was not right.

It began on Monday, when she hadn't been able to contact Hosea all day. By five o'clock, when she finally got through, he did apologize profusely.

"I'm so sorry, darlin', I just got caught up today."

"I understand," she said, although she didn't. He'd never gotten caught up like that before the trip to Oakland.

"I'll make it up to you tonight," he promised.

But it was after ten by the time he came home and collapsed into bed. He'd had few words for her—just said enough to tell her how exhausted he was.

It's just my imagination, she'd told herself when she'd laid beside him in bed, his back turned to her.

Then on Tuesday, he'd awakened, kissed her, and said, "I want to make up for yesterday. Can you meet me at the office for lunch?"

Jasmine had been thrilled, thinking that her concerns were unfounded. As she rushed to check on Jacqueline, she was already planning how she would order a picnic basket so they could stay in. There was no telling what would happen with a couple of pieces of fried chicken behind locked doors. She giggled just thinking about it.

Then she'd walked back into their bedroom and heard, "Okay, Natasia, I'll meet you at the Bistro at noon." But if that wasn't bad enough, it was the way he laughed afterward. Like he and Natasia shared something that she wasn't privy to.

He'd flipped off the phone, turned around, and when he saw

her standing there, all he said was, "Sorry, darlin', gotta take a rain check on lunch," as if she didn't deserve any further explanation.

By this morning, Jasmine's imagination and intuition had gone from zero to one hundred. So she turned to what she knew best—sex. Natasia may have had her husband in the office, but she trumped that—she had Hosea in bed.

She couldn't sleep, waiting for the clock to strike six, not wanting to wake Hosea too early. At thirty seconds past six, she had straddled her husband, ready to give him some good, old-fashioned loving. But he'd kissed her cheek, and gently nudged her away.

"I'm sorry, but I've got an early meeting."

Since the day they'd married, there hadn't been a meeting that had stopped him from a quickie. And they hadn't made love in a week?

Something was definitely wrong.

And she was sure that something was Natasia.

The ringing hotel telephone gave her hope. Maybe Mae Frances had uncovered something already.

"Hey, what did you find?"

"Uh, Jasmine, this is Brian."

She bolted up straight. "What do you want?"

He stayed civil although she'd done nothing to hide her contempt for him. "I want to meet with you and your husband."

"No way."

"I'm not trying to start anything. You said your husband knows about me and the baby. So I need to talk to the two of you. To discuss your intentions."

"Our only intention is to keep you out of our lives."

"That's what I want."

"Then it's done. Over. We don't need to meet, and you don't need to call anymore."

"Jasmine, I'm not going away. I need to see you, talk to you straight. And I'll keep calling until you agree to see me." He paused. "I'll call your husband if I have to."

She could not believe this was happening. Not now, in the middle of her disaster.

"What is this really about, Brian? Are you trying to get involved with my daughter?"

"No," he spoke so loudly, she had to move the handset a couple of inches from her ear. "I don't want . . . look, all I want is one face-to-face meeting so that we're on the same page. I want to let you guys know my plans and I want to know yours so that nothing comes up later. A quick meeting. In and out. After this meeting, you'll never hear from me again."

Jasmine wanted to just hang up, but she certainly didn't want him calling Hosea. She couldn't imagine anything worse than her husband getting a call from Brian.

"Okay," she said, anger still in her voice and her heart.

He gave her his number. "And Jasmine, if I don't hear from you, I'll be—"

She slammed down the phone before he could finish his threat.

FORTY-SEVEN

"GOTTA SEC?" NATASIA PEEKED into Hosea's office.

She wore that smile that still made him melt. "What's going down?"

"Wendy will be handling the meeting this afternoon. I just filled her in."

Hosea frowned. Since their return from Oakland, Natasia seemed to be avoiding him—passing off a meeting on Monday, canceling their lunch date on Tuesday, and then she'd been out of the studio on Wednesday and Thursday. She hadn't made a single pass, hadn't called him sweetie once. For the first time since they'd come together again, their relationship was totally professional. Exactly how it was supposed to be.

So why did he feel so bad?

"You don't have a problem with Wendy, do you?" She tilted her head in just that way that he used to say was so adorable.

"No," and then he wanted to kick himself for sounding like a disappointed teenager. He cleared his throat, brought the bass back into his voice. "You have another meeting?"

"Nope. For once, I'm putting pleasure before business." She leaned over his desk, her cleavage right in front of his nose. "You wanna know what I'll be doing?"

He had to look up to see her eyes. "If you want to tell me."

"I'm going on a date."

"With whom?" The moment he asked the question, he regretted it. Why did he want to know?

"With Mario. He told me I have a lot of making up to do since I canceled last weekend because of our . . . business in Oakland."

She paused as if she were giving him time to remember their trip, their kiss. "Anyway," she continued, "he has big plans for me."

"How did you hook up with him?" Again, more regret for caring.

"I met him a few years ago at the Emmys. But we weren't able to connect until I got out here." She paused, sat back, and looked straight into his eyes. "Seems like L.A. is turning out to be a very good place for me."

"Great."

"So, if there's nothing else . . ."

"Nope."

"Then I'm out." She stood, wiggled her fingers. "Enjoy your weekend. I'm sure I will."

She sashayed toward the door, moving as if she knew his eyes were on her behind.

For the rest of the afternoon and through the early evening meeting, the vision of Natasia walking away from him had stayed.

Even now, as he sat in his office trying to prepare for Monday's taping, he couldn't get her out of his mind.

What is going on? he wondered. Why was he spending so many hours thinking about a woman who wasn't his wife?

It had begun with that kiss.

Now everything about Natasia made him remember. Made him wonder. Made him yearn.

Made him sick.

He needed to go home. Apologize to Jasmine. Not that he'd really done anything, but that was the problem. He'd been distracted, pushing aside his wife and daughter.

All because of one little kiss.

He needed to get Natasia out of his mind and out of his marriage. He grabbed his jacket and headed toward the door. He had a lot of making up to do.

. . .

Even in the dark he could see most of her face. And to Hosea, his wife was still the most beautiful woman he knew.

This is the woman God chose for me.

He knelt down at the side of the sofa, kissed her cheek. Jasmine stirred, then her eyes fluttered open.

"Umm, Hosea. What time is it?"

"It's late. Were you waiting for me?"

She nodded; her eyes were glazed with sleep. "I needed to talk to you." She tightened her robe around her waist.

"I'm sorry, darlin'."

For the first time in days, he saw her smile. She put her arms around his neck. "That's okay. You were working, right?"

"Yeah." He kissed her nose, then sat next to her. "Did you have a good day?"

She shrugged. "It was all right. I didn't do much. Missed you, though. I've been missing you a lot."

"Spoken like a wife."

"Spoken like a wife in love."

He pulled her into his arms. Kissed her, then leaned back and held her. They rested on the sofa, in the quiet, in the dark.

"What did you want to talk about?"

He couldn't see her face, but he could feel her smile go away. "It's late. Let's talk tomorrow."

"No, I've been distracted enough this week. Tonight, it's all about you. Let's talk . . . unless . . . this is about Natasia."

"No."

"Good, 'cause like I said, no one can come between us." He stopped when he felt her stiffen. With his fingers, he lifted her chin. Made her look at him. "Talk to me."

It took a moment. "I got a call today. From Brian." Another pause. "Jacquie's fa—"

Now, it was Hosea's smile that was gone. "I know who he is. What did he want?"

"He wasn't calling for me, Hosea," she said quickly. "He wanted . . . he knows . . . he has some questions about Jacquie."

He tried not to push her away. Moved slowly, gently. Sat up straight. But he couldn't keep the shock out of his voice. "You told him he's Jacqueline's father?"

"No, I never said anything to him. But somehow he knew."

His eyes narrowed. "You told me you never spoke to him after that day . . ." He stopped, his mind swelled with memories. But he shoved them aside. He didn't need to focus on the pain of the past.

"I don't know how he found out, or how he knew that we were here in L.A. But he called . . ."

He waited for her to say more and then wondered why she stopped. Wondered what she was hiding. Was this the first call she had received from Brian? Had she and Brian been meeting all of this time? Had their affair . . .

He took a breath and threw those ridiculous questions away. Jasmine had not been with another man. She would never cheat on him, never lie to him again.

"Well," he began slowly, "I wanted Brian to know the truth when the time was right."

She exhaled as if she was relieved. Moved closer to him and spoke softly, "He said he wants to know our intentions. I think he wants to know if we want anything from him." She placed her hand on top of his, but he didn't move. "He wants to meet."

His doubts came rushing back. "He wants to meet with you?"

"With us."

He stayed still, considering the idea. Then, he nodded. "Let's do it." Gently, he nudged her hands away from his. "Let's handle this right here, right now." His hands folded into fists. "Brian needs to know *my intentions*—that I'm not giving anything to anybody."

Jasmine waited a moment. "Are you sure you want to do this? Because we don't have to."

"Yeah, I want to meet with him. Make it plain. Face him man-to-man. So he can look in my eyes and know where I stand." He could hear, feel his anger rising. And then he knew that time had not healed his wounds. He peered at his wife and tried not to think of her as the source of his pain. "Call Brian," he said, once again pushing aside his suspicions. "Set it up. As soon as possible."

"Okay." She paused. "Hosea, you know that I love you, right?" Gently, she pressed her lips against his. "Come with me," she said, lust filling her voice.

He had rushed home to see his wife, to be with her, make love to her. But the memories of Jasmine with Brian were poison. Made him not want to touch her ever again.

"Come on," she said again. "I've missed you."

He'd missed her, too. But now Brian was in his head. "You go on. I'll be there in a while."

Her eyes pleaded with him before the words began. "I'm so sorry, Hosea."

"Nothing for you to be sorry about, right?" He prayed that was the truth. "It's fine, Jasmine," he said, even though it wasn't. "I'll join you in a little while."

Slowly, she walked toward the bedroom, then stopped at the archway. She looked back with hope in her eyes, but he was right where she left him.

When he heard their bedroom door close, he sighed. He couldn't believe that Brian Lewis was back. He'd expected this day to come—but way in the future. When it was time for Jacqueline. He wasn't ready for it now.

He leaned back, closed his eyes, and tried to forget. But all he could do was remember. The day he'd been betrayed.

It should have been the best of times when he walked into that hospital, his pockets full of pink-cellophane-wrapped cigars. All he wanted to do that night was kiss his wife and new baby girl good night, then rush out to prepare for their homecoming.

But instead, his bride of six months had spoken words that had crushed his heart into pieces.

"Hosea, I had an affair."

Those five words had stopped him from breathing. "What did you say"? he had asked, sure that he had somehow had a stroke that had confused his brain cells.

"I had an affair. And the baby, our baby, is not—"

Jasmine had tried to stop there, but he had made her say it. Had forced her to tell him the whole truth.

"Are you saying that Jacqueline is not my daughter?"

"Yes." And then she started talking about how she'd been faithful from the moment they became engaged.

Like that even mattered.

In those minutes, she'd taken away what he'd wanted for a lifetime—a child of his own.

Even now, that was too much misery for him to bear. He needed to get away from these thoughts, this pain that could still bring him to his knees. He needed to be somewhere else. Another place. Another time.

He settled into the sofa. Closed his eyes and thought about Natasia.

# FORTY-EIGHT

It felt like old times.

Had been this way the entire week. Because of Tonya Brady, he had his wife back.

Alexis grabbed a handful of popcorn, then rested against his chest. "I cannot believe you got me to watch this movie again."

He pulled her closer. "Ssshhh. It's almost over."

"What is it with guys and *Scarface?*" she asked anyway.

"He's a real O.G."

"There's something downright wrong with watching all of this violence on a Sunday."

He chuckled. "Ssshhh."

Less than five minutes later, Alexis cheered. "And that's not because I enjoyed it any more than I did the last fourteen hundred times you forced me to watch."

Brian hit "Stop" on the remote. "Fourteen hundred times?"

"At least."

He grinned. "Ya gotta love it."

"No, I love you."

They stopped, her words surprising them both.

He said, "Thank you for loving me." He held her hand. "I'm just so sorry—"

She pressed her fingers against his lips. "No need to say that anymore. I've forgiven you."

He was filled with joy and pain hearing those words. She'd forgiven him; he was blessed with that. But inside, his lies still haunted him.

I did it for her.

"To be honest," Alexis said, "I didn't think it was possible to get to this place. But I thought a lot about Kyla. And how I'd counseled her when she was coping with Jefferson and Jasmine's affair."

The sound of Jasmine's name from his wife's lips made him shake. His secret was sitting right there in the living room with them.

She said, "And Pastor always says you have to forgive to be forgiven."

He couldn't find anything to say.

"And I have to thank you, too," she added.

"For what?"

"For being honest and telling me everything. And for continuing your therapy. I can't ask for anything more."

Slowly, Brian turned away. Folded his hands together under his chin. *Honest.*

"What's wrong?" Alexis asked.

He shook his head and pulled her close to him. "Nothing."

For long minutes, Alexis rested in his arms, quiet, and he prayed that from now on, this was how it would be.

His vibrating cell phone interrupted their peace.

"Want me to get that?" Alexis asked, but she was already moving toward the coffee table, reaching for the phone.

She picked it up. Glanced at the screen. Frowned. "The Fairmont Hotel," she said with a question in her voice.

Before she could flip it open, he snatched the phone from her. "That must be one of the doctors. There's a doctor who's here in L.A. From New York. I'm going to be doing a consult. He needs my help. A newborn. My advice. The baby, he was just born . . . He chattered until his cell stopped ringing.

Alexis's frown deepened. She folded her arms. "You missed the call."

Brian nodded. "Yeah. Let me take this in the office. I'll be right back." He kissed the top of her head, and tried not to move too quickly. But he couldn't get away fast enough. He bolted into the office, closed the door, breathless.

How close was that? If Alexis had taken that call . . .

Still shaky, he dialed the number, asked for the Bushs' room, then said, "This is Brian," the moment Jasmine answered.

"Hosea and I will meet with you," she said, without saying hello. "Tuesday morning. Here at the hotel, in the lobby, and then we'll go someplace else, if it's necessary."

"That'll work," he said, glad they weren't meeting in the city. He didn't want any chance meetings with Alexis. "How's nine?"

"Fine."

Before he thought, he said, "Will you bring the baby?" He was stunned by his own question and just as quickly, he said, "Never mind. I'll see you Tuesday," then he hung up.

He settled into the chair. Why had he asked about the baby? It wasn't like he wanted to have anything to do with her. Not that he was shunning his responsibility. Like with his two sons from his previous marriage, he would provide financially.

But from what Jasmine said, she and Hosea wanted to raise this baby on their own—without him or his help. And that's what he wanted, too.

He stood; he needed to get back to Alexis before she became suspicious.

At the living room entryway, he paused. Stared at his wife, engrossed in the Sunday newspaper. He settled next to her.

"Did you get . . . that call taken care of?" she asked without looking up.

"Yeah, everything's fine."

"Good."

Brian glanced at Alexis for an extra moment. She sat as stiff as her voice sounded. Still didn't look at him. *What's wrong?* But as quickly as his concerns came, he tossed them away. There wasn't a problem and he didn't need to look for one. It was just that close call with disaster that had him shaken up.

While Alexis read, Brian scanned the sports pages. But his mind was on Tuesday. If it went as planned, it wouldn't take ten minutes. He'd thank Jasmine and her husband for all that they'd done. And then they'd get to the important part—the three would agree that this was a fact that was best kept a secret until the end of time.

After that, he'd be able to walk away. For good.

FORTY-NINE

Jasmine sat on the bed long after she hung up the phone. The call had sucked all energy from her. But if God was on her side, this would end on Tuesday. And she would never have to speak to Brian Lewis again in this life or in the hereafter, if where she hoped he'd spend eternity was correct.

Tuesday had to be the end, because she wasn't sure how much more her marriage could take. If Natasia had been dynamite, Brian was a nuclear explosion. Because with his return, he brought the memory of her betrayal.

Since Friday night, Hosea's pain had been palatable. So many times, she felt him staring at her, his thoughts of her and Brian together right behind his eyes.

She'd apologized over and over. And over and over he'd told her he was fine. But then yesterday he'd worked long hours in the third bedroom he used as an office. Even when he came to bed last night, she could feel his distance.

The moment he laid his head on the pillow, she'd asked, "Do you want to talk?"

"No," was all he said. And even though he had wrapped his arms around her, she could feel that he wasn't there. In his mind, he'd gone someplace where she wasn't invited.

Somehow, she had to break through. Get Hosea to see that Brian's return made no difference at all—they were still a happily married couple.

"You spoke to him."

She looked up. Hosea stood at the edge of the bedroom, arms

folded. And she prayed that all of the hate that she saw in his eyes was for Brian.

"Yes," she said, "he's meeting us Tuesday. At nine. Is that okay?"

He nodded. In that moment, his face softened, now etched with a sadness that matched her own.

She said, "He asked if we were bringing Jacquie, but he hung up before I could tell him that there was no way he'd ever—"

"I think he should see Jacqueline."

Her eyes widened. "No! Definitely not. What are you thinking?"

"I'm thinking that we should live in the light."

"And that's what we're doing." She paced in front of him. "We're meeting Brian, and I don't even want to do that. But there's no way I'm exposing my daughter—"

"You mean our daughter, don't you?"

She stopped. Turned to him with eyes that were already begging before she spoke, "Hosea, I don't want to take her."

"What are you afraid of?"

"I don't want anything to happen to Jacqueline."

"Do you think I do?" He softened his voice. "Jacquie won't even know what't going on. Let him get a look at her now, so that he won't be calling us back two days later asking to see her."

"He could do that anyway!"

His eyebrows bunched together. "I thought you said he didn't want to be part of her life."

She shook her head and sank onto the bed. There was no way she was going to let Brian see her child. Because she could feel it—if they brought Jacqueline, something bad was going to happen.

Hosea said, "I'm just sayin,' we're going to handle this now. Out in the open. Then he'll go his way, we'll go ours. And when

Jacquie is older, if she wants a relationship with him . . ." He shrugged, although Jasmine could see the pain of that thought in his eyes. "But no one will ever be able to say that we didn't even let him see . . . *his child.*"

Those words stabbed her, but before she could take the knife out, the telephone rang. She grabbed the handset, wanting to hurl it across the room. She answered, "Hello."

"Let me speak to Hosea."

That voice was worse than fingernails on a chalkboard. Jasmine slammed the phone back in place. "Hosea," she started, picking up their conversation as if Natasia had never called, "Jacquie is your—"

He didn't let her finish. "Who was that?" he asked with a frown.

Then his cell phone rang.

He unclipped it from his belt, flipped it open. "What's going down, Natasia?"

Jasmine crossed her arms, glared at him. Their eyes stayed locked as Hosea talked.

"Did you call Triage?" he asked.

Jasmine seethed more.

"I'll be right there."

She was shaking her head before he hung up. "Hosea, why is she always calling you on the weekend?"

"It's work."

"Well, that's going to have to wait, because we're in the middle of this."

"We'll finish later, but I'm not changing my mind," he said before he turned away.

"Hosea!"

Seconds later, he closed the door to their hotel suite.

✳ ✱ FIFTY

TOMORROW. EVERYTHING COULD be different tomorrow. That was the fear that had settled in his heart. What was Brian's real agenda? Jasmine had said he only wanted to know their intentions. But what were *his* intentions?

Hosea's eyes moved to the photo of Jacqueline on top of his desk, and his smile came before he even had a chance to lift the frame.

Jacqueline had never met a camera she didn't like. Always laughing. Always posing. And she wasn't even two. His daughter was born to be photographed.

His daughter.

Not Brian's.

What would Brian think once he saw Jacqueline? Would seeing *his* daughter—who had come to life in his image—make him want a relationship? Maybe Jasmine was right. Maybe they should leave Jacqueline out of this. But there was something inside that told him it needed to be done this way.

Live in the light. That had always been his motto. That's what Jesus would do.

His heart was swollen with love as he kept his eyes on the photo. It amazed him the way he loved her more every day. He loved her as if she was his very own.

But every time she smiled, or laughed, or cried, or slept—he saw Brian Lewis. And tomorrow, he'd have to see that man in the flesh.

The tap on his door made him look up and Natasia asked, "May I?" before she stepped inside.

"I thought you'd gone home already."

"Nah, I'm a workaholic like you, and anyway, I wouldn't leave without saying good night." She tilted her head to glance at the picture he held. "Your daughter. I saw her on the plane. She's adorable." She reached for the frame.

"Yeah, she's my joy."

She frowned, just a bit. "She doesn't look like a Bush. Guess she takes after her mother."

He swallowed the lump in his throat; felt it float down and settle on his heart.

Natasia returned the photograph. "Hosea, what's wrong? You've been so distracted."

"I'm cool."

She squinted. "I know you. Was it because I had to pull you away from home last night? I hope it didn't cause a problem with your wife."

"No, I was glad to get out of—" He stopped. Couldn't believe he'd said that, even though it was true. He had been glad to leave the hotel right in the middle of his debate with Jasmine. By the time he'd returned, Jasmine was asleep. When he left this morning, he could tell that she was pretending to still be sleeping, which was fine with him. He didn't want to talk about Brian anymore. "No worries," he said to Natasia. "Everything's cool."

She stayed quiet for a moment. "I'm always here for you. No matter what happens, we'll always be friends. At least that's what I hope."

"We will be."

"So then . . . as a friend . . . talk to me."

He took a deep breath. It was building to a peak—his stress. He was trying hard with Jasmine. Trying hard not to blame her for a long-ago sin that he had supposedly forgiven. It was the for-getting part that tortured him. He wanted to, needed to forget.

And he was well on his way, until Brian came back and forced him to remember.

Maybe it would help to talk.

He looked up. Saw that smile. And a vision rushed him like a tsunami. Of him and Natasia in bed. Sheets disheveled. Legs entwined. Arms tangled. Tongues dancing. Bodies wet. Connected as one. The way they used to be.

He squeezed his eyes shut.

"Hosea, are you all right?"

"Yeah, yeah." He was almost afraid to look at her again. But when he did, the tsunami was gone.

She stood over him, lines of concern all over her face. "I'm really worried about you."

"Don't be."

She waited a moment before she sat back in the chair. "Okay, then maybe you can help me with something."

"Be glad too."

"Good, because I could really use a friend's advice."

Mario. That was the first thing that came to his mind. "How can I help?"

"Well—" She stopped, changed the subject. "You know, we've been in this office all day. And we're going to be back here," she glanced at her watch, "in about twelve hours. Let's go grab a drink somewhere."

He thought about Jasmine. Probably waiting for him, since they hadn't spoken all day. They'd called, but kept missing each other, he suspected purposely. Now, he was sure she was up waiting for him. To talk about tomorrow. To talk about Brian.

He couldn't do that right now.

"Sure," he said to Natasia. "We can hang out for a little while."

"Let's go to my hotel." Before he could protest, she continued, "Not my room. There's a great lobby bar and we could talk there."

Her words, her tone were innocent enough. But it was the memory of his vision—the bed, the sheets, their legs, their tongues that made him say, "Not there."

"Okay," she said slowly. "I've heard about this club, de Janeiro. It's a salsa club I've been wanting to check out."

De Janeiro. The sister club to Rio. Jasmine's club.

He shook his head. "Why don't we check out Pure? It should be cool on a Monday. And it's close. Better for both of us."

"Sounds good. Let's go." She stood, moved toward the door.

Again Jasmine came to his mind.

"Are you coming?" Natasia reached her hand toward him.

"Yeah, I'm with you." He took her hand, and together, they walked out the door.

The Kenny G look-alike was just a few feet from their table, caressing the saxophone and the melody. They'd been at Pure for almost an hour and had exchanged few words. Instead, they sat shoulder-to-shoulder, listening, enjoying.

Natasia spoke first, "I have loved that song from the moment I heard Celine sing it for *Titanic*." Now she sang along, "Love was when I loved you." She shifted on her stool, sang to him, "One true time I hold to."

Hosea smiled a little, then took a long swallow of his soda. When he put his glass down, he stared straight at the musician. Kept his eyes away from Natasia. But only for a little while.

He peeked at her, watched as she now hummed. Her eyes were partially closed, her mouth partially opened. She swayed to the music, took a small sip of wine, and then her tongue traced her lips as her fingers massaged her glass.

He needed to go home.

"Ah, Natasia, you wanted to talk?" His eyes moved to her gloss-soaked lips. He imagined the taste of wine that still lingered there. He cleared his throat. "I don't want to rush, but . . ." He glanced at his watch.

"I'm sorry, I just got caught up. This guy is good." She smiled. "And it hasn't been too bad sitting here with you." When he didn't respond, she got to her point. "I got a call last week. From a headhunter."

"Really?" He'd expected words about Mario. "Didn't know you were looking for another position."

"I wasn't, but this woman found me. She had a couple of things, but there's one in particular that's really interesting. In London."

Her words made his heart beat faster. "London. Wow."

"That's exactly what I said. Living abroad, with quite an increase in my salary."

"Sounds too good to turn down."

"Yeah, but here's the thing. I don't want to leave." She paused, looked straight at him. "*Bring It On.*"

"Nat, your career comes first," he said, wanting to say the right things. "And this position with us, it was temporary. The real question is, are you ready to leave NBC?"

She lowered her head, stared into her wine as if her answer was there. "My career isn't everything. There are some things in life just as important." Even in the dim light, he could see the sadness in her eyes. "My life," she continued, "hasn't gone the way I planned. I need to stay here." Her hand began to move slowly until it covered his. "I need to stay here until I'm sure—"

"Natasia—"

"I know there's no chance for us. But it's our friendship that I want to be sure of. Even when the show leaves L.A., I want you in my life. I want us to nurture our friendship and that's why I don't want to leave right now."

He wondered what Jasmine would think of that and whether

Natasia planned on being friends with his wife, too. "Your career is more important than our friendship."

"My career is fine. I make good money. I love working on the show. Being with you is an extra bonus. Right now, our friendship is most important."

"We can be friends from anywhere."

"So you think I should move to London?"

"I think you should give this serious thought."

She nodded. "Can this stay just between us?"

"Definitely." He peeked at his watch again.

"Yeah, it's getting late," she said. "Jasmine's probably wondering where you are." She waited for him to say something. He didn't. She said, "Thanks for listening."

"No problem. Glad I could be here for you."

"I wish that was an all-the-time thing." She continued before he could say a word. "As a friend. I'm really cool with our friendship."

"So am I. You ready?"

"Yeah, I don't need any more wine. Remember last time?"

He didn't want to remember. But he did.

Hosea led Natasia outside and they waited for her car to arrive. When the Town Car stopped, he opened the door, and she hugged him. Held him. For a long moment.

"Just know you always have me," she whispered in his ear. "My shoulders are your shoulders." She kissed his cheek, then slipped into the car.

He stood on the edge of the street watching until her car was out of sight. Then he strolled to the parking lot where he'd left his SUV.

Inside the car, he sat. And prayed. Prayed about the meeting with Brian tomorrow. And then prayed that he would never need those shoulders that Natasia had offered.

FIFTY-ONE

DRIVING WHILE CRAZY!

And Alexis blamed it all on the man she was following on the 134 Freeway. She couldn't believe she was back here, in her car, trailing Brian as he zipped from lane to lane.

What am I doing?

But she knew exactly what she was doing. This was a well-thought-out plan that had started on Sunday. When Brian had snatched his cell from her, then ran like he had something big to hide.

She hadn't waited a minute before she tiptoed down the hall-way, then stood outside the room with her ear pressed to the door as if she were spying on a cheating husband. She listened. She heard. Tuesday. Nine o'clock. Baby.

She had stayed right there until Brian moved toward the door. Then she dashed back to the living room and grabbed a newspaper just seconds before her husband returned.

This meeting could have been nothing more than what he said: a consultation with a doctor about a surgery. It could have been as normal, as innocent as that.

She doubted it.

And that's what drove her back to crazy. That's what had her once again tracking her husband as if she were a bounty hunter.

Twenty minutes later, the light flashed on the back of Brian's SUV. She wasn't surprised when he swerved onto Zoo Drive; it was exactly where she'd spent three days just two months before. And it was where the call on Sunday had come from. The Fairmont Hotel.

Her chest ached as she followed Brian until he twisted into the Fairmont's curved driveway. She drove past the hotel, then slowed at the end of the block. There, she waited. Took deep breaths and counted.

One, two, three . . .

She needed to give Brian enough time to make his move.

Nineteen, twenty, twenty-one . . .

What would she do when she found him?

Forty-two, forty-three, forty-four . . .

Suppose he was with another woman?

Sixty!

The tires screamed as she made her U-turn and swerved into the hotel's driveway. Brian's SUV was still there, but her husband was gone.

Her fingers tapped an impatient beat on the steering wheel as she waited for the valet attendant. What would she do now? She had no idea what room he was going to. Didn't even have a name to ask for.

She would just wait in the lobby. And confront him when he came down. If he'd been telling the truth and he was meeting a doctor, he'd just have to understand why she was acting like a fool. He'd driven her to this. He'd have to forgive her, the same way she'd forgiven him.

"Are you checking in?" the man asked as he opened her car door.

"No. I'll only be—" She had no idea how long this would take. "I'll be an hour or so."

She took slow steps toward the hotel and willed her heart to match her pace.

She stepped through the revolving door.

No matter what, she would never make a scene. She was, after all, an aristocrat by nature, if not by birth.

But if Brian was with a woman . . .

She entered the lobby.

Stopped.

Stared.

Jasmine Larson!

Anger flared up in her like a firecracker.

Detonated!

Alexis stomped across the Persian rug, past top-shelf-suited men and designer-label-wearing women. Decorum gone. Instead, all that was in Alexis's eyes was red—the color of the blood that would spill when her fingers strangled the life out of both of them.

"Brian!" she screamed. "What are you doing?"

Then she stopped. Noticed that Jasmine was not alone. By her side a man who looked familiar. And an older woman stood close behind them.

But it was the toddler, the little girl who held Jasmine's hand, that stopped Alexis cold.

She stared.

And the girl stared back. With Brian's eyes. Brian's brow. Brian's cheeks. Brian's lips.

Alexis gasped. Looked at Brian. Then at the girl. Back at Brian. Back to the girl.

Jasmine lifted the toddler. "Mae Frances, please take Jacquie upstairs."

"Mama," the girl reached for Jasmine. But the older woman grabbed the child.

"Mama!" The girl's cries faded as she was taken farther away.

"Wait!" Alexis exclaimed. She needed to look at the girl again. Figure out what she was doing with Brian's face. She turned to her husband. "Who . . . what . . ." But that's where the questions stopped. She didn't need any answers.

She knew.

Then she felt it. Bile from deep, rising higher. And higher. She pressed her hand against her stomach. Tried to close her throat. But she couldn't stop it.

All her disgust poured out right there in the middle of the lobby of the five-star hotel. With men dressed in top-shelf suits and women sporting designer-label garb looking on.

FIFTY-TWO

THIS WAS JASMINE'S WORST NIGHTMARE.

The woman she hated as much as she hated Natasia had come into the hotel—where she was not invited—and then had the audacity to throw up—all over her!

She turned on the faucet full blast, not caring that water splattered everywhere. Her raw silk dress was ruined. Still, she needed to get this filth off her.

Jasmine grabbed paper towel after paper towel. But even with the searing water, the paper did little to remove the stains. Or the stench.

Jasmine wanted to throw up herself.

She looked down the row of sinks. To the one on the other end. Where the culprit stood. Alexis was leaning over the basin, her water running full blast too.

Jasmine shook her head, still not able to believe this. She had to admit, she'd been a bit shaken when Alexis had stormed into the hotel, a crazed woman, stomping and screaming. But now, as she moved her attention from her dress to her three-hundred-dollar sandals, she wasn't afraid. She was just plain pissed!

She and Alexis had been enemies for a long time. Almost from the moment Kyla introduced the two of them. It was the day after Alexis had moved to Los Angeles, right after she and Kyla had graduated from Hampton University.

"Alexis and Jasmine!" Kyla had exclaimed when the two met. "My two best friends are now going to be best friends too."

That had never happened.

From the moment they met, Jasmine hadn't liked the leggy beauty who used her Southern drawl and feminine wiles to take away all the men Jasmine had an interest in.

Even Brian. Jasmine had had her eyes on him first all those years ago at Jefferson's fortieth birthday party. And Brian would have asked her out, if Alexis hadn't spun her web that night.

She remembered how she hated Alexis then.

She looked down at her shoes again and really hated her now.

Alexis turned off the water. Stood tall and held wet towels to her face. Through the mirror, she glared at Jasmine. "If I wasn't so sick . . . I'd beat you down . . . right here, right now."

Jasmine smirked. "And what do you think I'd be doing while you tried to do that? I told you before, I'm not afraid of you."

"And I told you before, that makes you one dumb trick."

Jasmine wanted to say it so bad—just say that *her husband* had loved every moment of being with this trick.

But she was trying to live right. So she kept her mouth shut.

"Tell me one thing," Alexis said.

"Why should I tell you anything?" Jasmine tossed the last paper towel into the trash.

Alexis ignored her words. "Is that child . . . the little girl . . ." She inhaled, as if she needed air to continue. "Is that Brian's child?"

Forget about living right. This day had been a long time coming, when she could get back at the woman who'd spoken down to her, made her feel inferior for years.

A litany of wonderful words that would crush her nemesis marched through her mind.

She opened her mouth, then stopped.

The look on Alexis's face. A look that she'd seen before. Pain. The same pain had been etched on Hosea's. And just like when she saw it on her husband almost two years ago, her heart ached.

That made Jasmine mad all over again. She didn't want to feel anything except anger and hatred toward this woman. But all she did was grab her purse. "You need to talk to your husband." She brushed by Alexis, and stomped from the bathroom.

✳ ✳ FIFTY-THREE

HOSEA STOOD STRAIGHT UP when Jasmine rushed from the bathroom.

"Is Alexis all right?"

Jasmine halted. Looked at Hosea. Looked at Brian. Standing side by side. Speaking the same words. At the same time.

She ignored Brian. Said to Hosea, "We need to get upstairs to make sure Jacquie's okay."

"She's with Mae Frances; she's fine. I want to make sure Alexis is all right."

Her eyes widened. "You're kidding, right?"

"No," he said, gently. "We're gonna wait."

He could see the steam rising from his wife, but he didn't move. Not that he wanted to upset Jasmine, but he couldn't leave Alexis. He saw her face, understood her pain. He wanted to let her know that she would make it through. Just as he had.

"Brian and Alexis need to be alone." Jasmine glanced at Brian standing behind them. She lowered her voice, "She asked me some questions. I didn't tell her anything, but she needs time with her husband."

"I only want to talk to her for a moment."

Jasmine folded her arms, glared.

He said, "We can't cause this kind of pain for someone and then just walk away."

A beat, and then, "I'll be over there."

He watched his wife trudge to the other side of the lobby, where maintenance men worked with vacuums and air fresheners to clean up the mess this situation had made.

Hosea took a deep breath, leaned against the wall, and kept his eyes away from Brian. He held back his disgust for the man who had almost ruined his relationship with Jasmine and who was now the reason for Alexis's pain. All Hosea wanted was one shot—just one uppercut to Brian's chin. And then he might have peace.

But he reminded himself that it wouldn't be a good thing to be on the front page of the *L.A. Times* tomorrow explaining why he had beat down his daughter's father.

He was a minister after all.

So he kept all the urges that had festered for eighteen months inside. And waited for Alexis.

✳ ✳ FIFTY-FOUR

HE HAD WAITED LONG ENOUGH.

Brian pushed through the bathroom door. And there was his wife. Glaring at him in the mirror. They stayed that way, eyes glued, saying nothing, saying everything.

Slowly, Alexis pivoted. Took small steps toward him. And then she hit him. Again and again. Beat his chest as if it were a drum.

He stood there, taking it.

Finally, he said, "I am so sorry, sweetheart." He wrapped his arms around her, even though she struggled to break his embrace. But he held on—needing to comfort her and himself at the same time.

How could this happen? He'd been so careful, and then in just one minute, it was over.

He kept his arms wrapped around her until she calmed.

"I'm so sorry."

She shoved his arms away. "Sorry about what?" Her voice was full of tears. "Sorry that you were caught? Sorry that you had a child? Sorry that you're a liar? Tell me, what exactly are you sorry about?"

"I'm sorry that I've hurt you again, but—"

She pressed her palm against his face. "Don't. Speak. Don't. Bother. It'll be a lie anyway." She crashed through the restroom door and he rushed behind her.

"Sweetheart, wait."

She whipped around. "I am not your sweetheart," she spat. "Stay away from me, Brian. If you know what's good for you, you'll stay away from me!"

Her venom froze him in place. And she dashed away.

He wanted to go after her, hold her and make her understand that this was all part of the disease.

But the way she'd looked at him . . . maybe she just needed space. That's what he would give her—space and a little time. Then he would be able to make her understand.

"Alexis," Hosea called. "Wait."

Brian watched as his wife stopped when she heard Jasmine's husband.

He was too far away to hear their exchange, but he could see his wife nod, soften. Brian's teeth clenched when Hosea took her hand. As if they were friends with much in common.

All he wanted to do was snatch his wife away from that man's clutches. But he didn't dare. Space and time. That's what he needed to give her.

From the side, he saw Jasmine staring. Mesmerized by the same sight. After some moments, Jasmine stood and crept closer to their spouses. But then suddenly, she stopped. As if she were burdened down by shackles, Jasmine stood as frozen by the sight as he was.

She turned. Their eyes met. Without uttering a word, Jasmine and Brian spoke. Said the same thing to each other—that betrayal made strange bedfellows.

And both knew, this could be big trouble.

FIFTY-FIVE

ALEXIS WONDERED IF ANYONE had ever died from trembling. Or would she be the first case on record?

Maybe her death wouldn't come from trembling at all. Maybe shock would be her demise. She was still stunned as she barreled south on the freeway. As stunned as she had been when she first looked into that little girl's face.

Brian's face.

"Brian has a daughter." She paused, let that thought settle. "With Jasmine."

She yelled those words into the wind, hoping that somehow a gust would sweep them away.

But the words stubbornly stayed right in the car with her.

"Brian has a daughter. With Jasmine."

How bizarre was this?

And then there was the man with the calming spirit, consoling words.

"I want to pray for you, Alexis," were Hosea's words. "You can get through this. I did."

"You knew?"

"Yes. Since the beginning. That's why I know you'll be fine."

She'd thanked him, before she turned away. Maybe he'd gotten through it. Because his wife had an affair with Brian. But she would never get over this. Because her husband had an affair with Jasmine!

Of all the women in the world.

Suddenly, Alexis laughed. Threw back her head and guffawed as if the truth was a joke. She laughed. And kept laughing so that she wouldn't cry. Knowing that if she shed even one tear her cries would never stop.

So she laughed at the fact that her husband was a sex addict. She laughed because he was a baby's daddy. She laughed at the baby's mama being Jasmine Larson.

She wondered if this was the only child who'd been born from this addiction. Not that it mattered. One baby with Jasmine was way beyond anything she could handle. Her life as the missus to the doctor was so over.

She wished she'd already been packed. Wished that she could just walk into their penthouse, grab her bags, and walk right back out. But no matter how long it would take, she was gone. Babies certainly weren't part of this deal. And a baby with Jasmine Larson? Please!

There was nothing to talk about. No psychologists to see. No pastors to pray with. No one could give her a reason to stay now.

FIFTY-SIX

JASMINE ROLLED OVER, THEN slowly opened her eyes when she didn't feel the warmth of her husband next to her. She reached out, touched the empty space. Still, it took a moment for her eyes to adjust and another moment before she saw him. Sitting across from her, in the chair, in the dark.

"Hosea." She turned toward the lamp on the nightstand.

"No, leave it off," he said, his eyes now focused on her.

"Are you all right?" she asked.

He nodded. "Just couldn't sleep."

Jasmine certainly understood. The air was still thick with tension when she laid her head on the pillow last night. It was only fatigue that allowed her to fall asleep and finally escape the horrid day.

The fiasco in the hotel lobby was just the beginning. When she and Hosea had returned to their suite, Hosea called the studio, then spent the rest of the day at home—with Jacqueline. He stayed inside her room where he read to her and held her. Not leaving her alone, as if he feared his departure might separate him from his daughter forever.

But while he laughed and played with their daughter, he had few words for his wife.

Jasmine's heart had ached—with her fear and his pain. She'd wanted to reach out, love him, and convince him that Alexis and Brian's mess had nothing to do with them.

But she'd said nothing, knowing the best way to handle her husband was to not to handle him at all. Hosea just needed space . . . and time. Soon enough, he'd realized that nothing had changed in their lives.

While Hosea was with Jacqueline, Jasmine had spent time with Mae Frances . . . and with God.

"Jasmine Larson, I cannot believe what you've gotten yourself into now," Mae Frances had exclaimed when Jasmine went to her friend's suite for a bit of consoling. "What did Preacher Man say?"

"He hasn't said anything. At least not to me. Just seems to want to talk to Jacquie right now."

"I don't know," Mae Frances had said, shaking her head. "Seems like there could be some big trouble coming."

Jasmine couldn't run back to her own suite fast enough.

Since Mae Frances hadn't given her a bit of reassurance, she hoped that God would. Inside her bedroom, with Jacqueline's giggles wafting across the suite, she asked God to make it all right with her family. Prayed that by the time Hosea came to their room, he'd be ready to make love and forget about the disaster of the day.

But Hosea was silent when he finally came to bed. Moved around with his head down as if his mind was heavy. With thoughts of her and Brian. And now, Alexis.

"Can you tell me something?" Hosea asked her now.

Jasmine sat up and pulled her knees to her chest. Even in the dark, she could see his eyes, focused on her.

"Weren't you and Alexis friends?"

Oh, God, she thought. She'd been right. He *was* still thinking about Alexis. "She was never my friend, Hosea. Not really."

"It came back to me," he continued as if she hadn't spoken. "As I was waiting for Alexis to come out of the bathroom, I remembered I met her in New York. At Tavern on the Green."

Jasmine closed her eyes and played in her mind the day when she and Hosea and Reverend Bush had run into Alexis and Brian. She'd been shocked when the three of them had walked into the restaurant and Alexis had called her name. And then, she'd almost fainted when she realized that Brian was there with his wife. Brian had greeted her that day as if he didn't know her. As if they hadn't been knocking boots every chance they got.

"Do you remember what happened that night, Jasmine?"

Slowly, she nodded. Softly, she said, "It was the best night of my life, Hosea. You were in the hospital, but you asked me to marry you."

"I thought we were going to have a wonderful life."

She swallowed her fear. Stayed calm. "We've had a few bumps, but we're still happy," she told him, feeling he needed to be reminded.

"Something else I remember," he paused for a moment, "is that Alexis said you'd known each other for a long time."

She wanted to scream. *Why are you still talking about Alexis?*

"How long have you known her?"

She had to get Hosea back to just the two of them. "I don't think—"

His voice rose, just a bit. "How long, Jasmine?"

She sucked in air. "For a lot of years. Almost twenty, I think." She paused when she heard his moan. "But we weren't friends," she told him again.

"So that's why it was okay to sleep with her husband?"

She winced. Tried to remember that this had been a tough day. That's all this inquisition was about. "Hosea, what I did was wrong. And I've apologized. But that happened years ago."

"It wasn't that long ago."

She had to keep him focused, on what was important, what was true. "It was long ago enough so that it's in my past. It's not who I am now."

"Turn on the lamp."

It took her a moment to do as she was told. And he stared at her. Looked as if he saw her differently in the light.

He pushed himself from the chair, and in his eyes, she could see it—the pain of what she'd done, rising up, the bad taking over the good.

He said, "I have to get ready for work. I have an early meeting."

If she wasn't trying to get him on her side, she would have called him a liar and demand to know what kind of meeting took place before the sun even rose. But she couldn't say anything, because it was her lies that had brought them back to this place.

When he closed the bathroom door, she lay down, feeling as if she was living in the middle of déjà vu—right back where this had all started.

She closed her eyes, prayed that the same blessings that had brought her and Hosea out of this before would bring them back together again. And then she repeated that prayer three times. Just as Mae Frances had told her to do.

Jasmine had come ready to fight, ready to remind Hosea just how wonderful their life had been and would be again.

She hoisted Jacqueline on her hip and balanced the picnic basket with her other hand.

"Oh!" Brittney jumped up from behind her desk and ran to the studio's door. "Your hands are full!" She laughed as she grabbed Jacqueline from Jasmine. "She is so adorable," Brittney cooed.

"Thanks for agreeing to watch her," Jasmine said. "Are you sure you'll be okay?"

"We'll be fine. Sharon will cover the phones while Jacquie and I will hang out in the break room. I made sure that Hosea's calendar was clear; he's free for the rest of the afternoon." She lowered her voice and peeked at the basket Jasmine had rested on her desk. "I didn't tell him a thing."

Jasmine kissed her daughter. "Be good, babygirl." Then to Brittney, she added, "Can you make sure we're not disturbed?"

Brittney giggled. "I can handle that. Just make sure you lock the door."

Jasmine laughed. *That* wasn't part of the plan, but it wasn't a bad idea. Anything to get Hosea back to where they used to be.

With a quick prayer, then a quicker knock, Jasmine stepped into her husband's office before he could invite her in.

"Hey, babe." She closed the door behind her.

From his desk, Hosea looked up, frowned, just a little. "What are you doing here?" he asked, confused. "Did I—"

"You didn't forget a thing." Holding up the basket, she added, "This is for you." She held her breath and then relaxed when his frown faded into a bit of a smile. "I brought all your favorites. All you have to bring is you." When he glanced down at the calendar, she added, "I hope you have some time for me," knowing that he did.

When he looked at her, in his eyes she could see his thoughts, his memories of yesterday. And she could see his battle, his fight to forget. "I have an hour or so."

She felt complete relief. "An hour is good."

In silence, they worked together, unloading the basket, stacking the sandwiches onto their plates, then setting the glasses to the side. Every time she had the chance, her fingers grazed his hands. She needed to touch him, wanted him to feel her.

She said, "Remember when we used to have these indoor picnics before we were married?"

"All the time." He drifted back on more memories. "This was one of my favorite things to do with you." Then he said, "Jasmine, I—"

At the same time, she said, "Hosea, I—"

They both stopped. Both chuckled. She breathed fully now, sure that they'd be fine. They were talking together, laughing together. On one accord.

She motioned with her hands for him to continue. "You first."

He nodded. "I'm sorry about this morning. It's just that yes-terday—" Before he could say more, his office door swung open.

"Oh . . . Jasmine." Then the grimace on Natasia's face changed from scorn to a smile. "How are you?"

Jasmine was not fooled by this show for Hosea. But she would not be outplayed. "I'm fine, Natasia." Her smile was just as wide, just as fake.

Natasia smirked, a look that Jasmine was sure her husband didn't see. "What's this?" she asked, looking down at the spread across the desk.

What does it look like, heifer? "Hosea and I are having lunch." She had to work not to add, *Mind your business.*

"Really?" Natasia's eyes were wide with innocence when she turned to Hosea. "You must've forgotten."

"What?" He frowned.

"The edits for the special. They have to be done by three today."

"That's tomorrow."

"Nope, today." She glanced at her watch. "In fact, we're run-ning late."

Jasmine's eyes narrowed. She could see right through this, but when she turned to her husband, she could tell that he didn't share her vision.

"Jasmine . . ." he began, his apology already in his tone.

It's a trick! But aloud, she said, "Baby, you still have to eat." She waved away Natasia with her hand. "We won't be long. Let me feed my husband and he'll get right back to you."

Hosea shook his head. "I can't. We pay by the hour for the editing room and—"

Natasia interrupted, "We really need to get going, Hosea," as if she were not the one intruding.

"You can delay it by an hour, right?" Jasmine asked Hosea.

"I'm sorry," he said. "I really have to take care of this." He paused, and then tossed her a bone. "Maybe we can do this for dinner?"

It was only God who made her act with good sense. "Okay," she said, although she made it clear with her tone and her stance that she was far from fine. She lifted the basket's lid, dumped the food back inside without wrapping up a thing.

"Let me help," Natasia sang.

Jasmine snatched the plate away from her, good sense now gone.

Hosea jumped in front of Jasmine as if he needed to stop whatever she might do next. "I'll be home early."

She didn't get the chance to accept his offering before Natasia said, "We'll probably be working late, Hosea. I need to go over the final budget with you."

His lips just grazed Jasmine's cheek as if he was in a hurry to make a getaway. "I'll call you later."

"Good seeing you again." Natasia waved.

That was more than she could take. Jasmine slammed the top of the basket shut, then stomped from the office. Ten minutes hadn't even passed before she was back in front of Brittney and Jacqueline.

"Seems like Hosea did have a meeting," she said to Brittney.

"I'm really sorry about that. I don't know how I missed it, but I knew something was up when Natasia came by and asked what Hosea was doing behind closed doors. I told her you didn't want to be disturbed, but when she still marched down the hall, I figured it had to be important. I'm sorry," she said again.

I knew it! "That's okay." She took Jacqueline's hand. "Do you want this?"

Brittney's eyes widened as she took the basket from Jasmine. "Thanks!"

As Jasmine rode down in the elevator, she marveled at Natasia's nerve. If she hadn't been the enemy, Natasia may have been a woman to be admired. Natasia had tricks Jasmine hadn't even thought of, and now she had timing on her side. With Brian back in their lives, Hosea could become weak.

Since Natasia had come to New York, Jasmine had feared her, but deep inside, she always knew she'd win. Now with Alexis and Brian in the picture and with Natasia's not-to-be-denied fortitude, Jasmine wasn't so sure anymore who would be the victor.

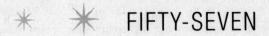# FIFTY-SEVEN

THE VOICE-MAIL MESSAGE CAME ON again. "This is Alexis, you know what to do." Then the beep. Brian hung up. He'd already left a year's worth of messages in seven days.

He stood, slid open the balcony, and stepped outside into the cool of the August night. He took in his $129-a-night, third-floor view of the parking lot filled with Ford Escorts and Chevy Impalas. This was not the kind of place he was used to, but when he'd left their apartment a week ago, he'd had no thoughts on where to go. He'd driven for hours until he circled back to Los Angeles, exhausted and willing to stay in the first place he saw—this motel. The plan had been to be here one night, because surely, after twenty-four hours he'd be home, working through this with Alexis. But this was the seventh day. And without speaking once to Alexis, he had no idea if this exile was ever going to end.

With a sigh, he stepped back inside and tried to keep his mood from matching the gloom of the room. He settled onto the overly firm mattress, closed his eyes, trying to stop the images. But the movie in his mind played, then rewound and played again. The memory of seven days before . . .

When he had walked into that hotel, it had been hard to keep his emotions inside. He'd greeted Jasmine and Hosea and then stared at the little girl. He couldn't help it, couldn't take his eyes away from this child who looked more like him than his sons did. And without hesitation, without explanation, his heart had instantly filled with love. How was he supposed to turn away from this child, his seed forever?

But then he thought of Alexis. His wife and daughter could

never coexist. But he'd hardly had time to ponder a solution before Alexis had barged in. A split second later, Jacqueline was gone.

The rest was a daytime nightmare that he wanted to forget. But he remembered it all—how Alexis had sped from the hotel. How he'd followed her, tossing aside his thoughts about giving her space.

He'd rushed home and breathed with relief when he saw her car parked in front of their condo. But when he stepped into their penthouse, rage met him right at the door. All he could do was stand at the edge of the living room and watch Alexis storm through, throwing items into her suitcase.

"Alexis, sweetheart," he finally whispered. "Please, let's talk."

She marched right by him.

"I want to explain. Jasmine was part of the disease."

She wouldn't even look at him.

"Baby, please. I love you."

She'd paused, for just a moment. Then, without looking, without speaking, she snapped one suitcase shut before she tossed more clothes into another.

Then, a thought came to him—if he left, at least he'd know where she was.

"Alexis, I don't want you to leave. I'll go, if that's what you want."

She stopped. Looked at him for the first time. "You'll leave?"

He nodded.

"That'll be the first decent thing you've done in our marriage." She grabbed her purse. "I'll give you one hour. When I come back, if you're not gone, I will be."

The pictures on the living room wall shook with her anger when she slammed the door.

As he packed, he'd wondered if this was the end, but then decided right there that this was not.

But now, seven days had passed, and she wouldn't take a single call. He didn't want to take this drama to her job. They were both too private—and bougie—for that. And he couldn't confront her at church.

He'd find a way, he was sure. Because giving up was just not in his nature.

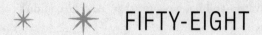 # FIFTY-EIGHT

SEVEN DAYS OF HEARTACHE.

That's how Hosea would describe the last week. Ever since he'd come face to face with Brian.

He'd done his best to hide his emotions at work and especially at home. He made a point to get home as early as he could. Shared as many dinners with Jasmine and Jacqueline as time allowed. Continued to walk and talk as if life was all normal.

But his misery was apparent, especially when he lay with Jasmine at night.

Of course he knew that Jasmine had been with other men before him, just as he hadn't been a virgin when they met. But it was the deceit behind her relationship with Brian that gripped Hosea's heart even after two years.

All he could think about was that she'd been with Brian while they'd been dating. She'd lain in Brian's arms while he had been falling in love with her. She had sex with Brian while he had been trying to honor her with the purest gift he could give—a celibate courtship.

She had poisoned all of that by cheating on him—with Brian.

Now, his head spun with doubts that he hated. Doubts that he tried with all his might to push away. But like a recurring cancer, his fears kept returning. He wondered, had Jasmine and Brian ever stopped? Were they sleeping together even now?

He shook his head. There was no way. She wouldn't lie to him. She wouldn't cheat on him. Not again. Never again.

The knock on the door rescued him and made him come back to

now. But he kept quiet, hoping silence would deter the intruder.

Still, the door opened, and Natasia peeked in. "You busy?"

"No. What's going down?"

"Thought you might be hungry." She held up a picnic basket just like the one Jasmine had brought him last week.

His eyes widened with surprise.

"So, are you hungry?"

Her smile brought him a bit of cheer. "Yeah, I am."

"Good." She stepped inside the office and locked the door. "Let's have some peace—at least for a little while."

He watched as she flung the tablecloth in the air, then spread it on the floor. "You didn't get to have your picnic the other day and it was my fault. So I want to make it up to you."

She spread the fried chicken, potato salad, and biscuits across the cloth. "I brought all your favorites, including this." She held up a carrot cake. "Food cures all wounds."

"I gave up that addiction long ago." He rose from his desk and joined her.

"I know, but this is still comfort food." She added softly, "And I think you need a little comfort."

She filled their plates before Hosea said grace. Then she leaned back against the wall, her stretched-out legs exposed by her rising skirt.

Hosea kept his eyes on his plate. Ate silently.

But after a while, Natasia asked, "What's going on with you?"

The doubts, the fears, the worries filled his mind. "Nothing."

"I know that's not true. Why don't you talk to me?"

He paused. "Let's talk about you for a moment."

"I'd rather talk about us." Then she added quickly, "You'll never guess who called me the other day . . . Chuckie."

Hosea laughed. He hadn't thought about their first landlord in years. "What's he up to?"

"The same. Still buying all those buildings in Chicago. He's gotta be a millionaire by now. You know what he asked me?" Natasia laughed. "How many kids we had."

Hosea stabbed a piece of chicken. Natasia thought that was funny, but he didn't. For days, he'd been wondering what life would have been like if he hadn't listened to God and hadn't left Natasia. What would his world look like without all this drama?

She said, "Chuckie was surprised to find out that we weren't married."

Hosea chewed.

"Everyone says that. Whenever I see people from the old neighborhood, they're shocked to know that we didn't make it."

All he did was nod.

The laughter had gone. Now, solemnly, she said, "We had some good times. Some wonderful times."

Hosea put his plate down. Turned to her. "Yes, we did."

"We were pretty happy, right?"

"We were." His tone matched hers.

She dropped her plate onto the cloth. "Hosea . . . you know I care about you." When he began to shake his head, she added, "I'm not going there. I told you from now on, it's all about our friendship. So, I'm talking as a friend. And as a friend, I'm concerned." She took a deep breath. "I've heard rumors." She paused. "About Jasmine."

He stared at Natasia, his jaw tight. In the past, he would have shut her down right there. Never allowed her—or anyone else—to talk about his wife.

But that was before Brian. That was before his doubts.

His hands squeezed into fists. He asked, "What kind of rumors?" then braced himself for hearing that his wife *was* cheating on him.

"Well, they're not about Jasmine. Not exactly."

His frown deepened.

"They're about your little girl. *Her* little girl." She paused for a moment, lowered her eyes and voice as if she cared. "That baby is not yours, is she?"

Where had she heard that? He spoke softly, "You know what? I'm not hungry anymore."

"Hosea."

He pushed himself from the floor. "You need to leave, Natasia."

"Hosea, I was just asking—"

"And I'm asking you to leave," he snapped.

Her head jerked back at his tone. "Okay." Still sitting, she raised her hands. "I'm sorry. I didn't mean to upset you." She paused and spoke the next words deliberately, "And I want you to know that I'm always here for you. I'm your friend."

"You need to leave," he said, letting her know those words, right now, meant nothing.

She reached to pack up the food, but he said, "Leave that, I'll take care of it."

He stood behind his desk, not looking up, until he heard the door close. His sigh was one of exhaustion when he slumped into his chair. He was tired . . . and pissed. Not that Natasia had done anything so wrong. She was just the messenger delivering the news that people were talking.

He didn't know why this bothered him. It wasn't like this was a huge secret. When he'd left Jasmine after he found out about Jacqueline, the few in his tight circle of family and friends were aware of Jacqueline's paternity. And he'd asked no one to be silent. Especially since as soon as it was time, he planned on telling Jacqueline the truth himself.

But that didn't stop the facts from hurting.

He needed to talk. Talk to someone who could understand all that he was going through. But no one knew his pain.

No one, but Alexis.

He grabbed his cell phone and made the first call.

✳ ✳ FIFTY-NINE

IT HAD TAKEN ALMOST TWO years, but now Jasmine felt just like a wife.

A suspecting wife. Of a cheating husband.

Not that Hosea had done anything to make her believe he'd been unfaithful. But the symptoms were there—the distance that was wedged between them. The way he talked without looking at her, the way she caught him gazing at the walls, staring at nothing, like someone else was on his mind. The way he rolled away from her in bed, at times hanging so close to his edge, she just knew that in the middle of the night she'd hear him fall to the floor.

Still, she was sure he hadn't cheated.

Not yet.

The moment Hosea closed the bathroom door, Jasmine sat up. Leaning against the leather headboard, she waited until she heard the spray of the shower against the porcelain, then she jetted to the closet in search of any signs of Natasia.

After three days, she had this down. First, she scanned the collar of the shirt he'd worn yesterday—no lipstick. She breathed in the scent; only a trace of his cologne was still in the cotton—no perfume. She exhaled.

She searched through his jacket pockets—nothing. Next were his pants. Quickly, she shuffled through the three loose business cards she found. More nothing. She stuffed the cards back into place. And exhaled again.

With a smile, she turned back to the bed. Then stopped. In the last days, she hadn't checked his phone. She paused, made sure that the shower was still running, then grabbed his PDA. Not too many calls, one to her, one to his father. Even the call to 411 didn't make her curiosity rise. It was the number that came after. A 310 area code. And it had been called twice.

She frowned. Surely, this didn't have anything to do with Natasia—unless the call was made to a hotel. Jasmine knew that Natasia was staying in some hotel in the Valley, but maybe she had moved. Maybe she'd found a place in the city where she and Hosea could meet far away from work and Hosea's family.

That is ridiculous, Jasmine told herself. Still, she jotted down the number, then stuffed the paper inside her nightstand drawer just as the shower stopped. Seconds after she slid back between the sheets, Hosea strolled from the bathroom wrapped in just a towel tucked at his waist.

Just looking at his still-damp chest made her forget Natasia. All she wanted to do was rip away the terrycloth and love him until all that was on his mind was her.

She swung her legs over the side of the bed. "Babe," she began softly in that voice that told him what she wanted.

But he shook his head. "I have an early meeting." Then he ducked into their walk-in closet.

She slid lower in the bed. There was a time when all she had to do was be awake and he wanted her. But now, she couldn't remember the last time they'd shared their bed that way.

She waited until he came out of the closet, dressed, before she asked, "Will you be home for dinner? I was hoping . . ."

He looked at her. "I'm sorry, Jasmine," he said, with sorrow in his voice. "I'm not sure, but I may have a meeting. A dinner meeting."

"Oh."

"I'll call and let you know."

Thoughts raced through her mind like a runaway train. The number. Was probably to a hotel. Natasia's hotel. They hadn't yet made their plans for tonight.

"Got anything planned for today?" he asked.

Just following you. "Nope. I'm going to take Jacquie to the park and then I'm going to check in with Malik. See how things are going at the club."

"Good." He grabbed his cell phone, kissed her forehead. "See you tonight," and then he left their room.

After she heard the door to the suite close, she waited a minute before she grabbed the phone and dialed the number. She was going to get the name of the hotel, find out Natasia's room, and then bust them both when they arrived tonight.

Three rings and then a voice-mail recording, "You've reached Ward and Associates. No one is available—"

She didn't need to hear anymore.

Jasmine's heart was pushing through her chest when she hung up. Ward and Associates. That was the name of Alexis's company.

Hosea had been calling Alexis.

This had nothing to do with Natasia.

Shaking, she laid back on the bed. She and Alexis had hated each other for a long time. And the way Alexis had looked at her when they were in the bathroom, Jasmine knew that loathing had deepened.

Was this payback? Was Alexis secretly meeting Hosea? Was that the meeting he had tonight?

Jasmine stood, paced the bedroom. She'd first found Brian so attractive because he was Alexis's husband. And now, Hosea was just as attractive to Alexis because he was married to her.

She snatched her cell, scrolled through the numbers, then dialed. Another voice-mail recording, but this time, she left a message. "Brian," she spoke through clenched teeth, "this is Jasmine. I need to see you this morning no matter what. If you want to stay married to your precious wife, you'd better call me!"

She slammed the phone down. She needed to get dressed, get

Jacqueline ready, see if Mae Frances could watch her while she took care of this business.

But the pounding in her head and in her chest made Jasmine lie back down. She just needed a moment to recover from the drama. She closed her eyes and tried to push away the stirring inside that told her that this drama was just getting started.

✳ ✳ SIXTY

ALEXIS SHUT HER OFFICE DOOR, glanced at the message, and dialed the number.

After they exchanged hellos, Hosea said, "I was hoping you'd call me back."

"Honestly, I was curious. I was surprised to get your message yesterday."

"I hope you don't mind my calling."

"I'm actually glad you did."

Then they shared a strangers' silence. Awkward. As if neither knew what to say next.

Hosea jumped in first. "I wanted to check on you. Make sure that you're okay."

"Would you like to get together?" she blurted out, then wondered if he was as surprised as she was by her invitation. "There are a few things . . . I just want to know . . ."

"Sure."

She smiled when she heard his smile. The wall between the strangers came tumbling down.

He said, "Got any plans tonight?"

"I do now."

"What about meeting at one of my favorite restaurants. Ever heard of Heroes?"

She paused. His favorite restaurant was hers. She remembered all the times Brian had taken her there—for birthdays, anniversaries, so many wonderful celebrations.

And tonight was certain to be a special occasion. She was

having dinner with the man who had the sad fortune of being married to Jasmine Larson.

"Heroes will be great," she said.

They made plans to meet at eight, and Alexis hung up feeling better than she had in a week.

SIXTY-ONE

JASMINE'S HANDS TOUCHED THE GOLDEN bar across the smoked-glass door of the Wellness Center. It was hard not to think about the last time she'd entered this building.

She didn't exactly remember how many years ago it had been, but she did remember her mission then. To become Dr. Jefferson Blake's wife. The only problem was he was already married. To Kyla, her best friend for over thirty years.

She shuddered. *What was I thinking?* Swinging the door open, she put those thoughts and that past behind her.

Good thing she'd been changed.

At the welcome desk, the receptionist asked her name and when she told her, the woman popped up from her seat. "Mrs. Bush," she spoke quickly. "Dr. Lewis asked me to walk you back to his office right away."

Jasmine smirked as she trailed behind her escort down the long hall. If he could have, she was sure that Brian would have met her in the alley behind the clinic at midnight. As it was, he was not happy about this meeting.

"What can I do for you, Jasmine?" he had asked when he called her back less than ten minutes after she'd left the message.

"I need to see you."

"For what?"

"So that we can talk about my husband and your wife. They're seeing each other."

He had paused. "No they're not."

"Yes, they are. Look, I'm not going to discuss this on the phone."

It had taken some time, but Brian finally agreed to meet.

"Not in public," he demanded.

At first, she'd been insulted. But then, she'd calmed, knowing Brian was right. Their last public meeting didn't fare well and neither one of them wanted Alexis—or Hosea—barging in on them.

So when he'd suggested the clinic, she'd asked, "What about Jefferson?"

"He's out of the office this afternoon. No one here knows you."

The receptionist tapped on the door once, then stepped aside.

Behind the desk, Brian stood, and Jasmine took a quick breath. The last time she'd seen him, she'd been standing in the middle of her family. And he'd been the enemy.

But now as she heard the door close behind her, Brian didn't look like the adversary she remembered. He looked like the man who—with his hands, and lips, and all his other parts—had given her bouts of pleasure that she could not deny.

She blinked those memories away. Because with that pleasure came pain.

Why am I thinking about him like that anyway? She despised this man.

She said, "We have a problem," with as much attitude as she could muster.

"Hello to you, too, Jasmine," he said, taking a seat behind his desk.

"There's no need to be nice, Brian." She sat across from him. "If you don't believe we have a problem, all you have to do is remember the way Hosea and Alexis looked at each other the day she found out . . ."

If she hadn't been so afraid of losing her husband, Jasmine would have been pleased with the shadow of doom that cast over Brian's face as he pushed himself from his desk and ambled toward the window. But she found no joy in his sorrow. His pain was hers too.

Still, she gave him no time to recover. "I found Alexis's number in Hosea's phone."

"That doesn't mean a thing," he said without looking at her.

"He's called her twice. Yesterday."

She couldn't see his face, but she could almost feel the heat rising beneath his skin.

She said, "So what are we going to do about this?"

He shrugged. "What can we do?"

Jasmine rolled her eyes. She could not believe he wasn't ready with a battle plan to win this war. She marched to where he stood. "You need to talk to your wife," she demanded. "Keep her away from my husband."

He faced her, but at first, he said nothing. His eyes wandered over her for seconds and now it was heat that rose beneath *her* skin.

She took a deep breath, tried to calm and cool herself. Tried not to pay a bit of attention to how the air-conditioned office had warmed.

Finally, he said, "What am I supposed to do? Alexis is a grown woman."

His tone sounded as if he'd given up. But Jasmine had no intention of being denied. "You can't control your wife?" she taunted him.

He stepped closer to her, fought back. "No more than you can control your husband."

"Look, Brian," she said, holding her place, not caring that only inches of hot air were between them. "Both Alexis and Hosea feel betrayed. And that makes them vulnerable. If we don't do something, a week from now, you'll be singing, 'She used to be my girl.'"

He glared at her. "This is your fault."

She reared back. "My fault?" Crossed her arms. "You must've forgotten." Her neck moved with each word. "All those times that you came after me? You should have just left me alone!"

He said, "And you shouldn't have gotten pregnant," with as much anger as she had.

She laughed, with no humor. "Both of us were there, Brian. You need to step back and remember."

Silence.

And in the passing seconds, they both remembered.

Jasmine was not sure what happened next. She wasn't sure if he had leaned into her. Or if she had fallen into his arms.

But their lips met. And then, their tongues. And then, their hands. Touching, fondling, stroking like all those times before that had brought them now to this place of trouble.

Jasmine could barely breathe, could hardly think. Could not push away.

She wanted more.

And Brian held her like he wanted the same.

His hands moved to the straps on her sundress, slipping them from her shoulder. Then, his tongue followed.

She moaned, and held him tighter.

Then . . . a sound. But not from him.

A knock. Then another.

And the door slowly opened.

Brian jumped two feet away from Jasmine. But not in time.

"Brian, I was just checking on—"

Kyla stopped. Stared at Jasmine. Then turned her glare to Brian. Her eyes were flashing with fury when she turned back to Jasmine. "What are you doing here?"

Jasmine's head was pounding hard, just like her heart. But as if nothing was going on, she said, "Hey, Kyla," because she couldn't think of anything else to say to the woman whose husband she'd tried to seduce into more than a one-night affair. To the woman who was once a best friend, but now was an enemy.

Jasmine straightened her dress, then grabbed her purse. She

turned to Brian. Her plan had been to give him a last warning— about her husband and his wife. But when she looked at him, all she could see were his lips.

With the back of her hand, she wiped away his taste from her mouth, brushed past Kyla, and without a good-bye, dashed from the room.

SIXTY-TWO

"BRIAN! WHAT WERE YOU DOING!" Kyla demanded to know.

He held up his hands. "It's not what you think."

She snatched a tissue from her purse, waved it in the air. "You need to wipe Jasmine's lipstick from your mouth." She tossed the tissue and it floated toward his desk. "And then tell me that nothing happened."

He picked up the tissue, wiped the ginger-berry gloss from his lips, and sank into his chair. He held his head in his hands.

"Brian," she said softly. "What are you doing with Jasmine?"

He couldn't look up. Couldn't stand to see the tears he heard in her voice that matched the ones in his heart.

She said, "I thought you were trying to work things out with Alex."

"I am." It took strength and courage to raise his head. "Kyla, please. I'm telling you. I love Alexis. There's nothing . . . going on with me and Jasmine."

"That's not the way it looked to me."

"*She* kissed *me*," he said, wanting to believe that. "I was pushing her away when you walked in."

Kyla folded her arms, twisted her lips.

He continued his defense, "I was so shocked I just stood there for a moment. But then I pushed her away. I was just asking her what that was about when you came in."

She stared him down.

"You've got to believe me."

"It's hard to do that with what I saw."

"But I'm telling the truth. It was Jasmine—she came on to me."

He could tell that she was considering his words. She had to—all she had to do was remember how Jasmine had trapped her husband, and she would know that the same had just happened to him.

"What was she doing here?" she asked.

He swallowed. "I . . . don't know. She said something about Alexis and Hosea getting together, getting hooked up."

"What!"

"That's what I said. I think it was just a trick to come to the office." He paused. "Kyla, you've got to believe me."

Seconds passed, then slowly, she nodded.

He took a deep breath. "I know this is a lot to ask, but . . . please don't say anything to Alexis."

She crossed her arms. "I can't make that promise. She's my friend."

"I know," he said quickly. "But I really want to work things out and if you tell her this . . . there'll be no chance."

She took a deep breath. Stood silently, contemplating.

And Brian prayed. Prayed that she wouldn't tell Alexis, but prayed even harder that God could make him understand what had just happened. He didn't even like Jasmine.

That woman is the devil.

He couldn't believe she had leaned into him. Put her arms around him like that. Pressed her lips into his.

At least that's the way he remembered it.

"Kyla, please," he begged again.

She exhaled a long breath. "I won't say anything to Alexis,"

Now he breathed, but she only gave him a short reprieve.

"But if you hurt her, Brian—"

"I won't. I'm telling you, I love her."

She nodded. "I don't know why, but I believe you."

"Thank you."

"No need for thanks. You get only this one shot from me." She leaned over his desk. Glared at him, said, "If I ever see you with Jasmine again and Alexis doesn't know about it, I'll make sure your marriage is over."

Brian pushed back in his chair a bit. This was not the Kyla he'd come to know over the years. Kyla Blake was always the gentle, kind, too nice, too sweet woman who loved everyone.

But there was no kind of love in her eyes right now. Instead, her gaze burned right through him with her rage, with her threat.

He swallowed, sufficiently admonished. "I won't see Jasmine again."

She stepped back. Nodded. Her point made. "I'm going to buy a little insurance."

He frowned. "What does that mean?"

She swung her purse over her shoulder. "I'm going to make sure that Jasmine stays away and in the process, it might just be time for a little payback."

She was gone before he could ask her anything more. Not that he wanted to know. At that moment, all he wanted to do was stay far away from Kyla Blake.

SIXTY-THREE

Hosea was such a gentleman.

That was Alexis's thought as he stood when she was led to their table. He held her chair, waited for her to sit.

A gentleman.

Just like Brian.

She shoved Brian out of her thoughts. He didn't belong there. Instead, she smiled at Hosea as if he were her new best friend. "Thanks for meeting me."

"No problem," he said, taking the menu from the hostess. "Have you been here before?"

She pushed those before times from her mind. "Yeah." She glanced at the menu that she already knew by heart. "I'm not really hungry. I think I'm just gonna have a glass of wine."

"Not on an empty stomach." Hosea gave their waiter the order for appetizers—the Blackened Shrimp Cocktail and Filet Mignon Carpaccio. Then ordered a Coke for himself and wine for Alexis.

When the waiter left them alone, she said, "Can we get right to this, or do we have to go through all the niceties?"

He laughed. "This is your party. Whatever, however."

She inhaled, ready to let loose a stream of questions. But she asked only, "How did you stay with Jasmine after you found out about their affair?"

He sat back, crossed his legs. "It happened before we were married," he said, just stating the fact. "We weren't even engaged."

"But the baby—"

She recognized the pain that wrinkled his face. She had a matching ache in her heart.

"At first, I thought she was mine. But Jasmine told me the truth—"

"*She* told you the truth? What did you do? Hold a gun to her head?"

He shook his head a little like he didn't approve of her words. "She told me that you two weren't big friends."

"More like big enemies. Especially now." The waiter had barely placed the food and her glass in front of her before Alexis took a sip. Then another. And another.

Hosea slipped a shrimp onto his fork, but she pushed her own plate aside. Pulled her wine closer. "So," she began, "the baby didn't make you freak out?"

He nodded as he chewed. "At first, I did. We'd been married for six months when I found out and left. I tried to get our marriage annulled right then. But God got in the way. He got all in my head, and the whole time I was away, He let me know that I was messing up His program. He badgered me until I went back to my wife." He shrugged. "Since then, we've been making it work."

"So, you just thought about God, and now you're over it?"

She could see his pain rise again. "Far from it. Don't know if I've gotten over it or if I'll ever learn to live with it. It's hard at times, but all I have to do is look at Jacquie—"

"That's her name?"

"Yes," he said with pride. "Jacqueline, the best thing in my life." He paused, and then an afterthought, "Along with my wife."

She squinted, trying to see him better. "I don't know how you still love Jasmine."

"It's a love that comes from God." He looked as if he was thinking about his own words. "You and Brian . . . how are you doing with this?"

"Can you spell divorce?" She emptied the wine that remained in her glass, then motioned to the waiter for another.

He said, "I'm sorry to hear that. That's where God's leading you?"

She shrugged. "I haven't spent a lot of time talking to Him about this. Guess you can say I'm kinda pissed off He let this happen."

"Can't blame God for our mistakes, but I know how you feel. Believe me, I was in the same place." Hosea sat back as if he needed a moment of thought. As if he wondered if he was still in that place. "Look, I'm not a fan of your husband," he started again, "but if God put you and Brian together, you've got to find a way to work it out. No man, no woman, no situation, no circumstance . . . not even a child should tear you apart, if it's about God."

Alexis peered at him closer. Wondered if this man was for real.

She'd always been so skeptical about men. Yes, Kyla had Jefferson, but even he—the good doctor, loving husband, doting father, man of God—had cheated. There was her father and his hobby—cheating. And the men she dated from her teens to her thirties. All cheaters. A good man—that was an oxymoron.

Then she met Brian.

Her knight had been married before, had fathered two sons. So if not even children could keep him and his wife together, then something had gone wrong. He'd said irreconcilable differences. She'd wondered if that was code for "I cheated." But he'd convinced her that he was the man God had chosen for her. And if that was the case, surely he could be trusted. For five years, that fantasy had been her truth.

But for five years he'd cheated on her over and over in the name of addiction. Made her know for sure that there were no good men.

Except for this one who sat across from her. Hosea Bush, who talked about God and forgiveness even in the midst of this madness.

She took a sip from her fresh glass and wondered if Hosea had ever cheated. If he had ever thought about cheating. Wished that he had. Wished that Jasmine could feel the kind of hurt that she wreaked on the rest of the world.

"Jasmine doesn't deserve you," she said when she finally put her wine glass down.

"There are lots of things I don't deserve, but I thank God for His grace and even more so, for His mercy. Remember that, and you and your husband will have a starting point."

She smiled, but inside she was shaking her head. That part of her life was over. She was just here, just talking, because she was curious.

"Tell me about Jacqueline."

His smile erased all of his pain. "She's a wonderful child. Has this great personality. Very inquisitive. Wants to know about the world. I'm sure she's going to be the one to find a cure for cancer and AIDS. And after she finishes with that, she'll be the first black female president, right before she flies for NASA and leads a space station on the moon."

Alexis laughed. "She's that special, huh?"

He nodded, but then his smile went away. "I know this is hard, Alexis, but remember that in the middle of this, God created a bright life. God has to have a reason. I can't believe that Jacqueline's here to tear you and Brian apart."

Alexis sighed. "I don't know how Jasmine does it. She always gets the perfect man."

"I'm sure she dated some duds."

"Doesn't matter who she's dated. All that matters is who she married. And when it comes to getting the ring, she's two for two for the good guys. Two great men married her."

Hosea frowned. "Two great men?"

"Yeah." Alexis chuckled. "What did she tell you about Kenny? Did she say that her first husband was a dud?"

Hosea grabbed his glass, took a sip, then returned the soda to the table. Spoke slowly, softly, "She doesn't talk much about her . . . first husband."

"I don't know why. Kenny was as great as you seem to be." She sipped more wine. "But I guess it's never a good idea to talk about the ex with the next, huh?"

"That's what Jasmine says." Hosea rested his arms on the table. "But I've always been a bit curious . . . about Kenny. How long were they married?"

Alexis squinted, trying to recall. "I can't remember, exactly." She took another sip of wine. "Ten, no, more like fifteen years."

"Why did they divorce?"

She drank more wine. "I don't know, but I'm sure it was her fault." She took another sip. "She never told you any of this?"

"Yeah, yeah, she did. But I like to get different perspectives."

"I don't like your wife, but I could learn something from her on how to marry a good man."

Hosea leaned back from the table and Alexis paused, peered at him through foggy eyes.

"I'm sorry," she apologized. "Seems like I upset you."

"Not at all."

"Guess I shouldn't be talking about your wife this way."

"You have no idea how glad I am that we had this talk."

She finished the rest of her wine, then stared at the bottom of her empty glass. "Maybe I should have another one."

"Maybe you shouldn't."

She looked up. Studied him for passing seconds. "Maybe you should come home with me."

It was his turn to let seconds go by. Without a bit of judgment, he said, "Maybe I shouldn't."

She shrugged. "Can't fault a girl for trying. I don't want you to get the wrong impression, though. I don't usually invite men home with me."

His face was soft with compassion. "I know that."

"No, you don't. You don't know me. But I just thought after spending a night with you, I might be able to do a little of that forgiving you're talking about."

He smiled, said nothing.

"And maybe we could have a baby of our own." She leaned back and laughed, a bit loudly. "That would fix 'em, huh?" But just as quickly, her sadness returned. "Brian and I never had any children."

"Do you want to talk about that?"

She shrugged. "No. Yes." She sighed. "Brian already has two sons that he hardly ever sees. He said he didn't want any more children. Said he wanted to focus all his love on me." She laughed some more, sadly. "That sounded great at the time, 'cause all I wanted to think about was my husband and my business." She stopped. Sounded now like she wanted to cry. "Guess my business is all I have now."

Hosea motioned for the waiter. "I think it's time for us to go." He paid the bill, then asked the waiter to call for a cab for Alexis.

"No," she protested. "I'm fine."

"You're not driving."

Alexis closed her eyes. There he was, doing that good man thing again. She thought about asking him to go home with her once more. Maybe he'd changed his mind.

"You can pick up your car in the morning," he said, helping her rise from the table. "If you need a ride back here, call me."

At the front, they stood side by side, silently waiting until the taxi rolled up. Before she slipped inside, she hugged him. Held him tight. And long. "I don't know how I'm going to get through this." Her reddened eyes watered with those words. "I don't think I can."

"You can," he whispered, his lips close to her ears. "I'll be praying for you. And that's what you need to do. Take this all to God."

She sniffed, then crawled into the cab. She gave the driver her address, then stared at Hosea through the window, wishing even more now that he'd gone home with her tonight.

Keep hope alive! That was Alexis's thought when her cell phone rang the moment the cab turned the corner. Maybe Hosea had changed his mind.

But as soon as she glanced at the screen, that hope deflated like a busted tire.

"Hey, girl," she sighed.

"Dang!" Kyla exclaimed. "Don't sound so happy to hear from me."

"I'm sorry. I'm just tired."

"You sound it. Where are you?"

"In a cab. On my way home. From dinner with Hosea Bush."

"Really," Kyla said, her voice filled with surprise. "What—"

Before Kyla could ask any more, Alexis said, "And I even asked him to come home with me." She lowered her voice. "And I wasn't talking about having tea."

"What?" Then Kyla sighed. "Okay, how much wine did you have?"

"It wasn't just the wine," Alexis said, before she told Kyla about their talk through the dinner. "He's such a nice guy, Ky. He really cared about how I was feeling and wanted to help me get through this. I don't know how he ended up with Jasmine."

A moment and then, "Alex, do you have Hosea's number?"

Alexis frowned. "Why? Don't tell me you want to ask him to dinner and then get him to go home with you?" She giggled.

"No . . ."

It was Kyla's tone—suddenly too serious—that sobered Alexis. Made her frown deepen. "What's up, Kyla?"

"I want to . . . look, just give me the number and trust me."

With a sigh, Alexis pulled the message slip she'd kept from her purse. "Everyone's asking for trust from me these days."

"Well, if you're talking about your husband, you and Brian will have to work that out. But me? I'm your best friend. Trust is automatic."

"Yeah, and remember when you trusted Jasmine?" Not a second passed before Alexis wished that she had just swallowed those words. "I'm sorry, Ky."

Time passed. "You're forgiven. I'll just say that it was the wine, not you."

Alexis gave Kyla the number, then clicked off just as the cab stopped in front of her condo. She tossed a twenty into the driver's hand and didn't wait for the change. She didn't care about that. All she wanted to do was get into bed. The problem was, she'd be doing it alone again. And tonight, that wasn't the way she wanted it.

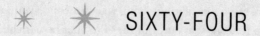# SIXTY-FOUR

HOSEA DIDN'T KNOW WHAT he was.

Hurt. Angry. Shocked.

His wife had been married before! For fifteen years. And when he did the math in his head—the years, her age, there was a lot that didn't add up.

As he swerved through the streets, Hosea tried to recall every conversation they'd had about their pasts. Tried to remember just how many times she said that she'd never been married, how many times she'd lied about her age.

When they met, he'd taken her out for what she said was her thirty-fifth. Maybe she wasn't lying. It was possible. She could have been married at nineteen, eighteen, seventeen, sixteen . . .

He doubted it.

His wife was a bona fide, straight-up liar.

But why? Why would she deny a first husband? Unless she was still married. Maybe she was a bigamist and he was part of her crime. Maybe she lied about her age to hide her identity. Maybe she was running from the law.

Maybe she wasn't even Jasmine Larson Bush.

But no, he'd met her sister, Serena. And knew her godbrother, Malik.

Seemed like all of them had kept the truth from him.

Who are you, Jasmine?

He swung into the circular driveway of the Fairmont Hotel, ready to demand answers. Tonight, Jasmine was going to tell him the truth.

He swung the car door open, jumped out, and his cell phone rang. He growled; he didn't want to talk to anyone—except for his wife.

But the 310 area code made him pause. Maybe it was Alexis. He flipped the cell open. "This is Hosea," he answered as he tossed the keys to the valet.

"Mr. Bush, you don't know me," he heard a woman say as he stomped across the lobby. "My name is Kyla Blake. I'm a friend of Alexis and Brian Lewis."

Hosea stopped moving. Had something happened to Alexis? He knew he should have taken her home himself.

"This is odd for me," Kyla continued, "but I'm calling out of concern—"

"Is Alexis all right?"

"Yes, well, no, actually, that's why I'm calling. Alexis and Brian are having challenges."

Why is this woman calling me? "Ms. Blake, I'm not friends with Alexis or Brian," he said, unable to keep the impatience out of his voice. He moved again, marched toward the elevators. "I don't even know them, not really."

"But you know your wife."

He paused, held the elevator open with his hand.

She said, "Alexis and Brian will never be able to save their marriage if Jasmine doesn't stay away from Brian."

Hang up now. That was the voice he heard, but he pressed the phone closer to his ear. "My wife hasn't had a thing to do with Brian."

"If that's what she's told you, then she's lying, because I walked in on her and Brian today."

His heart beat slowed. "Today?"

"Yes, and I don't know what was going on, but let's just say, I'm happy I got to his office when I did."

Now his heart stopped.

"I'm not trying to start any trouble, Mr. Bush. Just trying to help my friends make it through a tough time, and it won't happen if *Jasmine* keeps hanging around."

The way she said his wife's name—like it was a brand of poison—made him frown.

"Mr. Bush?"

"Yes. Thank you," was all he said before he hung up.

He backed away from the elevator and sank into the deep pillows of one of the sofas in the lobby.

Jasmine was seeing Brian. Just like he thought.

Even though he'd had those doubts for days, he wanted to believe that he was wrong. That Jasmine could be trusted. But how could a liar be trusted?

He shook his head. Chuckled, because he refused to be a punk and cry. Slowly, he pushed himself up and staggered back across the lobby toward the front door.

He'd been such a fool.

Exhausted, Hosea edged his car to the curb. He'd been driving through the unfamiliar streets for hours, and now he was just too tired to continue. Too tired to even think about this anymore. There were too many secrets, too many lies.

He was so hurt.

He needed someone to talk to. Someone who would just listen.

He was so angry.

But who could he call? It was too late to reach his father. And Triage—though that was his boy, he didn't know him like that.

He'd spent so much of his time over the last year focused on his family and work. Now, he had no one to confide in.

He was so shocked.

There was Alexis. But she'd left in such bad shape. Could she handle hearing this news tonight?

He revved up the engine and then snaked his SUV through the streets.

He knew just the place to go.

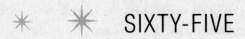# SIXTY-FIVE

THERE WAS THE GUN. THE barrel pressed hard against her temple. Jasmine couldn't move, even as Hosea screamed that he wanted her out of his house.

The gun cocked. And then the blast.

Jasmine bolted up in bed like she always did at that moment in her dream.

It took a minute before her heart slowed to its regular beat. For once, she knew why this dream had come.

Because of Brian.

She still couldn't believe that it had happened. She didn't even like Brian, so what was that kiss all about?

That man is the devil, she thought as she replayed the moment in her mind when Brian leaned into her. She had tried to pull away. But he held her and pressed his lips against hers.

At least, that's the way she remembered it.

Closing her eyes, she squeezed away that memory. She needed Hosea and his arms right now. She reached across the sheets. Felt nothing. Then, patted his side of the bed as her eyes adjusted to the darkness.

Her husband was not there.

She jumped up. Checked the bathroom. Then the living room. And Jacqueline's room.

A quick glance at the clock. It was after three. Her heart raced.

She dialed his cell phone. It went straight to voice mail.

"Hosea, where are you?" she cried. That was her message.

She hung up. Called again. And again.

Left more messages. Again. And again.

Where is he? She paced. Tried to think of the last time they'd talked. He'd called to tell her that he was having that dinner meeting he'd mentioned this morning.

"Sorry, Jasmine, I can't get out of it," he'd said. "But I shouldn't be too late."

She had wanted to demand that he tell her who was going to be at that meeting.

But all she'd said was, "All right," because not enough hours had passed between Hosea's call and Brian's kiss. And she wasn't ready to talk to her husband. Didn't want him to hear anything in her voice.

So she'd just hung up, and then prayed that God would put back together what seemed to be falling apart.

Where are you, Hosea?

Surely, he wasn't still with Alexis. It couldn't have been that easy for Alexis to get Hosea into bed. But why not? It had only taken her one chance meeting at de Janeiro when she was in L.A. for a business meeting to get Brian. Barely an hour after she ran into him, they were back in her hotel room, messing up the sheets. It had been quite easy to get Alexis's husband.

She shook her head. Hosea wasn't like Brian.

So where was he?

Maybe he was stranded. Hurt on some abandoned road. She needed to call the police.

She grabbed the phone, but then her mind told her to dial another number first.

"Brittney." She tried not to sound frantic when Hosea's groggy assistant answered. "I'm so sorry to wake you, but do you know who Hosea was meeting with tonight?"

"I'm not exactly sure. He had a dinner meeting. Maybe it was with Natasia. They walked out of the office together."

Natasia!

Her intuition had been right. This wasn't about Alexis. This was Natasia.

She hung up and slipped into her bathrobe, then tiptoed into Jacqueline's room. Her daughter slept the way she lived, with a smile. She kissed her cheek before she returned to the living room.

In the old days, Jasmine would have been in the streets tracking her husband down. And she would have done that tonight, would have wrapped Jacqueline up and strapped her into her car seat. But she didn't know where to find Hosea and Natasia.

She shouldn't have banned Natasia from staying at the Fairmont. She should have been smart enough to keep her enemy close.

Grabbing a blanket from the closet, Jasmine turned the over-sized chair to face the front door, then she settled into the cushions. She would just sit and wait. Wait for her husband to come home.

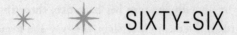# SIXTY-SIX

I<small>T HAD BECOME HIS HABIT.</small>

Brian rolled over, picked up the phone, and dialed the number. It would be his first call of the day. Always around six o'clock. By the time night came, he would have made at least a dozen more calls to her.

The phone on the other end rang. This was the point where he began to count. But not today. Instead, as the phone rang, he prayed that Kyla had kept her word about Jasmine.

He could hardly sleep last night, thinking about that kiss. But he'd given up searching for a reason. It didn't matter. It was a mistake. It would never happen again.

On the third ring, Brian sighed. After the next one, the machine would pick up and he would leave the same message he left every day, "Alexis, I love you. Please call me."

But today, on the third ring, she answered, "Brian?"

She was groggy, but just the sound of her made him sit up straight in the bed.

"Alexis." He didn't have any other words prepared. "How are you?" was all he could think to say.

"Fine." Her voice was thick with sleep. "I need to talk to you."

He searched her tone for any sign that Kyla had betrayed him.

"Do you have time to see me?" she asked.

There was no anger, no hostility. "Definitely." He jumped from the bed and calculated how fast he could get dressed and get home.

She said, "Can we meet for lunch?"

"I can come over right now." Plans were already in his head. He had a consultation this morning, but someone would have to cover him. And Dr. Perkins—she would understand when he told her why he had to cancel their session.

"No, lunch would be better for me," she said, stopping his roll.

"Okay." His thoughts turned to making this more than a lunch. "I'll pick up something and bring it to you."

"No, not here."

"Okay." Plan B—take her to her favorite place. "Let's meet at Heroes."

She paused. "Let's meet at Pink's."

"All right." It wasn't as good as he wanted, but Pink's wasn't bad. Another one of their favorite places to just hang out. "Is noon good?" He'd really wanted to ask her to meet him in an hour or two, but he didn't think she'd agree to an eight o'clock lunch.

"Make it two."

Two was too late. He needed to see her now. But he agreed and hung up without saying all the other things on his mind. Like how much he loved her, missed her, wanted to come home.

He'd save those words for later.

He couldn't stop grinning. He could feel it. By the end of this day, he'd be back home with his wife.

SIXTY-SEVEN

JASMINE'S EYES FLUTTERED open. A moment. Then she jumped from the chair. Ran into her bedroom.

At the door, she stood motionless. Stared at the bed that was the way she'd left it. Sheets tossed, pillows thrown.

Not a single sign that Hosea had come home.

She crumbled to the floor. He had spent the entire night away. With Natasia.

It wasn't until she heard her little girl's cries that Jasmine pushed herself up.

"What's wrong, baby?" she said as she rushed to her daughter.

Jacqueline stood in her bed, her arms raised in the air. "Mama," she cried.

"What's wrong, baby?" She held her before she lowered herself into the rocking chair. Resting Jacqueline's head on her chest, she rocked back and forth, trying to bring comfort to them both.

But together, they cried.

"Ssshhh," Jasmine continued, even though her own tears kept coming. "It's going to be okay," she whispered again and again to her little girl and herself.

Soon, Jacqueline's sobs subsided, and she slept, nestled in her mother's arms. Still, Jasmine rocked, held her daughter, trying to find reassurance in the normalcy of this act. But she couldn't stop crying.

Her mind was whirling with just a single thought—Hosea had spent the night with another woman. Without a call, without discussion, without explanation, he'd walked away from his family.

No! She wasn't going out like this. She wasn't going to just hand Hosea over. Her marriage could be saved—just like before. And she was ready to go to battle with every bit of life within her.

She laid Jacqueline back in the bed and wiped away her own tears.

It was time to fight.

Jasmine slowed her steps as she approached the studio. Calmed herself, then opened the door.

"Hey, Brittney," she said with a smile.

Brittney looked up, yawned. "Hey."

Jasmine began, "I'm sorry about that call last night or rather, this morning." She forced a chuckle. "Hosea and I got our wires crossed. He told me he was going to have a late night with some friends who came in from New York and I forgot."

"That's cool. I was worried at first, but when you didn't call back, I figured he was okay."

"I'm just gonna go back there—"

Brittney frowned. "Hosea's not in," she said, as if Jasmine should know.

Jasmine took a deep breath. Kept her smile. "He's not?"

"No. Natasia called about an hour ago and canceled all appointments for today, for both of them."

Jasmine didn't know how she kept standing, kept breathing, kept talking. Until that moment, she'd still held hope that her suspicions were wrong. "Oh, I forgot," she lied. "They had a . . . I'll just call him on his cell."

She turned toward the doors, her steps unsteady. She was going to find them. Find them and kill her.

"Brittney." She turned back, hoping that she wasn't showing any signs of the heart attack she was having. "Did Hosea tell you that we wanted to send flowers to Natasia?"

"No, but I'll send them. What's the occasion?"

"I'll do it. I have a couple of other gifts I need to send. Where's Natasia staying?"

"She's at the Rendezvous, room fourteen eleven. It's not far from your hotel."

Jasmine walked toward the elevator, marching to the battle cry in her head. Inside her car, it took a moment for her shaking hands to fit the key into the ignition. She pushed the car into drive and heard Mae Frances's voice in her head.

"Don't do anything that could get you in any kind of trouble, Jasmine Larson," Mae Frances had said when she'd come over to the suite to baby sit Jacqueline. Jasmine had filled her in on Hosea's night out with Natasia. "I can make a couple of calls and bring in one of my connections to handle that kind of thing."

Jasmine had turned her down then and was really happy about that now. She wanted to handle this personally.

She punched the accelerator and aimed her car toward the Rendezvous.

SIXTY-EIGHT

HIS BACK ACHED.

Hosea stretched, but there wasn't enough room. His eyes blinked opened and he wondered where he was.

"Hey, you." Natasia sauntered around the sofa, the hem of the short robe she wore fluttered high around her hips. Handing him a coffee mug, she said, "I thought you'd want some of this when you woke up," and she tossed the blanket that covered him onto the floor before she slid next to him on the couch.

"Thanks." Hosea took a quick sip, and tried not to stare at Natasia. But his eyes didn't oblige.

She leaned back and her robe spread open, revealing the barely there black teddy underneath.

He forced his eyes away. "Thanks for letting me crash here."

"Not a problem. I'll always be here for you, Hosea."

He glanced at her once more. Swallowed hard as he watched her chest swell with each breath. "You can go and . . . get dressed or something . . . if you want."

She looked straight at him. "I don't want." Leaned back, exposed more. "I'm fine."

He sipped more coffee and wondered if he needed something cooler.

Last night, when he banged on her door, she had been wearing a floor-length bathrobe. He took another quick peek and wondered why she'd changed. Then he wondered why he was being so stupid. He needed to get out of there.

"What time is it?" he asked, putting the cup down.

"A bit after eleven."

He stretched. "I can't believe I slept this late."

"Well, it was after four when you got here."

He remembered that. And everything else. Every bit of yesterday had stayed with him as he tried to sleep. He couldn't rid his mind of Jasmine and her lies. Of Jasmine and her affair with Brian. "I need to get . . . to the studio," he said, thinking that he really wanted to go home. But to what?

She touched his arm. "You have plenty of time. I called Brittney. Everything's covered."

He felt a bit relieved. Going into the office wasn't what he wanted to do right now—his bones still ached with fatigue. With hurt, and anger, and shock. Still, he couldn't stay here.

"So do you want to tell me what's going on?"

He had walked into this hotel with every intention of talking to Natasia. But the moment she'd opened the door, her inquiring eyes plagued him with guilt. Made him wonder what he was really doing here with a woman he once loved.

"I . . . just need a place to crash. Just for tonight . . . the rest of tonight," was what he'd said.

There was not one moment of hesitation. She opened the door wide and invited him in—and into her bed.

"No." He'd shaken his head when she tried to lead him that way. "I'll take the couch. If that's a problem, I'll just—"

"Not a problem," she'd said quickly. "I just wanted you to be comfortable. But if you're fine with the couch, I'll get a couple of blankets."

He'd taken off his shoes and leaned back. Thought about all that Alexis had said, all that Kyla had told him.

And every lie that Jasmine had ever spoken.

When Natasia had returned, he pretended to already be asleep. He didn't move when she draped the blanket over him. And kept the façade even when he felt her standing, watching him. Soon she'd left him alone and he'd spent a restless night with dreams full of lies and deception starring Jasmine and Brian.

He inhaled deeply and Natasia rested her hand on top of his, bringing his thoughts back to now. "Hosea, I want to help."

This time, he didn't hide his glance. Looked straight at her. Devoured her. Wondered how much of his pain she could take away.

She whispered, "You could have gone anywhere last night. But you came to me. So don't shut me out now."

My wife is a liar and a cheat. "Jasmine and I are having some problems," he began as a test.

She breathed, as if her relief was inside his admission. "She doesn't make you happy."

He thought about those words. He'd been so happy with Jasmine. Loved her with a love he'd never known before. But was that possible anymore? Did she love him, or had she fallen all the way for Brian?

Maybe Brian and Jasmine were getting together for the sake of their baby.

When he groaned with that thought, Natasia slipped from the couch and knelt at his feet.

"Hosea," she whispered in that voice that made his insides yearn. "You've been through so much with Jasmine. The baby—"

He winced, but she held his hands, made him stay. Made him listen.

"She can't make you happy. But I can."

He looked into her eyes and wondered if those words were the truth.

"I can make you forget about Jasmine."

Was it time to forget? Was it time to finally move on?

"Natasia," he said, knowing he needed to fight through these feelings, "I didn't come here for this—"

"You came here for something."

"I came here to talk."

"Is that all you really want?" She paused. "I don't think so . . ."

His breathing stopped. His heart stopped. Time stopped. Only Natasia moved—her lips aimed for his.

Commitment. That was his thought as her mouth met his. His commitment to Jasmine. And then he thought of Brian. Brian and Jasmine together.

It was a soft kiss. At first. And then his heartache raised his urgency. He held her as if she was his freedom from the hurt. The anger. The shock.

He leaned back, bringing her with him. Kissed her, held her, caressed her, like she belonged to him.

His heart banged against his chest. And he could feel hers pounding too. Their beats were in sync. First gently. Then suddenly loud. Pounding.

It wasn't their hearts.

He tried to push Natasia away. "The door," he breathed. "Someone's at the door."

"I don't care." Her tongue teased his ear. Driving him further away from sanity.

The knocking kept on.

"Yes," he breathed. "Get the door. It must be important."

"No." But her fingers said yes to everything else. She squeezed him. He moaned. Then she undid his belt, unzipped his pants.

His groans were as loud as the banging on the door. It was hard to think. Hard to speak. "Get . . . the . . . door." He pushed her again, this time like he meant it.

She struggled to her feet, then staggered, drunk with lust, to the door. Swung it open. Yelled, "What—" She stopped.

Jasmine busted inside like a keg of dynamite, her rage on the verge.

She stood for a moment, her glare on a stone-still Natasia, and then she turned her fury to her husband, who was just as unmoving in his shock. When she turned back to Natasia, Jasmine's fists were flying.

The first blow hit her target—the center of Natasia's eye.

Natasia shrieked. Fell back.

Jasmine plunged forward like a pit bull. As if her mind was filled with a single command—kill.

Hosea jumped from the couch. Corralled his wife from behind before she could land the knock-out punch. "Jasmine!"

"You stank ho!" Jasmine screamed, fighting to get loose from Hosea's arms.

"Jasmine! Stop it!" He squeezed her, held her, whispered, "Please, please, please," over and over until her breathing steadied.

He kept his glance on Natasia. And with his eyes told her not to move. She obeyed.

Jasmine twisted inside his arms. Looked at him. "How could you do this?" Her question came through tears.

"I haven't done anything, Jasmine." She fought to break his grasp, but he held her tighter. "Listen to me," he demanded. "I haven't done anything, I promise."

"Then what are you doing here?"

He looked at Natasia. "I needed a place . . . look, we'll talk about this. I need you to go."

Her eyes widened with his audacity. "I'm not going anywhere!"

"Yes. You are. Go back to our hotel. I'll be right there."

"I'm not going anywhere without you," Jasmine cried, her shoulders heaving with her own hurt.

Hosea spoke with a calm he didn't feel. "If you leave now and go home, I'll be right there, and we can talk."

She turned to Natasia; venom spilled from her eyes. "I'm not leaving you with her."

Natasia held one hand to her eye. But even with that injury, she wore the victor's veil. Didn't say a word, but her smirk—half pain, half triumph—showed she knew she'd won.

Gently, Hosea nudged Jasmine toward the door. "Please, Jasmine," he whispered. "You're not like this. We're not like this. Just go. I'll meet you in ten minutes."

She didn't move on her own accord, but somehow, in the next second, she was in the hallway.

Hosea gently closed the door on his wife. Inside, he leaned against it, his hands, his forehead pushed against the dark wood.

After a silent moment, he said, "I have to go." But he didn't move. Stood in the same place, resting on the door.

"No." Natasia shook her head. "Now we don't have anything to hide." She stepped closer to him. "What was happening, what was going to happen, was real, Hosea. And you can't deny it anymore."

He stayed still, not moving. Still not facing her.

She pressed against him. Her front to his back. And he felt all of her familiar places.

"Even if you leave now," her breath was warm against his ear, "it won't be over. So stay. Let's finish this."

Hosea imagined Jasmine on the other side, waiting for him, her heart, filled with agony.

Then he thought of all her lies.

Then he remembered who he was.

Swiftly he moved, slipped on his shoes. Snatched his wallet and keys. When he walked to the door, Natasia was right behind him. Her hand was on his when he grabbed the doorknob.

"No matter what you do, it's not over between us, Hosea. I've known that. And now you and Jasmine know that too."

He opened the door.

"I was your first love," she said.

He stepped into the hallway.

"Jasmine will never be able to change that."

He turned around. Looked at her now. Saw the mark that she wore—black and blue and red—the gift from his wife.

"I love you, Hosea," she said. "And I know that you love me too."

He closed the door before she could say anything more.

SIXTY-NINE

JASMINE'S BLOOD SHOT PAST BOILING.

Raging, she paced the length of the living room, watching the clock tick away seconds that turned into minutes. She counted the time passing, ready to jump right back into her car if Hosea wasn't standing in front of her within the next five minutes.

Watching the clock did little to keep her mind away from the images. Natasia, barely dressed. Hosea, pants undone. The one shot that she'd gotten on Natasia.

But what hurt her heart most was the way Hosea had held her and protected Natasia. And then, he'd pushed her out the door. As if she was the trespasser, the one loitering on their relationship.

Jasmine wanted to whip Natasia all over again. But that thought stopped when the front door opened.

Hosea stepped into the suite. Their eyes met. For seconds. Then with a grunt of disgust, he turned away. Dragged through the living room. Headed toward their bedroom.

"Where are you going?" she demanded.

He kept walking as if she'd hadn't spoken.

"Hosea!" she screamed, following him.

"Where's Jacquie?"

Now she wanted to whip him. Those were his first words to her? "She's with Mae Frances."

He turned to her. Said, "You shouldn't have come to Natasia's hotel."

His words were a stun gun, rendering every single muscle in her body motionless. But the shock wore off fast. "I find you half-naked in that woman's room after you were gone all night, and that's what you say to me? Have you lost your mind?"

He looked at her as if she'd lost hers. Then he turned away again. Moved inside the closet.

"Are you sleeping with Natasia?"

"No."

"I don't believe you."

He stepped back into the bedroom. His lips, upturned as if he was grinning. But his eyes were raging with wrath.

Made him look like a madman.

"You don't believe me? You're the liar."

"This is not about me," Jasmine screamed. "This is about you. And Natasia."

He laughed, a gurgle from his throat.

Made him sound like a madman.

"You want to know about Natasia?" He moved toward her. Halting steps. Eyes glaring. Mouth twisted.

He was a madman.

And now, she was very afraid. But stood stoic, like she had courage.

Standing right in front of her face, he said, "I am not having an affair. That's it. That's everything. Now you know."

She crossed her arms and returned his glare. Told him with her stance that she didn't believe him.

He said, "Now that I've told you, why don't you tell me?"

"Tell you what?" she spat.

"About you and Kenny."

She couldn't get enough air into her lungs. Couldn't feel the blood pumping through her veins. She needed to sit down to stay alive.

"Kenny?" she squeaked. Thoughts were already swirling, forming together to shape lies.

"Yes, Kenny." Hosea stood over her. A giant. "Remember him?

Your first husband. The one you forgot to tell me about. No," he held up his hands. "You didn't forget. You just straight-out lied." He pointed his finger in her face. "Like I said, *you're* the liar." He stomped away.

"Hosea, please," her voice, softer now. "I didn't know . . . I'm sorry."

"Are you even divorced?" he asked from the other side of the bed.

"Yes!"

"How do I know that? Give me one reason to believe you."

"I have the divorce papers—" She stopped. Remembered that she didn't have the papers anymore. Remembered how she'd burned them the night before their wedding so that he would never find them.

"You have divorce papers?"

She shook her head. "Of course not with me. I don't travel with them. But I was divorced here in Los Angeles. I can get the papers."

He looked at her, then at the bed where she sat. He backed away and sank into the chair behind him. Head down. Eyes closed. "After Jacqueline, there were supposed to be no more lies." He sounded so tired.

"There weren't any more lies, Hosea."

He looked straight at her now. "Really? Then tell me about Brian."

Now she wanted to stand up. Click her heels three times and wake up in Kansas.

How did he find out?

"Are you sleeping with him?" She could hear his heartache in his tone.

Slowly, she shook her head. *Was that why you were with Natasia?* But she kept that question to herself. Finally she answered, "No, Hosea. I'm not sleeping with Brian." She was grateful to be able to tell that truth. "I love you. I wouldn't do that to you."

"Didn't you love me when you slept with him before?"

She fought back her tears. "I was falling in love with you." Her voice quivered. "But I was different then. I'm not like that now."

"No, now you're just a liar."

Her sobs were stuck in her throat. "Kenny is an old lie."

He paused. And then he laughed. "I've never heard that before. I guess old lies are better than new ones."

"All I'm saying is that I haven't lied to you since we got back together. And I never told you about Kenny because I didn't know how."

"You didn't know how to tell the truth?"

She nodded. "I was afraid that I would lose you."

"The best way to lose me is to lie to me." He stood, snatched his jacket, then swiveled toward the door.

But she grabbed his arm. "You have to listen to me; you have to believe me," she pleaded.

"Really?" He snatched his arm from her grasp. "Why?"

"Because I love you."

"Is that another lie?"

"No."

"So now you know how to tell the truth?"

"Yes, I do. I'm different because of you."

He shook his head and she wanted to shrink away from his glare. "You're the same woman you were when I met you. And it's time we both accepted that. You'll always be Jasmine Larson."

Inside she screamed that she was Jasmine Larson Bush. But she said nothing. Just watched him march right out the door.

SEVENTY

ALEXIS DIDN'T KNOW IF IT was the wine or God that kept her up all night. Kept her thinking about Hosea's words.

Then in the still-dark hours of the early morning, she'd heard a voice. Again, she wasn't sure if it was the wine or God, but, she was clear on what she'd heard.

You do your part and I'll do mine.

She hated when God (or wine) talked to her. But she was old enough to know that when God spoke (even through wine), she had to listen.

It's the disease.

And then, even as God spoke, the telephone rang. She'd known before she answered that it was her daily alarm. At six o'clock. Every day. For the last week. Brian always called. She never answered. Until today.

Now here she was. In front of Pink's. Doing what was God's will, because clearly she was not here on her own. But she had to follow God—or else she might never again have a good night's sleep.

She pressed forward, around the white plastic tables and chairs, still filled to the hilt even though it was past the lunchtime rush hour.

Brian stood when she approached the table, his eyes bright with his smile. He scurried to hold the chair for her.

A gentleman.

"It's good to see you," he said.

She tried to smile, but couldn't. And for a moment, she wondered what God would do if she was to just march right out of that place. But then she thought about all the hours that she hadn't slept, and she knew she had to stay.

Brian asked, "Are you all right?"

She knew he could see it—all her reluctance and restlessness, maybe even the wine from last night. "I'm fine." She closed her eyes and willed her headache away. "It's just been rough."

He hesitated, then reached across the table and covered her hand with his. When she didn't pull away, he exhaled. "I've missed you."

She could feel it. His love was like a current, charging through him to her. It was real. She just didn't know if it was enough.

"Do you want to order?" he asked.

Around her, every seat was taken by Los Angelenos who always filled this famous hot-dog-stand-to-the-stars to capacity. The familiar chatter and clanking played in surround-sound, and the aroma of the chili and fresh buns overwhelmed her nostrils. But today, the sounds and smells of her favorite hang-out joint brought no joy. Only made her sick.

"I'm not hungry."

His lips turned down as if he knew he was the reason she'd suddenly rather starve.

She said, "I just want to talk."

He nodded and began, "Alex, I'm so sorry. I—"

She held up her hands. "You said that already. Now I need something new."

He frowned.

"I had dinner with Hosea Bush last night."

The light that had been in his eyes dimmed. His lips pursed like he was holding back words he didn't dare say. Then, "Alex, I don't think he's the best person. We need to talk to people who support us. Who—"

She stopped him. "If it wasn't for Hosea, I wouldn't be here." She relished his look of surprise and thought more about Hosea's advice. "He said that if God put us together, then I had to do everything in my power to make sure we stayed that way."

Now he nodded, as if he suddenly agreed with anything Hosea Bush had to say.

"The thing about Hosea," said Alexis, "the thing that really got me to listen, is that he doesn't just talk. Did you know that he's known about . . ." She paused; it was still hard to say. "He's known that the baby was not his all along."

"Jasmine told me that."

Brian didn't know how much those words hurt. The revelation that he'd been talking to Jasmine. Talking, and doing so much more.

It's the disease, the inside of her urged.

Alexis continued, "Hosea loves that little girl anyway. And he still loves his wife too." She shook her head, still finding that hard to believe. "Even though he felt what I'm feeling, he's living what he's saying. Hosea's the real deal. He's forgiven Jasmine for the affair."

"It wasn't an affair," Brian said strongly. Then backed down when her eyebrows raised. "It was just a few—"

"It was enough to make a baby."

He swallowed, sat stiffly. Didn't confirm or deny.

"Anyway," she said, like she was annoyed at his interruption, "Hosea impressed me. He left me wanting to do the right thing too."

Brian leaned forward. "Are you saying that you want to give us a chance?"

No. "First, there's something I want to know." She wondered if he would tell the truth. "Besides, Jasmine's . . . baby. Are there . . . others? Any more baby mamas?"

His answer was swift. "I don't know, but I don't think so."

She exhaled. Those were the first words he'd spoken in a long time that she completely believed.

"I think if there were . . . others," he kept going, "I would know by now . . . but even if there are, it shouldn't affect us."

They both knew that was a lie.

He said, "All I can do right now is deal with what we know. And that's Jasmine and Jacqueline."

The sound of those names from his lips made her ache.

"What are your plans with Jasmine and her . . . your baby?"

He sat back, surprised by that question. "I don't have any plans. She and Hosea have made it clear that they will raise Jacqueline as their own."

"You're fine with that?"

Alexis didn't like the way he hesitated before he said, "I told you a long time ago I didn't want any more children."

"Seems like you forgot to tell Jasmine."

He swallowed. "Hosea is Jacqueline's father. That's what he wants. That's how it is."

She nodded. "He'll be a great father. But Jasmine . . ." She shook her head. "This situation is still impossible to believe."

"I'm sorry."

She looked at him for a long moment. "I think you are. But I wish to God that you had told me rather than have me walk into that . . ." She stopped, shuddered as she remembered.

He took her hand again. "I should have told you, and from the moment I found out, I wanted to. But I was scared that it would end up just like this. That you would be hurt. That you would have a hard time forgiving me."

"I don't want to forgive you."

He flinched as if he'd just been struck.

"I am," she continued, "smart enough to know that's my flesh talking. And if I really want to walk this walk, I have to be fully into this forgiveness thing." She stared at him, her eyes piercing. "Even if I don't want to."

He frowned a bit, as if he didn't understand her double talk.

With a deep breath, she said, "I really want to do the right thing. I'm going to step out on faith. I'm going to go against everything that I'm feeling." She paused. "You can come home."

It didn't sound like much of an invitation, but that didn't matter to Brian. He grinned like he had his victory.

"There's more," she said, stopping him before he stood up and danced. "I don't want your disease to become mine. If you don't think you can beat this, if you think your addiction will . . . flare up again, you've got to let me know and let me go. Because I can't do this anymore. I can't take another secret."

He inhaled. "There's nothing more. The whole truth is out."

She squinted, wondered why his words sounded so stiff. *Could there possibly be more?*

He said, "I'm going to continue therapy to make sure that none of this . . . stuff happens again." He edged his chair closer to hers. "Alexis, I will do anything, because being married to you is what's important to me."

She took her breath. Wanted to believe. Really wanted to believe.

"I love you," he said.

That she believed. But she couldn't return his declaration of love. Wasn't sure how much of that she had left. She looked down at the red-and-white plaid tablecloth. Kept her eyes on the squares. "When you come back—"

"Tonight. I don't want to waste any more time."

She wondered if he'd think her next words were a waste. "I want to sleep alone. Until."

It took a moment for him to say, "I understand."

Now she looked up.

He caressed her fingers. "That's fine. I'm willing to do whatever it takes, for however long it takes."

She nodded, released a long sigh inside. She'd done what the voice had told her to do. Her part. Now it was up to God to do His.

SEVENTY-ONE

MAE FRANCES LEANED OVER THE railing of the bed, her eyes staying on Jacqueline. She whispered, "So what are you going to do?"

Jasmine slapped the tears that soaked her cheek. She was so tired of crying—she hadn't stopped since Hosea had stomped out of their suite this morning. "I don't know. But we have to do something. What about all your connections?"

Mae Frances stared at her granddaughter before she motioned toward the door.

With her arms folded, Jasmine followed her friend. "So," she began the moment they were alone. "Do you have any ideas?"

"I did make a few calls." Mae Frances sat on the sofa and let moments pass. "But I was thinking . . . what do you think about praying?"

Jasmine was so shocked it took her a moment to say, "Are you talking about that pray-three-times thing you told me to do?"

Mae Frances's face was long and solemn as she nodded. "That and a whole lot more. I think we really need to just get on our knees and pray this through. Maybe pray three times every hour! I mean, Jasmine Larson, we've tried everything else. I'm willing to try some serious prayer."

Jasmine shook her head. "You've got to be kidding!"

"You used to always tell me to pray."

"That was different."

"Why? It worked for you. You prayed me back to God. And I'm just sayin', we've tried *everything*, and that woman is still here. Maybe it's time to see what kind of plan God has."

This was not the time for the tables to be turned. Not the time for Mae Frances to get all Christian when what Jasmine needed was the pre-God Mae Frances, the woman who would have drugged Hosea and then dragged him home.

Jasmine said, "I have been praying. But we still need a plan."

"We're out of plans!" Mae Frances exclaimed, waving her hands in the air as if that might make Jasmine hear better. "We tried to get the woman to Africa, then you tried to find her a job in Russia. And those calls I made this afternoon—I was thinking about hiring a gigolo and—"

Jasmine sat up straight. "A gigolo? For Natasia? That might not be a bad idea."

"No! It *is* a bad idea. It was going to cost thousands."

"How many thousands?"

Mae Frances sighed, exasperated. "Are you listening to yourself? Why would you want to spend thousands of dollars on something that might not work? It's time for us to just take this to the Holy Ghost corner."

Jasmine rolled her eyes. It was hard to listen to this woman who had been crying so hard that Sunday over a year ago that she had to be carried up to the altar for prayer.

But that didn't stop Mae Frances right now. She kept on talking like she was a preacher's wife. "I've told you before, you are who I used to be, Jasmine Larson. So don't think I don't know what you're going through. Remember, Elijah Van Dorn left me, and we'd been married for only a couple of years."

"*You* were having an affair." Jasmine snickered. Maybe that would make her friend shut up.

Mae Frances raised her penciled eyebrows. "So? Doesn't matter the reason. When Preacher Man leaves you, the results will be the same. You will be by . . . your . . . self."

Jasmine glared at her.

Mae Frances returned Jasmine's stare, but she softened her

voice. "I'm just telling it the way it is. I don't want to see you and Preacher Man break up. I don't want my grandbaby growing up with just her mama. That's how I was raised, and it's no way for a child. So that's why I wanna give this prayer thing a chance. I wanna see if it'll work."

With a sigh, Jasmine released the little bit of hope she'd had. Not that she didn't believe in prayer—God had answered so many of hers, she was sure she'd used up her lifetime quotient. But still, wasn't there something in the Bible about faith without works? She had a lot of faith. All she needed was a plan to work.

"So are we gonna do this prayer thing?" Mae Frances asked.

She wondered if smacking Mae Frances would bring her old friend back. But the problem with slapping Mae Frances was that she'd slap back. And even though she had more than twenty years of youth on the woman, Jasmine was sure Mae Frances could still do some major damage.

Jasmine nodded, although in her mind the wheels had already begun spinning. Another plan was forming. "If prayer is all you've got, I'll do it."

"Good, 'cause prayer changes things."

No she didn't. Mae Frances, the woman who hadn't entered a church for thirty years until Jasmine had forced her to, was wasting her time with Christian clichés.

"I think you should spend some real time on your knees tonight," Mae Frances continued her religious rant. "If you want, I'll take Jacquie with me so you can focus."

At least her friend was coming through for her with that. "Thanks, Mae Frances. That'll give me all the time I need . . . to pray."

"Okay, I'll go get my grandbaby."

Jasmine watched her friend strut toward Jacqueline's bedroom. As if she'd just given Jasmine a good word. As if Christ had always been part of her life. As if.

It was a good thing that Jasmine still remembered some of those tricks the old Mae Frances had taught her. Because before Mae Frances was fully out of her sight, Jasmine already had another plan.

It was simple. It was easy. It was basic.

Just three minutes had passed since the last time Jasmine looked at the clock. It was exactly midnight now.

She'd given Hosea enough time to come home.

She jumped from the bed, fully dressed in jeans and a T-shirt. Then slipped into her Keds and covered her head with a baseball cap. With her hair tucked under, she wasn't easily recognized.

Part of the plan.

She called down for her car, then walked out of the suite as if she was running a quick errand. Inside the hotel's lobby, the Fairmont was middle-of-the-night quiet, and when the doorman signaled that her car was out front, she stepped into the dark.

Outside, she paused. A déjà vu moment. This used to be her life. Back in the day. She'd spent all kinds of nighttime hours creeping through Los Angeles, lurking in the shadows for some man she wanted.

Years had passed and here she was. Again. Still the middle of the night. Still searching for a man. But this time, it was her man she was chasing.

It didn't take ten minutes to get to her destination, but she didn't give her car to the valet. She parked on the street.

Part of the plan.

She strolled up to the Rendezvous as if she belonged there. In these early hours of the next day, there was no doorman. But inside, the lone security guard hovered over the space as if it was his kingdom. He peered at Jasmine, suspicion in his eyes.

Still, Jasmine strutted past, into the elevator, pressed the "14" button, and then breathed once the door closed.

At room 1411, she knocked, then stepped to the side, away from the view of the peephole. Natasia would be more cautious this time.

She was working this plan.

But after a minute, there was no answer.

Jasmine knocked again. Stepped back. Waited some more. Wondered if she'd have to do this every night. She would—if she had to. She'd come here, knock on this door until the prayers that Mae Frances was talking about kicked in.

Jasmine heard movement, and she jumped from the peephole's view.

"Who is it?" Caution was in Natasia's tone.

Jasmine took a breath, became a Jamaican. "I'm in charge of housekeeping, ma'am," she began in her best Caribbean brogue. "We're so sorry to bother you this late, but the people above you have reported rats. They're in the pipes and now they're in your bedroom."

A scream. "What?" The sound of the locks unbolting. "Rats? In my room?" Natasia jumped into the hallway. "Rats?" she screamed.

Jasmine pushed past her. "Just one. Just you." She marched into the suite. "Where's my husband?"

"Jasmine, get out of my room!" Natasia yelled from the hallway, as if she was still a bit unsure about the rats.

"Where is he?"

Now Natasia followed her inside. Turned on the light and tightened her bathrobe. "It's not my job to keep track of him." She folded her arms. "At least not yet."

Jasmine raised her eyebrows. Looked at the woman wearing the mark she'd left on her. Couldn't believe she was talking to her with so much attitude. Her eyes were narrow as she strode toward her enemy.

Natasia backed away and edged toward the bedroom. Disappointed Jasmine, just a little. Surely a woman with this much nerve would be willing to fight for the man.

Then Jasmine eyed the bedroom door. Closed.

"Don't even think about going in there," Natasia warned. "I'll call—"

Before she could say, "Security," Jasmine shoved Natasia against the wall. Heard her head hit hard. But she didn't look back. Just charged into the bedroom.

Natasia screamed, "Get out!"

Jasmine ignored her cries. Instead her glance settled on the bed. Sheets tousled, comforter sprawled on the floor.

But the bed was empty.

Behind her, Natasia shouted, "I'm calling security!"

Jasmine stomped into the bathroom, ripped the shower curtain from the rod, leaving the tub bare.

Nothing.

Now she headed to the closet. Slid the glass mirrors back and forth, searching for her hiding husband.

Nothing.

"There's an intruder in my room!" she heard Natasia scream.

Jasmine wondered if the police would come with guns drawn. But she wasn't worried. Hosea would explain it all—as soon as she found him.

She eyed the bed again and paused. That's where he was! She couldn't believe he would hide from her that way.

Jasmine dropped to her knees. Threw aside the comforter. Stared under the bed. Stared at the big empty space.

You're still Jasmine Larson.

Those words, Hosea's voice, overcame her like a fifty-foot wave.

No, she wasn't that same woman. she'd left this kind of lunacy behind. But here she was, on her knees. Searching under a bed. With a hysterical woman screaming in the next room.

This was some ghetto drama!

Jasmine pushed herself up and staggered from the bedroom. Past Natasia, still ranting. She swung open the front door, stumbled into the hallway. Natasia's shouts rang in her ears as she leaned against the wall, catching her breath and her sanity. But she paused for no more than a moment.

She dashed to the staircase, just as she heard the elevator doors open. She raced down fourteen flights, peeked into the lobby, composed herself, then snuck out the back door. Outside, she ran around the corner, to her car, and then slipped inside.

At any moment, her heart was going to explode through her chest—she was sure of that.

You're still Jasmine Larson.

She thought about her husband's words. Thought about how she'd torn through Natasia's suite. Thought about how the police were probably looking for her right now.

And she bowed her head and cried.

SEVENTY-TWO

HOSEA'S HEAD WAS POUNDING AS he gazed into the blue-black of the midnight.

His eyelids drooped, heavy with exhaustion—all he wanted to do was sleep. But God hadn't granted him one moment of rest. From the time he stepped into this four-hundred-square-foot motel room until he laid on the mangy mattress and scraggy pillows, God was in his head.

Forgive her! was what the voice said over and over.

And he had talked right back. Told God, "I can't."

I forgive you.

He had pushed himself up, turned on the light, and talked as if God was sitting in the room. "But she lied, and she just keeps on lying."

You've never lied?

"Not like this."

One lie is no better than another.

He folded his arms across his chest. Didn't want God's words to get anywhere near his heart. "Well, I can't get over this lie. I'm getting a divorce," he shouted.

The gentle, guiding voice became quiet.

Good! he thought before he laid back down. This time, he wasn't going to be stopped. He was tired of forgiving her.

I'm not tired of forgiving you.

That was when he'd jumped from the bed, hoping that standing up would turn Him off. He didn't want to hear God, didn't want to be talked out of it. His wife was a liar, a cheat, and probably a bigamist. She had brought him to this place of pain once more, and he was not going to be a fool again.

But his decision didn't erase his heartache. He ached for the loss of the woman that he still loved. And then thoughts of his daughter—that brought the first tears to his eyes. He had no plans of giving her up; Jacqueline was his, legally, and he would hire the best attorneys to make sure his rights were protected.

Divorce is not a punishment.

Hosea sighed. The voice could not be quieted.

You can't punish Jasmine by ending your marriage.

Grabbing his bag, Hosea searched for his iPod. He stuffed his ears with the plugs, selected his first playlist, and stood once again at the window.

Test her. She will do no wrong, the voice still came through.

Hosea yanked the plugs from his ears and laughed out loud. Jasmine will do no wrong? What did that mean? He didn't know what God was looking at, but from where he was standing, Jasmine was the walking definition of wrong.

Well, if God was going to talk while he was standing, he might as well lie down.

He rolled onto the bed, turned off the light, and prayed for sleep. But rest never came. God continued to speak. Even though Hosea was hell-bent on not listening.

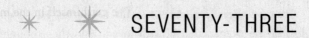

SEVENTY-THREE

HOSEA CLOSED HIS EYES, MASSAGED his temples. Wondered if God would ever let him sleep again. He glanced at his watch. The one o'clock production meeting was about to begin. He stood, just as his office door slammed hard against the wall.

Natasia was posed, under the frame, standing stiff, her hands on her hips, her eyes flashing.

He was drowning in her wrath—and he understood it. This was the first time they'd seen each other since he'd walked away from her and the mistake they'd almost made.

Even with makeup, the mark Jasmine had left—a black half-moon shiner under Natasia's right eye—was very visible. It was hard to look at her and not remember. All that happened. The before and the after.

"I need to speak to you." Her anger moved from her eyes. Now was in her voice.

"I didn't think you'd be in today," he said. He'd been relieved when she'd stayed home yesterday. Relieved that she wouldn't have to explain her bruise to anyone. Relieved that he wouldn't be filled with all kinds of shame every time he looked at her.

"I have a lot of work to do," she said. "And I'm tired of your wife getting in my way."

"Nat, I'm sorry—"

"Oh, don't apologize about this." She pointed to her eye. "Wait until you hear the latest." Her tone was tight.

He frowned.

"Your wife showed up. At my door. Again. Last night."

"What?"

"Came looking for you. But assaulted me. Again."

"Natasia . . ." was all he could say as he shook his head. He was a minister, a pastor's son; how did he get himself in the middle of this drama?

She said, "I tried to call you."

"My cell . . . it's off." It was hard to put words together, hard to believe any of this.

"Well, the only reason she's not in jail is because of how I feel about you." Her voice was softer now.

"Are you all right?"

"No. How can I be, Hosea? I'm going to get a restraining order."

"You don't have to do that."

"Yes I do, because I can't handle this."

"I promise, Jasmine won't bother you anymore."

"You can't stop her! She's a crazy woman."

He sat up straight. Spoke stronger now. "No she's not." He defended the woman who was still his wife. "She's just upset."

"Whatever she is, I don't want to be part of this soap opera any-more. Not unless—" She stopped, then took slow steps toward him.

It amazed him. Even with the blot on her face, even with her hair pulled back in a ponytail, her beauty, her class, still made his heart stop.

"I left you messages all day yesterday," she said, her tone so dif-ferent now. "Why didn't you call me back?"

He swallowed before he said, "Because." That was enough. She understood what he meant.

She said, "You owed me a phone call. You just walked out of my hotel room—"

"My wife showed up." That was his explanation and his apol-ogy.

"If Jasmine hadn't shown up, what would have happened? Where would we be now?" she whispered.

He stared at her, standing above him. But even though her questions had been his thoughts, he said nothing.

"Are you just using me?"

"No!"

"So, you're saying there *is* something between us."

"No!" he exclaimed again, thinking that lust wasn't an emotion.

She folded her arms and backed away a bit. "You can't have it both ways, Hosea. Either you're using me or—"

"I'm not, but I can understand how you might see it that way. I shouldn't have come to your hotel. I needed a friend, but I'm—"

"Don't bother to say it. Don't apologize anymore." She leaned close to him. "I just want one thing, I just want you to get this straight."

"I've told you—"

"I know what you've said. But what I know more is what you do." She moved so close now, there was barely air between them. He felt her breath as she spoke. "Why are you fighting us?"

He looked straight into her eyes and told her the truth. "There is no us," he said, sitting up. Defiant. But that didn't stop the stirring inside of him. It was their chemistry, their history that he just could not deny.

"You want me. I know you do," she whispered.

He shook his head, but didn't address her claim out loud. All he said was, "I'll take care of my wife. She won't bother you again."

She waited a few seconds. "That's it?"

He nodded.

She stayed in place as if she was sure there was more. Then she backed away. "Take care of your wife. And while you're doing that, be sure she's the one you really want."

She let her words settle and then turned and walked out the door.

. . .

Jasmine answered on the first ring. "Hosea, where are you?"

"At the studio." His voice was flat and tired.

She said, "I need to see you," doing nothing to hide her tears. "I'll be there—"

"No, I don't want what's private to be public."

"Then come here," she pleaded. "We have to talk."

He paused. He didn't call for this. But it was because of his dreams that he had to know. The dreams that he'd had last night during his intermittent bouts of sleep, where Brian had strolled through his mind like he belonged there.

"Brian—" was all he said before Jasmine jumped in.

"Hosea, I'm not sleeping with him. What do I have to do to get you to believe me?"

"So," he took a deep breath, "*nothing's* going on between the two of you?"

A long moment. Then, "He kissed me." The rest of her words spilled from her quickly. "The other day. I went to his office to tell him to keep Alexis away from you. But *he* kissed *me*. I pushed him away. And ran out of there." She sobbed. "That's all there was, Hosea. That's the truth."

The truth was what he wanted. But this truth slashed his heart.

"Please, Hosea, you've got to believe me."

He wanted to. But only said, "I need you to do something for me."

"Anything," she cried.

"Stay away from Natasia."

Silence. "Hosea, I'm talking about us, and you're talking about Natasia?"

"We'll talk . . . about us. Later. But I need some time."

"Because of what I just told you about Brian?"

"No. Because of—" He thought about their pasts. His, with Natasia. Hers, with Kenny. And Brian. "A lot has happened and I need time . . . just leave Natasia alone. She doesn't have anything to do with us."

"Are you . . . staying with her?"

"No."

"Then come home, please. What about Jacquie? She misses you, too."

He closed his eyes. "I want to see Jacquie."

She breathed. "Okay, I'll bring her—"

"I'll call Mae Frances," he interrupted. "*She* can bring Jacquie."

"Hosea, this is not the way—"

"I want to see Jacquie tomorrow. But only Jacquie and Mae Frances. Not you."

He could still hear her protests, even as he hung up. He sat and waited. Expected her to call right back. But after minutes passed, he was grateful that she'd left him alone.

"He kissed me."

He'd asked for it. And she gave it to him. The truth. At least, he thought this was the truth. Jasmine would never have admitted that Brian kissed her unless it was the truth.

Maybe she's trying to change.

No! With everything within him, he shook that thought away. There were so many more lies out there, the complete truth had still not been told. And anyway, she shouldn't have been near Brian, shouldn't have been kissing another man.

Hypocrite!

No matter how it happened. And how did he really know that's all there was between them?

You kissed another woman. Is that all there is between you and Natasia?

His own conscience ridiculed him. Made him pause and wonder if he were doing the right thing.

He grabbed the telephone. Before he did anything else, there was more that he had to know.

When the voice mail came on, he left a simple message. "Pops, call me. Important."

✳ ✳ SEVENTY-FOUR

BRIAN STOOD AGAINST THE wall, silently watching. Alexis leaned over the sink, rinsed the plates, then loaded each into the dishwasher. He could stand for hours watching his wife do this—or anything. That's how much he loved her.

From the beginning, it had been this way. He loved her intelligence, her strength, her independence, her feistiness. He loved all of those things that were keeping her away from him now.

A week. That's how long he'd been home. But he didn't feel as if he was back. Felt more like he was just one of the accessories in their apartment—a piece of furniture, not her husband.

How was he going to earn her forgiveness?

"Oh!" Alexis exclaimed, facing him. "I didn't know you were standing there."

He grinned.

She turned away. "Do you want anything?" She lifted two plates from the sink.

He edged toward her. All he could think about was feeling her, holding her. Making her want him again.

He reached out. Touched her shoulder.

She gasped. The plates she held crashed to the floor.

"I'm sorry!" he said.

"That's okay," she said.

Together they bent down, gathered the pieces. He touched her fingers and she cringed, snatched her hand away. As if the feel of him disgusted her.

"I'll get the rest of this." He grabbed the broom, swept the pieces toward the electronic dustpan. Then he stood to the side as she closed the dishwasher.

"Sweetheart—"

"Brian." She kept her eyes down. "I'm not ready."

"Ready for what? For me to touch you? That's all I want." He paused. "You can't even look at me."

"No, because," she turned to him now, her eyes misty with misery, "every time I look at you, I see Jasmine. And her baby. Your baby."

"I'm. Sorry. Alexis. But that's not what you should see when you look at me. You should see how much I love you."

"But . . . you . . . were . . . with her."

Brian wanted to comfort her. But he didn't move. Folded his arms to make sure he held back. "I wasn't with her, Alex. I wasn't with any of them—"

She took a deep breath when he reminded her that Jasmine wasn't the only one.

"Not the way I want to be with you."

She shook her head, as if she didn't believe him.

He said, "If this was about sex, Alexis, I would have been long gone. That's why I know being with you is different than being with anyone else."

She breathed deeply. Over and over. Eyes still glazed, she said, "You need to give me time."

He said nothing, did nothing, as she staggered away. Into the bedroom. She closed the door. And then he heard the sound that twisted everything within him—the lock turning.

Message sent. Message received.

In the years they'd been married, she'd never locked him out of their bedroom. Not even when she found out about his addiction. It was only after Jasmine. Jasmine and the baby.

Brian released a deep breath. His stress was rising, and Dr. Perkins's warning rewound in his mind.

It's not about sex, Brian. It's about stress. And with the tension of your marriage, this could be a challenging time. Be aware.

He'd told Dr. Perkins that he'd be fine. That there was no test that he couldn't pass. That was true—even with what happened with Jasmine, he knew he was fine. It wasn't like he'd gone after her. Jasmine had clearly been the aggressor. And he had fought it. Turned her down and walked away.

But how much longer was he supposed to be denied by his wife?

He opened the drawer where he kept the candy bars, his substitute addiction.

There was only one left.

He unwrapped the bar and broke off an end. Leaned against the kitchen counter, sucked on the chocolate, and stared at his bedroom door.

Locked.

This had been a long week. Three surgeries. And he still couldn't touch his wife.

Stressed.

He stared and chewed.

He needed to be understanding and give Alexis time. But how much more could he take? He was a sex addict. Not an excuse, just a fact. A fact of his life.

✳ ✳ SEVENTY-FIVE

JASMINE TWISTED IN THE bed. Looked at the side where Hosea was supposed to be. Seven nights had passed since her husband's head had touched that pillow. And what was worse was she wasn't quite sure why he hadn't come home. Was it because he'd found out that she'd been married? Was it because she'd told him about Brian's kiss? Was it because he'd fallen for Natasia? Was it all of the above? None of the above?

She just didn't know.

So how was she supposed to get him back?

I should have never told him about Brian. But she'd been trying to do better, be better. Just didn't look like the truth had worked.

Still, she couldn't let it end here. There had to be something she could do.

Then it came to her.

Jasmine reached for the phone and wondered why she hadn't thought of this before? Surely after she told Reverend Bush the whole story, he would be on the next plane to L.A. putting his family back together.

"Jasmine!" Reverend Bush exclaimed when he answered. "How are you, sweetheart?"

"I'm fine."

Then his tone that had been filled with cheer changed. Concerned now, he asked, "You don't sound fine."

It was his love that unlocked her tears. She cried, and along with her sobs, told her father-in-law the story.

He listened, without words, without judgment, to the lie she'd told Hosea. Then she told how she hadn't seen her husband. At the end, she wiped her face and tossed another tissue into the trash. "I can't believe Hosea didn't tell you."

"No," Reverend Bush said slowly, as if he was still processing all that he'd heard. "We keep missing each other. I've been at a conference—I was going to call him back today."

In the silence that followed, she could hear his questions. "I know I shouldn't have kept my marriage from Hosea," she said before he could ask her why. "But I was scared to tell him."

"Hosea wouldn't have cared about that."

"I know now. But once I told the lie, I couldn't get out of it. From the moment I said it, I wished I could take it back, but I didn't know how."

A pause. "I remember when Malik told me you'd been married before."

Jasmine inhaled.

"At the church picnic," Reverend Bush said, in a tone that told her he was reminiscing. "It was right after you and Hosea were married. I asked you about your first husband, do you remember that?"

She'd forgotten, but now she remembered. And now she wished she'd never made this call.

He continued, "But you said that Malik had gotten it wrong. That you'd never been married. And then Malik came back and told me that he'd made a mistake."

That was exactly what happened—in Bear Mountain Park— just months before Jacqueline was born.

"You brought a whole bunch of people into your lies, Jasmine." His voice was soft; his tone was not.

Oh, God. Could this get any worse? "I never meant to get Malik mixed up in this, but I was scared. And I didn't want to lie to you that day, but I'd already lied to Hosea and I didn't know what else to do." She paused. "I really am so sorry."

He listened to her tears. Then, "I believe that you are."

She exhaled with relief. Her father-in-law, always the merciful one. She hoped that the compassion in the father would find its way to the son.

"I believe that you're sorry, but I'm not the one you need to speak to."

"I've tried to talk to Hosea, but—"

"Before Hosea, you need to get this right with God."

Unlike Mae Frances, she expected these words from Reverend Bush. And she would listen, long enough to get to the point where she would beg him to make Hosea come home.

"You've come a long way, Jasmine, but you still lean on your own understanding. You get into trouble, and then get into more trouble by trying to handle it yourself."

"I didn't try to handle anything."

"You kept a lie alive. That's handling it. You're a child of the King, Jasmine, and you've got to start behaving that way. You can't have one foot in the kingdom and the other foot out. There's no such thing as a halfway Christian."

His words sounded like a scolding, but didn't feel that way. Sounded like he cared.

A halfway Christian. "That's not what I want to be," she said and meant it. But how was she supposed to change? And how could she change fast enough to bring Hosea back?

"If you really want to do this right, Jasmine, then turn it over to God. All of it and all the way. Get rid of the lies. That's who you used to be; that's not who you are now. Give this to God and really mean it. Let Him bring you and Hosea back together, if that's His will."

"The way you say it sounds so easy. But it's not. Just the wait-ing—"

"God's timing."

"It's hard to sit and do nothing."

"Don't do nothing. Pray. Pray for strength to be still."

Jasmine frowned. Pray to sit still? That didn't make a lot of sense. She thought you prayed to be empowered. Prayed to get things done, move mountains. Praying to sit still didn't seem to take much faith.

But if there was one thing she knew, it was that Reverend Bush had this God thing down. Her father-in-law knew the Lord, knew how to talk to the Lord, knew how to get things done through the Lord.

She said, "If I do that . . . if I really give it to God, do you think . . . Hosea and me . . . do you think Hosea will come back?"

"I don't know."

Those were not the words she wanted to hear. After the rebuke she'd just taken, she wanted words of comfort, reassurance that all would be well if she would just be still and let God handle it.

"But Jasmine, let me tell you what I do know. If God put you and Hosea together, with prayer, nothing is going to pull you apart. Just let Jesus take the wheel." Reverend Bush paused, letting the advice that he'd given her two years ago hang between them.

She pondered his words. Letting God take over had worked before. Jasmine knew it was God who had brought Hosea back home. But would He do it again? Didn't even God get tired of always having to fix her mess?

He said, "If you can leave it alone and leave it to God, I know you'll be all right. And I'll always be praying for you. Just make sure that you say a few good prayers for yourself."

Prayer. That seemed to be everyone's answer.

"And Jasmine, you know you can call me anytime, right?"

"I know."

"But I'm not going to do any more than encourage you and get you to pray. I'm not going to talk to Hosea unless he brings it to me." When she agreed, he added, "And one more thing."

She waited for him to give her some last advice about how she needed to grow up and take this like a Christian.

He said, "Make sure you give Jacquie a big kiss from her grandfather."

That almost made her cry again, but not from sadness. Reverend Bush had forgiven her long ago and so completely. He'd accepted Jacqueline as if Bush blood pumped through her. Could his son ever extend the same mercy? That would be her first prayer.

When she hung up, she imagined Hosea back home with her and Jacquie. Saw the three of them they way they'd been just weeks ago in New York. And that was when she closed her eyes and began to pray.

SEVENTY-SIX

HOSEA'S HEART BEGAN double-pumping the moment he glanced at the screen on his cell phone. Before he flipped it open, he said a quick prayer.

"Hey, Pops." His voice was steady, though his heart told a different story.

"How you holding up, son?"

"I'm hanging." *And waiting.* "Got something for me?"

"I just got the papers. Turns out Jasmine's married name is Larson. Her maiden name is Cox."

Jasmine Cox. A woman he didn't even know.

Reverend Bush continued, "She's divorced. Has been for seven years."

Instant relief. Now he could breathe. "That's legit? You're sure?"

"I had a copy of the divorce certificate faxed over."

"Thanks for taking care of this for me, Pops."

"Always. So . . ." Reverend Bush didn't finish, but Hosea knew what he wanted to know.

"I only asked you to check it out to make sure I wasn't married to a bigamist. This doesn't change anything, Pops."

"This changes everything. It means you and Jasmine are married. Period."

"Yeah, I'm married to a perpetual liar. It doesn't even make sense that she lied about this."

The reverend sighed. "You're right. It makes no sense. Sometimes I just want to shake Jasmine. She tries, but when things get rough, she gets drawn right back to her old ways. It's what she knows."

"So, if that's what she knows, then that's what she'll be. How am I supposed to live with that?"

"You live with it through love, patience, understanding, grace, mercy, forgiveness—"

"Pops, stop there," he said. He was agitated just thinking about forgiveness when there were other lies. He wondered if his father had bothered to add up the years. It was clear now—she'd definitely lied about her age too. And only God knew what else would pop up later. "How many times am I supposed to forgive her?"

"Good thing God doesn't ask how many times He's supposed to forgive you."

"Well, I'm not God."

"I thank Him for that."

Hosea ignored his father, continued his rant. "It won't work, Pops. A relationship has got to be built on trust. That's the foundation. And Jasmine and I don't have it."

"You can build trust back; give her a chance."

"And how will I know if she's telling me the truth?" He shook his head as if his father could see him. "I can't do it."

"Well, if you're talking about divorce, I can't agree. There's only one reason why God allows for that—unless you're telling me . . ."

Hosea closed his eyes. Thought about Jasmine and Brian. Just kissing. Thought about him and Natasia. Almost doing so much more.

His voice was softer now. "I don't think Jasmine's been unfaithful."

"Then the reasons you want to end your marriage are not good enough. God expects you to work through all that."

A beat. "I don't have enough in me."

"That's just pride talking. You're hurt, you're angry, and in your situation, most people would be. But you're not like most people. You're a walking Christian, not a talking one," he said, as if his son needed to be reminded.

Hosea hated these kinds of lectures. Sounded exactly like the ones God had been giving him every night.

The reverend continued, "One of the reasons I believe God chose you for Jasmine is so that she could *see* faith. See faith in the way you treat her."

"But what about the way she treats me?"

"Now come on, son. I'm sure there've been a few times when she had to show her faith with you. You can't tell me that in the two years you've been married, you've done everything right."

Visions of Natasia came back and all the things he'd done wrong. "When did you become such a fan of Jasmine . . . Cox."

"Son," the reverend began softly, "she's Jasmine Bush. Instead of doing what the world does—looking for a reason to leave—why don't you do what God wants, and find the reason to stay?"

He was so tired. Tired of hearing how he had to be the one to do right.

What about Natasia?

He shut his eyes and shut down his conscience. And said good-bye to his father. He didn't feel like hearing anymore do-right lectures tonight.

Hosea pushed himself from the bed and walked to the window. The summer sun had already set, leaving him only a view of a nighttime-traffic-light Ventura Boulevard. The days were getting shorter, just like their time in Los Angeles. In a few weeks, they'd be returning to New York. What would his life look like then?

At least his father's call had brought just a bit of good news. Jasmine was not a bigamist. Made finding out about her previous marriage not as big of a deal. At least it didn't feel as big as it did when he first found out.

But then, he shook his head, stood up straight, stuck out his chest. He wasn't going soft now. So what—Jasmine was divorced. This was about principles. This was about trust. And there would never be any trust between him and Jasmine again. He didn't see how there could ever be.

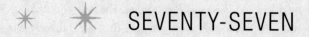# SEVENTY-SEVEN

THE PRODUCERS PUSHED THEIR chairs back from the conference table.

"Okay, that's a wrap," Hosea said. "Thanks for making this a quick meeting."

Triage laughed. "Yeah, we've had some marathons, huh?" He bumped knuckles with Hosea. "I'm out, on my way to the studio."

Hosea followed his friend to the door, but before he could get out, Natasia asked, "Got a moment?"

He turned around. Since her altercation with Jasmine, he'd stayed as far away from Natasia as work allowed. He said, "Sure," as if it wasn't a big deal. "What's going down?"

"Let's talk in your office."

That's not what he wanted to do. Really didn't want to be anywhere alone with her. But he agreed.

As they walked side by side, he had to work hard to ignore her scent, but the lavender and orchid fragrance was a part of her, became a part of him. He stared straight ahead, not looking at her until they were behind closed doors.

"So what do you want to talk about?" he asked in the professional tone, designed to keep distance between them.

She perched herself against the edge of his desk. Waited an extra moment, then said, "I'm gonna get straight to the point. I know what's going on."

He frowned.

"I know you've moved out of the Fairmont." She passed him a small smile when his eyes glazed over with surprise. "I know you're not with your wife."

At first, he was shocked. And wondered about her source. But there was no reason to be shocked. Even though this was a secret he'd worked hard to keep hidden, she was a journalist. Snooping was in her blood. And he was sure that she'd taken prying into his life to a new level.

"Why didn't you tell me?" She pouted.

His eyebrows rose. "It's none of your business."

"Oh, really." Her lips bent into a twisted smile. "I'm the reason you left Jasmine and it's none of my business?"

It was her nerve, her guts, her aggression that made her so attractive to him years before. But not now. Not while he was still married. "Natasia, you're not the reason, but whatever is going on is between me and Jasmine." His eyes narrowed. "I would never leave my wife for another woman."

She half-laughed. "Of course you wouldn't. Especially not if I were your wife." She paused. "So tell me, is it true? Are you and Jasmine separated?"

"Have you listened to anything I said?" he responded, his voice filled with his irritation.

As if he hadn't said a word, she asked, "You've finally realized that you haven't gotten over me."

He shook his head, turned his attention to papers piled high on his desk.

After a moment, she rose, moved toward the door, then stopped. When she turned back, her lips had curved into that smile. But there was more—an unbridled determination was etched in every line of her face.

"There's a reason why you never said good-bye all those years ago, Hosea. It's not over, and I'm not about to let you walk away this time."

He breathed with relief when she left him alone, but he could tell by her words that this respite would be short lived.

. . .

All Hosea wanted to do was get into the shower, read his Bible, and then make up for the hours of lost sleep from last night.

Turning off the lights in the studio, he was glad that he was alone. He was surprised that Natasia wasn't lurking around, after what she'd told him today. But she'd left hours ago. Good thing—he didn't have enough patience tonight.

His bones were aching as he dragged into the parking lot, his computer bag resting heavy on his shoulder. But as he neared his SUV, he slowed even more. Stared at the two back tires. Flat.

Frowning, he crouched down and inspected. Both tires had been slashed. *Great,* he thought, and wondered if he should report this vandalism to the police. But it was probably just neighborhood kids and calling the police would delay his getting home.

Sighing, he turned back toward the building, but then the sound of screeching tires made him stop. He frowned when a black Jaguar raced around the corner and lurched toward him. He jumped to get out of the car's path.

The car came to a sudden stop only inches away.

"Sorry 'bout that." Natasia looked at him over the rim of the dark glasses she wore, even though the sun had set an hour before. "I haven't driven in a while."

He looked at her. "I thought you were trying to kill me."

She laughed. "Why would I want to do that?" And then her laughter died when she looked at his tires. Putting her car in park, she slipped out and stood next to him.

"What happened?"

He shrugged. "I have no idea. I'm going to call a tow truck now."

"Geez," she said, peering closer. "This really looks bad."

"Yeah," he sighed. "One tire, I would have been able to change. But two." He shook his head. "And all I wanted to do tonight was get to the hotel and get some rest."

"Well, then, isn't it lucky that I rented this car?" She grinned.

"I'll take you to your hotel and you can handle this in the morn-ing."

He folded his arms, studied her. "Why do you have a rental? I thought you were using the car service."

"I wanted to do some stuff over the next couple of days. I was coming back to the office to . . . well, anyway," she waved her hand in the air, "I'm here, and I can take you to your hotel. Maybe we can stop and get a bite to eat first."

He shook his head. Stepped away from her and moved toward the studio. "That's okay," he began, talking over his shoulder as he walked. "I'm gonna call the auto club."

"Why would you want to do that?" she yelled to him.

He stopped, turned around. "Because." And then he kept right on moving.

Behind him, he could hear her sigh. "Hosea, it doesn't make sense . . ."

But the studio's door closed on her words. Within minutes, he had the auto club on the line, trying to find a tow company near him. As he was placed on hold, his mind wandered back to his car, the gashed tires and Natasia's sudden appearance.

"Nah." He shook his head. She didn't have a thing to do with this. What grown woman would knife tires just to get a man's attention?

"Mr. Bush," the operator came on the line, "it'll be at least an hour."

"Okay, thanks," he said, even though he was far from grateful. He leaned back in his chair, thought again about the tires. Won-dered again about Natasia. And prayed to God that she didn't have anything to do with this. Because if she did, he was afraid of what she might do next.

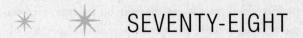

SEVENTY-EIGHT

"RING AROUND THE ROSIE," Jasmine sang and Jacqueline giggled as they jumped together. "All fall . . ."

"Down!" Jacqueline shouted, fell to the floor, and kicked her feet in the air.

Jasmine clapped and was still smiling when she answered the ringing telephone.

"Jasmine!"

That voice took all her cheer away.

"What do you want, Natasia?" she asked and then wondered why she didn't just hang up.

"I'm calling to see if you're going to be there this evening. Hosea wanted me to pick up a few things for him."

"What?" Jasmine shook her head, trying to understand this woman's words.

"I said," she spoke slower, "I need to come by and pick up a few things for Hosea."

Now she hung up. Slammed the phone down hard, then paced the length of the living room.

"Mama, all fall down!" Jacqueline clapped.

Jasmine nodded. She agreed with her daughter. She should have taken Natasia down the last time she saw her. Should have whipped that crazy woman until she was begging for a one-way ticket back to Chicago.

"Mama, down!"

"Yeah, baby," she said, though she couldn't turn her attention back to the children's game. Not when she had to focus on this grown-up game that Natasia had drawn her into.

Had Hosea really asked her to call to pick up some of his things? *No!* Her husband would never do that. This was just another skank ploy—get the wife off balance. Get the husband and wife arguing. It was something she used to do.

Still, suppose . . .

Jasmine grabbed the phone, but then stopped. If she asked Hosea about this, it would just make him mad. That was Natasia's objective. She needed to know if he was with Natasia—just had to find out another way. Still holding the phone, she dialed Mae Frances's room.

"Hey, can you come over here right away?" she asked when her friend answered.

She returned the phone to the cradle, and then sat on the sofa, waiting. Certainly, Mae Frances had some kind of connection who could help her handle this.

Jasmine was keeping her enemy close.

That was her thought as the phone on the other end rang.

"Quimby here," the man answered.

Jasmine paused. She hadn't expected the man to answer his own phone. Maybe she needed a larger agency. But then she shook her head. No need to second-guess. Mr. Quimby came highly recommended. "Hello, my name is Jasmine Larson, and I'm interested in hiring you to do some surveillance."

"Yes, Miss Larson, or is it Missus?"

"It's Miss," she said, wanting no connection to Hosea in this instance.

"What can I do to help you, little lady?"

Jasmine frowned. *Little lady?* Oh, she didn't like this man already. But according to Mae Frances (who had hooked her up with Mr. Quimby through a connection who had a connection), he was one of the best private investigators in Los Angeles.

So she swallowed her irritation and focused on her mission.

Gave the man Natasia's name, where she was staying, where she worked, and the car service she used. "Will your company be able to do twenty-four-hour surveillance?"

"Yeah, but that's going to cost some bucks."

"I'm not worried about money."

"Well, if it doesn't bother you, it won't bother me. How often do you want a report?"

"Anytime she does anything except go to her hotel or the station, I want to know. And I also want to know if anyone ever goes with her to the hotel."

"Okay, little lady. Give me your credit card and I'll scope her out on the Internet, see if we can get a photo, and we'll get started tonight."

By the time she hung up, Jasmine was smiling again. Tomorrow she would know if Natasia was lying or if she had really set up house with Hosea. After she found that out, she would take it from there.

She glanced at her watch. It was time to read to Jacqueline before she tucked her into bed. And then, for the rest of the night, she'd do exactly what her father-in-law had told her. She'd read her Bible and pray. And let Jesus take the wheel from here.

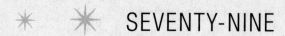

SEVENTY-NINE

"I AM HAPPY TO SEE you." Pastor Ford hugged Alexis before she led her to her couch in her office.

"Thanks for calling to check on me."

"Of course. I was just glad that you finally called me back." The pastor chuckled. "For a while, I thought you were avoiding me." She reached for the coffeepot. Filled one mug. "You still like yours black?"

Alexis inhaled. Lingered in the aroma of her addiction. Could feel the heat of it in her mouth. "I don't drink coffee anymore."

"Really? You stopped just like that?"

Alexis paused. Thought about their addictions—hers and Brian's. "Just like that."

"Good for you." Pastor Ford leaned back with her cup in her hand. "I saw you and Brian on Sunday." She sipped her java. "I was thrilled. So, all is well?"

Alexis shrugged. "Can't say that, but Brian's been home for almost three weeks and I haven't kicked him out again." She chuckled. Tried to make the truth a joke.

Pastor Ford smiled, sipped, said, "That's good."

"I'm trying to do the right thing." Alexis's eyes followed Pastor Ford's cup as she rested it on the table.

The pastor said, "What you're doing is huge. You're going to be an example for so many women."

"Believe me, Pastor, I want to do what every other woman would do and walk away. But I keep thinking about what you told us about God and divorce."

"I'm not sure that every woman would walk away, but you're

not like other women anyway. You know what I say, true believers have a hard time fitting in with the world."

"I just wish this walk was easier."

"God never promised easy. Just strength." She took Alexis's hand. "I know you've needed strength. Brian told me about Jasmine and the baby." She stopped, hugged Alexis again.

"Pastor, if you've got any really good prayers, I need them now, because the baby is the worst part of this."

"That's a big one. But remember it's all because of his disease."

It's the disease. The mantra that she lived by. Pastor Ford continued, "Brian would have never been with Jasmine if it wasn't for his addiction."

Maybe. "I know that."

"And the baby . . . what are you guys doing about her?"

She shrugged. "Brian says that Jasmine and her husband are her parents. He doesn't want to interfere."

"And you?"

"I'm fine with that. It makes it easier, actually. I couldn't imagine having a child with us now. We're not stable, we're not sure . . ." She stopped.

There was no scenario where she could imagine a future with Brian and Jasmine and their baby. She couldn't wrap her mind around every other weekend visits. Or talking to Jasmine about allergies and school projects. Couldn't see planning joint birthday parties. And the thought of breaking holiday bread together made her want to never eat another piece of turkey or stuffing or sweet potatoes again.

"You're handling a lot, Alexis. I'm proud of you."

"Don't say that too quickly. Brian's home, but we're not really . . . back together. We're still in separate bedrooms."

"That's totally understandable."

She exhaled. She'd walked in, expecting a lecture. "I don't know how long . . . we'll be this way."

Pastor Ford nodded. "Tell me, what's keeping you from being intimate with Brian?"

"Everything! I think about his addiction and all the women he's been with. And now the baby. I wonder if there are any more. Pastor, he could have ten, fifteen, thirty children out there."

"If he did, you would have heard about a few of them by now." The pastor paused. "I think it's Jasmine—"

Alexis cringed every time she heard that name.

"I think it's Jasmine and your history with her. The affair she had with Jefferson. And how she went after Brian. That's your challenge."

Alexis nodded. "I know I'm not supposed to have enemies, but if I did, she'd be the one. Just knowing that she was with . . ." She closed her eyes and wished that everlasting picture in her mind of Brian and Jasmine together would go away. But it stayed during every waking hour, during every hour she slept.

Pastor Ford said, "You know, it really shouldn't matter who Brian was with. It's all part of—"

"—the disease," Alexis finished. "Easy to say. Not to live."

"Alex, do you really want your marriage to work?"

I don't know. "I think so. Yes."

"Then I'm going to tell you what I tell all the couples I counsel who are working through infidelity. Once you're committed to making your marriage work, you have to get to the next level to heal. Find your way back to Brian. Get back into bed with him." She paused. "What can I do to help?"

With a sigh, Alexis said, "This is something I'm going to have to do myself."

"You're right about that," the pastor said with a slight smile. "But if you and Brian want to come in and talk this through—"

"We remember *how* to do it, Pastor."

Pastor Ford chuckled. "That's good to know. Now all you need to remember are the reasons *why.* Remember that no one is as bad as the worst mistake they've ever made. Not even Brian."

His worst mistake. Jasmine.

Alexis eyed the pastor's coffee again. Right now all she wanted to do was drink mugs and mugs of her addiction to take the edge away. But if Brian was leaving his obsession alone, she had to do the same.

Get back in bed with Brian. "I'm going to try, Pastor. Really try."

The pastor's phone rang. "Excuse me."

As Pastor Ford went to her desk, Alexis sat back, stared at the coffeepot. Maybe if she had one cup . . . but then she shook her head. She wasn't going to depend on her addiction to get her through this. She was going to handle her marriage. Do it right. No matter what it took, she was going to find her way back to her husband.

EIGHTY

"QUIMBY HERE."

Jasmine paused, wondering again if she needed a larger agency. The man answered his own phone and he hadn't even called her yesterday like he promised. "Mr. Quimby, this is Jasmine Larson," she said, her tone sharp.

"Hey, little lady," he sang as if she was his friend.

She cringed. "Do you have anything for me?"

Papers shuffled and then, "Yeah, Elliott gave me the report, but there's nothing to tell, which is why I didn't bother you yesterday. Ms. Redding hasn't done much. Just goes from her hotel to the studio and then back to the Rendezvous sometime between seven and eight. That's it."

I knew the heifer was lying. "And she's been alone when she goes to the hotel?"

"Yup. At least for the last two nights."

"She hasn't even gone out to dinner?"

"Nope. You're paying quite a bit of money for me to tell you this lady is boring. Are you sure you want to continue the surveillance?"

"Definitely. Keep following her."

"Okay. It's your hundreds."

I'd pay thousands.

"Oh, there is one little thing. She's not using the car service you gave us. She's rented a car."

Jasmine frowned. Any little change with Natasia meant something, and she wondered what this was about. But as long as she had Mr. Quimby, she would find out Natasia's moves before she even made them. "That's fine. Just keep me posted."

"You got it, little lady."

Jasmine hung up. She might not like the way he addressed her, but she loved the way he did his job.

So, that call—Natasia had just made it to upset her. Probably thought she'd go running to Hosea and then Natasia would have denied ever speaking to her. Would have made it look as if she'd made up the whole thing. A typical trick that could have worked. But not on her.

Well, at least Natasia's lie had worked in one way—it made Jasmine take more notice. Natasia was no slouch; she was a crazy skank who was not to be played with. But with Mr. Quimby, Jasmine had the control.

Jasmine laid back and opened her Bible. This reading, praying, letting God handle most of it was really working.

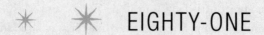# EIGHTY-ONE

IT DIDN'T SURPRISE HOSEA — the way God just kept on talking.

Days ago, the pounding in his head had ended, but still God spoke—through calls from his father, through guests on his show, and now, through the Bible.

All he'd done tonight as he prepared to read was say a little prayer asking for guidance. Then he opened his Bible—right to the Book of Hosea. To the verse where God told the prophet *Go show your love to your wife again.*

If it weren't so sad, Hosea would have laughed. There was no subtlety here—it was clear what God expected. The problem was, although they shared the same name, Hosea Bush was not Hosea the prophet.

The love part wasn't difficult. But the trust—he couldn't, wouldn't live with anyone he didn't trust.

The ringing hotel phone made him frown and glance at the clock. Who would be calling him so close to midnight? He sighed. Jasmine. She was the only one who knew where he was staying. She'd probably tried to reach him on his cell, but he'd turned that off. After the questions he'd had about his tires being slashed, he didn't want Natasia to have any way of reaching him.

He stared at the phone, still ringing, not wanting to answer. But then he remembered Mae Frances. And Jacqueline. He was supposed to see his daughter the day after tomorrow. He grabbed the telephone.

"Hosea, this is Natasia." She spoke succinctly. "I'm downstairs in the lobby."

He pushed himself from the bed. "What are you doing here?"

He didn't bother to ask how she knew where he was staying. She was a journalist. So that wasn't the surprise. The shock was that she had actually come to his hotel.

"I have some papers I need you to sign," she said, her tone still professional.

But he was not fooled. "Whatever it is," he began, shaking his head as he spoke, "we'll do it in the office, in the morning. I'll be in early."

"I have a couple of meetings off-site tomorrow; I won't be in until late." When he didn't say anything, she sighed and continued to explain, "This is the contract for the extended use of the studio. I just left Triage, got his signature. And now I need yours before I FedEx them to New York tomorrow."

"I still—"

She interrupted him, "Look, we need to do this," not trying to hide her irritation. "I'll be in and out in five minutes. What's your room number?"

"I'll come down."

A pause and then, "Whatever!"

He jerked back at the sound of the phone slamming in his ear. But he didn't care how upset she was; he was pissed too—that she would think he was dumb enough to believe this.

He slipped into jeans and a shirt, and five minutes later he was in the lobby that was furnished with only a worn plaid sofa and single table.

With her lips pursed, she slowly glanced around the small space. "Nice digs," then she handed him the envelope without a smile.

He sat, and while he reviewed the first pages, he could feel the heat of her fury as she walked back and forth in front of him. He worked to keep his focus on the contract. Tried not to think of the times in their past when she'd lost her temper. Didn't want to remember all that great make-up sex.

By the time he got to the sixth page, she couldn't hold back anymore. Still pacing, she said. "You know, Hosea, I drove all the way over here to take care of business. Nothing else."

He looked up. "If it's only about business, Natasia, I apologize."

She didn't change her stance. Stayed with her arms folded, glaring at him until he finished reading and signing.

When he stuffed the papers back into the envelope, she grabbed it, then turned away without saying a word. But she'd only taken two steps before she slowed.

Hosea frowned as Natasia's hands searched the pockets of her knee-length jacket. Then she stopped completely and rummaged through her purse.

Hosea moved behind her. "What's wrong?"

She shook her head, without looking at him. "My keys . . . I don't know where . . ."

The memory was instant—another time, another place, missing keys.

She sighed. "Where the heck are the keys?" And then just like all those years before, she said, "Maybe I left them in the car." She marched toward the front door.

He was right behind her when she stood in front of the Jaguar. The doors were unlocked.

"I must have left them inside," she said.

But even after they searched together, behind the seats, under the mats, no keys were found.

"What am I supposed to do now?" She slammed the door.

"The keys have to be here somewhere," Hosea said. "You just drove over."

"I don't have them," she said slowly. "Do you want to search me?" She held out her arms as if she were about to be frisked.

"Of course not. I was just sayin'." He stopped, motioned for her to walk in front of him. "I'm sure the clerk has a number to a cab company. We'll call for one inside."

She looked at her watch. "At this time of night? We're in L.A. I'll be waiting for hours."

Inside, Hosea rang the bell sitting atop the counter.

As they waited, Natasia said, "Look, it doesn't make sense for me to take a cab tonight. I'll just have to be back over here in the morning to get the car. It would make more sense if I just stayed in your room." She rolled her eyes at his expression. "I wish you would stop accusing me."

"I haven't accused you of anything," he said, his voice steady.

"It's the way you're looking at me. It's the way you wouldn't let me come up to your room when I called you about these." She held up the envelope. "It's the way—"

He held up his hands. "You're right. Just stay here. No need to take a cab back tonight."

It was a tiny smile that she gave him, but then she frowned when he rang the bell again. This time, the night clerk shuffled from the back room. "May I help you?" the man asked before he yawned. "Oh, Mr. Bush." The white-haired man stretched his arms above his head. "How ya doing tonight?"

"I'm great, Ralph. Sorry to get you up. Do you have any rooms?"

The old man frowned. "Something wrong with yours?"

"No, this is for a friend."

The clerk gave Natasia a long glance, then turned back to Hosea. With a crooked-teeth smile, he said, "I think I can gather up something for ya."

Natasia's mouth was open, but not a word came out, until, "Ah, thank you." She grabbed Hosea's arm. "Can you excuse us for a moment?"

"Sure, this will take a minute on my end." The clerk clicked keys on the computer.

"Hosea," she whispered once she'd pulled him to the side, "why are we spending money for another room? It doesn't make sense."

"It makes plenty of sense, Natasia." He didn't say more; he knew she understood his message.

"But it's not like I'm trying to get with you. This was really just work. Doesn't this," she held up the envelope again, "prove it?"

He shook his head.

She blew out a long breath of frustration. "I'll sleep in my clothes, I'll sleep on the floor, whatever you need."

"You don't have to do any of that. I'll get you a room."

She folded her arms. "Just let me stay with you," she challenged. "No need to waste money."

"Look around," he whispered. "This isn't the Rendezvous. It's not going to cost that much." He didn't give her time to say another word. Turned back to the desk and chatted with Ralph. But even as he talked, he could hear Natasia's deep breathing behind him.

"Here you are." The clerk offered Natasia the sleeve with the key.

It took a moment for her to grab it, then she glared at Hosea before she swung her bag over her shoulder.

"The elevators are over here," Hosea called behind her as she marched toward the staircase.

She shook her head. "I'm just one floor up. And don't worry. You don't have to escort me." She paused, as if she was trying to get him to remember the last time he'd walked her to the room. That last time in Oakland—that was the beginning.

But he kept his face blank, pretended that he remembered nothing. She turned, stomped up the stairs. And despite her protests, he followed her to the second floor. Standing in the cut of the staircase door, he watched until Natasia slammed into her room. Waiting for just another moment, he smiled. Then turned and trotted up the steps.

. . .

Hosea slapped the alarm clock off, then glanced up, just to make sure that it really was seven o'clock. It surprised him that he slept through the night. He'd expected at least one phone call from Natasia. Or one knock on his door. Or even someone shouting, "Fire," in the hallway—anything to get into his room.

But in the almost seven hours that had passed, she hadn't tried a thing. He wondered if she was already awake, if she'd already called the car company.

He picked up the telephone. When the clerk answered, he asked, "May I have Natasia Redding's room?"

"Hey, Mr. Bush, this is Ralph. Your friend is gone."

"Gone?"

"She checked out about ten minutes after you guys checked her in. Said something about finding her keys. I'm not even going to charge you for the room."

"Thanks, Ralph."

Hosea was still shaking his head long after he hung up. He'd known the keys were a trick, and now he wondered if that had been her trick all those years ago. Had their entire relationship started with that scheme? Seemed like neither one of the women he'd loved could be trusted. And he wondered what that said about him.

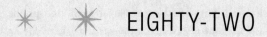

EIGHTY-TWO

SLOWLY, JASMINE CLOSED HER BIBLE. For the seventh time in as many days, she'd read the complete Book of Hosea. Somehow, she found peace inside those pages. Maybe it was seeing her husband's name over and over. Or maybe it was that she saw a little bit of herself in Gomer. Not that she was a whore like Gomer, but it was clear that Gomer, like her, had been so misunderstood.

Now, all she needed was for Hosea to have the same heart of forgiveness that Gomer's Hosea had. Could her Hosea—like the prophet—forgive her twice?

She sighed and wondered what she could do to make that happen.

Let Jesus take the wheel.

That's what she really wanted to do, but it just seemed as if sometimes God could use a little help. Especially when it came to making life happen faster.

"Mama, look."

Jasmine glanced at her daughter and couldn't do anything but smile. While she'd been reading, Jacqueline had been doing the same with her picture book, turning the pages slowly. Her eyebrows were bunched together, exactly the way Hosea frowned when he was in deep thought. *She really is his daughter.* And then she felt the ping of pain. That little ache that always made her wonder if prayers would be enough to bring Hosea home.

"Here, babygirl," she said, taking the book that Jacqueline held upside down and turning it upright. "Let's read this together."

But before she could share a word, her cell phone buzzed. She flipped it open quickly when she recognized the number.

"Mr. Quimby," she said, without saying hello. The private investigator never called her.

"Yeah, little lady. I got something for you."

Already, her heart was beating fast with fear. He would only call if Natasia had changed her routine. And that couldn't be any kind of good news.

"Your friend changed her plans last night. She drove over to the Extend-a-Stay Motel in Burbank around midnight and—"

Oh, God. Jasmine stood, paced. Held the phone to her ear with one hand. Clutched her Bible with the other.

She had been doing exactly what Reverend Bush had told her to do. She had tried to be still. But that hadn't done a doggone thing. Natasia had still spent the night with her husband and . . .

"She was there for about twenty minutes and then she drove back to the Rendezvous."

His words stopped her descent into misery. "What?"

Even though he repeated what he'd said, it still took her a moment to digest the private eye's words. *She didn't stay with Hosea?*

Jasmine sank back onto the sofa next to her daughter. "She left and went back to her hotel—alone?"

"Yup, she was alone. I figured I'd call and tell you. Can't imagine that it would mean anything, but that's what you're paying me for—information, right?"

"Thank you, Mr. Quimby." If he was standing in front of her, she would have kissed him. "Please keep me informed."

She hugged the Bible closer to her chest and imagined how the scenario had played out. Natasia had gone to Hosea's hotel and she was out in twenty minutes. Nothing could have happened. Natasia had gone after Hosea and he had turned her away.

She looked at the Bible she held, thought about all those prayers she'd been saying. Maybe God was handling this.

She lifted Jacqueline onto her lap and then opened the Bible again. "You want Mama to read something to you?" she asked.

Jacqueline nodded.

This time, Jasmine opened her Bible to the chapter that Mae Frances had told her about this morning.

"When you're reading," she'd said as she glanced at Jasmine's open Bible on the couch, "make sure you check out Proverbs thirty-one. Start at verse ten."

"Why? What's that about?"

Mae Frances had rolled her eyes toward heaven as if she couldn't believe she had to deal with this heathen. "Chile, don't you know nothin' 'bout your Bible?" She shook her head as if she'd been reading her Bible every day for thirty years. As if. She said, "That's about that virtuous woman. Whew! She was no joke. Take a few lessons from her, and when Preacher Man comes home, he'll never leave again."

Jasmine would have grabbed her Bible right then if she and Jacqueline weren't on their way to the park. But now that she'd read about the prophet Hosea again, and she had this great news from Mr. Quimby, she was ready to check out this Proverbs woman.

Jasmine found the scripture. "Who can find a virtuous wife?" she read to her daughter. She paused, read those words again silently. This was going to be interesting.

She sat back, hugged Jacqueline to her chest, and shared with her daughter the scriptures that Mae Frances had told her to read.

EIGHTY-THREE

"YOU SURE YOU DON'T WANT me to stay, Preacher Man?"

Hosea smiled. Kissed the top of Jacqueline's head again as he held her and shook his head. "Nope, Nama. My pumpkin and I are going to be just fine."

"Hmph. You and your pumpkin would be better off—"

Hosea held up his hands, stopping her before she could even begin her rampage about him and Jasmine. "Mae Frances, please. Let me work this out."

She glared at him. "Are you praying?"

He smiled. Of all the people to ask him that. "Yes. I am."

"Then, I guess it'll be all right eventually."

He kissed her cheek. "Have the driver take you wherever you want. You got money to do some shopping?"

She pushed her shoulders back. Stood taller. "Yes, I do. I got a job, you know. I don't need you and Jasmine Larson looking after me like I'm an old woman."

"You're not old. But we'll always look after you, because we love you."

"If you loved me so much, you would—"

Hosea directed her out the door. "Bye, Nama. I'll see you in a couple of hours."

Once alone, Hosea held Jacqueline in his lap. "So, how's Daddy's pumpkin doing?"

She giggled when he tickled her.

Then he held her close. God, how he missed her. He wanted his life back—wanted to be with his daughter all the time, every day. But he couldn't get his heart to move.

The knock on the door startled him.

"Hey, Boss." Brittney stepped inside. "I know you didn't want to be disturbed, but Steve is here with some guys he wants you to meet."

"Now?"

She nodded. "He just walked in. They're dressed casual, so I don't think he wants a long meeting or anything. Looks like he just wants to make some introductions."

Hosea frowned.

"I'll watch Jacquie," she said, reaching for the girl. "She and I get along just fine."

"I don't know."

"I've watched her before. Lots of time with Jasmine."

But this was different. This was his time with his daughter. "All right. Keep her in here." He lifted her off his lap, handed her to Brittney. "I'll be right back, my pumpkin." He kissed her before he dashed from the room.

He'd make this quick and get right back to his daughter. He took a breath before he opened the door to the conference room and with a smile, he stepped inside.

Hosea glanced at his watch. It had only been twenty minutes, but to him that was too much time. He said his good-byes to the network executives, then rushed back to his office.

He stepped inside with a grin, then frowned. Quickly, he scanned the empty room. He dashed down the hallway, chuckling a bit. If Brittney had to return to her desk with Jacqueline, he could only imagine how frantic she must be. His daughter and telephones just did not mix.

"Hey," he said before he turned the corner. But when he did, his smile was gone. Brittney was on the phone, but there was no sign of Jacqueline. "Where's Jacquie?" he whispered.

Brittney held up a finger, asking him to wait.

He shook his head. "Put them on hold," he demanded. "Where's Jacquie?"

His tone made her press the hold button. "She's with Natasia."

"What?" He didn't know why his heart raced.

"The phones were ringing off the hook," Brittney spoke quickly, "and Natasia said she would watch Jacquie for me. I didn't think you'd mind." But now, Brittney sounded as panicked as he felt.

He barely heard the last of Brittney's words before he ran toward Natasia's office. Another empty room.

His heart was pounding; even the deep breaths he took didn't calm him. But then he wondered, why was he worried? Jacqueline was with Natasia—she was a friend. A woman he once loved.

The tires on his SUV—that's what he thought about first. And then her missing keys.

I'm not about to let you walk away this time.

He had wondered then what that meant. And now he prayed Jacqueline wasn't part of her plan.

"Your imagination is in overdrive," he whispered to himself. "Jacquie's fine." That became his mantra as he searched through the studio, finding nothing.

She'd left the building, with his daughter. Where could they have gone?

And then he heard the sweetest giggles. Behind him.

He turned around and Natasia was coming through the studio doors. Her arms full—with Jacqueline and a bag stuffed with toys.

"What are you doing?" He grabbed his daughter and the little girl frowned.

"Hosea!" Natasia's eyes were wide with shock. "What's wrong?"

Feeling Jacqueline's eyes on him, he kept his voice soft. "Where did you take her?" His teeth were clenched.

"I didn't take her anywhere." She tried to calm him with her tone. "I was helping Brittney and I had some toys in the car. I took her with me to the car to get the toys."

His glower deepened. "You just happened to have toys in your car?" *What kind of crap is that?*

"Yes, I had toys." And then she glanced around. Saw Brittney and Sharon staring at them. Natasia lowered her voice. "You're making a scene."

He glared at her for a moment longer. Turned and carried his daughter away.

Natasia was right behind him. "Why are you making a big deal about this?"

He didn't say a word until he was in his office. "Because *this* is my daughter. And I didn't tell you to take her anywhere."

"I didn't take her *anywhere.*" Natasia folded her arms. Now her tone matched his. "I took her to my car."

"Without telling anyone? That was some fatal attraction—" He stopped. Thought about all the times that Jasmine had warned him that Natasia was crazy.

Natasia looked at his daughter and smiled. "I was only trying to help," she said softly. "I wanted you to know that Jacquie and I were friends." She reached toward the girl and Jacqueline buried her head against her father's chest.

"Natasia," he began, composed now, "I'm sorry. Thank you for watching Jacquie. But you can go now. We're fine."

"I thought the three of us could hang out—"

"No." He stopped her. "I just want . . . to be with Jacquie."

She nodded slowly. Held up the bag. "What about these?"

"You can take them."

"I can leave them and then next time—"

"Take your toys," he said sternly.

She shrugged, waved at Jacqueline, and then left them alone.

Hosea sat down, and sighed as he rocked his daughter back and forth. Wondered why this had upset him so much. Was it because he didn't know where Jacqueline was? Or was it because she was with Natasia? Or both?

Or maybe it was just discernment.

He leaned back, looked at Jacqueline. Now, she smiled. And he did the same.

—*Thank God,* he thought. Thank God that she was safe.

He strapped his sleeping daughter into the back of the Town Car and kissed her.

"So, Preacher Man, everything okay?"

"Yeah." He slammed the door and turned to Mae Frances. "Why're you asking me that?"

Mae Frances shrugged. "That gal at the front desk said there was some confusion earlier with Jacqueline."

He pressed his lips together. He'd have to remind Brittney that what happened in the office, stayed in the office. Then said, "There was no confusion." He paused. Wondered how much Brittney had said. Looked into Mae Frances's eyes and prayed that she would say nothing to Jasmine. "Please don't start any drama, Nama."

"What you talking 'bout, Preacher Man? Do you know me to ever start drama?"

He rolled his eyes and walked Mae Frances around to the front of the car. He kissed her before she slipped inside.

"You still praying?"

"Yes, Mae Frances. I pray all the time."

She nodded. "Good. Make sure that you say each prayer three times. And then say them over again if you have to. After you've prayed all that you need to pray, then you need to say what you need to say and ask what you need to know." She held up her hand in a "Hallelujah" motion and closed the car door before the driver edged away from the curb.

Say what you need to say? Ask what you need to know? What did that mean?

Hosea stood on the street, watching the car roll away. Thinking about Mae Frances's words made him shake his head. He wouldn't ever be able to figure out Mae Frances. Anyway, he had other things to do. He had to get back in the studio and explain some things to Brittney. And at the same time, he had to figure out a way to stay far away from Natasia.

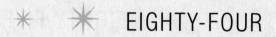

EIGHTY-FOUR

ALEXIS HAD COME HOME EARLY just to do this.

She lay back on the bed. Closed her eyes. And imagined.

Imagined Brian next to her. On top of her. Beneath her. Imagined his lips on her lips. His flesh on her flesh. Imagined his fingers and his tongue doing what she used to love. Imagined again loving it, loving him.

And then, there was Jasmine.

Right in the middle of her fantasy, Jasmine arrived. Lay between her and Brian. And stayed.

Alexis pushed Jasmine and her image away. Sat up, disgusted.

A week ago Pastor Ford had given her the advice to get back into bed with Brian. But every time she imagined herself with her husband, Jasmine was there.

She just couldn't figure this out. She'd been able to find her way back to Brian after she'd found out about his addiction and all the other women. But none of them had faces. Even Tonya had a face that she couldn't remember.

But Jasmine had a face.

And Jasmine had a baby.

Get past this. That's what she kept telling herself. To get back to Brian, she had to get rid of Jasmine.

She smiled and counted the ways Jasmine's extermination could happen. But since she wasn't willing to spend time in a federal correctional facility, she'd have to come up with something else.

She would.

Tonight. I'm going to make love to my husband. Tonight.

Determined, she lay down again. And imagined. Imagined hard. Imagined love with her husband. Love before Jasmine.

EIGHTY-FIVE

THE ICE CUBES CLICKED together as Brian twirled the glass in his hand. Then in one quick motion, he turned the glass up and emptied his drink. The vodka burned a trail down his throat and after a moment, he turned and faced the dance floor. A merengue beat pulsed through the club.

He couldn't remember the last time he'd come to de Janeiro. Certainly, it had been way before he'd made that fateful trip to New York where he'd found a pregnant Jasmine. Just the memory of that moment made him want to order another drink—a double.

Brian turned back to the bar. Raised his glass toward the bartender.

He'd have one more drink. Then go home. He didn't have any reason to be here.

Except for Alexis.

He shook away that thought of blaming his wife. She was not the reason. He was in this place because this decadence was already in him. Just a part of who he was.

No! he protested. He wasn't that man anymore. He was overcoming his addiction. The fact that Jasmine had kissed him and he hadn't let it go any further proved how far he'd come.

So what am I doing here?

He sipped his drink and kept his back to the dance floor. He didn't need to see any of those legs kicking or hips swaying. He kept his eyes behind the bar. Trouble wasn't waiting for him there.

"Is this seat taken?"

The voice was throaty, sexy. He didn't want to see those lips. So he just shifted a bit so that she could sit.

He kept his eyes away. Stared at the rows of liquor bottles that lined the shelves.

And the music kept on bumping.

"I haven't been to a place like this in a while," the voice said. "What about you? Do you come here often?"

Flirting words. Pick-up words. Ones he used to say.

He took a sip of his vodka. Still didn't look at her, but didn't want to be rude. Turned slightly. Gazed instead at her legs.

Big mistake.

"I've been here a few times," he said to her limbs that were crossed at her knees. Shapely legs that he could already imagine wrapped around him.

Not as shapely as Alexis's.

The voice said, "Is it always like this? Always this loud?"

Now he looked at her. A beauty. Even though she sat, he could tell that she was long. And lean. The way he liked. Her beige knit dress broadcasted her curves, told him that he wouldn't be disappointed.

He thought again of his wife.

She tilted her head. "Great. Of all the guys in this place, I had to pick the quiet one." She shook her head. "And that is not what I need tonight."

What he needed was to get out of there. But it was her skin that kept him in place. Her skin that—even in the dim light—looked so silky, he had to fight not to reach out and touch.

"I'm not quiet," he said finally, cupping his glass inside his fingers to keep his hands occupied. "It's just that the music is loud. Kinda difficult to hold a conversation."

"Then we need to get closer." She scooted the barstool over until they were almost one.

He didn't back away.

The woman said, "This seems like a fun place. Do you salsa?"

He took another sip of vodka. Felt the burn. And then felt his shoulders ease. "I don't dance much." He chuckled. "I stick to what I do best."

"And what is that?"

Alexis. "Lots of things."

"Care to share?"

He took another sip, glimpsed at her over the rim of his glass. "I don't share anything without knowing a name."

She chuckled. Held out her hand. "Natasia Redding."

"Nice name."

"And what about you?"

He leaned against the bar, his arm touching hers. "What about me?"

"What's your name?"

"Call me Doc."

"Doc?" She chuckled. "Is that what you do, or is that the games you play?"

"That's what I do."

"Too bad. I was thinking we could just play." She leaned closer. "I make a great patient."

He laughed. "I haven't met anyone like you in a while."

She motioned toward the jammed dance floor. "I know that's not true. This place is full of people looking for a one-night hook-up."

He took a final swig of his drink. "That's what you're looking for?"

She raised her eyebrows and looked to the sky. "After the few weeks I've had. And then yesterday," she blew out a long breath, "I need a quick hook-up to release this pressure. And then, I can get focused again on what I have to do."

"What is it that you have to do?"

She rolled her eyes. "It's a man thing." She waved her hand.

"But I don't want to talk about him. Tonight, it's all about you."
Before he could respond, she pulled her cell phone from her purse
and glanced at the screen. "I've gotta take this call."

"Leaving already?"

"I didn't say a word about leaving." The tip of her tongue
grazed her top lip. Made Brian shudder. She called to the bartender, "Get him another one of those and I'll have a glass of
white wine." Then she slipped off the barstool, whispered in his
ear. "Do me a favor and watch my drink. I wouldn't want anyone
slipping something into it."

She was pressed against him, but Brian didn't budge. His hand
touched the flesh of her arm. And he felt it—the familiar stirring.
"How do you know *I* won't slip something into your drink?"

"Oh, you won't," she said, stepping away just a little. "You
already know you don't have to." She took his hand into hers.
Leaned so close, their lips almost touched. "I'll be right back."
But she didn't move, just stayed, letting him inhale the fragrance
of her. Daring him to press his lips against hers.

He felt it—his stress—rising.

As if she knew she'd done enough, she pirouetted, then slowly,
sensually, swayed along the edge of the dance floor. Gliding,
knowing his eyes were plastered on her.

"Here you go," the bartender said, sliding a fresh glass toward
him. Brian heard his voice, but didn't move until he couldn't see
Natasia any longer. Then he faced the bar. His vodka was there.
And next to it, Natasia's wine.

Brian stared at the drinks—side by side. A pair. A couple. Like
husband and wife.

His wife didn't want him.

But this woman, Natasia, she did. At least for tonight. He
thought of her legs, her arms, her lips. And what they could be
doing in an hour. Playing doctor.

It would be such relief.

Alexis.

He was tired of telling her that he loved her.

Alexis.

How many more times was he supposed to say it?

Alexis.

But he loved her—always had, always would.

He pulled three twenties from his wallet and laid the bills next to the drinks, then glanced back to where he last saw Natasia. There was no sign of her.

Maybe that was the sign.

He pushed through the crowd and didn't look back. He had at least one more "I love you" within him. And he was going home to say it again to his wife.

EIGHTY-SIX

ALEXIS GLANCED AT THE clock once again. Two hours ago—that's when she'd expected Brian to walk through the door and into their apartment. He was supposed to take one look at the candles glimmering, inhale the fragrance of lavender, then lift her into his arms and carry her back to the place where they used to be.

For two hours, this had been her dream. She and Brian. Alone. With no signs of the others. Or Jasmine.

But he'd never come home.

Alexis pushed herself from the sofa where she'd been waiting. Slowly, she strolled the perimeter of the living room, blowing out candles, even though most had already lost their flicker.

She kept her mind on the task at hand. Didn't want to give into the thoughts that were taking her to a place where she didn't need to be.

But it was difficult keeping the questions at bay. Hard not to wonder if Brian was locked up in some hotel. With some faceless woman who was taking her time and her pleasure in meeting every single one of his needs.

This is my fault.

No. There was no fault here. Brian just had an emergency and he wasn't in a place where he could call to explain to his wife who was loaded with doubts. He wasn't with another woman. And he certainly wasn't with Jasmine.

She had to close her eyes to rid herself of that image. Jasmine. Why was she always thinking about her? Surely she wasn't on Jasmine's mind. Jasmine had moved on with her happy life and her happy husband. Hosea—he was the kind of man that she should have married. Jasmine never had to worry about him being with another woman.

"And I don't have to worry about that either," she whispered. Brian had a disease. He was fighting to be cured. Fighting for their marriage. Fighting for her to love him again.

She inhaled, blew out the last candle, when the front door lock clicked. She stood in the darkened living room, covered only by her camisole and matching thong. The soft light from the balcony was behind her.

The moment he opened the door, he stopped. Took in the clouds of fading smoke that remained from the now unlit candles. Then took in his wife.

"Sweetheart . . ." His eyes traveled up her body, then down again. "Baby, you look beautiful."

It took effort, but she found her smile. "I've been waiting for you." She took slow steps, and then without any more words, wrapped her arms around him.

Their kiss was gentle at first. But then he pressed against her and she felt his passion rise.

She squeezed her eyelids tight, keeping away the images. All she wanted in her mind was her husband.

Brian lifted her up—just like she dreamed—and carried her into the bedroom. He broke their embrace long enough to rip her camisole away.

He moaned as he caressed her bare skin. "I want you so much," he panted.

She invited his tongue to hers and they kissed as if they'd never done so before.

As she held him, he slipped from his shirt, then tossed his pants aside. He lay his body against hers, flesh against flesh.

He was fire hot.

She was shivering cold.

Still panting, he raised up for a moment. "Do you want the blanket over us?"

She shook her head. "I want you." Grabbing him, she pulled him back to her. Kissed him. Deeply. Urgently.

He touched. He caressed.

She felt him. Tasted him.

But it wasn't enough to keep the pictures from her mind's eye. The women. *Their* hands. *Their* lips. All. Over. Him.

It wasn't a moan of pleasure that she released. She fought to push all of it away from her.

And she won the fight. The images were gone.

But now, there was the sound.

She flinched when she heard it. The baby—gurgling, giggling. Pushing Brian up, she whispered, "Did you hear that?"

His lips, his tongue were on her neck and he moaned his no. With the way he groaned, with the way his hands danced over her, he told her that he hadn't—and didn't want to—hear a thing.

He recaptured her lips.

But it came again. Louder this time. So close. The sound of a baby. Crying. Jasmine's baby. Her husband's baby.

She shifted and shoved Brian so hard that he grabbed the sheets to hang onto the bed.

"You didn't hear that?" She rocked onto her knees; her eyes darted around the room. Where was the baby?

"Sweetheart," he said, his voice deep with longing. "There's no one here."

But he was wrong. They were not alone.

"Sweetheart, it's all right," he spoke softly as he leaned forward, his lips on target toward hers once again.

He came closer, closer. And she looked into his eyes. In the reflection, they were there. Jasmine. The baby. Staring right at her. From inside him.

She screamed. Jumped from the bed. Grabbed her bathrobe.

"Alex, what's wrong?"

She heard his concern, his confusion. But she couldn't look at him.

"Alexis!"

At the door, she stopped. Turned back. And let him see what he'd never seen before. Her eyes wide—filled with tears and fear. She was losing her mind because of him.

In that moment, she knew there were not enough "I love yous" or "I'm sorrys" left to save them.

EIGHTY-SEVEN

IT HAD TAKEN HOSEA A couple of days to figure it out. But with time and discernment, he finally had.

For as long as he could remember God spoke to him. Yet, it still amazed him every time he heard Him. But what was even more astounding was that this time, God had used Mae Frances.

"Say what you need to say. Ask what you need to know."

Those were her words, but God's guidance.

He stopped his car in front of the Rendezvous, nodded to the valet attendant, and then took a deep breath before he entered the hotel. As he stepped into the elevator, he kept his mind on his mission: *Say what you need to say. Ask what you need to know.*

In the fourteenth-floor hallway, he glanced at his watch. It was late, not quite midnight. But he had no doubt that she would still be awake.

At the door, Hosea raised his hand to knock, but before his knuckles touched the door, it opened. As if Natasia knew he was coming and was gladly expecting him.

Only, she wasn't.

Natasia stood there, covered only with a sheer robe. And next to her, a man. With his shirt undone at the collar and his tie and jacket flipped over his arm.

"Hosea!"

Her tone told him that she was as shocked as he was.

"Ah . . ." He didn't have any words.

"Wow," the man said, looking from Hosea back to the woman he'd just met a few hours ago at de Janeiro. "This is awkward." And then, as if he wasn't sure, he added, "Isn't it?"

"Nah, man," Hosea said. He stood taller, pushed back his shoulders. "It's not awkward at all."

"Uhmmm." Natasia pulled the belt of her robe tighter. As if that would hide her bare skin beneath. "Hosea, come on in. Uhmmm . . ." She paused, looked at the man, squinted as if she was trying to recall his name. Finally, she gave up. "He was just leaving."

"No, that's okay," Hosea said. "You guys can finish . . . your business. We can talk tomorrow."

She pulled her arms tightly around her chest, trying to cover herself even more. "No, now is good. Come in."

The stranger brushed past him and said, "I'm outta here," and then dashed down the hall.

"Come in," she said again, her voice shaking now.

He wondered why she trembled. Did she know what he had come to say? Or maybe she was cold—just naked and cold.

"I don't need to come in." It was easier now than it had been in weeks to keep his eyes on her eyes. "I just wanted to apologize for the other day. With Jacquie."

"That's okay." She tried to smile. "I shouldn't have taken her away without talking to you." She paused again. "I just wanted you to know that your daughter and I could be friends." She motioned toward him again. "Please come in."

He shook his head. "The reason I came by, Natasia, is to say good-bye."

She frowned.

"You've told me a couple of times that I never said good-bye. And you were right. I think that's why you came back. Because I never released you. I never said good-bye. But now, you can put the life we shared behind you. Now you can go forward."

She shook her head. "No, Hosea." She reached for him. "Please, come in. I can explain what this—"

He held up his hands. "You don't have to explain a thing. I

said what I came to say." He paused. Looked at her again. Repeated, "Good-bye," so she would surely understand.

"Hosea!"

She called his name over and over, but he kept walking. He rang for the elevator, and when he stepped inside, turned around, she was there. Standing in the middle of the hallway. Almost naked.

"Hosea, please."

He didn't say a word as the elevator doors closed and the car descended.

He inhaled deeply, then exhaled. He'd done what he was supposed to do—he'd said what he had to say.

Now he had to ask what he needed to know. Had to find out if he could ever trust Jasmine again.

But he wasn't ready to do that. Not yet. He needed time, because Jasmine's answer could change his life.

He needed a few more days to pray.

✳ ✳ EIGHTY-EIGHT

ALEXIS LIFTED HER DELTA Sigma Theta mug from her desk and sipped. She moaned softly. Inhaled and savored another sip of her coffee. This was as close to heaven as she'd been in a long time.

She caressed the half-full mug as if it was her lover, and then she buzzed her assistant. "When you get a moment, can you bring me a cup of coffee?" It was always good to have another waiting.

"More coffee?"

"Yup," she said, and clicked off the intercom. Sure, this was probably about her fifth cup in an hour. But she had a lot of catching up to do. She'd been back in her addiction for only a week.

She punched in the Web site for her real estate broker and scanned the available apartments. The hotel was getting old. And even though Brian told her that she could have the condo, she had no plans of returning there for anything more than to pack the rest of her clothes. Her goal was to have her own place by this weekend.

The knock on her door came more quickly than she expected. "Come right on in," she said without turning around. "Just put it on my desk."

"Okay."

She whipped around in her chair, shocked that he was standing there. "Brian."

He held up the mug. "Your assistant gave this to me to bring in. Is it okay?"

She nodded.

She watched him close the door, place the cup on her desk, and then slip into a chair across from her.

"I hope you don't mind my stopping by."

"Not at all. I knew we'd have to see each other . . . eventually." She paused, did a quick scan of the man she still called her husband. Dressed casually, in jeans and an open-collar shirt, he certainly looked as if he was handling this well. "How are you?"

He nodded. "I've been better. But you look great. Better than you've looked in months." He held up his hands when she frowned. "That's a compliment."

Now she gave him a small smile. "I'll take it as one."

"You look happy. At peace."

"I am." *Finally.* "You look good too."

"It's not because of the way I feel." He pulled an envelope from his shirt pocket. "I got your letter."

She bit the corner of her lip. "I'm really sorry. I tried."

He nodded. "So this is really it. You want a divorce?"

"Yes. Definitely, this time."

He lowered his eyes. Nodded again. "I have a question," he said, looking up at her. "If it wasn't for Jasmine, if it wasn't for the baby—"

She shook her head. "I don't know, Brian. Before all of that, I thought I could do it."

"But once Jasmine came into the picture, you couldn't. You couldn't forgive me."

She didn't answer right away. The worst part of all of this was that she didn't feel like a very good Christian right now. Didn't feel like she had a forgiving heart. "I think I've forgiven you. The problem I have is trust. I know you didn't mean to hurt me, and I know that you're sorry, but I don't know how I'd ever trust you again."

In the quiet, he thought about her words. "I really did love you, Alexis. I still do. You can trust that."

"I never doubted your love. It's all my other doubts that would have kept us from having the kind of marriage we had before and the marriage we deserve."

He nodded, but she could tell by the way his lips were pressed together that he didn't agree.

She said, "We can both do so much better."

"There's no one better for me than you."

She smiled. "I have a feeling you won't be saying that in a couple of months."

"You're kidding, right?"

She shrugged.

"Do you think I'm going to get over you like that?" He shook his head. "It'll never happen. That's why I'm hoping we can stay friends."

"It'll never happen." She laughed. "Maybe. I don't think I can love you anymore. But I do like you. And everything that you tried to do for me. For us."

"But everything I did—it was just too little, too late. It wasn't enough."

"I don't know. Maybe I was the one who wasn't enough."

He sat forward, his eyebrows pinched together. "Don't ever think that. This was never your fault. Never about you."

She nodded. "Are you going to continue therapy?" she asked.

He grinned. "You sound like you care."

"I can't turn that off and on. I want you to be well."

"I'm definitely going to continue. I don't want to be that man anymore."

"That's not who you really were, Brian," she said, shaking her head. "It was the—"

"Disease," he said before she could finish. "I'm not sure you ever really believed that."

"I did. It was just the consequences of it that I couldn't handle." She paused. Asked, "What are you going to do about the baby?"

"Nothing's changed. I agreed to let Hosea and Jasmine raise her."

"Can you really live with that?" she asked softly.

He shrugged. "For now." He pushed himself up. "Well, I didn't want to keep you. Just wanted to stop by and see you for a moment." She didn't move as he came around to her side of the desk. "I'm not happy about this, but I'm going to give you the divorce, Alexis."

"Thank you."

"But you know me." He leaned over her. "There's something inside that doesn't let me lose. Doesn't allow me to give up."

Maybe she'd thanked him too soon. Was this a warning that they were headed for battle?

He smiled. "Don't worry," he began. He was still her husband, so close, he could almost read her thoughts. "I'm not going to fight you." He inched toward her and when she didn't back away, he pressed his lips against hers. Softly. For a long moment. Then he turned away.

But at the door, he stopped. Looked back. "Have your attorney call me. But keep him on retainer. Couples have been known to remarry, you know."

He walked out of the office without looking back. Without seeing the smile that he'd left on her face.

✳ ✳ EIGHTY-NINE

JASMINE LEANED BACK IN the bed and played the message again.

"Call me as soon as you can," Annika said, her excitement bursting through. "The skussy left me a message a couple of days ago, but I was out of the office and just got it. Seems she wants a new job. And if I can help it, she'll be in Timbuktu."

Jasmine pressed "four" on the phone to listen again.

Natasia was going away? Why? Had she given up on Hosea? Had he given up on her?

Jasmine had prayed and read her Bible and left Hosea alone. Sat still, just like everyone told her to do. But it had been almost a month since he'd walked away. And for the last week, neither she nor Mae Frances had heard a word from him. He hadn't even called for Jacqueline. That broke her heart the most.

But now that Natasia was out of the picture . . .

Jasmine grabbed the phone, dialed Hosea's cell. After the first ring, she breathed. At least his phone was on.

Then it rang again. She imagined him looking at the screen.

And rang again. By now, he knew it was her.

And then, it rang for the last time. He was not going to answer.

Jasmine hung up when his voice mail came on.

Natasia may have been gone. But that didn't change a thing. Why should it? Their separation was about a whole lot more. It was about Kenny. And Brian. And all the lies that she'd ever told. How much was a good man supposed to take?

"I get it now," she said to herself, fighting her tears.

But it seemed as if her revelation was too little, too late. That realization made her roll off the bed and drop to her knees.

"God, please forgive me." And then she stopped, knowing that was all she had to say. But she added, "I want You to know that I'm sorry. I've done some dirt in my life, and this is payback. It's just hard to accept because You sent me such a good man. The only man I've ever loved. —And because I didn't trust You, he's gone.

"But I'm making this promise now, God. If You ever give me the chance to love someone again, it will be all about You. And all about trust. I know I won't be perfect, but I will trust You to take care of me. I will trust You always."

Jasmine stayed on her knees for moments longer before she pushed herself up. All she wanted to do was lie in her bed and cry. But what would that do? No amount of tears was going to bring Hosea home.

She sighed. If there was anything good to come out of this, it was that she would never have to tell Hosea about her age or any other lies she'd ever told. She would have never been able to face him with that truth, anyway.

But there was no need to lament over her past deception. All of that would remain a secret and she'd be able to start over, fresh.

The first thing she had to do was get herself and Jacqueline and Mae Frances back to New York. She reached for the phone, but then paused when she heard her daughter's giggles. Jasmine smiled. At least she'd still have a wonderful life, as long as she had Jacqueline.

She tightened her bathrobe before she hurried to her daughter's bedroom. But she stopped suddenly. Stood still in the doorway and pressed her hand against her throbbing chest.

"Hosea," she whispered.

He didn't look up, though she could tell he knew she was there. He held Jacqueline in his arms as he rocked in the chair.

"Daddy!"

It was one of her new words—Daddy instead of Dada. Jasmine watched Hosea's face brighten.

"Say that again." He laughed and tickled her.

Jacqueline laughed with her father. "Daddy!"

Jasmine half-laughed, half-cried with them, but she stayed where she was. Scared that if she moved a muscle, Hosea would go away.

Finally, Hosea placed Jacqueline down and watched as she grabbed her dolls. Then, for the first time, he looked at Jasmine. Stared at her for a moment, before he walked past her, into the living room.

She followed, praying that he wouldn't leave without saying a word. But in the living room, he paused in front of the windows. She kept quiet. Just watching. Just waiting.

When he finally turned, he looked straight into her eyes. "I hate liars," he said, as if it was just a fact.

It was hard to breathe after those words. All she wanted to do was cry. But she didn't let a tear fall. Didn't even blink.

He continued, "Because, if you lie, you'll cheat. And if you cheat, you'll steal. And I don't even know what you'd do from there."

She began to shake her head. She needed to deny that she was anything more than a liar.

But he held up his hand, stopping her. "I know you're not a thief, Jasmine. But you are a liar."

She tried her best to hold her sobs in. "Hosea," his name came out in a whisper, "baby, I am so sorry. But I have changed. Really, I have."

He stared, like he was trying to study her, believe her. "I can't do this anymore."

It was harder now to fight back the tears.

He said, "I can't live with you and wonder if you're lying. I have to know that my wife is telling me the truth. I have to be able to trust that." He took a deep breath. "I have a question." But he let moments pass, as if he was afraid to ask. As if he was afraid to hear the answer. Finally, "Have you told me any other lies?" he whispered. "Is there anything else . . ."

No! she screamed inside. Why did he have to ask her that? She didn't want him to know. Didn't want to see the look of disgust in his eyes if she told him. She would never have a chance at getting him back if she told him the truth.

But there was a part of her that wanted to plead guilty to all that she'd done. "I . . ." She stopped. She just couldn't tell him.

"Jasmine?"

Then she remembered—the promise that she'd made to God.

"Is there—"

Before Hosea could finish the rest of the question, she was singing like a jailbird. "I'm not thirty-eight," she cried. But her tears weren't going to get in the way of her confessions. "I'm forty-three. I think that's why we haven't been able to have a baby. And I haven't gained twenty pounds, I gained twenty-five, maybe even thirty. And I don't wear a size seven shoe anymore. But I think that's because of the weight I gained. And I did grow up in Inglewood, not Ladera. Although there are a lot of people who say that Ladera is Inglewood. And . . ." She stopped, trying to remember all the words she'd ever spoken. Trying to make every wrong right.

But then, through her tears, she saw him. And his slight smile. "Is that it?" he asked softly.

"I don't know," she cried, her mind still searching. She wanted to tell him everything. But her head hurt. And her heart ached. "It's all I can remember right now. But if I think of anything else, I will tell you, I promise."

He nodded. Said nothing for a moment. "I didn't know about your weight or shoe size, but I knew how old you were."

Her eyes and her mouth widened.

"I didn't know your exact age, but I knew that you had lied. And I needed to know if you would tell me now. I had to ask, I had to know, if you had really changed."

"I have, Hosea. There's a lot more I have to work on, but I've really changed. You can trust me. I'll never lie to you again."

Slow seconds ticked by. "I believe you now."

A sob of relief rushed from her throat.

He said, "And I won't lie to you, Jasmine." With a breath, he added, "There are some things that I have to tell you. Some things that we're going to have to work out." He reached for her. "But first, let's go in there and get our daughter."

She stared at his hand, waiting for hers. And she wondered what secrets he had to tell. Was it about Natasia? Had they slept together?

But when she looked up at him, all she could see, all she could feel, was his love. She took his hand. And when he squeezed hers, she started crying all over again.

If he had slept with Natasia, it would hurt, but it wouldn't matter. Because Natasia was gone. And he had come home.

Together, they walked back into Jacqueline's room, and their daughter looked up. She pushed herself from the floor and wad-dled toward them.

"Mama, Daddy!" She clapped her hands as if she knew this was a miracle.

Hosea laughed. Lifted his daughter. Kissed her cheek. And then, kissed his wife.

Jasmine closed her eyes while Hosea held her. And in her mind, all she could say was, "Thank you, God," over and over again.

Acknowledgments

I've said this before, but I mean it this time. I'm not doing acknowledgments anymore! I took so much flak for my last acknowledgments that I've yet to recover! So, from this point forward, I will only say to my family and friends: you know who you are and you know I love you. That's it for personal acknowledgments.

Now that that's done, I can breathe and move on to the acknowledgments I must make.

First, as always, to Jesus Christ, my Lord and Savior. You gave me the gift of using words, but I've yet to come up with anything that can thank you enough for what you've done for me. So my mouth says thank you, but my heart says so much more.

For the ten years I've been writing, God has blessed me with the best of the best!

I've had the best editors: first, Adrienne Ingrum, who in the very beginning taught me how to write, giving me an incredible foundation to build. (She was my editor for *Temptation*, y'all!) Then, I was blessed with Cherise Davis Fisher (congrats again!), who gave me such a gift by bringing me to Touchstone, changing the direction of my career, and teaching me how to broaden my thinking with my writing. And my blessings continue to flow with Trish Grader, who challenged me with this novel more than I've ever been challenged before. Because of you, I've continued to grow and I'm excited about that!

I have the best publicist in Shida Carr, whose hard work and commitment never ceases to amaze me. (You're not the president yet?) And I have the best publishing home with Simon & Schuster, and everyone there who always makes me feel like I'm part of that fantastic team.

Talking about the best, I have to thank my agent, Elaine Koster, whose belief in me seems to grow every day. "Thank you" is not enough for all that you do.

I have to give thanks to my pastor, Dr. Beverly "Bam" Crawford. I often get credit for being the first African American to write in this genre, but the thing is, I wouldn't have had anything to write if I hadn't been under your spiritual guidance. You've taught me, prayed for me, loved me, and because of you, my gift was released. Because of you, this genre began. (And for those who don't know, the pastor in my books, Pastor Ford, is based on my pastor! And she really, really is like that!)

Finally, to the readers who keep me and so many authors in this game—nothing happens without you. I thank you for casting your vote by purchasing and reading my novels, but I'll never be able to thank you enough for passing the word. You have no idea how important your telling others about my books has been. I am forever grateful. Thank you! (And if I can ask one teeny-tiny favor —can you tell just one more person, please?)

Too Little, Too Late

Discussion Points

1. In *A Sin and a Shame,* Jasmine reached a major turning point in her life when she told Hosea the truth about her affair with Brian—a point she refers to as the distinction between the Old Jasmine and New Jasmine. In *Too Little, Too Late*, how does Jasmine's "inner Jezebel" threaten to reemerge?

2. Hosea and Jasmine both are guilty of lying by omission when it comes to past relationships. What reasons do each of them give for never mentioning their former loves? Were you surprised to discover that Hosea had secrets of his own? Why or why not?

3. Why does Jasmine hesitate to travel to Los Angeles with Hosea? How does Natasia's presence turn the tables on her?

4. In what ways do both Jasmine and Brian reconcile their respective "fresh starts" with the secrets they continue to keep? What kind of compartmentalization do they each have to create in order to convince themselves that they are making the right choices?

5. The author splits the novel into parts that exclusively follow each of the two main couples in this story. What effect does this have on your reading experience? In what ways do the two couples' stories parallel each other? Where do they diverge? Explain why you did or did not like this technique.

6. Brian challenges Alexis: "If I had cancer, would you leave me?" Do you think this is "playing fair"? Why or why not? What effect do his words ultimately have on Alexis? Why, in the end, does she leave him anyway?

7. Like Jasmine, Natasia is smart, beautiful, and manipulative almost beyond imagination. How does she set her trap for Hosea, and how does Jasmine play right into it? What lessons do you think the author is trying to illustrate with this scenario?

8. On page 311, Hosea tells Jasmine, "You'll always be Jasmine Larson." What does he mean by this? Jasmine swears that she's changed—all because of Hosea. Has she really? Why or why not? What finally makes Jasmine realize the truth?

9. Both couples in this novel perform recommitment ceremonies. As with any ritual, these ceremonies have the power to effect change. What do the characters hope will happen when they renew their vows? What actually does happen?

10. Hosea is named for a prophet to whom God speaks. Identify moments in the novel when God is speaking, either directly or indirectly, to these characters.

11. Reverend Bush counsels Jasmine to stop trying to control her life and to let Jesus take the wheel. How does trying to take control work out for the various characters?

12. In some sense, this novel bears the message that it is never too late to ask for forgiveness. So what relevance does the title, "Too Little, Too Late," have for these characters?

13. At the conclusion of *A Sin and a Shame,* Jasmine's husband Hosea asked her if there were any more secrets she was keeping from him, and she said no. *Too Little, Too Late* ends with a similar conversation. How is this ending different?

Enhance Your Book Club Experience

1. Dr. Perkins emphasizes to Alexis the importance of her acceptance of Brian's sex addiction as a "real illness." Unconvinced and hurt, Alexis rages that claiming a sex addiction seems too convenient for a cheating man, something that men, in fact, probably made up. Do some of your own research and present your findings to the group. You can start at the Sex Addicts Anonymous web site: http://saa-recovery.org.

2. Victoria Christopher Murray is praised for her storytelling. Try tracing the intricate web of lies spun by the four main characters in this novel—Jasmine, Hosea, Brian, and Alexis— using a visual chart to help you appreciate just how intricate a plot Murray has concocted.

3. The characters in this novel all believe that God speaks to those who listen, and that He is trying to help them live a good, Christian life. But God isn't always so direct. At your next book club meeting, go around the circle and share your own stories about moments when you've thought God was communicating with you, describing what happened when you did or did not heed Him.

A Conversation with Victoria Christopher Murray

Fiction often imitates life. Were there events in your life that inspired you to write this story? What personal elements might fans find in *Too Little, Too Late*?

Actually, this is probably the one story I've written that has absolutely no personal elements. This was not a novel I planned to write, but after A Sin and a Shame, *I received so many e-mails from readers that I knew I had to continue the story. It was not my plan—I truly thought Jasmine's story was over, but readers told me it was not. So, I developed this plot to reveal the answers to questions that were left open at the end of* A Sin and a Shame.

Paralleling the stories of the two couples—the Bushes and the Lewises—was an interesting choice. What were you hoping to accomplish using this technique?

When I write, I don't think of techniques. I'm not thinking of what I can do to make the story different. Once I decide the story line, all I try to do is tell that story in the best possible way. I decided to write the story in three parts—first Jasmine and Hosea, and then Alexis and Brian, because I felt that was the best way to get the reader totally invested in each couple's story before bringing all four characters together.

As it was in *A Sin and a Shame*, forgiveness is a major theme in this novel. Would you share with your readers a time when you struggled to forgive someone for a wrong they did to you, or had to ask to be forgiven yourself?

Forgiveness is the major theme in all my novels. Not because that's what I set out to do, but when you're writing books with these inspirational messages, that's the basis of the Christian doctrine. As far as personally, I work very hard not to hold unforgiveness in my heart because I truly believe that I have to forgive to be for-

given. And, at this moment, I can't think of a time when I've struggled with forgiving someone. About asking for forgiveness myself, I can think of a situation with one of my best friends, Lolita Files. While I will not share that situation specifically, I will say that her forgiveness of me was instant! In fact, I think that even though she was really hurt by what I'd done, she forgave me before I even asked.

Jasmine has long been your premier schemer, but Natasia really gives her a run for her money. What is it like getting inside the heads of women like these?
I love these kinds of characters, whether male or female. The bad girl/bad boy is so much fun to write because there are no limitations. These characters have no ground rules and are so self-centered that you are free to put them in all kinds of situations. That's what makes it such fun.

Too Little, Too Late takes place primarily in Los Angeles. How does Los Angeles compare to New York City as a backdrop? What was it like to bring your characters back to the origins of the series—where Jasmine's story began?
It's easy to write novels that take place in both Los Angeles and New York because I've lived in both cities. This time, bringing Jasmine back to L.A. was necessary for the story—for Jasmine and Hosea's interaction with Brian and Alexis.

In *A Sin and a Shame*, Brian Lewis is just another smooth operator, a cheating husband that Jasmine hopes she'll never see again. What made you decide to portray him so sympathetically this time?
Readers reacted so strongly to Brian in A Sin and a Shame *that I decided to take the challenge and make them feel differently about him. I wanted to show that we make judgments about people with-*

out knowing anything about them. I wanted to challenge readers to understand that no one is all bad or all good.

Alexis struggles with the concept that no one addiction is more terrible than any other, that her addiction to coffee is in essence no different than Brian's addiction to sex. How do you think this plot element will be received by African American women, for whom infidelity seems to be a major concern? Aside from the obviously juicy twist it provides, what prompted you to create this situation for your characters?

First, I find fascinating the statement that African American women have a major concern with infidelity. I don't accept that statement as fact. I think past experiences as well as personal insecurities play a huge factor in issues of infidelity and those have nothing to do with race. But I digress—I chose the sexual-addiction story line for the reason I mentioned above. I wanted Brian to be a sympathetic character and, at the same time, it gave me a chance to explore a topic —sexual addiction—that I knew nothing about.

On page 341, Reverend Bush tells Hosea, "Instead of doing what the world does—looking for a reason to leave—why don't you do what God wants, and find the reason to stay." That's a pretty strong critique—does it reflect a personal opinion? What else does this novel tell readers about your own views on marriage and divorce?

I didn't write about my views on marriage and divorce at all. I went straight to the Bible for those views.

In many ways, all of the Jasmine novels tell an entertaining story while imparting some robust food for thought. How do you use your fiction to challenge readers? What do you hope to achieve?

I don't see my "Jasmine" novels being any different from my other ones. With my novels, I hope to challenge readers to think about their views. To get the readers to question long-held beliefs, or to perhaps answer a few questions.

Despite all the talk about doing what God wants and practicing forgiveness, Alexis does eventually leave Brian for good and files for divorce. And yet, we leave them on a somehow hopeful note. Their situation is so complicated and extreme—what do you think readers will relate to? What do you hope they will take away from this aspect of the story?

I never try to guess what readers will relate to because I am always so surprised what readers eventually take away from a story. I wasn't writing for any deep lessons to be learned. I wasn't sure if Alexis was going to leave Brian until I got to the end of the story. I allow the characters to tell me what they're going to do and Alexis said that for now, she had to walk away.

Jasmine may be the woman readers love to hate, but it's her humanity that makes her sympathetic. As her story unfolds and she grows as a Christian, she seems more desperate and confused than diabolical. How have the reactions from fans changed with each Jasmine novel?

Readers are becoming more and more sympathetic to Jasmine.

This is the third novel that follows Jasmine's escapades. Have we seen the last of her, now that she finally seems happy and lie-free?

You know, I had never planned to even write a Jasmine sequel. I'd had enough of her after Temptation *and then, I was sure the story was finished in* A Sin and a Shame. *I tried to leave Jasmine happy and lie-free in* Too Little, Too Late, *but I don't know for sure. These characters come to me in the middle of the night, never leaving me alone! I know these people still have issues—like, will Brian truly walk away from Jasmine and his daughter, Jacqueline? And knowing Jasmine, it's hard to believe that she doesn't have deeper, darker secrets that could destroy not only her life, but Hosea's as well. I don't know—like I said, my goal was to stay away from sequels. But who knows . . .*